THE LOVEDAY FORTUNES

A sweeping Cornish family drama in the bestselling tradition of Poldark.

Cornwall: 1791. Charles Mercer – Edward Loveday's brother-in-law – has been found dead, the reputation of his eminent bank in tatters, leaving the Lovedays facing emotional trauma and financial ruin. Adam finds refuge in his passionate relationship with the gypsy-bred Senara – whom he is determined to marry. His twin, St John, decides to throw his hand in with the notorious Sawle brothers, smugglers who rule Penruan by intimidation, and the vengeful Meriel Sawle, now St John's wife, has her own vendettas to solve. Each one of the Lovedays must sacrifice personal ambition and unite – but to some, sacrifice does not come easy.

THE LOVEDAY FORTUNES

The Loveday Fortunes

by

Kate Tremayne

Magna Large Print Books
Long Preston, North Yorkshire,
BD23 4ND, England.

British Library Cataloguing in Publication Data.

Tremayne, Kate
    The Loveday fortunes.

    A catalogue record of this book is
    available from the British Library

    ISBN   0-7505-1808-1

First published in Great Britain in 2000 by Headline Book Publishing

Copyright © 2000 by Kate Tremayne

Cover illustration © Ben Turner by arrangement with
P.W.A. International Ltd.

The right of Kate Tremayne to be identified as the author of this work
has been asserted by her in accordance with the Copyright, Designs
and Patents Act, 1988

Published in Large Print 2002 by arrangement with
Headline Book Publishing Ltd.

Magna Large Print is an imprint of Library Magna Books Ltd.

Printed and bound in Great Britain by
T.J. (International) Ltd., Cornwall, PL28 8RW

As always my love to Chris – my long suffering husband who puts up with all the idiosyncrasies inflicted on our partners by writers.

For my children Alison and Stuart who have achieved so much and for my dear brother Alan.

ACKNOWLEDGEMENTS

Heartfelt thanks and appreciation to my editor Andi Sisodia and agent Teresa Chris. They are the Guardian Angels of the Loveday family, who anguish over their suffering, delight in their adventures, care for them, and above all ensure that the Lovedays' passage through the intricacies and mysteries of the publishing world is blessed by their professionalism, support and enthusiasm.

To Rhian Bromage who is always cheerful and helpful when I press the panic button. Also the support and encouragement of Jane Morpeth and Amanda Ridout has been immeasurable.

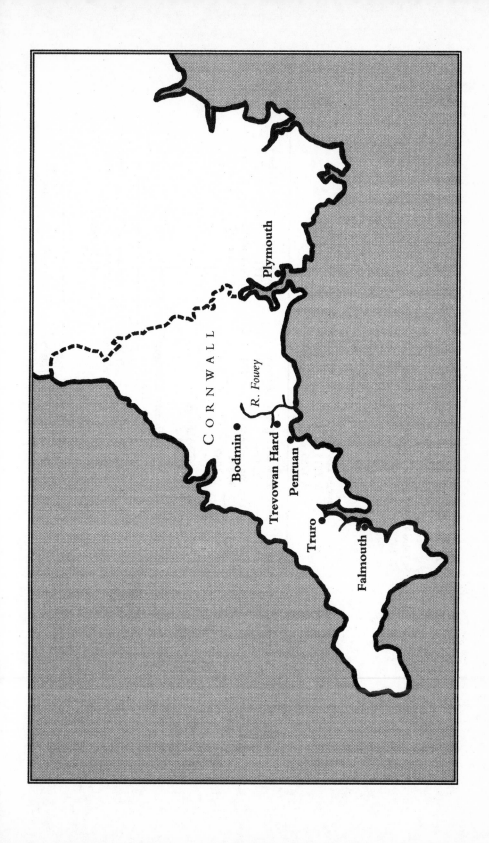

CORNWALL

Plymouth

R. Fowey

Bodmin

Trevowan Hard

Penruan

Truro

Falmouth

THE LOVEDAY FAMILY

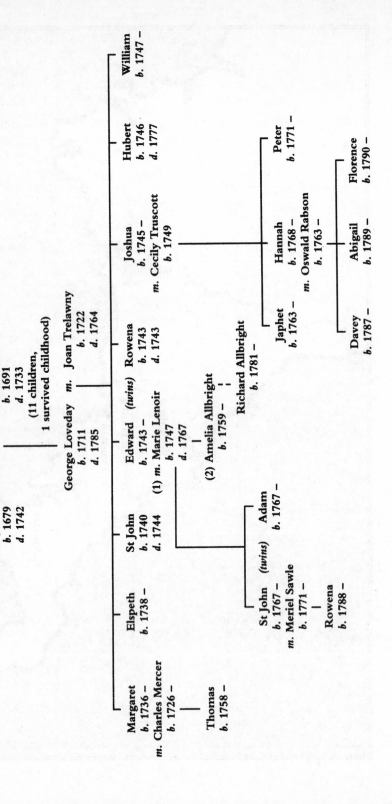

Arthur St John Loveday **m.** Anne Penhaligan
b. 1679   b. 1691
d. 1742   d. 1733
(11 children,
1 survived childhood)

William
b. 1747 –

Hubert
b. 1746 –
d. 1777

George Loveday **m.** Joan Trelawny
b. 1711   b. 1722
d. 1785   d. 1764

Joshua
b. 1745 –
m. Cecily Truscott
b. 1749

Rowena
b. 1743 –
d. 1743

Edward *(twins)*
b. 1743 –
(1) **m.** Marie Lenoir
b. 1747
d. 1767

(2) Amelia Allbright
b. 1759 –

Richard Allbright
b. 1781 –

Peter
b. 1771 –

Hannah
b. 1768 –
m. Oswald Rabson
b. 1763 –

Florence
b. 1790 –

Abigail
b. 1789 –

Davey
b. 1787 –

Japhet
b. 1763 –

Elspeth
b. 1738 –

St John
b. 1740
d. 1744

Adam
b. 1767 –

St John *(twins)*
b. 1767 –
m. Meriel Sawle
b. 1771 –

Rowena
b. 1788 –

Margaret
b. 1736 –
m. Charles Mercer
b. 1726 –

Thomas
b. 1758 –

Prologue

June 1791

The flame of the single candle flickered over the ravaged features of the man studying his ledgers. The once-proud figure was slumped and despondent. He threw down his quill and rubbed his hand across his eyes. The flame spluttered and died and the room became as dark as an abyss.

As Charles Mercer stared into space, unmoving, gradually the faint light from the rising moon penetrated the gloom. In Charles's tortured state of mind the open pages of the ledgers on the desk became pale spectres. The ghosts of his ancestors stared at him from the open pages: the men who had all sat at this desk at the family bank and brought it to greatness. They pressed around him, condemning, accusing, judging his failure, until Charles felt that his head would explode.

Mercer's Bank had risen to become the fifth most prosperous bank in the City. How could it all have gone wrong so quickly? How could his judgement have failed him when he had needed it most?

He reached for the brandy bottle and refilled his glass. The liquid splashed over his shaking hands as he lifted the glass to his lips and downed its contents. It burned in his throat and scalded a trail to his stomach. He closed his eyes to savour the brandy's warming breath and felt his optimism return. He was renowned for his business acumen, and astuteness in assessing an investment which could yield a high return. He was worrying in vain.

There was yet time to recoup his losses. Charles took a second ledger from a drawer in his desk, with the Loveday name written across it. So far ethics had stopped him from chancing the Loveday wealth; he had thought to protect his wife's family. The Lovedays trusted him to invest their finances and bring a high return for their money.

Charles hesitated. Would his wife, Margaret, see the use of her brother's money as a betrayal? She was proud, as were all the Lovedays. Margaret was also passionate about her family home, Trevowan. This venture could put it at risk and for that Margaret would never forgive him. And what of Amelia, so recently married to Edward Loveday, whose fortune was bound to the family? Her money had saved the Loveday shipyard and Edward still had the high interest on loans to be met. And Amelia was Margaret's closest friend. Would this seem a double treachery on his part?

His torment increased. Could not this latest scheme bring untold riches? According to his sources it would. It was his last chance. His final bid to save his family from disgrace.

Still Charles hesitated, and eventually he pushed the Loveday ledger aside.

No, he could not risk it. What if he failed? His judgement, once so sure, was shredded with the memory of recent failures. If he did not use the Loveday money there was only one other honourable way for him.

He opened another drawer and lifted out a box inlaid with mother-of-pearl. He unlocked it and opened the lid to stare at its contents for several despairing moments. Better that honour was served by his death – for that would atone for the ruin which was facing his bank – than he risk the Loveday money on one last investment to recoup his losses.

Then, with glazed eyes and fierce determination, he lifted out the silver powder flask. The pistol was cold in his hands as he primed it and inserted the bullet. He checked the flintlock system and took a steadying breath as he put the muzzle to his head. His hand was firm upon the trigger...

There was a dull echoing click.

Charles Mercer's head slumped on his chest, then with a snarl of pain he flung the pistol across the room. The powder was damp and it had not fired. Dear God, he had even failed to kill himself. Was fate truly against him? After failing so many investors, honour demanded that he took his life.

Or was fate finally on his side? He had been spared. Did that mean he could yet recoup his losses?

With renewed vigour, he reassessed the ledgers and also the papers of the investment in the South Seas. The company looked solid enough, and the returns would be enormous from the emerald and diamond mines in South America. The profits would be so high because many investors were still wary of such ventures, remembering the lost fortunes of the South Sea Bubble of seventy years earlier. But had not then the initial shares of one hundred pounds risen to the value of over a thousand before the bubble burst?

Excitement pulsed through Charles's veins. His grandfather had invested and got out as the shares rose, and his grandfather had avoided the disastrous fall in prices which ruined so many speculators. Charles Mercer was determined to do the same.

He opened the Loveday ledger and now saw this money as the means not only to save Mercer's Bank but to make the Lovedays one of the wealthiest families in Cornwall.

Charles no longer paused to contemplate failure. He dare not. Too much depended on his success.

Chapter One

August 1791

From her point of vigil on the headland rock, Senara Polglase tipped back the hood of her long cloak, and lifted her arms as though to embrace the dawn. Her unbound brown hair streamed

14

over her shoulders to her waist, and her body tingled with expectancy. Her intuition had not failed her.

The horizon glimmered in the blue and gold aura of the rising sun. Towards the east was a tiny speck, the white sails of a brigantine barely distinguishable from the white flecked crests of the waves.

She stood, patient as a sentinel, her cloak and skirts whipping around her in the breeze, until the ship turned into the Fowey estuary. Although she could not see the rearing figurehead of *Pegasus*, with its gilded hoofs, she knew she was not mistaken. Captain Adam Loveday had come home after three seasons at sea.

Happiness swelled her heart and, with the fleetness of quicksilver, she ran down from the headland to the shelter of the coombe where she lived with her mother and sister, Bridie. It could be hours before Adam would come to her, perhaps even a day or so. His first obligations were to his family, and from them Senara would always be an outcast.

She entered the sanctuary of the clearing. She did not mind the isolation, preferring its peace to facing the cruel tongues of a village. Her sister was a cripple with a twisted back and had been taunted all her life for her deformity. The one-room, dilapidated cottage which had once belonged to her grandfather had been transformed in the three years they had lived there. Gone was the sail which had weatherproofed the leaking roof. It was now thatched, and a second room built on as a bedroom for the women. That had

15

been at Adam's insistence, and had been the only gift she had accepted from him in the two years he had been her lover.

When Senara entered the stable and rubbed the nose of Wilful, the donkey, her mother looked up from milking their goat.

'He be back then?' Leah observed, knowing that the glow on her daughter's cheeks would only come from one cause. Now round-shouldered, Leah remained slender, her face showing few lines despite the hard life she had led. Her grey hair was hidden under a linen bonnet which tied under her chin.

Senara nodded, her head lowered to hide her flushed face.

Leah straightened and rubbed her swollen finger joints. She was Adam Loveday's housekeeper, although she did not live in his home within the shipwright's yard. 'Then I best ensure Cap'n Loveday's house and linen be properly aired, and a meal ready for him. Though no doubt he be dining at Trevowan with his family this day. I'll take Bridie with me to help. Or would you rather be there to greet him?' Leah was rarely ruffled by anything life dealt her and had never judged her daughter's relationship with Adam Loveday as wrong. Happiness was a rare commodity for the poor and you took it with an open heart when it blessed your life.

'That wouldn't be right. Ten months is a long time; his feelings may have changed.' Senara picked up the wooden pail of milk, and carried it past the garden that was fenced to protect the herbs and vegetables from the animals. Bridie

16

was busy weeding with a hoe, her thin, adolescent body bent awkwardly over her task.

'Cap'n Loveday loves you,' Leah stated, following Senara. 'You were a fool not to wed him when he asked.'

'Our backgrounds are too diverse. He will one day marry his own kind.'

Leah studied her daughter. Senara was beautiful, with an oval face and high cheekbones. There was a sensuous sweep to her brows and tilt of her full lips. Such beauty was dangerous for a woman who was half-gypsy. Women became jealous and saw her as a rival, and men too easily desired her, believing her lowly status made her easy sport. Captain Loveday adored Senara and treated her with respect.

'Captain Loveday's twin brother did not wed his own kind,' Leah provoked. 'St John Loveday wed a tavern-keeper's daughter.'

Senara rounded on her mother, and her green eyes flashed in a rare show of anger. 'Meriel Sawle was a scheming fortune-huntress who married for money. She got herself with child to snare St John. Would you tar me with such a brush?'

'No! You love Cap'n Loveday. Meriel Sawle, hussy that she be, never loved anyone but herself. It's not the same.'

Senara glanced at Angel, the scarred mastiff that she had rescued from death after a bull-baiting. He lay in the sunshine, his legs twitching, making whimpering noises as he dreamed. When she walked on, Senara added, 'I know my place, Ma. It be here, not in any fancy house owned by

17

the Lovedays. Besides, I've my trade as a potter and need to make more jugs before market day in St Austell.' The words were defiant, but Leah could see behind them to the passion and vulnerability beneath. Adam Loveday was handsome and charming enough to turn the head of a princess. Yet could he bring her daughter lasting happiness? She shook her grey head and sighed, fearing the couple's love was ill-fated.

Senara was not the only woman to witness the homecoming of the *Pegasus*. Meriel Loveday was also sleepless. Her expression was mutinous as she stared through the diamond panes of the window of her bedchamber in the Dower House at Trevowan. She was angry at not getting her way in an argument with her husband the previous evening. St John had refused to buy her a diamond and sapphire brooch she had admired in Truro. She had been married for three years, and the jewels and riches she'd envisaged would be hers by marrying a Loveday had not materia-lised. One would think they were paupers the way St John tightened the purse strings.

She glared at her husband's sleeping figure on the rumpled bed. The rose-pink damask hang-ings were pulled back to reveal a handsome, well-built man, but there was no tenderness, only resentment in her eyes. Her blonde hair waved around her shoulders with sensuous abandon, and her full lips pouted with the invitation of a Venus. Yet Meriel, with her hourglass figure and beauty, was without passion, her emotions roused solely by ambition and the need to surround herself with riches.

Meriel now took for granted the expensive Turkish carpet, the red velvet curtains, and the elegant gilded walnut Louis Quatorze furniture imported from France. Had she made an error in taking St John as her husband, even though she had been pregnant and given little choice by her brothers? Born the daughter of Reuban Sawle, the innkeeper in Penruan, she had set her sights on bettering herself in marriage. To many she appeared to have succeeded. She lived in an imposing grey-stoned, ten-room house which had been the home of the Lovedays before Trevowan House was built. Yet she remained discontent.

As the sky brightened, her stare returned to the triangle of sea visible from the window. She paid scant heed to the brigantine, her sails golden in the brightening sun. With Plymouth to the east and Falmouth to the west, this part of the Cornish coast was crossed by many ships.

A dog fox barked from the direction of the orchard which linked the dower land to that of Trevowan House. The sound made her shudder, and when her gaze returned to the sea this time the vessel came more sharply into focus. Her pout deepened and her eyes narrowed.

He owned such a ship. A smouldering rage flared in her breast. Adam had won his coveted prize, to captain a ship of his own. No doubt the black-hearted rogue was returning to reap a handsome profit from his voyage. Why could not St John be as successful? The fool of a man she

19

had wed had even failed to turn a profit from the smuggling she had urged him to invest in. For all St John was Edward Loveday's heir to Trevowan, he worked like a common labourer upon the land. That might have been necessary when they first married, but since then Edward himself had married a wealthy widow. The investments Amelia had made in the yard and on the estate should have released St John from his toil. Except Edward insisted that St John prove himself as a worthy heir to the estate.

Meriel folded her arms across her chest, and her foot, in a crimson silk slipper, tapped with frustration. It would never have crossed her mind that, by her family forcing their marriage, she had been part of St John's fall from grace. Neither would she admit that she encouraged his wastrel and spendthrift ways, which Edward so frowned upon. Brought up by a miserly father, Meriel had vowed that every luxury would be hers once she wed. She was not a woman who lowered her expectations. Her eyes sparked with malice. If it wasn't for Adam, St John would be the undisputed heir to both estate and yard, but St John's twin was the favoured one now.

She dug her nails into the flesh of her arms. How she hated Adam Loveday. Yet once she had loved him with all the blind passion of youth. Although he was the younger son, without expectation of a fortune, his dashing looks, and the air of wildness and danger that surrounded him, had captivated her. Even when Adam had become betrothed to his French cousin Lisette, Meriel still believed she could win him. Her beauty had enslaved many men, and for Adam she would have sacrificed the wealthy marriage she had planned to marry the pauper son. That had been when Adam was in the navy – during a leave when, betrothed to another or not, Meriel had set her heart on winning him. And had succeeded, or so she thought. Then he had rejoined his ship.

Her dreams had shattered. Disaster struck. Her father had insisted that she wed Thadeous Lanyon, an ugly toad of a man. With Adam at sea for several months, her only hope of escape had been to seduce St John.

Her silent laughter was cruel and bitter. How easy that had been! There had been triumph in the power her beauty could wield over men. Yet it had proved a hollow victory, for she had found no joy in her marriage.

A spasm fringed with pain circled her heart. The brigantine had disappeared from view when it entered the Fowey. Was it *his* ship? There was a momentary soaring of her spirit and excitement heated her blood. Then she swallowed against an overwhelming sense of loss.

The emotion caught her unawares. She ground it down and reminded herself that the love she had once felt for Adam was long dead. She hated him now. Hated him with a vengeance for spurning her. She brushed at a tear which formed in the corner of her eye. A tear which mocked her hatred, her resolve, and the power over men which she saw as her right.

An hour later Edward Loveday broke his fast

21

alone in the pale oak-panelled dining room at Trevowan. A copy of the *Sherborne Mercury* was open beside him on the century-old, solid oak table. The long table had been set for four at one end and the early sunlight was reflected in spears of light on the silver-lidded tureens on the serving dresser along the far wall. Edward's eleven-year-old stepson, Richard, had eaten and gone to feed the farm animals, a task he relished. Edward would miss the lad when he returned to his studies, boarding at Winchester School.

The sound of a stick tapping on the floorboards diverted his attention from the herring he was eating. Elspeth Loveday limped into the room, carrying her tricorn riding hat.

'Good morrow to you, sister. You are abroad early.'

'You have forgotten the hunt rides out from Lord Fetherington's at ten. A day in the saddle would do you good, brother. You spend too long cooped in your office at the shipyard.' Despite an injury to her hip some years earlier, Elspeth never missed an opportunity to ride to hounds. Having not married, her five mares were her passion and she fussed and cosseted them as though they were her children.

In her early fifties and five years Edward's senior, Elspeth was a doughty and stalwart woman, her thin face often pinched with the pain of her injury. It was only the waspishness of her tongue which marred Edward's pleasure in her company.

This morning she was dressed in her favourite navy velvet riding habit, which was worn and

22

shabby with use. Her dark hair was dressed simply in a chignon, with two grey streaks arching back from her temples. She looked pointedly at the empty place opposite Edward.

'Amelia still abed? Is she unwell again?'

Edward had been worried about Amelia's health. Usually his wife rose with him, but for the last month she had been tired and pale, and kept to her bed until late morning. She had been acting strangely of late, her manner abstracted as though her mind was elsewhere. Did she miss her life in London?

'I took the precaution of summoning Dr Chegwidden,' he stated.

Elspeth ran a finger along the gilded frame of the portrait of their parents, painted when the couple's seven children were between the ages of twelve and six months. She tutted at the light smear of dust on her finger, then lifted the lid of a tureen and spooned some coddled eggs on to a plate.

'Better to allow the Polglase wench to tend her. Her balm for my hip is a miracle, far better than Chegwidden's blood-letting and purges.'

'Competent as Senara Polglase may be, she is quite rightly ill at ease attending us when Chegwidden has been the family physician for years.'

'Poppycock!' Elspeth snapped. 'It is the health of your wife we must put first, not Chegwidden's feelings. Though I sometimes wonder if the old leech-purveyor possesses any. He puts me through torture with his blisterings and noxious poultices which strip the flesh raw.'

23

Edward smothered a tart retort. Elspeth could be a martinet at times, but despite her acidic tongue she had the welfare of the family at heart. Following the death of his first wife when the twins were born, Elspeth had run his household for twenty years.

'I have nothing against the balms and tinctures you procure from Senara Polglase to treat your horses or the family of any minor ailment,' he informed her. 'They always seem to work.'

'Indeed they do. Look how she cured Richard's cold...'

Her sharp voice faded into the background as Edward allowed the words to wash over him as he had done during so many of her tirades over the years. He saw himself as a progressive man, and did not have the same faith as Elspeth in ancient gypsy lore.

'...so I shall send for Senara then.' Elspeth lifted the handbell on the table to ring for a servant.

Edward took the bell from her, and exasperation harshened his voice. 'You will not! Chegwidden will examine Amelia. Her health is precious to me. I would rather entrust it to an educated physician who has practised for forty years than to a woman who can barely scrawl her name.'

Elspeth peered at him over the top of her pince-nez. 'Who was it saved Adam's life when he was shot whilst riding to Trevowan, and left for dead? It was Senara, not that fool Chegwidden. He would have made a cripple of your son.'

Edward looked away from the forthright glare. That was a time he preferred not to dwell upon.

They had never discovered the identity of the assailants who had attacked Adam. At least Adam's near-fatal injuries had healed the rift between St John and his twin. His sons had been at loggerheads with one another for as long as he could remember.

He sighed. 'Chegwidden will make his examination. If Amelia has not improved after a day or two, then by all means send for the Polglase woman.'

Dew still sparkled on the grass as Edward Loveday rode out of the stableyard, surrounded by outbuildings set at right angles to the three-storey house with its tall chimneys and high gables. Once past the protection of the wooded hill behind the house, a sharp wind from the sea sabred through him. The sunshine was already fading behind gathering clouds. It would rain within the hour. He rolled his shoulders against the twinges in his joints. At six-and-forty he was beginning to judge the weather more by the ache in his shoulders and knees than by the colour of the sea and sky.

His thoughts returned to his wife. He had never expected to find love again with such intensity of happiness. Cornish winters could be hard for those not bred to them. Though it rarely snowed, the storms, constant rain and mists plagued the lungs. Amelia jested that after being used to the noisome smogs of London, where she had lived during her first marriage, Cornwall was as invigorating as a physic. It had certainly made her son, Richard, more robust – though that could be due to the exercise of constant riding, his love of helping with the farm animals, or sailing Adam's old dinghy in the cove.

Three years ago, when Amelia and Richard first came to Cornwall, Richard had been a sickly child. Now he thrived. So why was Amelia ailing? She was a dozen or so years younger than himself, and should expect to enjoy good health yet awhile.

To ensure Amelia returned to full health he would insist that they attend a London physician. With Adam due home at any time, Edward could entrust the running of the yard to him while *Pegasus* was in the dry dock having the barnacles scraped from her hull.

After a three-mile ride, Edward had reached the brow of the hill overlooking an inlet of the River Fowey. Below him was the sprawling shipyard, and cluster of a dozen labourers' cottages which formed a hamlet. A small distance from the other houses was the extended cottage, Mariner's House, where Adam lived. There was also the Ship kiddleywink, a tavern which also sold general goods. And Amelia had built a schoolhouse for the children, which also served two nearby villages.

The grate of saws and ring of hammers accompanied Edward's arrival. A score of men were working on the scaffolding cradles around the ships being built. A cutter, constructed to the new lines designed by Adam, would be launched in a month. Her narrow lines would race throught he seas, sleek as a porpoise, and she would carry three masts and a jib for greater

26

speed. She had been commissioned by Thadeous Lanyon, ostensibly for his new trading company, but Edward guessed the cutter would be used as often in Lanyon's smuggling runs. She was to be named *Sea Sprite* and her hull, at Lanyon's insistence, had been painted black to blend in with the night sea. She would be faster than any revenue ship yet afloat.

Another keel was having the outer planks nailed to the skeletal ribs, and rose up like a giant mammoth's carcass. Piles of cut planks lay each side of the vessel. The carpenters were painstakingly measuring and trimming each plank to create the tightest fit before drilling and securing it to the ribs. The sight brought an ironical twist to Edward's lips. This was to be a revenue vessel which would one day be a match for Lanyon's ship.

A third, smaller, cradle held the keel of a fishing sloop, but work had been abandoned on this, for the men were needed in the dry dock where a naval frigate was being refurbished after an Atlantic storm. Edward wanted the work completed so that the dry dock would be free on Adam's return.

The yard prospered. Yet three years ago, before his marriage to Amelia, Edward had despaired that he would lose the yard to meet his debts. Even now, he needed loans to cover the extensive cost of materials needed for an expanding yard. His experienced eye scanned the work in progress, and it was several moments before he noted the brigantine riding at anchor in the river channel beyond the bank of the yard.

Her sails were furled and a long boat was tied to the jetty. Edward's handsome face lit with pleasure and he spurred his gelding, Rex, to a canter. The ache in his limbs was forgotten as he leapt to the ground. Adam ran forward to meet him from where he had been listening to the overseer, Ben Mumford, explaining the latest developments in the yard.

Edward could not stop his grin of pride as he regarded the broader shoulders and mahogany sheen to his son's face, after months in the West Indies and the old colonies of America. Adam's long black hair was caught back in a ribbon, and tendrils had escaped and curled around his lean, handsome face. There was a heavy gold hoop in his ear and several days' growth of beard on his cheeks.

'Hail, the adventurer returned from the sea,' Edward grinned, and slapped his son on the back. 'Or is it Blackbeard himself? You look like a veritable pirate.'

Adam scratched his beard self-consciously. 'I intended to shave and change before coming to the house. I would not want to scare the ladies. Neither had I wished to present myself to you in such a manner, sir.' He spread his arm wide to encompass the yard. 'I was diverted. Mumford has told me that the order book is full for the next year.'

'I have no complaints.' Edward surveyed his son from top to toe. Apart from his broader shoulders, there was greater strength in the bronzed forearms which showed beneath the rolled-up sleeves of his shirt. Also his voice had a deeper maturity. There were white lines around his blue-green eyes where he had squinted against the glare of the sun. And a greater knowledge was within their depths. He was a man who was now his own master, his hands firmly on the tiller of his destiny.

'The family are all well, I trust?' Adam walked with his father towards the stone-built office, raising his hand several times in greeting to any worker he recognised.

'We will all be the better for seeing you. Ten months is a long time away, my son. How was the voyage?'

'Without serious mishap and profitable enough to keep my investors happy. We unloaded at Bristol and my agent expects a good price for the cotton. For the next voyage I should be able to put up a third of the price of the cargo myself.'

'The higher the investment the greater the risk,' Edward was moved to caution.

'Everything in life is a gamble.' Adam smiled, showing white even teeth. 'And I do not intend to be on the high seas all my life.'

Edward chuckled. He doubted that the wildness which drove Adam to seek adventure had yet dissipated. 'There is work aplenty for you here, but I expect for some years your mistress will remain the sea. It is in your blood.'

'For the moment it is good to have my feet on land which does not leap and caper like a March hare,' Adam grinned. 'We weathered several storms. *Pegasus* rode them out as though they were no more than a squall.'

'You designed her well.'

'She was well-tested and not found wanting. She was built by fine craftsmen.' His pride was in the workmanship, not his own design. 'Now, sir, if you will excuse me, I shall make myself presentable.'

He hoisted the sea chest to his shoulder and proceeded to Mariner's House. The limewashed building stood apart from the other dwellings and work sheds. Adam deposited his chest on the wooden floor of the narrow hall and entered the bow-windowed parlour. Though spartanly furnished with worn, comfortable leather arm-chairs, a mahogany round table and sideboard, and books lining a recess by the fireplace, he welcomed the peace and privacy it brought him. The parlour was his favourite room with a commanding view of the yard and the river beyond. Trevowan was the home he loved, but it would never be his, and Mariner's House within the yard was a haven from the family turmoil caused by his twin. It had been one of the shipwright's cottages and had been extended before Adam moved in, with a parlour, a study, kitchen and two further rooms above. The smell of a rabbit turning slowly on the spit over the kitchen fire made him realise how hungry he was. It was over a month since he had tasted fresh meat. He could hear movement in the kitchen and soft voices.

Against reason his heart pounded harder and when he leaned against the doorframe his disappointment was hidden. He watched Leah Polglase roll out an oval of pastry while Bridie, with her tongue peeping between her teeth, concentrated on peeling an apple for the pie.

Leah looked up and dropped the rolling pin with a clatter on the flagstone floor. 'My, Cap'n Loveday, you fair gave me a turn. How long you be standing there?'

'Adam!' Bridie's elfin face lit with pleasure as she hobbled towards him with her arms outstretched.

'Bridie, that be no way to greet Cap'n Loveday,' Leah said with horror.

Adam laughed and lifted Bridie high, then pretended to sag under her weight. 'Our little turnip has sprouted.' He spun her round until she squealed with pleasure.

Leah shook her head and wiped a surreptitious tear from her eye. Adam was the only person outside her family to treat Bridie like any other girl, ignoring the deformity of her twisted shoulder and leg, and showing her affection. Bridie worshipped him. 'How be I able to teach her the proper respect due you, when you treat her like that?'

When he set her down, Bridie stepped back and, raising the side of her skirt, dipped into a wobbly curtsy. 'I knows how to be respectful to Cap'n Loveday, but I forgets when I bain't seen him for the longest age.' She then rubbed the side of her face which was reddened from his beard. 'What you growed that hair for? Makes you look fearsome.'

'A cutthroat razor and a stormy sea do not make merry companions.' He rubbed the stubble. 'You do not think it improves my visage?'

She pulled a face. 'I don't know nothing about

31

no vizzy – what you do call it, but you be more handsome without that hedgepig nesting on you.'

Adam roared with laughter, then swept her a mocking bow. Over her head, he winked at Leah, who was clearly appalled at her daughter's audacity. 'Then I shall remove the hedgepig. I cannot have my favourite girl thinking me a sight to frighten the devil.'

'Your pardon, Cap'n,' Leah said, flustered. 'I don't know where she gets such a wayward tongue. They be a beating for her when she gets home and no mistake.'

'Do not beat her for her honesty.' Adam knew that Leah would never raise a hand to her daughter. 'Father said I looked like a pirate. Now if there is hot water I will make myself presentable.'

When Leah brought the water to him in his bedchamber, Adam could not stop himself asking, 'How is Senara?'

'She be well.' There was no embarrassment in Leah's regard, having long ago accepted that Adam and Senara were lovers. 'No doubt you hoped she'd be here today. That bain't her way.'

Adam had always found it hard to accept Senara's stubborn streak where their relationship was concerned. She was content to be his mistress, but refused to flaunt her position. While Adam applauded her discretion and respected her too much to make her the cause of gossip, it made being alone with her difficult. Yet it also added a mysterious quality to their loving, the moments all the more special. Except that the impermanence irked him. He loved Senara, but until now she had refused to wed him. It was time that changed. Before he again took to sea, he was determined to court her, and with such ardour that he could not fail to win her consent.

That it would bring censure from his father he was prepared to accept. The hardest hurdle would be convincing Senara.

Chapter Two

By the time Adam was ready to join his family, the weather had changed. An earlier shower had been replaced at midday by hot sunshine. The rapid changes of weather, and the way it altered the mood of the sea and land, was part of the enchantment of the county. He loved this land, and like many a true Cornishman, there was a part of his heart which regarded it as a separate kingdom from the rest of Britain.

After weeks cramped on his ship, Adam had mounted his gelding, Solomon, and ridden for an hour across the moor. The crag-peaked tors were interspersed with the deep channels of coombes, the purple of heather and saffron of gorse, the sanctuary of rabbits fleeing from Solomon's hoofs. He even startled a small herd of roe deer to flight.

When Adam passed the ancient circle of stones, with the tall monolith under whose protection he and Senara had first made love, the memory increased his longing for her. He was tempted to visit Senara before returning to Trevowan. Yet he knew that once in her arms he could not bear to drag himself away. The reunion must wait until later, and he veered Solomon towards Trevowan.

Gradually the countryside became less wild and isolated. Cattle and sheep grazed the fields of the scattered farms and in the distance the tall chimney and engine house of Traherne mine were silhouetted against the skyline. Further along the coast were other mine housings, long unworked, the roofs stripped by gales and the walls crumbling.

The sight of his birthplace, majestic on the cliff top, filled Adam with pride. The tall chimneys and high gables rose towards an azure sky. Trevowan House stood imposing as a citadel against the violent storms which buffeted it from the channel in the winter, but this was no hostile fortress. The ivy which trailed over the west wing softened its contours, and the glass in the mullioned windows now glowed golden in the sun's rays.

A familiar ache gripped Adam's chest as it did whenever he had been long from his home. Trevowan beckoned like a beacon, for ever a part of him, yet for ever denied him: it would be St John who inherited the house and estate Adam loved.

He pushed aside a twinge of jealousy. His twin was the elder by three minutes; by a twist of fate – which the Caesarean birth had played upon Adam – it had been St John lifted first from their dying mother's womb. His full lips thinned as he regarded the weathered stone of the three-gabled

34

house with its golden lichen covering the shingled roof. No other place could move him as Trevowan did, and there was a persistent voice within him which maintained that Trevowan was part of his destiny.

At least not all was lost. Adam had set out to prove to his father that he was the son worthy of inheriting the shipyard. To that end during his voyages, both as a midshipman and lieutenant in the navy, he had studied and drawn all types of vessels, and the way they were constructed. The sleek lines of the *Pegasus* had been his own design. She was the largest vessel ever built in the Loveday yard, and paid for by the legacy left to Adam from his great-uncle Amos.

If Trevowan was Adam's mainstay, the Loveday yard was the tiller and rudder. He was born to be a shipwright. Although he had chosen to spend some years at sea as a merchant adventurer to establish his own fortune, it would be the yard which would anchor him on shore.

Yet it was wrong to deny St John his right to possess Trevowan. In the last two years his twin had been more diligent in his work and interest in the management of the estate. He had also curbed his gambling. During Adam's last visit home there had been a lull in the rivalry between them. St John was at pains to be pleasant when in his company. Adam suspected it was more to please their father than from any love for Adam on St John's part. But easy-going by nature, Adam had no wish to be at constant odds with his brother.

He was level with the circular fountain of

35

Neptune, the sunlight sparkling like polished crystal in the falling water, when barking broke out from the back of the house. Scamp, his own dog, in a streak of black, tan and white tore across the grass towards him. Hot on Scamp's heels was Faith, Richard's dog. Both came from the same litter which had been saved by Senara from drowning, after being tossed into the River Fowey in a sack. He dismounted to ruffle the long spaniel ears of the cross-bred dogs and waited as the older wolfhound, Sabre, shambled towards him at a more dignified pace. There was no Barnaby to greet him: the old spaniel had died during his last voyage. Their welcome over, Scamp and Faith shot off across the fields and Sabre flopped down in the warmth of the sunlit courtyard by the fountain.

Adam threw Solomon's reins to Jasper Fraddon, who had been drawn by the dogs' barking.

'Welcome home, Cap'n.' A face as lined as the bark of an ancient oak creaked into a smile.

'How are you, Fraddon?' The groom and gamekeeper grew yearly more bow-legged and stooped. 'And how is Winnie?'

'We be fine, Cap'n. The wife be cooking up a mountain of dishes all morning once we heard you'd docked.'

Adam marched into the house. The sound of his boots rang on the black and white sun design on the marble floor of the hall. The smell of beeswax on the oak staircase and the scent of lavender, rosemary and rose petals in a large bowl on an Elizabethan chest were a familiar welcome.

He paused, as he did on his return from every voyage, to feel the essence of the house around him. Portraits of several generations of ancestors lined the curving staircase, their fixed gazes silently questioning his absence. He swept his tricorn from his head and executed a mocking bow, his voice low with homage. 'The prodigal returns. Try and keep me away. Trevowan will always draw me back.'

The family were assembled in the Green Saloon.

At his entrance, Richard cried out, 'Adam, at last you are home! Wait until you see how well I sail your dinghy.' He flung his arms round him, and as Adam hugged him he looked over the youth's head to the others.

Elspeth rapped out, 'Richard, a gentleman does not deport himself in such an unruly manner. You should shake hands with your brother.'

Chastened, Richard slunk to the window seat and fidgeted with the fringing of the green velvet curtains. St John had moved to stand behind Meriel's chair, a proprietorial hand on her shoulder. There was no warmth in his eyes when he remarked, 'Father says your voyage was profitable.'

'Tolerably. You look well, St John.' Adam bowed to Meriel, who inclined her head in curt acknowledgement. He passed by her to kiss the cheeks of Aunt Elspeth and Amelia, seated together on a padded settle.

The greetings of his family over, Aunt Elspeth eyed him sternly. 'You return brown as a field-hand, and what is that nonsense in your ear?' She

37

flicked at the gold hoop with her finger. 'Lord, you look like a gypsy brat. It is not the correct attire of a gentleman.'

'Adam looks well enough.' Edward smiled with pride and indulgence as he wound the ormolu clock on the marble fireplace.

Amelia laughed. 'I think Adam looks very dashing. Did not his grandfather always wear a gold earring? He does in his portrait.'

'Papa was a law unto himself,' Elspeth sniffed.

'And you admire Adam the less for being the same?' Amelia chided.

Elspeth gave a dry laugh. 'I suppose not. But the days are gone when it was acceptable for a gentleman to be a buccaneer. These are more civilised times.'

'Not so civilised if you are living in France,' St John observed. 'Since the National Assembly abolished all titles and privileges of the nobility, the peasants continue to attack their châteaux.'

Elspeth energetically rapped her stick on the floor. 'I will not have politics discussed tonight. What the French do amongst themselves is their affair, not ours.'

Adam ignored her command. 'Later I would have all the latest news. What happens in France should concern us all. Insurrection is contagious. We would not want the same happening here.'

A gong sounded from the rear of the hall. Elspeth rose stiffly. 'I forbid talk of politics over dinner. It agitates the spleen and gives rise to evil humours in the body.' She took Adam's arm as they walked to the dining room. 'Forget not that we once decided to rise up against our anointed

38

King, and it brought sorrow to every family in the land. Our cousins in Helston were killed to a man: a father and son fighting for Parliament and another son died for his King.'

Edward surveyed the diners as the soup dishes were cleared by the short, rotund Sarah Nance and her equally plump sixteen-year-old daughter Molly. The dining room was bathed in a peach light from the sun, which reflected off the crystal drops of the central chandelier. Elspeth had become quite pink with excitement as she quizzed Adam about his voyage. St John had been polite, though there was little warmth in his regard of his brother. Edward, who had great affection for his own brothers, Joshua and William, was at a loss to understand the antagonism which had always been between St John and Adam. Meriel had hardly spoken. The woman was sulking over some matter, for usually she demanded to be the centre of attention. There was an over-bright glitter in her eye whenever her gaze fell upon Adam, which disturbed Edward. He was aware of the rivalry which his sons had once shared over this woman before St John had wed her.

Lines furrowed his brow as he noted that Meriel was ignoring her husband. Had they quarrelled again? Her moods were vexing, and he was glad she no longer lived under his roof but in the Dower House on the estate. His attention turned to his stepson. Richard was flushed with excitement as he hung on every word Adam related. The youth's adoration of Adam amused Edward. The boy was a fine lad, still rather shy,

39

but he had his mother's gentleness.

Edward's gaze returned to his wife seated at the far end of the table. Amelia was listening intently to the conversation, but her pallor was disconcerting. There were times when her stare became abstracted, her concentration wavering, which was unlike her. A rainbow sphere darted from her cheek to the pale wall panelling as she twirled her crystal goblet which was catching the evening sun. His fear mounted that she was sickening for something.

Amelia saw Edward's worried gaze and forced a reassuring smile. She struggled to appear at ease in the company of her family. She had barely touched her beetroot soup before it had been taken away, and now the pungent smell of the jugged hare in its rich gravy, potted pigeon with pickles, and roast lamb was making her queasy. She sipped delicately at her wine, but as she tried to concentrate on what Adam was saying, to her horror the portraits on the walls began to swerve and dip unnervingly before her gaze. A strong hand touched her arm and Adam's face blurred.

'Amelia, are you unwell?' Adam asked with concern. Immediately Edward was beside her.

'I do feel a trifle faint.' She dabbed at her neck with a lace handkerchief, unable to meet her husband's gaze. 'It is warm in here and the excitement of your return, Adam... There are some smelling salts on the mantel. They will revive me.'

Edward waved the phial under her nose. 'Perhaps you should lie down, my dear.'

She shook her head. 'No, it was but a momentary weakness. Please do not worry.' Amelia rallied her spirits, unwilling to spoil Adam's homecoming with her misgivings. Suddenly a wave of nausea overwhelmed her. With a cry she pressed her napkin to her mouth and staggered from the room. Edward hurried after her.

Amelia knew she would never make the privy at the back of the house and staggered across the hall to the front door. She gripped the warm stone wall of the house for support and vomited over a bed of marigolds. Edward put his hand round her waist. When she straightened from her bout of nausea, she leaned weakly against him. He led her to the Neptune fountain and wetted his handkerchief in the cool, splashing water and pressed it to her brow.

'I will send for Chegwidden again,' Edward insisted. 'Did his ministrations or physics not help you this morning?'

'Young Dr Chegwidden attended me. His father was indisposed.'

'Simon Chegwidden is a naval surgeon,' Edward looked shocked. 'It is hardly appropriate that he attend upon you.'

'He has left the navy. He is taking over his father's practice. Dr Chegwidden took his wife's death badly when she died last year and his own health has suffered. Simon Chegwidden was most solicitous, and better-mannered than his father. There is no need to send for him. He did not tell me anything which I have not known this past month.'

She hesitated and stared across the gardens and hard-packed earth of the tree-lined drive before

41

continuing. 'I am with child, Edward, but I have this fear that all will not be well. I should have told you that I miscarried a daughter the year before my late husband died.'

Amelia kept her head buried in his shoulder. In the last two years she had been fretful that she had been unable to conceive a child, while Edward had accepted long ago that the twins would be his only progeny. Now a grandfather to St John's Rowena, he did not regard another child as a necessity, but rather as an added blessing. Gently, he stroked her auburn hair, his fears for her welfare overriding all else.

'Does Chegwidden believe you will miscarry?'

'He said there is no reason I should not carry a child full term. But the sickness persists though I am now past my third month.'

He kissed her hair as he strove to conceal his own fears for her welfare. Edward had lost one wife he adored in childbirth, and was tormented that he could also lose Amelia. His love for her made him hold her close, and when he led her into the parlour, he had controlled his emotions. 'You must take every consideration of yourself. Do you wish to lie, down instead of rejoining us at the table?'

'Chegwidden advised that I rest at every opportunity. But I have not the patience to make of myself an invalid. Though for the sake of the child...'

Her uplifted gaze was filled with such anguish that he held her tighter, his murmur impassioned: 'This time all will be well, my darling.' His eyes screwed shut in a fervent prayer.

She relaxed and pulled back from him, her smile tremulous. 'I am being foolish. I will take some tea in the parlour until you have finished your meal and can join me.' Her smile faltered. 'Are you not pleased, Edward?'

'I am delighted.' He hid the fear which over-rode his joy. His emotions were again under control when he left her. Assured that she was comfortable, he rejoined his family.

'What ails Amelia?' Elspeth demanded, when he returned to the dining room. She signalled to Sarah Nance to bring Edward's plate, which had been taken away to keep the food hot.

'It is nothing untoward,' Edward began, then found himself grinning as he explained, 'It appears I am again to become a father.'

'I knew the filly was breeding. Saw it in her eyes.' Elspeth chuckled. 'Glad to hear it.'

Adam leapt to his feet and congratulated his father and was joined by St John.

Meriel remained seated and in a state of shock. The words droned like a demented hornet through her head. Amelia was with child. This was what she had feared ever since the wedding. She had prayed that Amelia would not conceive. A son would have a claim to the Loveday money, for did not Edward support his brother the Reverend Joshua Loveday with a substantial allowance? Edward would not leave a third son unprovided for, and a daughter would be given a large dowry which would further deplete the Loveday fortune before St John could inherit his father's wealth and estate.

The specially prepared meal to mark Adam's

homecoming lost all taste as Meriel focused on her resentment. Elspeth was watching her. The old harridan wore that pinched look of disapproval she so often favoured.

'I think on this occasion the men may bring their port into the parlour,' Elspeth announced. 'Amelia has been left too long on her own, and this is an occasion for rejoicing.'

Meriel put a hand to her brow. 'If you would all excuse me, I have the headache and shall return to the Dower House.'

She was subjected to a condemning glare from Elspeth, who declared, 'Pass Meriel the smelling salts, St John. We can not have her deserting us. I would have thought she had more sense of family unity than to allow the headache to deprive us of her company. For the sake of good manners one is expected to endure such afflictions.'

Meriel scowled behind her napkin before she rose from the table. The old dragon never lost a chance to deride her. 'We know you are a martyr to the pains which afflict you, Aunt Elspeth. Though sometimes to retire from company would relieve us from suffering the sting of your ill humours.'

'My sting is but a flea bite compared to the blistering society you will give to any who does not pass muster.' Elspeth hobbled to Meriel's side. Her frail, willowy figure as she leaned on her cane was deceptive. She was a formidable woman. Her once striking looks were thinned by years of duty and her sentimentality soured by spinsterhood. Above her hooked nose her unblinking stare was as all-encompassing as a hawk when she continued, 'Your false airs do not impress us. No gentlewoman wears her emotions on her sleeve. I doubt not that Amelia's news is a grief to you. You have not conceived in recent years. Do not take your barrenness to heart. Rowena is a delightful child.'

'St John expects a son.' The tartness in Meriel's voice raised Elspeth's eyebrows.

'I see no lowering of his regard for you. We are blessed when the Lord sees fit to bless us.' Elspeth's expression softened as she stared into the parlour. 'Oh, how charming! Rowena has been brought over from the Dower House.'

In the presence of Rowena, Elspeth showed rare compassion. Elspeth often visited and gave lavishly to the parish orphans. She had a patience with children – and her mares – which did not extend to adults.

Meriel resented the aunt's interference in Rowena's upbringing. Rowena had won an unconditional acceptance by the Lovedays, which she herself had yet failed to achieve.

Everyone fussed around Amelia congratulating her. Three-year-old Rowena was sitting on the end of the chaise longue on which Amelia reclined. Her dark curls fell over her face as she played with a doll. She hugged it to her with her right hand; her left remained at her side, the all but useless arm which had been damaged at birth hidden by the long sleeve of her dress.

Meriel flounced to the far side of the room ignoring Amelia and her own daughter. She picked up and examined a shepherdess figurine which was amongst several others Amelia had brought with her from London. As anger and frustration ground through her she felt like hurling it at the huge turquoise and gold Chinese vase on a pedestal in the corner of the room. That she had been unable to produce a son was a personal failing. It made her vulnerable, her position at Trevowan insecure. She was not used to accepting failure for it depleted the power and position she craved.

The parlour, with its faded Chinese wallpaper of strutting peacocks and blue velvet drapes, which were bleached with pale stripes by the sun, was the cosiest but least grand room at Trevowan. Meriel's expression remained sullen as she watched Adam place a red coral necklace, which he had brought back from his voyage, around Rowena's neck. Rowena cried out in pleasure and scrambled up, her arm held out for him to pick her up. She kissed him, then wriggled to be put back down so she could proudly show everyone her new treasure. St John fingered it, and there was a possessive jealousy in the way he lifted Rowena to kiss her cheek, before sending her to the kitchen where the maid would take her back to the nursery. St John doted on his daughter.

Meriel looked into the large Venetian looking-glass over the marble fireplace. Its gilded frame was carved with vine leaves and grapes. Covertly, she studied the twins reflected in it. St John was an inch taller than Adam's six foot, and her husband was heavier in build, although his labour on the estate had thinned the waist which had once begun to thicken. They did not look like twins. St John had lighter hair and had inherited the classical features of his father. Adam was angular of face with black hair. Yet his striking looks were sensuous and masculine in a way which set women's hearts fluttering. There was an untamed air about Adam, and a twinkling in his eye which was irresistible.

Still angry with St John after yesterday's quarrel, Meriel watched Adam through lowered lashes. There was a self-possession about him, whereas St John could appear merely arrogant. A spark of the love she had felt for this man since a young girl flickered in her heart, and was rapidly doused. It mocked the irony of her marriage, for she had never loved St John. Thadeous Lanyon had wanted to wed her and she had panicked. Adam was away at sea. To escape marriage to Lanyon, she had seduced St John, who had been in competition with Adam all summer to win her affections.

Believing Adam was as much in love with her as she was with him, she expected on his return that he would continue as her lover, despite her marriage. The twins had always been rivals. Instead he had turned from her in horror and her love for him had turned to hatred.

The emotion writhed and twisted like a nest of vipers in her breast. She had plotted Adam's downfall and had failed. Adam had risen higher in his father's regard. The yard which provided the wealth of the Loveday fortune would go to Adam.

Remembering, her hatred intensified. The yard should be St John's. His inheritance had been halved and that she could not tolerate. Outwardly, she pandered to Edward Loveday's demand for a reconciliation between the twins. She had learned patience and greater stealth since her marriage. She might have failed once in her scheming to prevent Adam inheriting, but she would succeed. Upon that she was determined.

The undercurrents running through the family reunion were not missed by Adam. Since St John had married Meriel the atmosphere at Trevowan had had an edge to it. He was used to friction when Elspeth's sharp tongue scythed the air with recrimination. But this was more incisive, like a termite lodged in the wainscoting, its gnawing silent and insidious but totally destructive.

Adam could guess his father's concern for Amelia. It was obvious that St John still resented the loss of the yard, but at least he was prepared to be amiable in front of their father. Meriel was more beautiful than ever. Yet her false smile did not reach her eyes, and knowing her from childhood, Adam recognised the danger signs. She was bored and ill content. Her beauty now left him unmoved. He had tasted the power of her seductive wiles, and also seen the depths of her cold-hearted calculations. Her presence within his family troubled him.

The Lovedays were not saints. His ancestors had been buccaneers, smugglers and notorious rakehells. Most had sown their wild oats in their youth, then settled down to an orderly mid-life. So why did Meriel continue to disturb him? Was it because she was a Sawle – a family of rough hot-heads any man would be unwise to trust?

He shrugged off his unease. St John remained besotted with her. Judging by the expensive silk of her gown and emerald pendant and earrings, her husband indulged her notions of grandeur. A dissolute nature governed St John. Meriel would encourage his worst excesses, and manipulate his weaknesses to ensure her own will prevailed. Therein could lie disaster.

Adam sat in an upholstered chair and attempted to lighten the mood in the room. 'The comforts of home are sorely missed whilst I am at sea. Even now, if I close my eyes, I feel as though my body is still swaying to the rise and fall of the ship.' He frowned as he realised that not all the family were gathered as he had expected.

'Is Aunt Margaret not down from London this summer? She never misses her seasonal visit.'

The lines deepened about his father's eyes and for a moment he looked strained before answering. 'We expected her as usual ten days ago. There has been no word.'

Adam leaned forward. 'There is nothing wrong, is there?'

Elspeth tapped the silver top of her cane with a fingernail. 'That ingrate Thomas has been causing his mother no end of misery since you sailed. Got some notion that he will be a playwright. He has left the bank. Your Uncle Charles is furious. He disowned him. Margaret has been distraught, and who can blame her?'

Adam let out a surprised breath. 'I knew

49

Thomas was not happy working in the family bank, but I never thought he would go against his duty.'

'Margaret blames those poets and ne'er-do-well actors he has been mixing with,' Elspeth snapped. 'It is a disgrace. At four-and-thirty, Thomas has shown no sign of marrying and settling down. And now this!'

St John chuckled. 'On her last visit Aunt Margaret had her eye on a match between Thomas and Lady Traherne's sister, Gwendolyn. Perhaps she is hunting higher game for Thomas in London. Aunt Margaret is a passionate matchmaker.'

Elspeth shook her cane at St John. 'This is no matter for levity, nephew. That Margaret has not come to Cornwall makes me fear that all is not well with the family in London.'

'Her departure may have been delayed,' Amelia reasoned. 'There has been much rain of late, making the roads hazardous. Do you agree that is most likely the case, Edward?'

'It is possible.' Edward forced himself to appear unconcerned for he did not want Amelia worried. But he was ill at ease. Nothing in all her years of marriage had delayed Margaret's annual visit to Cornwall. His last visit to London had been six months ago. Many of his business affairs were handled by Charles Mercer's bank, and also those of Amelia. He had been shocked to see the change in Charles since Thomas had walked out. Charles was drinking heavily and in other ways his behaviour had been erratic. Edward had attributed his manner to the pain Charles must

50

be feeling at his son's conduct. God knows he himself had suffered similarly over St John from time to time.

'Margaret will be here in a day or so,' Elspeth declared. 'Amelia is right: the rain will have made travelling difficult. None of us is getting any younger to endure such long journeys.' She rang for Sarah Nance to bring them in tea.

Edward did not have Elspeth's conviction. Charles's strange behaviour troubled him. What worried him more was that Margaret was to have brought with her a draft for the moneys earned on Amelia's investments. The expansion of the yard had devoured Amelia's annuity. The money was needed to meet debts for the next delivery of timber, and the brass fitments for the cutter once it was launched. He could, of course, request that Lanyon paid a further instalment but he did not want any speculation to spread that the yard was in trouble. Competition was high amongst the many small shipbuilders in the area. Adverse speculation could make a nervous owner cancel a vessel waiting to be built, and place their order elsewhere.

He had another month before the repayment was due on the loan. There was no need to panic yet.

Chapter Three

It was dusk when Adam left his family, refusing their invitations to stay the night at Trevowan. He preferred the independence he had at his house at the yard. Scamp came with him as he cantered along the cliff top, the dog chasing across the fields on the scent of rabbits and foxes. The ever-present pounding of waves upon the granite rocks of the coast was a sonata Adam never tired of hearing.

At the crossroads leading to the Fowey inlet Adam turned away from the yard and skirted the edge of the moor with its craggy leviathan outcrops of rocks on the horizon. Finally, he would be reunited with Senara. The sky was free of clouds and the moon was full. It was bright enough to light his way as night masked the landscape.

In the wood which bordered the Polglase cottage a badger scurried across his path. To his right was a fast-flowing stream, its water gurgling over boulders, and the occasional croak of a frog accompanied his ride. When the trees thinned into a clearing protected by a rock outcrop, a cottage was outlined in the moonlight. The amber light of a single candle was visible through the square of an unshuttered window.

There was the smell of smoke and burning charcoal in the air from the pottery kiln at the rear of the building mingling with the sweet scent of wild honeysuckle which Senara had grown around the cottage door.

A bark from the mastiff within was taken up by the higher-pitched chorus of Charity, another dog from Scamp's litter. Scamp padded up to the door and barked. It was opened and he disappeared inside. Adam swung down from the saddle. The pale outline of three thatched beehives was new since his last visit. As he eased Solomon's girth, a tawny owl flew by his head to alight on a fence post. Its single eye marked it as a new member of Senara's animal infirmary. Any injured animal found by her was always treated and many survived. Adam stabled Solomon and rubbed the nose of Harriet the goat, who peered over the top of her pen at him.

Without hearing a sound, Adam turned, sensing Senara's presence. Through the stable doorway he saw a cloaked figure emerge from the woods, sylvan in its silent step.

'Senara...' His voice was husky with need.

They gazed at each other across the moonlit space for several heartbeats. Tall, slim and dressed in green, with her brown hair flowing loose to her hips, she was indeed a spirit of the woods – ethereal, magic. With the moonlight pearling her features, Senara was more lovely than he remembered. She gave a joyous cry and ran into his arms, the sprite transformed to a woman of earthly passion.

From her observation place by the open door Leah smiled with resignation at the lovers. They were well suited, yet she could not but believe the union was ill-fated, and would lead to heartbreak for her daughter. She closed the door, knowing they would want their privacy this night.

'Oh, Adam, my love...' Senara began, the rest of her words smothered by the ardour of his kisses.

She clung to him, light-headed with desire. His lips trailed along her neck and she breathed in the scent of him, the smell of soap on his skin and the pleasant musky tang of orris root he favoured. Beneath his jacket, she could feel the hardness of muscle. Then coherent thought deserted her as his lips were again upon hers and their senses were caught in the maelstrom of their reunion.

She took his hand and led him to the hayloft of the stables. There he threw his cloak over a pile of sweet-smelling straw, which had earlier been strewn with rosemary, lavender and honeysuckle, in anticipation of this moment. They were again locked in each other's arms as he drew her down beside him. This had long been their trysting place, for Senara would not come to his house in the yard. Neither would she allow him to provide her with a house of her own away from her family.

Moonlight streamed through the tiny window above them, bathing the naked lovers in an opalescent light. Ardour was a millrace in their blood, their passion rising to a tempest which, even at its height, was never without its tenderness and reverence. The exultation of sighs faded with breathless wonder. The scudding of twin heartbeats calmed, and the sweat cooled on their glowing, satiated flesh.

Adam levered up on one elbow to smile down at her. He could smell on her skin the lavender and calendula soap which she made herself, and the wild rose petals she had rubbed in to her hair. No woman of his class, with their overpowering perfumes and pomanders, smelled as sweet and enticing as Senara did to Adam. This night he had been captivated by her all over again.

In their passion Senara had pulled free the restraints of his hair ribbon and his black hair fell around his shoulders, the gold earring glinting in the moonlight. It also revealed the contours of honed muscle which sculptured his upper body and flat stomach. At four-and-twenty, he now had a maturity in his powerful form. The pale light reflected the sparkle in his sea-green eyes and the roguish flash of white teeth.

Senara touched the rough outline of the crescent-shaped scar on his cheek which he had received when saving Bridie from an insult by ruffians. There was another scar on his shoulder and thigh from the attack which had almost killed him, and also the slash of a sword wound on his arm. They were old familiar scars attesting to his courage, and she was relieved that her inspection revealed no new ones.

'You have lost none of your buccaneering looks, my love.' She fingered the earring. This was how she loved him most.

'Indeed, so Elspeth commented earlier. She did not seem so well pleased.'

'Being half gypsy, it is the adventurer who won my heart, for I can never be the equal of the son of a gentleman.'

He expelled a harsh breath loaded with impatience. 'Have I ever treated you as less than my equal? I love you, Senara. It is time you put these foolish notions aside. I want us to marry before I sail again.'

A look of intense pain flickered across her lovely face. 'This is the only way. I'll bring disgrace to you if we wed. Your world is not my world.'

'My world is empty without you beside me. I care not for the opinion of others. My family and society have accepted Meriel. They will accept you.'

Her eyes remained shadowed, their stare unwavering and resolute. 'And you must accept that I want none of that life. *Has* society accepted Meriel? Towards your family they appear to, for the Loveday name is an old and revered one, but behind your backs, they gossip and whisper. They see Meriel as a fortune-huntress. And what of her own kind? The villagers laugh at her haughty airs. She is an outcast amongst them too.'

He sat up and looped his arms over his knees. 'You will live at the yard and none will mock you, or they will know my wrath. Better still, you will sail with me as my bride.'

'Then you would be mocking fate, for are not women considered ill omens upon a ship?' She rested her head on his shoulder. 'Besides, what would I do to occupy myself on a voyage? I am fulfilled by my work here. I could not be idle and be content.'

'Am I selfish to want you at my side?' he challenged. 'Is that not how it should be between lovers?'

'I miss you so much that there are times when I feel but half alive,' she countered. 'But that is part of life. Why can things not remain as they are? Nothing can change our love. Here I can live with dignity. I know my place as Meriel did not.'

'Then you cannot love me as I love you.' His exasperation exploded. 'I want you always by my side and openly in my bed. Not this stealing moments of love like a thief in the night. You deserve better, as do I. I am not ashamed of you.'

'How can you doubt my love?' she disputed before his words of devotion could sway her. 'You are being stubborn, the rich man expecting to get his own way. I can never fit in to your world, so pray let the matter be.' There were tears in her eyes and she turned away.

Her words were unjust, but he battened down an angry response, and put his hands on her shoulders to draw her round to face him. The tenderness in his voice was teasing and persuasive. 'It is you who are being stubborn. I love you. My life is hollow without you to share it.'

He wiped the tears from her cheek with his thumb and kissed the damp trail they had made. She closed her eyes and swallowed against the emotion which was cramping her throat.

Wilful blew through his nose as he contentedly pulled at the hay in his manger, and Harriet bleated softly, rustling the straw with her hoofs as she settled for the night. There was an air of peace and tranquillity in the stable which had become their lovers' bower. Senara's body glowed with the warmth of Adam's lovemaking.

Here she felt safe and secure, and at one with her world and lover.

'Please, let us enjoy each other while we can,' she pleaded. 'In a few weeks you will be at sea again. That is your life and this is mine.'

She put her hand to his face and drew his head down to kiss her. Loving him more than she loved life itself, it would be so easy to agree to marry him. Her greatest joy was to be in his arms, or just simply in his company. But that was only a small part of his world. She had been hurt by a previous lover, a handsome captain in the army, who had shown her the prejudice and persecution his kind were capable of once their love paled. That experience had left her wary of all men, and she had fought her attraction for Adam for many months before finally yielding to him. But there was always a shadow in her mind. Her gypsy blood gave her a sense of knowingness. Twice she had dreamed of Adam walking out of a church with his bride. The face of the woman at his side was indistinct, and she was convinced it was not herself. To marry him would be to tempt providence.

As the family continued to fuss over Amelia and her condition, Meriel's discontent increased. In the privacy of the Dower House parlour, she ranted at St John. She was seated by the oriel window in a high-backed rocking chair and was struggling with some needlepoint. It was a genteel occupation which Elspeth insisted that she master. The light was fading fast as storm clouds gathered on the horizon. The wool knotted and she flung the hand frame on the floor, her patience frayed.

Out at sea lightning flashed, illuminating her angry face, and the delicate Sheraton furniture crowded into the room.

'I knew it was an ill day when Edward married,' Meriel fumed. 'That brat when it is born will take even more of your inheritance. Is it not bad enough that Adam has stolen the yard from you?'

'Hardly stolen, my love. Father decided to split the yard and estate in his will,' St John reminded her with sarcasm. He was stretched out on the day bed in moleskin trousers and shirtsleeves after a strenuous day mending fences on the estate. He was in no mood for Meriel's recriminations which always roused his own anger and frustration at the injustice of Edward making Adam heir to the shipyard. He had never forgiven his father for halving the property he would one day inherit. His resentment festered against Adam, who could do no wrong in his father's eyes. St John dismissed his own incompetence as a shipwright and ignored Adam's skill and flair for design. He saw his father's decision as a sign of favouritism towards Adam. His father had ordered that there be a reconciliation between them. Outwardly, St John played the dutiful son, but he was determined to find a way to regain his entire inheritance. He could afford to bide his time, for Edward was only in his mid-forties and in robust health.

'There are times when I despair of you, St John. And what of this child? Do you not realise how it will be a blight upon our future?' Meriel stood up and kicked the needlepoint across the floor.

At seeing the angry colour on her cheeks, St John sighed. Her temper was a daily trial. 'You upset yourself unduly, my sweet,' he attempted to appease her. 'As for the new child, it could be a girl.'

'Which will be given a handsome dowry, no doubt.' Her antagonism flared and she regarded her husband with disdain. He was so weak at times. She paced to the hearth and drummed her fingers on the mantel, which was crammed with exotic vases, gilt candlesticks and porcelain figures. 'Sometimes I wonder if I have married a man at all. Adam has taken your birthright now Edward has named him heir to the shipyard. My brothers would not let such injustice go unavenged. Clem and Harry are but simple fishermen, whilst you have been educated and have a position in the world.'

'The Sawles rule by brutality,' St John sneered. 'Clem served a year in Bodmin Gaol for assault. Is that anything to be proud of?'

She spun away and continued to stride around the room, kicking a footstool and an embroidered fire screen from her path. 'My brothers are men to be reckoned with.' Her hands clenched and she thumped a side-table. A Venetian glass vase of gillyflowers wobbled precariously. Her hand raised to sweep it to the floor, but she checked herself. The vase was a favourite of hers and her temper had cost her too many pretty objects in the past. Her eyes glittered as she looked around the room, surveying the landscape paintings, fine furniture and expensive ornaments that she had acquired. She hankered for so much more. There should be a full-length portrait of herself, which St John said they could not afford. And she wanted the ceiling plastered with a cherub motif depicted in gold. St John had laughed at the idea, saying it would make their home look like a bordello. That had sent her into such a fury that she had not spoken to her husband for a week.

Once she had been desperate to escape the drudgery of her life at the Dolphin Inn, and had suffered her father's beatings when their wills crossed. Yes, her family were brutal at times, but she admired their strength. The Sawles had forged their own kind of power. They thumbed their noses at the law on their smuggling runs and, if any defied them, they ruled by the threat of their fists. Few men would be foolish enough to cross the Sawles.

St John watched with trepidation as his wife worked herself into a frenzy. When thwarted she was a virago, hurling both objects and accusations at him. At the same time she excited him. Now her eyes blazed with an incandescent light. The sight of her breasts straining against her bodice as they rose and fell roused his desire. Too often he had suffered her indifference and been denied her embrace. When the flame of angry passion transformed her into a woman of fire, her beauty was entrancing.

He was more in love with her with each year. When she chose to grant him her favours, she was unlike any other woman he had made love to. That she was calculating and scheming, he

61

knew to his cost. But he was bewitched by her, and life was intolerable when he held out against her wishes. Though she could be cruel and cold, he found it impossible to deny her anything if it was in his power to give to her.

'I was planning a visit to Truro. Lord Fetherington has invited us to dine on Monday.'

Her fists unclenched and she looked at him through lowered lashes. Her swift mood changes could still take him unawares, but he was reassured by her slow smile.

'And there is that divine brooch I saw in Truro,' she said. 'You are not going to be so mean as not to buy it for me this time?'

Sinuous as a cat she moved towards him, her expression now inviting. He braced himself against displeasing her.

'My purse will not stretch to the brooch. But I had thought you in need of a new pelisse and perhaps a hat.' When her smile turned sullen, he added, 'And of course a new gown would be appropriate. You are seeing more of Roslyn Traherne of late. I would not have my wife appearing dowdy in society. It pleases me that Lady Traherne has taken you under her wing.' St John had recently had a streak of luck at the gaming tables and he felt that he could be generous. He caught her arm and drew her down beside him on the day bed.

Meriel pouted. 'I have been honoured by her Ladyship's interest.' There was a sarcastic ring to Meriel's voice. At first she had been delighted when Lady Traherne had shown an interest in her. It was some months before she realised that

62

Roslyn demanded constant praise and attention which was lacking from her family. Her husband, Sir Henry, was absorbed in making a profit from his mine. Since she had produced two children – one the necessary son and heir to continue the family line – he paid her little attention. It was rumoured he had a mistress in Truro, and his wandering eye often enticed local girls, or married women, to indiscretion. Lady Traherne's friendship with Meriel was because her Ladyship desired a companion who was lavish in her compliments and whom she felt she could manipulate to her wishes.

Meriel was prepared to humour her, for she was adept at using Lady Traherne for her own ends. She was prepared to ignore her shrewish temper and pander to her whims, for association with Roslyn meant she was accepted by society in a way marriage into the Loveday family alone could never achieve.

'A gown would be most acceptable,' Meriel answered her husband. 'But the brooch would not be out of reach of your purse if you invested again in the free trade.'

His hand that had been caressing her neck withdrew. 'We near lost everything last time. I was lucky to escape with my life. And if Papa had discovered my involvement, I would be disowned for certain.'

The fervour remained in her eyes. 'I think you wrong, Edward. In the past your family have profited from the trade. Their involvement in the sea and connections with France have always been strong.'

'Times were different then. We were at war and the navy too occupied to help the revenue men. There have been many arrests in recent months. It is too risky.'

'My brothers prosper. Though they lack the ambition to do more than drink and gamble their money away.' She pressed closer against him, her manner coercing. 'Think how much better we could live. You are forced to turn down invitations from Lord Fetherington and other of your friends, for you have not always the funds to engage in their card parties. It is your right as a gentleman–'

'To squander my inheritance.' He gave a bitter laugh, 'Most times I have precious little luck at the tables.'

'Then what of your tailor?' She refused to be distracted. 'How long is it since you had a new waistcoat or dresscoat? You cut such a fine figure in your fashionable clothes. Why, there was that thoroughbred gelding you were taken with at the horse fair. You were convinced it could have won you a fortune at the races, but you could not afford its price.'

That touched a raw nerve and St John's expression became fierce. 'You're right. I regret not having had the means to purchase him. He has proved to be a splendid animal and has won his owner a fortune, as I predicted.'

She knew he missed his old ways of carefree gambling and the entertainments enjoyed by his wealthier friends. With his finances curtailed by his father, St John was frequently bored when forced to stay at Trevowan. 'St John, would not the trade enable you to pursue your pleasures? You do not have to be directly involved with a run as before. You could raise a loan.'

St John glared at his wife. The last such venture had cost him his legacy from Great-uncle Amos. Adam had received the same legacy, and from it the *Pegasus* was built. His brother prospered on his voyages, while the share he, St John, had purchased in the smuggling vessel the *Merry Maid* had been a disaster. The ship and cargo were impounded by the revenue men and the *Merry Maid* broken up as a warning to others. He had been present at the landing and was almost captured. It had frightened him into sobriety. There were nights when he still woke in a sweat, reliving the nightmare.

Yet until that last run the profit had been substantial, his wilder side reasoned. Financial restraint did not sit well with him. He craved excitement – not like Adam in the form of adventure, but at the gaming tables and races, and mixing with other young bloods who knew how to take pleasure in life.

'I have done with the trade.' His voice was not as firm as once it had been.

Meriel noticed the hesitation and smiled.

To pacify his wife and to stop her pressing him to take up a life which, though rich in rewards, was dangerous, St John took Meriel to Truro and hoped to divert her by visiting the playhouse.

Truro was a port and an affluent coinage town where the tin was brought to be weighed and stamped so that duty could be collected. Its

65

narrow lanes between the main streets provided shelter from the strong winds and its shops were amongst the most fashionable in Cornwall. The Assembly Rooms had opened two years ago, with the renowned actress Mrs Siddons appearing in a play, and horse races were held on the downs outside the town.

St John treated Meriel to an emerald velvet pelisse embroidered with silver braid and a matching hat complete with a trailing ostrich feather. He also purchased enough pink dimity for the seamstress to make into a new gown. Fortunately, the diamond and sapphire brooch she wanted was no longer in the jeweller's.

They stayed overnight as guests of Lord Fetherington at his four-storey, red-brick house in the centre of town known as High Cross, which was opposite the gothic-style St Mary's church with its imposing spire. Lord Fetherington, an ageing roué of fifty, had encouraged St John to visit since his marriage. A keen huntsman, he also owned a house and estate to the north of Trevowan on the borders of Bodmin Moor. For years St John had been friends with his Lordship's son, the Honourable Percy Fetherington, though there was little honour in some of Percy's wild and despotic ways.

They were greeted by liveried and bewigged footmen, and Meriel gasped in wonder at the splendour of the black marble pilasters lining the square hall. Everywhere was gilded plasterwork, which set Meriel complaining that the Dower House was dowdy in comparison.

That evening they dined in generous style, and

once the ladies had adjourned to the drawing room, Lord Fetherington passed round the port.

'You are looking very fine this evening.' Percy eyed St John through a monocle as they finished their port. The room was hot from the light of thirty candles which reflected off the panes of the tall windows and five mirrors on the walls. Percy was stout and, like his father, had haughty rather than handsome features, with a large hooked nose, wide mouth and heavy-lidded stare. 'How about a turn at the card tables later?'

'Would you have St John abandon his dear wife?' Lord Fetherington wheezed. The years had not been kind to his Lordship and his skin was pock-marked from the disease which had also caused one eyelid to droop. He wore a grey wig which curled in three tight rolls above his ears. Five of his front teeth were missing, which gave a high-pitched whistle to his speech. 'A pretty filly like that should not be left alone. She does not play, does she?'

'Only whist,' St John explained. He did not want to encourage Meriel. She could be an impulsive gambler and on the occasions she had played in company had lost more money than himself. 'I doubt Percy had whist in mind.'

With twenty-five guineas to spare St John was eager for a night of gambling, although Meriel would not relish an evening tied to Lady Fetherington, who was prone to drinking heavily and then falling asleep in front of her guests.

Seeing St John hesitate, his Lordship insisted, 'An evening of whist would be admirable entertainment. Penelope never plays but she will insist

Meriel makes up a fourth.'

The card room was decorated with salmon-coloured wallpaper with a green fleur-de-lys design. Lady Fetherington declined to join the card game but insisted that Meriel play. The room smelt of brandy and tobacco smoke, which irritated Meriel's throat. Lord Fetherington had politely asked her permission to smoke in her presence which she had readily given as she wanted to be a part of the gaming party and to give the men no excuse to abandon the cards.

To St John's surprise Meriel won several hands and her original stake money of five guineas, which he had reluctantly given her, had increased to thirty guineas. Lord Fetherington was playing haphazardly, his skill perhaps affected by the half-dozen brandies he had drunk since dining. He threw in his last hand.

'That is me wiped out for the evening. I have lost fifty guineas and I never gamble more. Sound advice from my father, that. For only a fool thinks his luck will turn when the cards are clearly against him.'

'Would you break up the evening, my lord?' Meriel had hoped to win more guineas from his Lordship.

Lord Fetherington smiled at her. 'Let the young men play. For myself I would like nothing more than to hear you sing. You have a delightful voice, my dear.'

'But I do not accompany myself, my lord.'

'A voice like yours needs no accompaniment. Humour me. We shall adjourn to the upper saloon and partake of a nightcap before retiring.'

St John eyed the pile of guineas in front of Percy. His own luck had held so far. He could double his winnings if it continued. He smiled at Meriel. 'We will join you shortly, my love. Percy and I will have a few hands of *vingt-et-un*.'

Lord Fetherington held out his hand to escort Meriel to the upper saloon. The candles had burned low in the vast room. The yellow walls, gold curtains and upholstered chairs made Meriel yearn for something similar. A liveried footman stood by the door to open it for them. He was one of five she had seen ready to attend the Fetheringtons' needs. They also had four maids, one allotted to Meriel during her stay, and at least a half-dozen servants for the menial household tasks. In comparison to the sumptuous elegance here, the Dower House was little more than a cottage. It irked her that they had only three servants – a cook, maid of all work and a nursemaid for Rowena. How could she have once thought that life at Trevowan was so grand? Her discontent rose against her husband. She would make him rejoin the smugglers – it was his only chance to gain such lavish wealth for her to spend on their home.

Lady Fetherington was sound asleep in a corner chair. His Lordship cursed. 'I thought she'd be long abed.'

He pulled Meriel behind a Chinese screen and kissed her with urgent passion. When he thrust his hand inside her bodice to tug at her breasts, she pushed against his chest in protest, but her lips remained captured and his embrace was like a vice around her arms. Finally he broke for breath and murmured, 'Let us away to my rooms. We will return before St John is any the wiser. They will be an hour at cards.'

She wrenched free of him. 'My lord! You mistake me.'

'Why so coy? You permitted me more than a few kisses when you last stayed. Though you took flight when that stupid maid came upon us. I dismissed the wench for ruining our sport.'

'My lord, that was after your summer ball. I had drunk too much and you were too persuasive. I should not have permitted you such liberties.' She had been relieved at the maid's intervention, for Lord Fetherington had frightened her with the power of his passion, and had been intent on more than flirting and stealing a kiss. He had torn open her bodice and she had been struggling with him when the maid arrived. 'You were too bold, my lord, and you would have shamed me.'

'But did I not make amends? You accepted my gift of the diamond earrings.' They had been too expensive to refuse and Meriel had told St John she had won them from one of the women guests at cards.

Lord Fetherington's leer told her he expected payment for his gift. She glared at him with scorn. 'I accepted your gift as your apology, my lord. Was I naïve to have done so? I had not expected to be beholden to you. But then I am unversed in many ways of the gentry. Aunt Elspeth taught me that a gentleman's word is his bond. Is it less so for a nobleman?'

'No lady would accept such a gift.' He allowed

70

his own scorn and frustration to show. 'A true lady would be aware of the donor's intent and of the conditions. Time to pay for my generosity, sweet wench.'

He tried to kiss her again but Meriel stamped on his foot and wriggled free. 'Then it is for me to apologise to you, my lord. Clearly, I am no lady, but then I am more aware than most that I hold my place in society through the generosity of my husband. I have too much honour and respect for him to shame his name.'

'Do not play the innocent with me,' he accused. 'You tricked St John into marriage and were carrying his child. You are an opportunist, madam, but a beautiful one. I am prepared to be generous.'

A low muttering from Lady Fetherington warned them that her ladyship had woken up. Lord Fetherington released Meriel with a scowl and whispered, 'Your type can always be bought for the right price, and I can be very generous, Meriel.'

When her initial indignation wore off, Meriel, considered his Lordship's words. He could be right, but her place in society was at present too insecure for her to risk falling from grace.

Luck remained with St John that evening and he left Lord Fetherington's house the next morning the richer by seventy guineas. He bought two embroidered waistcoats and a gold horsehead stock pin for himself, plus a gold ring with two large aquamarine stones for Meriel. Out of her own winnings Meriel purchased two new hats.

Meriel was in good spirits and St John hoped

the new clothes and jewellery would satisfy her cravings and make her forget about the smuggling venture with her brothers.

While St John was in Truro, Adam was working in the yard. He spent the morning with Ben Mumford, climbing over scaffolding and walking through partially completed decks as he inspected the work in progress. The afternoon was more onerous, spent in the small office with his father.

They sat at a battered oak desk with the shipyard ledgers opened. In cubbyholes round the walls were rolled parchments of plans of earlier vessels built in the yard, and charts of the oceans which Adam had collected. The walls were bare of decoration and the desk and heavy wooden chairs were practical rather than ornamental.

'Outwardly, we look prosperous,' Adam observed, 'but the ledgers tell a different story. We have only received half the payment for Lanyon's cutter and there has been massive expenditure on the other vessels, with only the initial costs met by the owners. Bills for iron ore for the nail-making and timber are unpaid. Has our expansion been too fast?' A weight seemed to be pressing down on his chest as he tried to stave off a growing feeling of alarm. He studied his father closely.

'It was a necessary risk which was beginning to pay off—'

'But is the expansion proving a problem?' Adam interrupted, sensing his father's reticence.

'I thought Amelia's money was meeting some of the costs.'

Edward stared out of the window at the panoramic view across the dry dock and the ships being built. A frown pinched his brows together. He rubbed the back of his neck, which was a sign that he was troubled, and he did not meet Adam's stare.

'I was always loath to use Amelia's money. Most of her late husband's estate is tied up in trust for Richard, as is right and proper. Amelia has a generous allowance. She has been lavish in using it to build the dry dock and refurbish both the Dower House, your own Mariner's House and provide a school here.'

He paused before proceeding in a weightier tone, 'There has been trouble in London over the collection of rent moneys which your Uncle Charles deals with for her. And apparently dividends on her investments have drastically fallen in the last year.'

Adam felt his foreboding increase. 'That must have been a blow after you were committed to so much expenditure at the yard.'

Edward nodded. 'It could not have come at a worse time. I raised loans with a bank in Liskeard to cover the costs and the interest is due next month. I need three hundred pounds to meet it, and there are the men's wages also to pay.'

'When are the next dividends due?' Adam could see the tension in his father. Edward was trying to make light of the matter but the ledgers showed that their situation was grave.

'Margaret will be bringing a banker's draft with

her to be drawn on my Truro bankers, which should settle everything.'

Adam was not deceived by his father's bravado. There was a hollowness in his gut and his heart was beating suffocatingly fast. 'And if there are no dividends?'

Edward jolted up straight and his eyes were haunted. 'Then the yard will face a financial crisis. But I doubt it will come to that. Charles Mercer has never failed us in the past.'

'Yet Aunt Margaret has sent no word as to the cause of her delay? I have a bad feeling about this, sir.'

'It is unlike her.' Edward picked up a quill and fidgeted with it. 'A social engagement may have delayed her departure, but I fear that my creditors cannot be put off much longer.'

Adam sprang to his feet and paced the room, too disturbed to sit still. 'Will you have to mortgage the house, sir?'

Edward shot him a fierce look and Adam saw the anguish in its depths. 'The house is already mortgaged. I can raise no more money unless I sell some of the land. That, I pray, will not be necessary. Margaret will bring the money in time.'

Adam felt fear spiral through him like a whirlpool. To lose any part of Trevowan would be as painful as losing a limb. 'I should receive my profits from the cargo at the month's end. You must use them to tide the yard over.'

'Nonsense! I will not hear of it.' Edward was adamant. 'You need that money to buy your next cargo. You cannot afford for the *Pegasus* to be laid up and neither will your other investors tolerate it. Your reputation will also suffer and reputation is everything in such a trade.'

Now was not the time for Adam to inform his father that his biggest investor had backed out of putting his money in the next voyage. He was a mine owner and the price of tin and copper had fallen drastically.

'What money I have is yours if you need it, sir. Keeping Trevowan intact and the yard continuing with its work is what is important.'

Edward closed the leather-bound ledger and frowned at the now ragged plume of the quill. 'Generous as your offer is, it will not be enough and I would not endanger your future.'

In his fear and passion to keep Trevowan intact, Adam rounded on his father, his voice rasping with pain. 'And what of the family reputation? How can you sell any land without gossip and speculation becoming rife that the yard is in trouble? We could lose customers. It will destroy all you have worked for.'

Edward stood up. 'It will not come to that. We have a month before the loan is due. If Margaret does not arrive by the weekend then I will go to London. We could be worrying unduly. I should not have burdened you with my doubts.'

His father was making a valiant show of being optimistic but Adam was not deceived. Edward remained deeply troubled.

Chapter Four

On Sunday Meriel donned her new finery and insisted that St John and she attend Penruan church instead of the service conducted by Joshua Loveday at Trewenna. The family set off for Trewenna church in the coach. Meriel, who in the last year had learned to ride, was perched side-saddle on the quietest of Elspeth's mares. St John rode Prince and led Rowena on her pony. As they neared the headland with the fishermen's cottages of Penruan spread in a horseshoe below them, Meriel smoothed her skirts and tilted her head higher.

The church bell was calling the congregation to prayer. Its resonance echoed around the cleft in the cliffs made by the coombe which led down to the harbour. The tide was out and the fishing luggers were tilted on their keels in the mud. The drying and fishing sheds were shuttered and silent along the quay, while overhead the gulls swooped in noisy search for any morsels discarded from the last catch.

A crisp wind blew off the sea, and the sky was garlanded by feathery clouds which allowed the sun to warm them. Meriel loved to arrive at her old village in style. No other woman there had risen so high. Others of her age continued to live in drudgery, their hands calloused from cleaning the catches of herring, mackerel and pilchards, their skin and clothing forever reeking of rancid fish. She had been adamant that such a life was not for her. In her new clothes and with the aquamarine ring glinting in the sunlight, she felt very much the lady of the manor. Her head was too high to notice the denigrating glances from the villagers who trudged through the streets to attend a Methodist meeting in the next valley. Even if she had seen them she would not have cared.

Meriel always delayed her departure from Trevowan to arrive at Penruan church only minutes before the service began. That ensured everyone noticed her entrance. The last of the villagers who had gathered in the churchyard trailed through the porch as St John lifted Meriel and Rowena from their mares and tethered the horses by the lych-gate.

It had been several weeks since they had last attended a service here. As they entered the square-towered Norman church, the drone of conversation hushed. Meriel nodded to her mother, Sal, the only Sawle present. Her father and brothers would be supping ale in the back room of the Dolphin and waiting for Sal to serve their lunch.

Sal became yearly more wrinkled, her back rounded from long hours of cleaning and cooking at the inn. Her grey hair was pinned under her Sunday lace cap, and her smile, with its gaps from lost front teeth, was full of pride as she regarded her younger daughter.

'Done well for herself, has my Meriel.' Sal nudged her neighbour and patted the red

77

woollen shawl Meriel had bought her last winter. 'And she sees her old ma don't go without.'

The neighbour, Ginny Rundle, who had delivered both Meriel and Rowena into the world, sniffed and scratched the side of her large breast. 'It wouldn't harm her to visit her ma more. Meriel spends time aplenty at Traherne Hall dancing attendance on her Ladyship. My Sarah do visit me twice a week. Never fails to bring us a basket of food and the like. It bain't been easy since my Alf lost his arm.'

'It be different for Sarah.' Sal was defensive. It saddened her that she saw so little of Meriel, but whenever she came to the inn, Reuban or Clem would demand some favour or money from her. Reuban reckoned that since his daughter had married a Loveday he was entitled to special privileges. His attitude had become worse since his joints had become swollen and stiff in the last two winters. Edward Loveday had sworn on the day he learned of his son's forced marriage to Meriel that the Sawles would get nothing. Edward Loveday was a man of his word, but it did not stop Reuban raving at his daughter. Sal did not blame Meriel for staying away.

Sal regarded Ginny Rundle with resignation. 'Your Sarah be the wife of the bailiff of Trevowan. My Meriel will one day be its mistress. She has responsibilities: a big house to run and she helps Miss Elspeth with the orphaned children. She do right by me, never you fear.'

Meriel passed by the congregation and ac-knowledged the greeting of Martha Snell, the rector's wife, who ran the ill-attended village school. Too many of the children were needed to help with the catch, or at home, to attend to their education. Meriel was proud that she could write her name, but had not the patience to master her letters fully. During the early days of her marriage, St John and Elspeth had insisted that she learn to read and write as befitted a gentlewoman, but she had soon grown weary and refused to persevere.

The Chegwiddens were also present and St John paused to say a word to the Lovedays' physician. He was shocked to see the way the old man's hand shook as though from a palsy. Simon Chegwidden, a young widower, received many curious glances from the unattached women of the village. He was in his mid-thirties, with a beakish nose, close-set eyes and carried himself with a military bearing. His reputation as a physician had yet to be proved. William Loveday, St John's uncle, who was a captain in the navy, had once derided him as an arrogant sawbones. At Simon's side was a sullen-faced girl of about ten years, dressed in pink taffeta.

'This is my daughter, Clarice,' the doctor proclaimed.

The girl curtsied but her expression remained bored. There was a look of disgust in her eyes when they alighted upon any of the village children.

'Have you lost your tongue, Clarice?' The prim, grey-clad governess at the end of the pew whispered to her charge. 'Say good day to Mister and Mistress Loveday.'

The girl stared at her feet in silent defiance.

Simon Chegwidden flushed with anger. 'Clarice misses her mother – though the poor woman passed away two years ago. The move to Penruan from Plymouth has unsettled her.'

'Once she makes friends with the village children, she will feel more at home,' Meriel remarked.

The girl scowled. 'They are dirty and stink of fish. Who would want them as friends?'

'They are your father's patients and deserve respect,' Meriel reminded the child.

Clarice pouted. 'My father's patients are Sir Henry and Lady Traherne.'

'But I doubt Lady Traherne invites her physician's daughter to her nursery,' Meriel quipped. The girl needed to be taught her place. Meriel studied Simon Chegwidden and disliked his weak chin and close-set eyes. With a brittle smile, she added. 'Penruan is a close community. Reverend Mr Snell and Mr Lanyon, who are both childless, are the only villagers of your social standing. Clarice may find it lonely here. I trust not.'

She hoped that Simon Chegwidden would not be a regular guest to dine at Trevowan. Both he and his daughter were too aware of their own importance for her taste.

Ginny Rundle's voice carried to her. 'That Clarice Chegwidden reminds me of your Meriel at her age, Sal.'

Meriel sucked in her breath at the midwife's impudence and with her head held high proceeded to the family pew. Her eyes widened in shock. Opposite the Loveday stall an ornate pew had been erected. The figure of an angel was at each end of the seat, which was cushioned in red and gold velvet. The Loveday pew was shoddy by comparison, having served the family for a hundred and fifty years. The wood was scuffed and cracked with age and the cushions thread-bare. It had not been renovated as Edward always attended Joshua's services.

Meriel tried not to stare at the impressive structure which was taller and more dominant than their own. Who owned it? No new family had moved into the district, and where was the parson? The bell was no longer ringing and it was past the time the service should have begun. She fidgeted as they were made to wait.

St John had cast a suspicious eye over the pew opposite. 'Who the devil thinks to take such precedence?' he snapped. 'It cannot be Sir Henry, for Traherne Hall is within Uncle Joshua's parish and Roslyn prefers Joshua's sermons. Not one for the fire and brimstone, Uncle Josh, and he knows to keep a sermon short. Unlike Snell who witters on for an hour or more. I do not see why you must attend here.'

'The people look to your father as the local squire. It is fitting that we show ourselves on occasion.'

There was another lull from the congregation and expecting to see Mr Snell process down the aisle, Meriel's eyes widened. Thadeous Lanyon had entered with a woman on his arm. Lanyon was the wealthiest man in Penruan. Apart from the drying and smoking sheds, he owned the Gun, a rival inn to the Dolphin, and the general store. He was notorious for his involvement in the free trade, acting as the smugglers' banker and organiser behind many of the runs in the district.

Thadeous Lanyon was squat of figure, with a thick neck and large balding head. His lascivious, bulbous eyes had always repelled Meriel. Even now she shuddered that her father had once intended that she wed this man. Thank God she had seduced St John and escaped such a fate.

Belatedly, Meriel recognised the woman in blue velvet, and almost choked. It was Hester Moyle, the chandler's eldest daughter, and her brother Harry's intended bride. They had been courting for five years. Why was Hester on Lanyon's arm? And more strangely, why was Harry permitting it? Last she had heard, Harry was talking of a wedding at the end of the pilchard season. Though he had said that for the last two years, then found excuses to hang on to his freedom.

Hester saw Meriel's scowl and, gloveless, wriggled her left hand. A huge cluster of diamonds sparkled on her wedding finger. She held Meriel's glare as it took in her attire, calculating its cost. Realising that the fine velvet elaborately embroidered in gold thread would cost twice as much again as her own outfit, Meriel paled. There was no mistaking the smirk on Hester's lovely face. The two most beautiful women in the village had never been friends. Meriel had hated Hester from the moment Harry had taken an interest in her. She adored Harry, who was less brutal than Clem, and closer to her in age than her younger brother, Mark. Hester had stolen Harry's affections from Meriel when she was fifteen, and Meriel could never bear to be second place in anyone's affection.

She glanced towards Bart Moyle, Hester's father and the owner of the village chandlery. He was looking smug, as was Hester's younger sister, Annie. Bart Moyle had never approved of Harry as a suitor and thought the Sawles, as innkeepers, were too lowly for a chandler's daughter.

Thadeous Lanyon paused by the rood rail and turned to face the congregation.

'People of Penruan, may I present my wife. Hester and I were married in Truro on Friday. Mr Snell has kindly consented to bless our match this day. There will be free ale and refreshments at the Gun after the service. I hope you will all join our celebration.'

'But you can't be wed to Lanyon.' Sal stood up and shook her fist at Hester. 'You be set to wed our Harry.'

Lanyon grinned with triumph. 'There was no formal betrothal.'

'The whole village understood they were to wed,' Sal shouted.

'Informal understandings have a way of being overridden. As you should be aware, Mrs Sawle.'

There was a spate of spiteful whisperings as the villagers sniggered at her family's discomfort. Meriel glowered at them. The grand impression she had wanted to make on these people this day had been ruined. She was mortified at the way so many were gloating.

Meriel glanced at her mother for her reaction. Lanyon had never forgiven her family for the humiliation after Meriel had married St John instead of himself. Sal was clearly shocked. Obviously Harry did not yet know of this marriage. Would there be hell to pay? Or would Lanyon's influence curb her brother's retaliation? Harry and Clem had taken over from their father and were in charge of the smugglers who ran Lanyon's cargo. Knowing Harry he would want revenge. Neither would he work for Lanyon again.

'I see naught but ill feeling raised by this,' Sal prophesied. 'You both be fools if your think my Harry will let this insult ride. And I won't be part of any blessing on your marriage.' She pushed her way to the end of the bench and marched from the church.

Thadeous Lanyon watched Sal leave, his thin lips clamped into a harsh line. He never allowed a slight or insult to pass. The Sawles were a dangerous family to strike against, but he was their match – not in brawn, but by other means. By wedding Hester he had hit them hard. He had avenged himself upon the Sawles for Meriel's rejection, and won himself a beautiful bride in the bargain.

Thadeous Lanyon turned to St John, who since his marriage to Meriel he had regarded as an enemy. His smile was false. 'It would be an honour if you and your dear wife would attend.'

'Well, I...' St John blustered. He had no liking for Lanyon, who after his marriage to Meriel had called in a loan to his father which had almost been the ruin of his family. Lanyon was an upstart, the pew proved that. St John's manner became chillingly arrogant. 'Honoured as we are at your invitation, Lanyon, I fear we have to decline. Rather short notice. We have Sir Henry and Uncle Joshua and his family dining with us.'

Meriel was tempted to follow Sal's example and leave, but she hesitated as the spindly figure of the Reverend Mr Snell approached the altar. Her angry stare swept over Hester, who had now taken her place in the pew opposite. It was then that Meriel saw the sapphire and diamond brooch which she had coveted in Truro adorning Hester's bodice. Her fury intensified. It was not to be suffered. Hester and Thadeous Lanyon must be taught their place. How dare they seek to usurp the Lovedays' position in the village!

Mr Snell began the service. No matter how dearly Meriel would like to storm out of the church, St John would not tolerate an ill-mannered scene. There were other ways to get back at the couple.

She stared fixedly at the golden cross on the altar, her mind working furiously. St John had fallen foul of her brothers during their last smuggling venture. It was time the rift was healed between her family and her husband. Smuggling was in the Sawles' blood. Clem would demand that St John put up at least a one-half share in the cargo. That was another problem to overcome.

Last time they had been unfortunate and she had always suspected that one of Lanyon's spies had tipped off the excise men that night. There was more than one score to settle here, for she, no less than her brothers, believed that revenge was the only form of justice against an enemy.

Ten days later there was still no word from Margaret. The silence disturbed Edward for there was no reason Charles Mercer could not have forwarded Amelia's investment dividends by messenger. Charles knew the extent of the loan Edward had taken out, and that the high rate of interest was now due.

It was a warm evening and the Loveday family strolled in the rose arbour at Trevowan which Amelia had replanted last summer. Joshua Loveday and his wife, Cecily, were with them. The arbour was circular with stone benches around its perimeter, and at its centre on a plinth was a life-size statue of the Goddess Diana holding her bow, with a tame wolf at her feet. Hundreds of red, pink, yellow and white flowers wove a tapestry of rich colour across the trellis work and sheltering brick wall. In the heat, the air was heavy with the flowers' scent and the drone of bees.

'It is several weeks since we last heard from Margaret,' Joshua said, his hand threaded inside the opening of his black coat. His tall figure had thickened around the waist. He was dressed in black knee-breeches and hose, a long black frock coat over an amber waistcoat, and wore a powdered bagwig. Unless performing a service in church, he did not conform to a cleric's attire. Also rare for a clergyman, a mischievous twinkle was never far from his eyes, though at this moment they were serious as he continued, 'It is not like our dear sister. Margaret writes more letters than I do sermons and keeps the mail coaches well supplied. She would write if she had changed her usual plans.'

'She could have been set upon by cutthroats and thieves on the highway.' Elspeth was visibly agitated. 'I cannot shake from my mind the feeling that something is wrong.'

The women seated themselves on a stone bench surrounded by red and yellow roses. Edward cleared his throat. 'Of course this trouble with Thomas could have overset Margaret. There are matters I should attend to with my business agent in London.' He kept his voice matter-of-fact so that the women would not detect his concern. 'Since Margaret does not appear to be on her way here, and there is the chance that her letter has gone astray, I will call upon her to reassure us all that nothing is amiss. I intend to leave for London tomorrow.'

'London, by Jove, Uncle!' A voice boomed from behind them and Japhet Loveday strode into their midst. 'I have a mind to journey there myself. I shall accompany you.'

'Japhet, where have you sprung from?' his mother, Cecily, gasped. 'St John said you had been away from Truro for a month when he called at your lodgings last week.'

'Bath is a grand place, Mama.' He swept a high-domed beaver hat from his long dark hair tied back in a queue. Side whiskers added to the rakish handsome features. At seven-and-twenty he was three years older than the twins and at three inches over six foot, he was taller than his cousins by two inches. He bowed his slim figure to the ladies present. Then straightening, he frowned. 'Is Aunt Margaret not here? Do I play the diligent nephew in vain? How vexing.'

'Margaret has not come to Cornwall this year.' Elspeth held her pince-nez to her nose to scrutinize him from toe to head. Her breath whistled through her teeth. 'I never took you for a preening fob, Japhet. What are those extraordinary clothes and manners you have brought back from Bath?'

Always ready to turn a situation to humour, he laughed and played with the intricate twists of his stock from the centre of which gleamed a large sapphire pin. In cream breeches, expensive leather knee-boots, black embroidered waistcoat and burgundy cutaway tail coat with a high standing collar, he was a commanding figure. 'For years you have berated me to dress like a gentleman instead of a ragamuffin. I have donned my Sunday best in your honour, dear Aunt. I am distraught that I have failed to please you.' He blew her a kiss across the garden.

Elspeth hrmphed and shook her head. 'I am too old to fall for your slick charm, my boy. Though I fancy many a poor wench has been foolishly smitten to her cost.'

'They do not have your insight and wisdom, Aunt Elspeth,' Japhet parried.

'I think Japhet looks most handsome.' Cecily glowed with pride as she regarded her eldest son. 'You are always too harsh on him, Elspeth.'

Japhet laughed and embraced his mother with true affection. 'And you grow more beautiful each time I see you, Mama.' He raised first Amelia's and then Meriel's hand to his lips and acknowledged the greetings from the men. After surveying his family, he added, 'I see that my pious brother does not grace this gathering. Surely the term has ended at Cambridge.'

'Peter has chosen to work amongst the poor in Bristol during the next month,' Joshua explained.

'Heaven help the poor,' Japhet said with a laugh. 'They will be getting hell and damnation sermons delivered with every ladle of charitable gruel. Still, I shall be spared him trying to exorcise my devils.' He rested his foot on a stone bench and turned to Adam. 'Glad to see you back on shore. Are you also going to London?'

Adam looked at his father; the speed of Edward's intended departure had surprised him. 'There is work in the yard–'

'Yes, Adam will accompany me,' Edward interrupted. 'We have yet to finalize plans.'

'Splendid. All the more reason I shall join you. You do not object, Uncle?'

Edward sighed and raised a brow at his brother.

Joshua shrugged and replied, 'London did not smile kindly on your visit two years ago, Japhet. I recall you left in somewhat of a hurry.'

'A family trait, Papa, is it not?' Japhet could not resist referring to the incident where Joshua, as a young man, had killed a highwayman and fled the capital. The experience had led to him reforming his old life and taking the cloth.

'Would that you could learn from past mistakes.' Joshua eyed him in exasperation. 'I pray daily that in time you will put your wild ways behind you.'

'And your prayers are gratefully appreciated,

sir.' Japhet spoke with humility, but there was an unrepentant sparkle in his eyes. 'I am not without hope of redemption, yet the life of a sinner has so many merits to recommend it.'

His joking tone raised both laughter and a shake of heads, except from St John who rapped out, 'I was not informed of this excursion to London. I have long promised Meriel a visit to the capital.'

'I am sorry, St John,' Edward said. 'I want you here in charge of matters.'

'Why must St John always be left behind?' Meriel demanded, her hands clenched in anger. 'It is not fair.'

Edward regarded Meriel sternly. 'You will have your visit to London. Amelia will open her London house and you will be the toast of the season. But not this time. Amelia is not well enough to undergo the arduous journey. It is five days' hard travelling and our visit is for but a few days.'

'Even a few days would be–' Meriel challenged.

'Meriel, it is not your place to question Edward's decision,' Elspeth interrupted.

Meriel stood up, her head flung back in defiance. 'St John has as much right to visit London as Adam. More so. He is the one who slaves on the land while Adam roams the sea at his leisure.'

'Right has nothing to do with it,' Edward corrected. 'We go to London on business. Adam will visit warehouses to acquire merchandise for his next voyage.'

'It still is not fair,' Meriel raged. 'Are our wishes

of no importance? Obviously not.' She ran from the garden.

Elspeth tutted with displeasure. 'Just as I believe she is learning a semblance of decorum, that baggage resorts to her fishwife tactics. It will not do, St John. Blood will always out, I fear. Displays of temper will not get her to London. Rather the opposite if the woman had the wit to fathom it. How can we trust her to act properly and not shame the family?'

'She is upset, Aunt.' St John was white with anger. 'And is it so unreasonable? There is room enough for us all in the coach if Japhet did not travel.'

Japhet held up his hands. 'Do not blame this on me. I am content to ride alongside the coach. It is more comfortable than having your bones rattled by every pothole and rut.'

'I agree with Elspeth,' Edward declared. 'Meriel's display today is not what we expect from her. And our trip is a short one. It will be arduous and bring little pleasure.'

'Speak for yourself, Uncle,' Japhet chuckled. 'I intend to make merry in London.'

St John scowled. 'In her disappointment Meriel may have acted badly, but you use it as an excuse. When will you accept her as an equal? We have all felt the sting of your tongue, Aunt Elspeth, in public. More than once you have left the room when you have been bettered in an argument. When has that ever brought shame to our family? It is your prejudice against Meriel's birth which is against her. And that she can do nothing about.'

91

He bowed to Cecily and Amelia. 'Your servant, ladies, but my wife is justifiably upset, and I will go to her.'

A stunned silence followed his departure. Japhet gave a low whistle and added in an undertone to Adam, 'St John is showing his mettle at last.'

Elspeth looked ruffled. 'Edward, I despair of St John. Without loyalty to each other a family will flounder.'

Adam had been silent throughout. The undercurrents of tension in the house had deepened since he'd embarked on his voyage. He was driven to remark, 'Surely St John's first loyalty is to his wife.'

Elspeth sniffed, her stare accusing as it moved from Japhet to Adam. 'I trust you two know your duty and will wed more suitable brides. It is time you both settled down.'

'My freedom is worth more than gold,' Japhet declared. 'Time enough for marriage when the blood runs less hotly in my veins. Is that not true, Adam?'

Adam declined to reply. He was watching his father in conversations with Uncle Joshua and recognised the lines of worry etched deep around Edward's mouth and eyes. There was a great deal at stake in this London visit.

Chapter Five

'How was your sojourn in Bath, Japhet?' Adam braced himself against the side of the swaying coach. A vicious lurch threw his head against the glazed window, and even the padded leather upholstery provided little comfort as they were jolted by the deep ruts in the London road. He was bruised from collarbone to knee. Since they had left Cornwall, two days of rain had churned up the road, making craters a regular hazard. Twice they had alighted to put planks beneath the wheels when they had become stuck.

They had left the steep valleys and hills of Devon and Dorset behind them and this morning the countryside was flatter as they approached Surrey. Here, in the drier climate, the grass was baked to ochre rather than the emerald brightness of the meadows of Cornwall.

'Judas, these roads grow more shocking,' Adam groaned. 'A buffeting from a tempest at sea is scarcely more injurious to one's person.'

Japhet's complexion was tinged greyish-green. He removed his hand from across his mouth. '*Mal de mer* is not confined to travel by sea. When is the next halt? I fear I am dying.'

'Tell me of Bath and take your mind from your sickness,' suggested Adam.

Japhet made an effort to rally his spirits; a swig of brandy from a silver hip flask brought some colour back to his face. 'Bath is a splendid city in the season but in recent weeks it has become somewhat dull.' Japhet glanced across at Edward, who was again dozing after the last violent jolt and lowered his voice. 'And the husband of an accommodating viscountess suspected our liaison and also my tailor's bills, which she had put on his account.' He flicked the triple cape on the burgundy greatcoat he was wearing and patted a black and silver embroidered waistcoat. 'She insisted I wore only the best.'

'Is not the acceptance of such gifts from a woman shaming?' Adam was shocked. But then he often was at Japhet's behaviour, which too often took him the wrong side of the law.

Japhet lifted a dark brow, his expression sardonic. 'I have not the benefit of your affluence. Your father prudently used the legacy which all the Loveday cousins received from Great-uncle Amos to build the *Pegasus* for you. My own legacy rather slipped through my fingers, lost on reckless ventures and beautiful women and a taste for the high life. I have all the prestige of the Loveday name, but not the capital to live the extravagant life of my ancestors.'

'Many of whom, without such capital, chose the sea,' Adam replied.

'I would have been keelhauled for insubordination within a year. You were often in trouble with senior officers who were less competent than yourself.' He shook his head and gave a mock shudder. 'Similarly the poverty-stricken years of an apprentice to some trade held no thrall. When needs must, I make a tolerable living

94

as a horse-dealer. If all else fails Mama shall have her heart's desire and see me wed to an heiress.'

'Have you someone in mind?'

Japhet took another swig of brandy and offered the flask to Adam. 'It is no more than a passing notion. Though finding a woman who will overlook my reputation, who is pretty enough to make bedding her a pleasure, and is malleable enough not to try to change my life, will not be easy. In the meantime I take the opportunities which come my way. If a woman of beauty, wit, title and fortune enjoys my company, and is generous with her gifts, that is her privilege.'

He lifted a heavy leather pouch from inside his greatcoat. 'Name and appearance are everything when gaining entry to a game of hazard where the stakes are high, but fortunes can be won.'

'Or lost,' Adam counselled.

'At present Lady Luck smiles on me.'

'Long may she continue to do so for she is a fickle mistress.'

Japhet chuckled. 'Capricious as all women, but therein is the sport.'

Edward opened one eye to regard his nephew. There was as much the rogue as the gentleman in him. No wonder Joshua despaired that his eldest son would end his days in gaol. Yet Japhet's easy charm and wit were without malice. He had a love of life and of women, and women adored him. Though he loved them and left them with unerring frequency, that devilish charm of his had made no enemies among his ex-lovers. If only the same could be said of their husbands.

To Edward's knowledge Japhet had been the

95

victor of a dozen duels already. He had never killed an opponent, his honour appeased once he had drawn first blood. His reputation was making him notorious. It was time that Japhet took a wife and became respectable, but Edward doubted his headstrong nephew would ever become truly conventional. That was what made him such a fascinating rascal.

The brandy had revived Japhet, and he began to rib Adam. 'So what of your life, coz? Having escaped from the clutches of matrimony once, have you any notions of taking up the shackles again?'

Adam frowned. The memories of his betrothal to his French cousin Lisette were still able to rouse conflicting emotions: first relief that he had escaped matrimony when he was already in love with Senara; and then guilt that he had failed Lisette Riviere. Family duty had made him agree to the betrothal when his uncle Claude Riviere was fatally ill. With the seeds of discontent so strong in France, Claude Riviere had feared for the safety of his young daughter.

When Adam had learned that Uncle Claude was dying he'd gone to Paris to honour his obligation and wed Lisette. His father had travelled with him. There they had found Claude Riviere already buried and Aunt Louise being nursed in a convent after suffering a paralysing apoplexy. Adam had been told that Lisette's brother, Etienne, who had always been against the betrothal, had married Lisette to the Marquis de Gramont – a man Adam knew to be cruel, lecherous and capable of evil.

Adam had raged that the marriage was not legal, but before he had been able to attempt to rescue Lisette from Gramont's clutches, the events in France had become volatile and dangerous. He had been in Paris during the fall of the Bastille. When he discovered that Lisette had been taken to the Marquis's estate in Auvergne, Edward had urged Adam to return to England. His father insisted that now Claude was dead, Etienne had become Lisette's guardian.

'Sometimes I feel my freedom was ill won,' Adam confided. 'Lisette was so trusting and such a child. And Uncle Claude wanted her out of France for he guessed the mood of the people could turn to rebellion. In that he was right. France remains a powder keg with the fuse ready to ignite.'

'It is certainly that,' Japhet replied. 'Since last October when King Louis was forced to remove his residence to the Tuileries in Paris, the number of *émigrés* has risen. Did you hear that Louis tried to flee France this June? His coach was stopped and he was sent back to Paris a virtual prisoner.'

'I have not heard the latest news. But that is disturbing. Do you think they intend to end the monarchy?'

Japhet shrugged. 'It would not surprise me. Last month revolutionists were massacred in Paris by the National Guard. Then they say that the Emperor of Austria and the King of Prussia want Louis restored to full power.'

'I had not realised the situation had become so serious.' Adam let out a harsh breath in disbelief. He touched his father's arm, waking him, to ask,

'Sir, Japhet has been telling me of this summer's events in France. Has there been news of Lisette? Or of Aunt Louise?'

Edward stirred and replied, 'The last letter was over eight months ago. Your aunt is much improved in health. I had intended to visit the convent to ensure that all is well but business matters kept me at home. There has been no news of Etienne or Lisette. That nephew of mine has much to answer for. He has not visited his mother.'

He regarded Adam before adding, 'My mind would rest easier if I sailed to France. Perhaps I shall do so next month, if all is well with Margaret, and you could accompany me, Adam. *Pegasus* will still be in dry dock. We can take passage from Falmouth.'

At the Dower House Meriel was deciding the placement of two Sèvres shepherdesses which had been given to her by Amelia when she'd admired them at Trevowan. A spindle-legged table in the window recess of the parlour set them off to their best advantage and could not fail to be noticed by any visitor.

'They think I am a child to be bought by gifts,' she complained to St John, who was smoking a clay pipe and reading the *Sherborne Mercury*. He lounged on the day bed with one foot resting on its upholstery. 'We had as much right as Adam and Japhet to go to London.'

'And you will, my love,' St John placated. He was unwilling to provoke her after a long day helping with the coppicing of Ten-Acre Wood.

'Amelia did say she felt it was her fault that her condition prevented her travelling. And you have long wanted such figurines which are beyond my income.'

'As it seems is so much,' Meriel pouted. 'You promised me a proper riding habit months ago.'

He resumed his reading, ignoring the tirade of complaints which had become a daily routine. It was a balmy evening, without even the customary sea breeze to bring relief. His shirt stuck clammily to his shoulders and the pigeon pie and oversweet raspberry syllabub he had eaten was leaden in his stomach. The four brandies he had drunk had not helped his digestion. Suddenly the newssheet was snatched from his hands.

'Damn you! You are not listening to me, St John.'

'Every word, my dear. You find me an inadequate provider and forget that when we married I took you with just the clothes you stood up in. Now you have a wardrobe full.' He retrieved the newssheet from her and carefully refolded it.

'But what of the other matter? Do you agree it is a matter of respect?'

'Respect? Ah, there you have me, my love. In what way a matter of respect.'

'About Lanyon,' Meriel ground out. 'I knew you were not heeding me. He is an upstart. That pew shows he would put himself above us.'

St John stifled a yawn. 'It is a matter of small consequence. The Lovedays prefer to worship at Trewenna. It is only you, my dear, who insist on attending Penruan church.'

She threw up her arms, her eyes dangerously bright. 'As ever, St John, you miss the point. Many of the villagers pay rent on cottages owned by the Lovedays. Lanyon would usurp our influence and power in the village.' Meriel picked up a fan she had tossed on the rocking chair and waved it in furious agitation.

'I do not think we have ever considered our interest in the village was one of power,' he corrected. 'Our family has always been the one the people of Penruan look to as their benefactors. Lanyon has become a man of property over the last dozen years. Many of the villagers are in debt to him.'

'Does that not trouble you?' Hands on hips she planted herself before him. 'Would you see him rise above your family? For that is his aim. The man has no principles. He has slighted the Lovedays by erecting that pew.'

St John pressed his fingers to his lips, his eyes wary as he studied her. 'This is not just about our family, is it? It is about Lanyon marrying Hester Moyle, who was to be your brother's bride. No doubt Lanyon found satisfaction in robbing Harry of Hester. Lanyon lost face when we wed, for he had intended you as his bride.'

'I never agreed. That was my father's idea. But remember how Lanyon's spite almost ruined your father by calling in a loan. It is about justice. Lanyon grows yearly more important. Have you forgotten that it was he who tipped off the revenue officers with such disastrous consequences to your last smuggling run?'

'There was no proof of that.'

She threw the fan at him and it struck his chest. 'Who else gained from it? Lanyon wanted to ruin you and he almost succeeded. Do you not want revenge?'

St John shifted uncomfortably as he recalled the humiliation of that night. 'Revenge is an unpleasant word, but if he was guilty, then he deserves to pay for that night. Three men were shot and one killed. And he cost me every penny I had.'

'You were not the only ones who lost money that night. My family did as well.'

Anger chased the tiredness from St John's body. He slammed down the newssheet. 'They lost little compared to me. And they stayed in thick with Lanyon to continue their smuggling.'

'That will have changed now. It is time to settle your differences with them and work together against Lanyon.' Meriel's manner altered. She softened and placed her arms round his, neck and kissed his cheek. 'You had one misfortune in the trade, yet before that your venture had gone so well. You had money for fine clothes and could gamble with your friends. Do you not want those days back?'

He hesitated. They had made handsome profits for a year but there was also the danger. The memory of two encounters and battles with the revenue men could still cause him to break out in a cold sweat.

The Loveday coach passed the ancient palace of Lambeth on their approach to London over Westminster Bridge. They were greeted by a watery sun breaking through the afternoon clouds. It played upon the scores of baroque churches and Palladian palaces built in white Portland stone. The skyline ahead was dominated by the twin-towered Abbey, the medieval hall of Westminster Palace and, in Whitehall, the impressive grandeur of Inigo Jones's banqueting house. Barges and wherries scurried like water beetles around the scores of two- and three-masted ships moored at crowded wharfs, or anchored in mid-river to await unloading.

Beneath the elegant façades of grand houses, the runnels in the cobbled streets were awash with effluent from overflowing drains. Throughout London outbreaks of typhus, cholera and smallpox were prevalent; dysentery and consumption added to the misery of the poorer population in their evil-smelling garrets and basements. Thousands of chimneys belched soot and smoke into the air and often a miasma of yellow smog hovered malignantly over the city.

Today after the recent rain, the air was clear. Even so, the odour of drains and the dank smell of narrow streets with their press of unwashed bodies, took the breath from the travellers' lungs. At least they were spared the stench of the tanneries and glue, soap and candle-makers further eastwards. They soon came to appreciate the more pleasant aromas wafting from the chop- and coffee-houses, the smell of freshly baked bread and pies, reminding them that it was several hours since they had eaten.

Passage through the jostling vehicles and populace which filled the streets to the Strand was slow. The Lovedays were surrounded by a cacophony of shrill voices, selling wares, or raised in argument as tempers frayed from the congestion of vehicles.

Edward pressed a handkerchief to his nose. 'The stench and noise is more obnoxious with every visit.'

It was Adam's third time in London. Used to the overcramped conditions on a ship, the press and noise of the people did not trouble him. He was enthralled by the diversity of life here. In the riverside streets, gin-sodden bawds sprawled in doorways, and young apprentices, in their leather aprons, ran errands for their masters. In contrast, beautiful women and dandified fops rode in carriages. Every stratum of society was present, their every need catered for by the victuallers, tailors, wigmakers, distillers, jewellers, silk-weavers, watchmakers and trades of every description.

'I have visited many ports but there is nowhere to match London,' Adam observed. 'There is an energy within its people: sometimes desperate, often exuberant, but always vibrant.'

'This is how life is meant to be.' Japhet gave a low whistle. 'I've lost count of the beautiful women I've seen unaccompanied. Where shall we go this evening? The playhouse or Vauxhall Gardens? At Vauxhall the entertainments are more diverse and assignations easily arranged.'

'I would not like to upset Aunt Margaret by deserting her on our first evening.' Adam was tempted to revisit the pleasure gardens, but was aware that that was not their purpose in coming to London.

'Margaret will not curtail your pleasure,' said Edward, 'though since I sent ahead saying we would arrive today, she may have planned an entertainment of her own.'

Japhet gave a theatrical groan. 'You mean she will have selected some unmarried ladies with the intent of making a match for one of us. She is an insatiable matchmaker. I will have none of her interfering.'

Japhet let down the window on the door of the coach to talk with an expensively dressed, middle-aged beauty in a yellow landau which had drawn level with them.

Edward shifted in his seat with impatience. Adam waved aside the opportunings of a one-eyed beggar-crone, her scabious, clawlike hands with grime-infested nails, held out. To give to one would be to encourage scores of others, and the coach would never get through the crowds.

A cheeky orange-seller with cascades of red hair and a buxom figure called out to Adam. 'Good day, me handsome. Buy me fresh, sweet oranges. Good fer yer love life. Fer another crown we could make merry in me rooms, darlin'. If you've a mind fer some fun, that is.'

He declined with a grin. When they finally drew up outside the Mercers' house, one of an imposing terrace of four-storey houses in the Strand, Adam was surprised to see that the downstairs shutters were closed. He glanced at his father.

'You do not think we have missed Aunt Margaret on the road, sir?'

'That could be possible, but her coachman

would have recognised our carriage. We stayed overnight at the better coach houses, which Margaret would also have chosen.'

There was a long wait before their rap on the door was answered by Henderson, the major-domo. On recognising them, he looked flustered. 'Mr Loveday, this is...' he faltered and cleared his throat. 'Madame is indisposed. I will inform her that you have arrived.'

He led the visitors into the smaller saloon at the back of the house and opened the curtains, which, strangely for so early in the afternoon, were drawn. Edward felt a spasm of unease. The room, furnished in red with leaf-green walls, had an air of neglect about it. Even the paintings – by Hogarth and Canaletto – did not brighten it. The atmosphere of the house was different, less welcoming than usual.

It took several moments for Edward to realise that there was a musty smell to the place as though it had been shut up. Also there were no fresh flowers anywhere. Margaret adored them, and was always lavish in using large arrangements to decorate every room.

A maid brought the visitors a decanter of claret and a plate of saffron biscuits, and then hurried out without more than a sketchy curtsy. She had been with the family for years and Edward had greeted her warmly. Edward poured them all a glass of the claret, and as they lifted it to their lips Thomas entered the room.

'This is a surprise, my dear boy,' Edward enthused. 'I had no idea you had settled your differences with your father and returned home.

I am delighted to see it. But we seem not to be expected. I sent word of our arrival...' His words trailed off at seeing that Thomas looked pale and drawn. He was without a jacket and his shirt looked crumpled as though he had slept in it.

'Uncle. Adam. Japhet.' He seemed to find it hard to go on and dragged a hand through his blond hair, tied back in a queue.

Last time Adam had seen Thomas, he had been fashionably bewigged, but now the younger men about town had abandoned their wigs in favour of a more natural style. Thomas was also now more soberly dressed than the usual popinjay colours he favoured.

'This is all very difficult,' Thomas said. 'You find us in the most ... well, most damnable circumstances.'

Edward looked alarmed. 'Is Margaret ill?'

'No, Mama is coping extremely well. She will be down shortly. It is Papa...' His voice broke and he turned away, his hands covering his face. He drew a shuddering breath before continuing. 'Papa is missing. He left the bank over a week ago and has not been seen since. Neither has there been any word.'

'Charles would not just vanish.' Edward was aghast. No wonder Margaret had not come to Cornwall, although the dividend cheque had been due several days before Charles's disappearance. Puzzled, he pushed aside his fears about his finances, his greater concern now for Charles's safety. 'I assume you have contacted the authorities. London is thick with footpads. Or he could have been taken ill and is somehow unable to notify you.'

'We have made discreet enquiries. That is all Mama would permit. There is the reputation of the bank to consider.' His hand shook as he raised it to his brow.

Adam sensed that Thomas was not telling them everything. 'There is more to this, is there not, Thomas?'

Thomas looked even more stricken and nodded. 'Mama wants to be here when–'

'I am here, Thomas.' Margaret Mercer stood in the doorway. Adam scarcely recognised her, she looked so haggard. Her greying hair hung lankly about her shoulders. Margaret never usually left her bedchamber unless immaculately attired, with her hair elegantly coiffured and powdered. Her cheeks were sunken and her red-rimmed eyes bruised with shadows. She was hunched as though shielding her body from pain, and although it was four in the afternoon she was still in her dressing robe. 'I have never been so glad to see you Edward. Nor so–'

At that moment there was a strident banging on the door. Margaret flinched. 'Send those dreadful men away, Thomas. I will not see them. I can bear no more.' She sank on to a chair and burst into tears.

Edward hurried to comfort her and with an ill-at-ease glance at each other, Japhet and Adam retired to the garden. They wandered along the formal walkway to a Chinese-style summerhouse surrounded by topiaried bushes cut into pyramids and spheres. From here the clamour of the street was dulled but they could hear raised voices from the front of the house.

'Rum do, all this.' Japhet nodded towards the house. 'You do not think Uncle Charles has run off with an actress or something equally scandalous? Somehow I never had him marked as a libertine.'

'Charles has strayed on one or two occasions during their marriage, but he would never leave Aunt Margaret.' Adam frowned. 'But it is serious. More than they are saying. I have never known Aunt Margaret give way to tears. She is as stalwart as Aunt Elspeth, though less of a termagant.'

'Do you think we should go back in?' Japhet sounded reluctant.

Adam shook his head. Through the window he could see his father with his arm around their aunt. His head was bent as he listened intently while she struggled to speak, her shoulders shaking with sobs. 'Best not interrupt Father. But Thomas might find it easier to talk to us.'

They found their cousin slumped on the bottom step of the staircase, his head clutched in his hands. He looked up as they approached and his handsome face was ravaged with pain.

'Sorry you had to witness that. Those damned parasites were creditors. Word is out that Papa is missing, and they are baying for blood.' He took a crumpled piece of paper from the pocket of his open waistcoat. 'This arrived about an hour ago. It's from Miller, the chief clerk at the bank. There have been near riots there, with customers demanding to withdraw their money. They have had to close the doors. But the mob will not go away.'

'You must go to reason with them!' Adam advised. 'A run on the bank in such a fashion could mean its ruin.'

'I tried yesterday when the numbers were fewer. You know how these rumours get out of hand. One of our chief investors, Sir Absalom Grimshaw, who owns a fleet of merchant ships and is an alderman of the city, was denouncing the bank for failing to pay out dividends on a South Seas investment.' Thomas looked pinched and haunted. 'Grimshaw was after Father's blood. I told them that father was convalescing after a sudden illness; that he would be back at the bank in a few days and that there was no reason for them to fear for their investments.'

'But it did no good?' Adam asked. 'Surely an eminent merchant like Grimshaw would listen to reason.'

'Grimshaw is a bad lot. Most of his money is from the slave trade.' Thomas rubbed his temple. 'They set upon me like madmen, my coat and shirt were ripped to shreds. Only the arrival of the constables saved me from further harm. Of course, they insisted on seeing Father. When they learned he had not returned home, they threatened to put out a warrant for his arrest. Now they want to interview him on suspicion of fraud and God knows what other trumped-up charges.'

'Good Lord, I have never heard anything so absurd!' Japhet exclaimed.

Thomas glanced at the door where Edward had appeared and heard his last statement. 'So now you know the worst, Uncle. I pleaded with the constables that my father was honourable. Two eminent bank customers vouched for him, and the constables agreed to wait another three days.' Again his head sank in his hands. 'Why has there been no word? We fear the worst. Yet no reports of a man of father's description having been attacked, murdered, or taken to one of the hospitals have been made. Also Grimshaw's lawyers are demanding to see the bank ledgers.'

'This is grave indeed.' Edward let out a harsh breath. His face had drained to the pallor of a tallow candle and he was shaken by the news. He now feared that more than the interest moneys on the Loveday and Amelia's investments were at stake. He swallowed to overcome an icy thrust of panic. Charles Mercer was an honourable man: these rumours must be lies. 'I cannot believe Charles capable of any misconduct. I fear he has been injured in some way. I will consult the authorities and ensure a thorough search is made.'

They spent a sombre evening. The meal remained untouched. Margaret retired to her room and Thomas, Adam and Japhet had left the house. Not for a night of carousing as Japhet had planned, but to visit all of Charles Mercer's friends, his club or any place he favoured. Drawing a blank, they proceeded with the gruelling task of visiting the City mortuary and hospitals.

Edward remained at the house. Thomas had given him a copy of the bank's ledgers, saying, 'You more than anyone have a right to see these, for Amelia's money as well as your own entrusted to Father's care. I would value your advice.'

The candle was burning low in the study when Edward shut the ledger. He slumped back in the chair and closed his eyes. Emotions overwhelmed him and he battled to keep his darkest fears in check. It was worse than he had feared.

The clock on the marble mantelshelf was chiming eleven when there was a discreet tap on the door and Henderson entered. 'Sorry to disturb you, sir, but there are two gentlemen without. I think you should see them.'

Edward nodded for Henderson to admit them.

The younger of the two held back to stand by the door; the other, a portly man of middle years, bluntly announced, 'That servant said I weren't to disturb Mrs Mercer. You a relation or something?'

'I am her brother. My sister is indisposed. Can I be of service to you, gentlemen?'

A tic fluttered erratically, distorting the older man's eyelid. 'I have to inform you that a body matching the description of Charles Mercer was found an hour ago on the Thames mudflats at Queenhythe. I have to ask you to identify the corpse, sir.'

Chapter Six

The funeral was four days later on a hot September day when the City sweltered in bright sunshine. Over eighty mourners crowded up the steps and through the outer columns of the baroque church of St Martin-in-the-Fields, which gleamed golden in the sunlight. Many of these mourners filed back to the Mercers' house, where hushed conjecture about Charles's death dominated the conversations. The word suicide was on too many lips for Edward's comfort.

'Charles Mercer was a man of honour. You do him a great disservice,' he defended when a group of mourners broached the subject. They were in the blue drawing room on the first floor. Extra servants had been engaged to polish the furniture, floors, silver and windows to restore an air of prosperity. The cream furnishings and curtains had been beaten free of dust and the air sweetened by large arrangements of roses, pinks and lilies. Edward hoped the mourners would absorb the atmosphere of wealth and security. Any hint of a scandal and these vultures would withdraw their money from the bank, and then it would fail indeed.

Edward continued more sharply, 'Charles was murdered and you should be more concerned about bringing his assailant to justice than maligning an honourable man's name.'

Margaret was protected from the gossip by Adam and Japhet, who flanked her on either side. Though she tried hard to rally her spirits, she frequently withdrew into a cocoon of sorrow.

Thomas adeptly parried questions about the stability of the bank, which the less sensitive mourners and investors broached. Sir Absalom Grimshaw was the most phlegmatic and insistent, his bulldog body braced for attack and his small eyes antagonistic with distrust.

'I trust you will bear with me, gentlemen.' There was an iron thread which ran through Thomas's voice which was at odds with the abundance of lace at his throat and wrists. 'The murder of my father has been a great shock. Business will resume as usual at the bank tomorrow.'

'Then the late dividends will be paid out to your investors,' Sir Absalom Grimshaw accosted him. 'I shall expect my draft at ten sharp, when I shall personally collect it. My lawyer will attend with me.'

Edward, aware of the strain Thomas was under, came to his side. Like so many with Loveday blood, Thomas had a fiery temper. He was also over-ready to defend the family honour with his sword. He was an accomplished wrestler and pugilist, and prone to lambast any man reckless enough to deride his foppish attire or manhood.

Edward regarded Grimshaw with a stony countenance. 'In the circumstances, Sir Absalom, your tone and manner is offensive. This is neither the time nor the place.'

Thomas intervened. 'You may call at the bank

113

tomorrow, sir. However, midday would be more convenient. I will be spending this evening and the morning going through the ledgers and checking the figures as to the exact amount of dividends payable.'

Sir Absalom Grimshaw thrust his thick neck forward and prodded Thomas's waistcoat with his stubby finger. 'Midday and not a minute later. I have been patient enough.' Without even stopping to take his leave of the widow, he stamped from the room. Several others followed, their gazes no longer meeting those of the family.

Thomas glared after them. A muscle pumped along his jaw, warning Edward, that his nephew was in danger of losing his temper. 'If I hear one further slur upon my father's honour, I swear I shall call the blackguard out.'

'Take a grip on yourself, Tom,' Edward cautioned. 'This must be dealt with delicately.'

Lucien Greene, who had kept discreetly in the background, put his hand on his friend's shoulder. Slightly below average height and with his flaxen hair tied in a long queue with the front cut and curled, he was a man whose finely chiselled features were as pretty as any woman's. He had been the cause of the rift between Charles and his son. Although married, the poet was an effeminate, and his liaison with Thomas had always disturbed Edward. But he knew that you could not change a man's nature. His concern was for his sister's future, and he knew Thomas would do nothing to jeopardise that. At least Greene's royal-blue cutaway tail coat and cream nankeen breeches were less dandified than usual, although his rose-pink waistcoat had caused several raised eyebrows.

'Men like Grimshaw make vindictive enemies.' Lucien warned. 'The bank's customers must be kept sweet however loathsome they are.'

Somehow they managed to get through the next hour and when the last of the mourners had left, Margaret escaped to her room to be alone with her grief. Lucien, after an intense conversation with Thomas, tactfully took his leave.

He bowed to Edward. 'My condolences at this difficult time, sir. I have tried to convince Thomas that he has nothing to feel guilty over. He blames himself for his father's death by leaving the bank.'

Edward nodded. 'You did right. Thomas will need the support of his friends and family in the days ahead.'

Once Lucien left, Thomas asked Edward and his cousins to join him in his father's study. His step was heavy and as he perched on the end of the Sheraton desk there was a slump to his shoulders. He gripped his hands together, the knuckles white with tension, and he kept his gaze on the Persian carpet as he spoke.

'...So there you have the truth,' he finally concluded. 'A string of disasters and high-risk investments by my father mean that there is no money to meet any of the dividends. Indeed, there is not sufficient to meet any of the large investors' demands if they decide to withdraw their money.'

It was dark outside and the light from the three candles they had lit flickered over their faces, emphasising the deep lines of worry etched there.

'And that includes the Loveday money and Amelia's investments?' Adam asked.

Thomas hung his head. 'Before Papa's disappearance I had no idea that the bank was in trouble. The records I have seen show that Papa sustained heavy losses when a South Seas venture failed last year. Most of Amelia's money was also invested. He tried to shore up the loss by investing in higher-risk ventures, using the Loveday money to do so. He expected these to yield a greater return. But instead there was one disaster after another.'

Thomas had difficulty meeting Edward and Adam's stare. Both of them looked haggard, their eyes bleak as they gauged their losses. His voice cracked as Thomas forced himself to continue, 'I fear that you have lost nearly everything. Amelia keeps her property, which is tied up in trust for Richard, but the rents for the next five years were used as collateral in Papa's last desperate venture. That also failed.'

'Judas!' Japhet stroked his side whiskers. 'The family is done for.'

Edward rounded on him. 'Do not be so defeatist. Yes, the family faces a financial crisis. But together we can find a resolution.'

'How much do you think can be saved, Uncle?' Japhet persisted, unabashed by the show of anger.

Edward looked at Thomas. 'You know the situation better than I. Can the bank and our money be saved?'

'If a run is not made on the bank, we can in

time rebuild our reserves.' Thomas forced some optimism into his voice. 'And with careful investments, again in, time, I hope to recoup the losses.'

'But that could take years,' Adam groaned. He could see the yard falling into decline and half of Trevowan sold off before the money was recouped.

Edward rubbed the back of his neck, his face pinched with anxiety as he considered the matter. 'Our only hope for success is for the bank to remain stable. We will help you in any way we can, Thomas.'

'Thank you. That means a great deal to me.' His voice broke and he felt his eyes sting with tears. 'You must hate us for this.'

Edward sighed and spread his hands in resignation. Inside he was raging that all he had worked for had been destroyed by Charles Mercer, but what use was it to rant, or blame Thomas? Decisive action was needed if they were to win through. 'What use is hatred or recrimination? Whatever has happened we are family. The Lovedays have always stuck together in a crisis. United we can put up a front which should detract from the rumours. But first I would spare Margaret from learning how dire matters are. She has suffered enough. She loved Charles dearly.'

Thomas nodded, looking less harassed now that his family would stand by him. 'I shall stall for time at the bank. I would like to get Mother out of London before those carrion strip us clean. But how much do I tell her?'

'For the moment she need only know about the loss of some of the money,' Edward advised. 'She must go to Trevowan to help her through her grief. She need not yet know that the authorities have passed a verdict of suicide on Charles's death, for there was no sign of violence done to his body. I think we must accept that, rather than face disgrace, Charles chose to end his life by jumping off Westminster Bridge.'

Thomas looked crushed. 'We cannot avoid a scandal. We will have to declare ourselves bankrupt and, unless I flee the country, I will spend the rest of my days in a debtors' prison. There is no hope I can ever be free of my father's creditors. That you also should suffer through Papa's dealings makes matters worse.'

'We will overcome this.' Edward insisted, concerned that there was now a note of hysteria in Thomas's voice. So much depended on Thomas remaining strong. If he cracked under the strain they would indeed lose everything.

Thomas swung about and struck out at the wall with a fist. He then slumped his head against his grazed knuckles, his head to the wall. His groan was heartfelt. 'It is my fault. If only I had not quarrelled with Papa. He hated how I spent my life and despised my friends, and my desire to become a playwright. If I had stayed at the bank perhaps this would never have happened.'

'Uncle Charles made those investments with the best intentions.' Adam was still reeling from the shock. 'You must not blame yourself. You hated anything to do with the bank.'

'And we will do all in our power to prevent you

being arrested for debt.' Japhet was emphatic. He had felt the shadow of a debtors' prison threatening him too often to want to see his cousin so fallen. 'The Lovedays never abandon one of their own–'

Edward interrupted, 'Thomas, you must reconsider your future. To recover from this, Mercer's Bank must appear stable. People like Grimshaw have to be convinced that the bank is strong and their money safe. For that you must take over and give up your life as a struggling playwright.'

'You are right, of course, Uncle.' Thomas battled to keep his voice even and not show his despair.

Edward was not deceived; there was dejection in the slump of Thomas's shoulders and his hands were trembling. Edward tried to rally his nephew's spirits. It would take all of Thomas's strength of character and will to overcome the problems the bank faced.

'I know it will be hard for you, Thomas,' he said. 'But it is not only our money which is at stake. It is the savings of hundreds of people who trusted Mercer's Bank to keep their money safe. Once the bank is stable, it will be possible to arrange a merger. The bank has many influential customers. It has been a name in the banking world for five generations. That counts for a great deal.'

'Papa *was* Mercer's Bank,' Thomas groaned. 'If he failed, what chance have I?'

'Do not talk that way,' Edward commanded. 'You have a keen head on your shoulders. Win your customers' respect. Charles has often been approached by Carrs and also Lascalles Bank to form a partnership. Ride through this crisis and you can sell out, or become a sleeping partner.'

'I have no choice, have I?' Thomas looked haggard but resigned. 'I disappointed Papa in many ways, but in this I will not fail him.'

'He would have been proud of you,' Edward encouraged. 'But it will not be easy. Consult your lawyers. They will advise you more appropriately than I can in this matter.'

Thomas signed. 'There are no funds to meet any dividends. This house has already been mortgaged to its current value. If I cannot meet the next payment we will lose it.'

'That must be avoided.' Edward frowned. 'It will cause speculation in the City that the bank is in trouble.'

Japhet shook his head, his tone ironic. 'Tom, it seems you have no choice but to marry an heiress. Aunt Margaret has no doubt several in mind.'

At Thomas's look of horror, Edward said sternly, 'Japhet is right. News of an engagement will boost your customers' confidence in the bank. Do you truly prefer dishonour and Marshalsea Prison?'

'You ask too much,' Thomas stated, again refusing to meet any of their gazes. 'I would do any woman a disservice by wedding her. Lucien is more than a friend. I will not abandon him. There, I have said it.' With an antagonistic tilt to his chin he regarded each of them, expecting recrimination.

'Greene is married, is he not?' Edward dismissed his reasoning. Now was not the time to pass judgement on his nephew's sexuality.

Thomas nodded. 'Yes, but he has not seen his wife in years. She lives with another man.'

'Tom, you will give a wife a home – status,' Edward persisted. 'A spinster is too often an object of pity. And marriage is about forging alliances. The Mercer name is a revered one.'

Thomas struggled to remain composed. He chewed his thumbnail and there was a hunted look in his eyes which showed his fear of entrapment.

'Good God, Tom, do not look such a martyr.' Japhet lost patience. 'Even I will succumb to the inevitability of marriage one day. Though the Lord knows, I will be doing the wench no favours, for I doubt the wedded state will stop my roving eye.'

Thomas shuddered and sighed. 'If there is no other option I will consider it.'

Japhet raised a brow, his dark eyes mocking. 'Many men like yourself wed. Good lord, man. You've had women in the past. It was you who took me to a bordello in Truro when I was fifteen. Fortunate is the man who feels lust for his wife. Marriage is an alliance–'

'Tom must make his own decision,' Edward interrupted before an argument broke out.

Thomas spread his hands in supplication. 'I will do whatever is necessary. Now I must prepare myself to visit our lawyers. I would welcome your company and advice uncle. The meeting is arranged for an hour's time.'

'I will help you all I can,' Edward said.

Thomas left the room, and Japhet also made his excuses.

'If there is nothing I can do here, I could do with some fresh air.'

'Go and enjoy yourself, Japhet.' Edward waved him away. 'There is no point in all of us being gloomy. This hardly affects you.'

'Yes it does.' Japhet was indignant. 'Uncle, you may see me as a wastrel and black sheep, but I have no less loyalty than any Loveday when the family is in trouble. I have no money to help you, but I will do anything I can to aid you or Thomas.'

Edward nodded. 'We could well need you later, but for now enjoy yourself, Japhet.'

'Are you coming, Adam?' Japhet invited.

Adam shook his head. His head was too full of questions and fears for his home and the yard to seek entertainment.

When he was alone with his father he shifted in his chair. 'And what of our own position, sir? We also have lost so much. Amelia now has no income.' Adam knew the loans on the yard were high and that he and his father would struggle to meet the interest repayment without Amelia's money. Ships took a lot of expenditure and a long time to build before a profit was made on them.

'I cannot deny that it is serious. Very serious. Sir Henry has been after the meadow adjoining his land. Now that the mine prospers he wants to extend the new lode which runs towards our land. Such a sale will not cause too much speculation. It will pay off the immediate interest

122

on the loans.'

'But to sell part of Trevowan...' Adam protested.

'It will be the first of many sacrifices to be made in the next months.' Edward remained grim and there was anger in his voice. 'Sacrifices which will extend to each member of the family. God willing, we will survive this crisis. But how to break it to the women? I feel I have failed Amelia. She was a wealthy woman when she married me. Now she must endure hardship.'

'You must not blame yourself, sir,' Adam tried to comfort his father, who must be feeling just as devastated and horrified as himself. 'Amelia banked at Mercer's before she met you. The outcome for her would surely have been the same. At least now she has you to safeguard her interests.'

Edward let out a sharp breath. 'There will be a lean year or two ahead for us all. We have weathered financial storms in the past, but this is the worst.'

'And we will win through.' A steeliness governed Adam's determination. He was struggling with his own feelings of anger and panic that everything he prized and held dear would be wrenched from the family.

At Trevowan, the letter sent by Edward informing them of Charles's death, and his need to stay in London for another month to help with legal matters, stunned the family.

The Lovedays were gathered in the glazed orangery at the rear of the house, which looked out across the fields of the estate and the distant

123

spire of Trewenna church. The rows of potted shrubs and trees diffused the glare of the harsh sunlight. It was one of Amelia's favourite rooms, but its beauty was now lost on her. She was shocked by the contents of the letter and, knowing Edward so well, feared that because of her condition he had not told the family the full situation.

'Charles has died tragically,' Elspeth announced. 'It seems there is some crisis at the bank which will have repercussions on us all.'

Amelia felt the tiny fluttering movements of the baby within her and placed her hand protectively over her stomach. She must be calm. For the baby's sake, she must not worry unduly. Edward had told her all would be well. She clung to that knowledge, but the baby's movements echoed the flutterings of an insidious fear which would not be stilled.

She re-read the letter to reassure herself that her fears were unfounded, but the disquiet remained. According to Edward there would be no dividends paid on her investments this year. Her throat dried and tightened with gathering panic. She suppressed it. The lost dividends were not the end of the world. Edward had advised that some cutbacks in household expenditure should be made. They would present a slight inconvenience, no more. He wanted these put into effect at once, and Adam, on his return, would explain further.

Her hand shook and the words on the parchment blurred. With an effort she steadied the tremor. Edward urged her not to worry, but

124

without his reassuring presence, every fear became a forbidding spectre, lurking in the dark recesses of her mind to surface and magnify her sense of dread. A sharp pain stabbing her side sent a shiver through her. Worry would harm the baby. The baby was what was important, not the money.

It was several moments before either St John or Meriel spoke. Both looked shocked but Meriel's complexion was deepening to an angry flush and her eyes sparkled with accusation.

'What sort of repercussions?' she demanded. 'And why the devil are *we* supposed to make cutbacks, when it is Mercer's Bank which seems to be in trouble?'

'They are our bankers,' Elspeth snapped. 'Is it not obvious that the Loveday money has been jeopardised in some way and that our future is also at stake?'

With a distraught cry Meriel sank down on to a chair with a whoosh of silk from her gown and petticoats. She stared in horror at her husband.

'I think you exaggerate, Aunt,' St John scoffed. 'How severe are these cutbacks?'

Amelia felt Meriel's accusing glare turn upon her. She did not want to face one of the young woman's tantrums, but she had to be firm. 'Each of us will make some sacrifice. It would make sense for the Dower House to be closed and you and Meriel to live here.'

'No!' Meriel shouted. 'I will not give up my house.'

'I must say, that is a bit steep.' St John backed her.

'In which case drastic economies will have to be made,' Amelia hedged. 'Your cook and house-maid will have to go. You may keep Rachel Glasson as general maid and to help with Rowena. Winnie Fraddon will prepare your meals too. I shall also be cutting back on the staff here. Two maids, a gardener and groom at the very least. Of course, there will be no visits to the dressmaker or any entertainments planned.'

'It is not to be tolerated,' Meriel complained. 'We have our status in society to maintain.'

'Have you no sense of duty or loyalty, girl?' Elspeth rapped out, her cane beating on the floor to emphasise each word. 'We are a family in mourning. And apparently in financial crisis.'

'And how many of your precious mares will *you* be giving up?' Meriel retorted with a sneer. 'Will you not hunt next season?'

Elspeth gave a choking sound. 'Give up my mares! They are family. My allowance pays for their upkeep. I will sell my jewellery, and happily so, before I part with a single one of them.'

She took a diamond brooch from her bodice and handed it to Amelia. 'I have no use for fripperies. I shall give Adam my jewels to sell on his return.'

'That may not be necessary,' Amelia placated. 'Edward advises that we must economise and be careful. Adam will explain further.'

'Then it is clearly more serious than Edward is saying.' Elspeth sucked in her cheeks and glared at Meriel. 'If you want to keep your house, what are you prepared to give up? St John has brought you a pretty trinket or two.'

'I will give up nothing,' Meriel snapped at St John. To Elspeth she said stiffly, 'We will wait until Edward returns before turning ourselves into paupers.'

'The servants will be given notice this evening.' Amelia was emphatic. 'I assume that as Reuben Sawle's daughter, you are capable of looking after a house and tending to your own needs.'

Meriel reddened with anger.

Elspeth countermanded any further complaints she was about to make by stridently changing the subject, 'Poor Margaret. Her loss is so much greater. How can she bear it? She could lose everything, even her home. We must rally ourselves for her sake. I will hear no word of recrimination in her presence, and we will make light of the change in our circumstances. We must hope that it is but temporary.'

Amelia dabbed at her eyes with a handkerchief, relieved at the change of conversation. 'One never believes murder can touch one's own family. I am glad that Margaret will arrive next week with Adam. To escape London and her memories there will be beneficial for her.'

Meriel jabbed St John in the ribs with her elbow and scowled as she muttered in an undertone, 'How typical that Margaret, whose stupid husband is the cause of our troubles, should be cosseted. We are the ones who will suffer.'

'Did you speak, Meriel?' Elspeth rapped out. 'Any word of complaint and the Dower House will be shut up.'

'Margaret is fortunate to have such an understanding family.' Meriel's sarcasm was thinly veiled.

Elspeth snorted, her stare hostile. 'It was a mercy that Edward was there when they found the body.'

Elspeth tried to quench her own fears for the future. Meriel's words had hit her hard. It was unthinkable that she might have to sell any of her mares. They were her darlings, as precious to her as any child. Panic tightened in her breast and she felt physically sick. She breathed deeply. Meriel had spoken out of spite. It would not come to that. She relaxed but the doubts persisted and could not be entirely banished. Bravado carried her through. 'Fortunately, young Thomas has come to his senses, and has returned to the bank. I have faith in Edward.' She reached over and patted Amelia's hand.

Amelia stared across the fields of golden corn stooks. Her pregnancy drained all her energy and this was a time when she needed her strength. 'The harvest looks a good one. St John has done well with the crop this year. For that we are grateful. But there has also been the expense of feeding and paying the extra labourers. Meriel, Elspeth and I will help Winnie in the kitchen.'

As Meriel and St John walked back to the Dower House, Meriel vented her outrage. 'How dare they tell us that we must give up our servants? You work hard on the estate to make it profitable. Unfairly hard, in my opinion. Why should we be made to suffer? It is not to be borne. Indeed, I will not allow it.'

'The upkeep of the Dower House and servants are paid for by Amelia's money, my love,' St John appeased. 'I have not the means to–'

'No, you do not have the means,' Meriel raved. 'That is because they keep us tied by their purse-strings.'

'That is unjust.' There was a harshness to St John's voice which reminded her of his obstinacy over family loyalty.

'Elspeth would wrap us all in dust sheets for the duration of your aunt's stay. With your father away, you must reconcile with my family. They have the connections to make us rich.'

She felt him tense and ploughed on, refusing to let the matter rest. 'Would you see your wife working like a common skivvy? For your family seem determined that I must.'

'You exaggerate, my dear. We will still have Rachel to help with Rowena. Her duties will be increased. What need have we of a cook if Winnie prepares our meals?'

'It means that I am no longer mistress in my own home. If news of it reaches the village I will be a laughing stock.'

St John's face clouded. 'Father would not ask for such economies unless the situation was serious. Be grateful they have for now compromised, and allowed us to keep the Dower House.'

She rounded on him, her eyes narrowed with, determination. 'And then we shall use it to good purpose. Adam will be busy at the yard. Elspeth and Amelia will be too concerned about your aunt's welfare to notice your absence. A smuggling run or two will put an end to our financial problems.'

When St John did not answer, she bridled her anger. The set of his jaw was infuriatingly stubborn. To pursue her tirade would only make him more so. They had left the shelter of the trees and the wind, straight from the sea, like fronds of icy kelp lashed their bodies. She hooked her arm through St John's and leaned her head on his shoulder. 'I shall visit the Dolphin tomorrow. The tide is at midday so Harry will be there. Ma says he's furious with Lanyon for stealing Hester from him. She fears he means to harm them both. Harry and Clem refused to be part of Lanyon's last smuggling run.'

'If Harry raises a hand to either Lanyon or his wife, he will find himself before the magistrate and will rot in gaol,' St John jeered. 'He is a hothead and his own worst enemy.'

'Then use his anger to your profit. I do not want to see Harry in prison. Nor do I want us to lose the Dower House. There are other ways to hit back at Lanyon and for us to retain what is ours. Hit Lanyon through his purse and his standing in the community and at the same time we shall prosper.'

Now that the family were in financial trouble, Meriel was more determined than ever that St John must boost their finances by smuggling. She did not intend to go without the luxuries she now took for granted.

St John's head ached from his wife's nagging and persuasive arguments. He guessed that matters were serious for Edward to have insisted on cutbacks. But just how serious was what worried him. If money was tight, his father would decrease his allowance; that would bring an end to any gambling or nights in Truro with his friends. He could be tied at Trevowan with little or no entertainments to divert him. Frustration ground through him. Why should he be made to suffer? He had worked hard. He cursed Charles Mercer. Now Meriel's proposition could be his only means of escape to lead the life of a gentleman as he wished.

Even so, he remained hesitant, for the dangers would be many. 'Clem and Harry swore never to be involved in another. smuggling venture with me.'

'That was three years ago. Lanyon's marriage has changed their views. They will want to be in charge of their own runs. Meet with Harry; he will convince Clem.'

'You forget I have no money to fund such a venture.' St John's exasperation burst forth.

'There are other ways. Ways which will also strike at Lanyon. There is no need for money if Harry and Clem raise a gang of men to steal the next cargo landed by Lanyon.'

'Are you mad, madam? All hell will break loose if we try that.' His heartbeat quickened and he felt an icy sweat trickle down his back.

'The gang will be masked.' There was scorn on Meriel's eyes at what she perceived as his weakness. 'No one will be recognised. I've thought it through. You will have surprise on your side. Think of it as reclaiming the cargo Lanyon lost for you.'

St John suppressed a quiver of excitement. Icicles of fear slithered through his intestines. Such a plan could work. But the dangers were high. Yet the rewards... Avarice beguiled him. Temptation whispered as potent as any siren's lure in his ear. *The rewards could be immense.*

They had entered the Dower House and Meriel no longer ranted but became soft and enticing. She pressed herself against him, her breath hot against his throat as her hands spread across his chest. 'Think of all the money which will be ours,' she wore the last of his defences down with ardent kisses. Kisses too often withheld from him. 'And Harry will respect the man who goes to him with such a plan,' she coerced in a seductive whisper. 'As I will be proud of the man who shows that he will not let another beat him.'

St John surrendered to her manipulation, and through the onslaught of his passion retained just enough sanity to insist, 'I will meet Harry. But not at the Dolphin. Let it be at the cave in Trevowan Cove.' He did not want to be seen in the village consorting with his wife's family.

In her excitement at achieving her ends, Meriel kissed him with unrestrained passion. 'You will not regret it.'

He laughed and began to bunch up her skirts and pull her to the floor of the parlour. 'Show me how much you appreciate my sacrifice of family honour.'

Meriel tensed. 'It is daylight. The servants or Rowena could come upon us.'

'You want me to place my life in danger to satisfy your greed.' His hands were insistent as he kicked the parlour door shut. 'You have withheld yourself from me for too long.'

She submitted with ill grace and prayed that since she must suffer his advances, she would be blessed by conceiving a son.

Once the elation of passion no longer ruled his mind, St John found himself unable to settle. Ebullience was replaced by apprehension which grew to a deep, dark, unassailable fear. A fear so stark it all but unmanned him. He had entered his first smuggling forays with youthful enthusiasm, an almost romantic notion of high adventure and daring. The truth had been brutal. Smuggling was no gentleman's sport. Men died, not through any sense of honour but through greed. The excise men were too fond of using their pistols to end a smuggler's life. Death was as likely to be his reward as riches.

Chapter Seven

Meriel chose with care her timing to visit the Dolphin Inn. The wind swung the faded sign on its creaking hinges, and squawking seagulls circling the harbour were mirrored in the tiny panes of the windows in the timber-framed building. The inn could do with a coat of white paint to make it stand out against the stone cottages and emphasise its importance. Reuban was too much of a clutchfist to spend money on anything he did not consider a necessity.

Her father's temper had grown worse in the last year as his hands and knees became twisted and swollen with the rheumaticky joint. With Harry and Clem out most days with the fishing fleet, the responsibility of running the inn fell on Sal and Mark's shoulders. Mark did the heavy work, while Reuban sat in the taproom serving the customers and drinking the profits.

By midday Reuban was usually in a mellow mood, by two he would become argumentative, and by four he had usually passed out. Then Mark and Sal carried him to his bed until he woke at seven demanding his food and began to drink again.

Meriel tethered her mare in the stable. The other stalls were empty, which meant that Mark was using the old horse and cart to collect provisions either in St Austell or Liskeard. Reuban had forbidden his family to buy anything from Lanyon's shop.

The mud-packed ground of the yard was more cluttered than usual. Reuban had taken to collecting anything he thought of value. There was a water pump with a broken handle, a rusting old Cornish range with the oven door missing, a hand cart with a broken wheel and a covered wagon with no wheels and its side crushed from a collision. There was also a pile of worm-eaten ship's timbers from an old wreck, and a stack of beer kegs with broken iron bands awaiting repair by a cooper.

The wind blew straight inland from the harbour. Meriel wrinkled her nose against the stench of fish being gutted on the quay by the fishwives.

She lifted her skirts above her ankles and picked her way carefully across the yard, avoiding puddles from an early morning shower. A funnel of sunlight appeared through oatmeal clouds. By the vegetable plot a line of patched sheets and shirts flapped in the breeze. Three crows swooped down from an outbuilding to attack a feral kitten carrying a dead rat. The kitten dropped its prey and fled with a terrified yowl into the stables. The crows tore at the rat's bloody carcass until they were driven off by four scavenging gulls.

The kitchen door was open and a dozen flies and wasps buzzed around a cooked ham which had been left uncovered on the scrubbed table. The bunches of fresh-cut tansy spread around the kitchen were clearly failing to keep all the insects outside. From the open door leading to the taproom wafted the smell of stale ale and tobacco smoke.

'You there, Ma?' Meriel called, unwilling to venture into the taproom and face coarse comments from any fishermen.

'That you, Meriel?' Sal replied. 'Come through. Bain't no one here. Though there's been a rush and only me to deal with it.'

Meriel lifted a pomander of dried lavender to her nose. The smell of stale ale and tobacco smoke haunted every room of her old home. It was as bad as the stench of fish from the quay. Upon entering the dimly lit taproom, Meriel almost tripped over the prone figure of her father stretched on the flagstone floor. He snorted loudly, an arm swinging out as he mumbled, 'Ger

135

orf, you buggers.'

'Are you leaving him there?' Meriel asked.

Sal stepped into the light and hung the brass-handled bellows she had been cleaning on to the hook by the hearth. The low-timbered ceiling of the inn was yellowed from the years of fires and smoke. There were two wooden high-back settles along one wall. Other seats were provided by benches or three-legged stools set round up-ended beer barrels, which were used as tables.

Sal squinted at her daughter through a swollen, purple eye. 'He can stay where he falls. The drunken sod belted me yesterday when I tried to move him. Mark is at market. Harry can put Reuban to bed when he comes in. For what reason do we have the pleasure of this visit, daughter?'

'I need to talk with Harry. How has he been since he learned of the wedding?'

Sal sighed. 'He be as bad as his pa when it comes to the drink. And he be threatening to kill Lanyon. Fortunately, Clem can reason with him. Yet I fear the lad will do something foolish. He be so eaten up with jealousy and pain.'

Two fishermen came through the door and shouted for ale.

Sal served them and Meriel went back into the kitchen. She threw a cloth over the ham and stirred the fish stew which simmered continuously in the pot over the fire.

Sal waddled in to the kitchen and there was a cry for more ale. She dragged herself back to serve them, then flopped down on to a chair by the range and wiped her brow with her sleeve.

'You look wore out, Ma. Pa can't be much use. Where's Tilda? She should be helping you.'

'Don't mention that slut to me.' Sal looked fierce. 'She be out. God knows where. She's been acting strangely lately.' She dropped her voice, aware of the fishermen supping ale in the taproom. 'I reckon the young fool is breeding. And I wouldn'a be surprised if it bain't Clem's. Not that he's owning to it.'

Suddenly Sal's face crumpled and to Meriel's alarm, she burst into tears. 'Once Reuban would have kept them boys in line. He's as good as useless now. What did I do to deserve such a family? Your sister, Rose, disgraced us all by running off with a soldier. Now Clem will shame us. As for Harry–'

'Don't take on so, Ma. This bain't like you.' Meriel lapsed back into her old way of speech, upset to see Sal lose control. 'If Tilda be with child, Clem must wed her.'

Sal shook her head. 'Clem has set his sights higher than a tavern wench. He be courting a farmer's widow over Helston way.'

'Then why is he fooling with Tilda?' Meriel lost patience with her brother.

''Cause she's always been after him and what man bain't gonna take what is eagerly offered?'

'Tilda has always been flighty, Ma. Likely Clem is no more the father than a half-dozen others.'

Sal still looked uneasy as she wiped her eyes. 'Tilda has worked for us a long time. She's not a bad lass. Bit simple. How's she gonna look after herself, let alone a kid? Her father won't stand by her. I feel responsible if it be Clem got her into this mess.'

A year or so ago, Sal would have dismissed Tilda without a second's thought, and given Clem, big as he was, a beating with a poker. Life had worn her down and taken the fire out of her.

'Ma, when did you ever have any sway over what Clem does?'

'My boys bain't as black as people paint them. I know them: they have good hearts. They do, don't they?'

Through the open door of the food store, Meriel noted the brace of pheasants and a rabbit hanging on hooks. Harry or Clem had been poaching again. 'Aye, Ma. My brothers are perfect angels,' Meriel mocked. Then seeing that Sal remained close to breaking point, and at a loss as to how to cope with this weakness in her mother, Meriel brewed a pot of tea from the contraband store kept in a wooden caddy on the shelf above the range. Handing the cup to her mother she reassured her, 'Clem and Harry know how to look after themselves.'

At that point Tilda sidled in to the kitchen. She was pretty enough, though she was skinny, and now her skin was sallow and her hair lank and unwashed.

'Where have you been?' Meriel raged. 'Ma cannot cope on her own.'

Tilda flinched as though Meriel had struck her. Her face was pale and her eyes red from weeping. 'I'd to see someone.' She threw her apron over her face and burst into tears.

Meriel groaned. Coping with her mother had been hard enough, now she had an hysterical barmaid to deal with.

'Shall I send someone for your sister up at Trevowan, if you are so upset?' Sal suggested. 'Meriel won't mind the lass taking an hour from her duties.'

Tilda shook her head beneath her apron. 'Pa won't have me in the house. I wish Ma were still alive. She'd help me. I'm gonna have a baby. It be Clem's and he'll not own it.'

The servant sobbed harder. Sal hauled herself to her feet and put her arm round her.

'You be certain it be Clem's? He won't take kindly to you spreading such talk.'

Tilda nodded. 'He don't want to know. He told me last night I couldn't work here no more. Now me dad's found out. He won't tackle Clem, but he's thrown me out of the house. What am I to do?'

'I'll have a word with Clem,' Sal said with a shrug, 'though what good it will do–'

'He said he won't wed me. He's already set the date to wed that widow from Helston.'

'First I heard of this,' Sal muttered. 'Those boys and their secrets.' She wiped her nose on her hand and it was a moment before she added, 'Is there no one else who might wed you, girl? Clem bain't the only man you've been seeing.'

Tilda's sobs grew in strength. 'I bain't a bad girl like you think. It be Clem's all right.'

Meriel put her hand to her ears, which were beginning to ring with the sound of Tilda's crying. 'Have you tried the Polglase woman? She has a knowledge of potions. Are there not some which can rid you of an unwanted child?'

'I went to her. I were desperate. She refused to help me,' Tilda wailed. 'Said what did I mean by asking her to do such a thing. Got real mad, she did. I thought she'd set that devil's hound on me.'

'Perhaps you did not offer her enough money,' Meriel snapped.

'I offered her all I had. She said to keep it to look after the child when it comes.' Tilda sobbed against Sal's wide bosom and finally lifted her tear-smeared face to implore, 'What am I to do? Do I have to leave here as Clem says? I've no home now. Where can I get work to support the child?'

Sal walked away from the barmaid and her face was set. 'If Clem says you must leave then that is how it will be. I think it would be best if you were gone from Penruan before he returns. You don't show yet. You'll get work for three or four months yet. Take care you put some money by for when you can't work.'

Sal took down a chipped pot from a shelf and tipped out its contents on the table. There was about two pounds in silver and copper. She pushed it towards Tilda. 'Take it. It will help you pay for lodgings until you can find work. And if I hear you've spread rumours that Clem be the father of that child, then you had better watch the shadows, that someone bain't waiting to teach you a lesson in honesty, my girl. I've seen the times you've slipped out of the taproom with Davey Smeaton, and he wed with two children.'

Tilda dried her eyes, but did not defend her reputation as she scooped up the money into her apron and left the inn.

Sal sat at the table with her head in her hands. 'All I ever wanted was a quiet, respectable life. What can any mother do with sons like mine?'

'Clem seeks to better himself. Would you really want him married to a woman like Tilda? And Harry will get over Hester in time.'

An hour later with Sal's spirits revived, Meriel left the Dolphin for the quayside. The village women were gutting fish in the sheds, their laughter carrying to her. The men were either swilling down the decks of their luggers or seated on the quay mending their nets. Harry was hunched over the winch which hoisted the triangular sail of his lugger. 'Damn things jammed,' he explained, and dabbed a handful of grease on it.

'Walk up to the headland with me, Harry. I need to talk, and not near prying ears.'

Harry wiped his hands on a rag, put his tools away and jumped on to the quay. They spoke of inconsequentials as they walked to the headland. Away from the village, Harry put a foot on a granite boulder rising from the grass, and stared down at the turquoise sea breaking in white crests over the rocks.

He turned and stared for a long moment at the Traherne mine, its engine housing and chimney clearly visible further along the cliff. A grey spiral of smoke rising from the chimney marred the otherwise clear sky. Down the coast were other chimneys, their engine rooms silent and rusting, long closed as the price of tin plummeted.

'So what is such a secret?' he said without

turning to her.

First she explained about Tilda. 'Ma needs someone to help her at the Dolphin. Will you make sure Clem hires someone soon?'

'Bit late for you to be worried about Ma.' Meriel could smell the ale on Harry's breath and once the drink was in him he became belligerent. 'You rarely lifted a finger to help her before you wed.'

'Ma were younger then and capable of taking on an army. Haven't you noticed how ill and tired she's looking?'

'Haven't noticed much at all these past weeks.'

Meriel saw the pain in his eyes and heard the despair in his voice. It angered her to see Harry this way. She hated Hester Moyle for what she had done to her brother.

'No woman is worth what you are suffering, Harry.'

'I never thought she'd wed Lanyon. I could kill him. I could kill them both.' The pain changed to a manic glitter in his eyes.

Meriel took his arms. 'I am also worried about you, Harry. If you harm Lanyon they will hang you. That does not make you the victor, but the victim.'

'The grand lady of the manor condescends to trouble herself about the welfare of her family. Honoured, bain't we?' His sarcasm whipped her and he pulled his arms from her hold. 'You bain't no better than Hester. You sold yourself to the highest bidder same as her. Lanyon weren't powerful enough to challenge St John Loveday when you decided on a grander match. But I

142

bain't gonna let Lanyon get away with what he's done. Or her.'

Knowing Harry's volatile temperament, Meriel chose her words with care. 'Do you think Hester is happy now she is wed to Lanyon?'

He stared at her in disbelief. 'She's dressed up like a duchess. Got a grand house. Like you she aimed high. Why shouldn't she be happy?'

'Because she is a passionate woman who would need a real man to love her. A man like you. How could she be happy with a toad like Lanyon?' Meriel shuddered. 'Just to look at him makes my flesh crawl.'

'She made her choice,' Harry ground out.

'And could easily be regretting it.'

'I hope she is. I hope she feels sick every time he touches her.'

Meriel stood close to him, her voice low and insidious. 'I expect she is. She probably dreams of the comfort and love of your arms about her. And what better way for you to avenge yourself on Lanyon than by cuckolding him? You can always drop Hester once she's disgraced. Show the world that no one gets the better of Harry Sawle.'

Harry studied her. The wind was lifting his dark blond hair around his head and making a pennant of his stock as it fluttered over his shoulder. The sun was behind him, his body dark and solid as a mine tower against the sky.

Meriel put her hands on her hips, her voice sly. 'But even to cuckold Lanyon would be too easy a victory, and too light a sentence for his treachery. Lanyon is a miser. This recent display of his

143

wealth is to thumb his nose at the Lovedays and the Sawles. He worships money. St John has devised a plan to make you both rich at Lanyon's expense.'

'You mean you've devised a plan.'

'No, this was St John's idea.' For St John and Harry to be reconciled Harry must respect St John, therefore he must believe St John had changed and was a worthy partner in their venture. 'My husband has never forgiven Lanyon for informing the revenue men of his last venture. He plans to ambush a cargo of Lanyon's.'

'How?' Harry sneered.

'By stealing it. How else? It is time that the rift was healed between our families. I persuaded St John that you would not want to miss the chance to be revenged upon Lanyon.'

'I don't trust Loveday. The man is craven.'

'You mistake him. He wants to meet you at the cave in Trevowan cove. This is your chance to get back at Lanyon.'

'Not with any Loveday's help.'

'Then you are a fool,' she railed. 'This plan will make you a rich man. It will also destroy Lanyon's credibility as a smugglers' banker. At least meet with St John.'

Harry kept St John waiting a half-hour after the appointed time. There was a stiff wind which bit into St John's flesh as he sat on the rock outside the mouth of the cave. The two spaniels, Scamp and Faith, had followed him when he left Trevowan. The dogs were running through the bubbling waves barking at a large piece of driftwood. A whistle summoning the dogs drifted from the cliff, and St John dodged out of sight as Amelia's brat, Richard, appeared.

St John hid in the cave while Richard launched Adam's old dinghy and sailed round the headland to the next bay. The dogs followed the young lad's progress by running along the cliff path.

When Harry finally climbed down the cliff, his unsteady gait showed that he had been drinking. His complexion was a ruddy brown from its exposure to the sun, sea and wind, and his broken nose was testimony to his many fights. The same age as St John, he was broad-shouldered; his muscular body in his battered leather breeches and homespun shirt presented a menacing figure.

Harry halted some distance from St John, his arms folded across his chest and his expression assessing.

'I bain't your lackey to be so summoned, Loveday.' He was deliberately antagonistic.

'But you came none the less,' St John provoked. 'Meriel has spoken to you of my plan. Secrecy at this stage is all important.'

Harry hawked in his throat and spat on to the dark rocks. 'Aye, the plan has merit. And secrecy be one matter. Trust another. After the last time, how do we know we can trust you?'

'I lost more than anyone on that venture.' St John's own anger surfaced.

'And made sure you saved your own hide before the others. We expect more from our leaders.'

St John checked his temper. 'I was less experienced then. I made mistakes, I admit. It is different now.'

'Why should that be? What grudge have you against Lanyon?'

'Is it not enough that his spies informed on us to the revenue men that night? Lanyon is an upstart. If he wishes to play the gentleman, then he must learn to act like one. He begins to see himself as lord of the manor instead of our family. He has gone too far.'

Harry kicked a stone and his face twisted with fury. 'He stole what was mine. He had better watch his back.'

'Why did you not wed Hester when you had the chance?'

'That be my business.' His fists bunched and he struck out at an invisible opponent. The violent movement toppled him and he pitched across a large boulder. He lay prone for a moment, clearly winded. When he pushed himself up to sit on the rock, the anger had left him. 'Damn the wench!' he mumbled, barely coherent. 'I wanted something better for her than life at the Dolphin. Besides, she would not live there. She were scared of Pa. But I would have killed him if he dared raise a hand to her. As I could kill Lanyon now.'

'And swing for your actions. Is any woman worth that?' St John reasoned. He had been carefully schooled by Meriel as to what to say. And if he wanted to share her bed tonight he must return home successful. 'You can hit Lanyon hardest by stealing his cargo. It proves he is not

146

as invincible as he believes.'

'He'll suspect me, but not you. Why should I risk so much for your benefit?'

'The profit from his cargo will set us up as a rival gang. Is that not a better vengeance upon him?'

Harry regarded him with sullen distrust. He needed time to digest this new venture, but the gleam in his eyes showed his interest.

'There be a landing soon.' Harry grudgingly imparted the information he had overheard two fishermen discussing. 'I don't yet know where. But Lanyon don't usually use guards. He bribes the excise officers to be on duty elsewhere when he lands a cargo. We will need men from places other than Penruan. Too many are in debt to Lanyon to risk falling foul of him. The Jowetts on Bodmin Moor will raise a gang of tubmen to carry the goods away.'

'I'd rather keep the Jowetts out of it.' St John did not like to be reminded of the time he had engaged the Jowetts to settle a score with Adam. They had all but killed his twin and he had feared that he would be implicated and then disinherited by his father. 'They are known horse thieves and have no respect for a man's life. I want no killing. Also suspicion will fall too easily upon them.'

'Clem will keep them in line. The Jowetts can bring men in unknown to Lanyon. 'Tis the only way.'

St John remained ill at ease. The Jowetts were the worst kind of trouble, and he was not convinced that even Clem Sawle could control them.

They followed no law but their own.

Shouts and commands were heard from behind the headland and the sails of a revenue ship came into view. St John shivered as he watched it sail past, a portent of danger for the success of any smuggling venture.

Harry scowled at the vessel and raised a finger in a gesture of insult and defiance. He ignored St John's hesitation and went on, 'The Jowetts will want a one-third cut to pay off their men. The same for Clem and myself.'

'That is steep,' St John protested.

'We all take the same risks for the same money.' Harry was again antagonistic. 'But you be right about Lanyon. Death would be too easy for him. I want him broken.'

Harry's thoughts were centred upon a greater retribution. He wanted far more than he had said. He wanted not only Lanyon's death but his wife, his grand house up on the hill and he wanted Lanyon's position of the smugglers' banker. Lanyon had risen from nothing. Harry saw himself as no less cunning and ruthless. He was a better man than Lanyon, so why should he settle for less than what Thadeous Lanyon had achieved?

St John saw the obsession in Harry Sawle's eyes and suppressed a shiver of apprehension. Harry had a sharp and devious mind. He was also completely ruthless.

Chapter Eight

The situation in London was as bad as the Loveday men had feared. The investors in the bank were nervous and several insisted that loans were called in. One of those held another loan against the Loveday yard which Edward would find impossible to meet.

While Edward remained in London to renegotiate with the investors, and sort out the tangle of finances which Charles had left, Adam had returned to Cornwall. It had taken three weeks and all Edward's tenacity to get his sister away from London.

Japhet had insisted on staying in the capital until Edward returned to Cornwall. When Edward refused his permission, Japhet disappeared from the house and had not returned when Margaret Mercer's coach left for Cornwall.

'What will you do about Japhet?' Adam had asked his father as Aunt Margaret settled in the coach.

'Pray the rapscallion turns up before I too must leave and then turn his ear blue with a lecture. That cousin of yours is a bane to us all. But I could not look Cecily in the eye if anything happened to him.'

'Japhet will turn up in a day or so. He knows you mean to remain another month,' Adam said, with misplaced optimism.

'I have lost the most devoted of husbands,' Margaret declared to Elspeth and Amelia on entering the hall of Trevowan. 'A friend. A wonderful man. And now people whom I believed were friends would see me ruined. They act as though Charles had cheated them. That he was dishonest.'

'Lud, I have never seen you in such a taking, sister.' Elspeth was at a loss as to how to comfort her. 'Charles was an admirable man. We will all miss him.'

Amelia put her arm around Margaret as her friend's maid, Josephine, was ushered up the stairs by Isaac Nance carrying Margaret's trunk. 'I have been distraught with worry. Charles was a wonderful man and to have his life taken from him in such a brutal way... It is too shocking.'

'Yet there are men who would revile my husband,' Margaret struggled against tears. 'They are wolves seeking to destroy all he has worked for. Poor Thomas. My darling boy has had to cope with so much. Thank God Edward is there.'

'Edward will not allow Charles's name to be blackened,' Amelia soothed as they entered the parlour with its peacock wallpaper. 'He will support Thomas in all that must be done. And you will stay here as long as you have need of us.'

Elspeth looked deathly pale in her mourning gown, but remained stalwart. She could not believe that Margaret, who was always so strong and resilient, looked so ill and weak. 'Get to your bed, sister. The journey has taken all your strength. Winnie Fraddon will prepare a posset which will sustain you.'

Suddenly all three of them began to weep. Adam tried to rally them. 'Aunt Margaret, Father and Thomas will see to everything in London. Aunt Elspeth is right, you do need to rest.'

'I should not have left my dear boy to cope with so much.' Margaret would not be calmed. Since the funeral she had hardly spoken and now the floodgates had been breached, she could not contain her pain and sorrow.

'Thomas will not fail you or his father,' Adam assured, and watched with sadness as this once indomitable woman was led away, broken-hearted, by Amelia, and helped up the stairs to her chamber.

Elspeth also looked about to crack from the strain. She leaned heavily on her cane, her eagle stare fierce when it settled on Adam. 'There's something I have not been told if Edward is staying in London. He has too much at stake here to leave the yard. What is it? He would not insist on household economies without reason. His letter said that you would explain further what has happened.'

Adam was not prepared to face an inquisition from his aunt. Better to leave the explanations to his father on his return. 'There are many legal matters which need attention. Thomas was grateful for his support. A huge responsibility has been unexpectedly thrust on Thomas. Papa would not leave him to face that alone.'

Elspeth did not look convinced. 'Do we face ruin?' Adam was about to protest, when she demanded, 'I want the truth. I know Edward well enough to know he would want to protect Margaret in her grief, and Amelia because of her condition. Neither of them is a fool. For the time Margaret is too upset to know what is happening around her, but Amelia is worried. Edward would not have suggested household cutbacks if we were not in severe financial difficulties.'

'Father is being cautious as the yard is over-extended at the moment,' Adam prevaricated.

Elspeth banged her cane on the floor. 'Do not insult my intelligence, young man. Edward would not lay off staff if it was a matter of a couple of hundred pounds, would he?'

Adam shifted uncomfortably. No admiral in the navy, when as a young man he had faced disciplinary hearings, was as intimidating as Elspeth.

'There are heavy loans to be met and no funds at present, and the yard must be kept going to provide an income for the future. It can be done ... but not without some sacrifices made. I have only been told what is needed at the yard. Father will explain more fully when he returns.'

Elspeth tapped the silver head of the cane upon his chest. 'You are a loyal son, but a poor liar, Adam. What are you keeping from me?'

Adam glanced up to the landing. It was deserted. Elspeth would not be satisfied until she had prised the truth from him, but Edward has insisted that the women were not to be worried about finances and that Adam was to stall their enquiries and reassure them. His father hoped that something of their fortune could be salvaged before he returned from London, though Adam believed it to be a forlorn hope.

Adam eased the pressure of his stock, which had become uncomfortably tight. 'You are right, there is more. Quite shocking news which Father does not want Amelia or Margaret knowing yet. Uncle Charles was not murdered. It is possible that he committed suicide. He made some bad investments, some with our money. The bank could fail at any time.'

Elspeth put her hand to her mouth. 'Good God, are we done for?'

'It means some cutbacks so that we can meet the loans.' Adam feared he had said too much; Elspeth looked badly shaken.

'I will not have to get rid of my mares, will I?' She began to tremble. 'I have jewels – they can be sold. I will not give up my mares. Edward could not make me.'

'I trust it will not come to that, Aunt.'

She relaxed and the moment of vulnerability had passed. 'No, of course not. Poor Margaret. Edward is right that Amelia should not be told. She is worrying as it is. Does Margaret know about Charles?'

Adam shook his head. 'She was in a terrible state in London. You can see how ill she looks. She was not told that the bank is in trouble either. Papa thought the shock would be too much.'

'Thank you for telling me.' Elspeth's attention was caught by the reappearance of Amelia at the top of the stairs.

Adam made a hasty exit to avoid any more

awkward questions.

'Oh, Adam has gone!' Amelia was disappointed. 'I wanted to speak with him.' She was holding her side and her complexion was pale and transparent.

'Are you ill?' Elspeth was now more concerned for Amelia's health than in questioning Adam further. She suspected that her nephew had evaded some of the issues. If she showed her own fears at how serious their situation could be, Amelia would worry and that could damage the health of the child.

'I do feel rather faint,' Amelia admitted. 'All this upset is so exhausting. I wish Edward was here.'

'He is needed in London. He will soon be home. And from the look of you, Amelia, you should be resting. Is Margaret settled?'

'I took the liberty of giving her some of the sleeping draught Senara Polglase prepared for you. It has calmed her.' Amelia winced and clutched at the newel post for support.

With growing alarm Elspeth saw Amelia sway and there was the starkness of fear in her eyes.

Elspeth groaned, 'Dear God, it is not the child, is it?'

There were beads of perspiration on Amelia's brow as she managed to straighten. 'I do feel quite unwell. I have hardly felt the child move all day.'

'Get yourself to bed. No, better yet, lie on the day bed for now and recover your strength. I will send for Chegwidden or Senara if you prefer.'

'I think it should be our physician.' Amelia

staggered into the peacock room and lay on the day bed. The pain in her side eased, but increased each time she moved. 'If only the baby would move. Then I would know that all is well.'

'I'll also send for Ginny Rundle; she has more knowledge of these matters than Chegwidden. Now you rest.'

Adam's step was weary as he walked to the stable to collect Solomon and ride to the shipyard. St John was in the stable yard, his tan breeches smeared with grime and his shirt sleeves rolled back. He had just finished ploughing a field and his face and hair were streaked with sweat.

'You're back then,' St John said. 'Rum do, by all accounts. Put paid to your gallivanting in the playhouses and also to Thomas's plans for his future. What was Uncle Charles about that we must now lay off servants and the like? Father had better not have any ideas of selling any land. I won't stand by and see my inheritance lost.'

Adam's temper snapped. 'You have no thoughts but your own selfish needs.' He kept his voice low as he hissed. 'Uncle Charles was not murdered. He killed himself and the bank could collapse at any time. Along with that of so many of his customers, Uncle Charles has lost Amelia's and our money in bad investments.'

'Then we too could face ruin!' St John's eyes rounded in alarm. 'Damn Uncle Charles! This is outrageous–'

Before he had time to consider his reaction, Adam had punched St John on the jaw. His brother lay spread-eagled on the cobblestones, his hand in a pile of horse droppings freshly deposited by the plough horses. With his fist still clenched Adam stood over his twin.

'All Thomas has inherited is debts. That is why Father is in London, to try and help Thomas rescue something from this shambles. And we may well lose a field or two, if not more, to meet our creditors.'

St John scrambled up. 'You mean the debts of the damned yard must be met.' He swung a fist at Adam and caught his eye. 'Damn you! Father broke the covenant between the estate and the yard when he made you heir to the business. I've slaved to make Trevowan prosper. How dare he consider selling the land? You'll be rich and I'll get nothing.'

He raised his leg to knee his twin in the groin but Adam nimbly avoided the blow, and St John again reeled back from the impact of Adam's fist as it split his lip.

'Damn you for a useless cur!' Adam raged as he threw himself at St John and the two men wrestled on the ground. 'Trevowan and the yard are bound together while Father lives. If you were not so damned selfish, you would realise that it is the yard which can save Trevowan from further debt.'

Fists slammed into flesh. Years of past rivalry, too long restrained, demanded release. They were evenly matched for St John was strong from his years working the land and Adam from the rigours of life at sea and the manual work in the yard. They rolled across the yard and St John pressed his thumbs into Adam's throat.

'You stole the yard which was mine,' St John panted. 'You always were Father's favourite.'

Adam grabbed St John's wrists and, with his face contorted against the pain, managed to fling off his brother's hold. His knuckles cracked as they hit St John's jaw. 'If you wanted a fortune you should have wed one instead of seducing Meriel.'

St John rolled away from Adam and staggered to his feet. Adam was now also upright and was crouched low, ready for another attack.

St John bared his teeth as he circled his brother and taunted, 'But the better man won her.'

'Or did she win you?' Adam rained three blows in succession to his twin's stomach. He stood back as St John went down on his knees, holding his torso. 'Meriel was the winner. You took her out of her poverty. Had you wed an heiress as Father wished, then Trevowan House would not be mortgaged or the yard in such debt.'

'I won the woman you wanted.' St John scowled and flung himself at Adam, bringing them both to the ground.

Adam grinned up at his brother. He doubted St John knew that he had been Meriel's lover before St John had seduced her. Even in the heat of temper Adam kept his triumph secret.

Faith and Scamp returned from romping in the freshly ploughed fields after the harvest. They barked with excitement, seeing the fight as a game which they wanted to join in. Adam's head was licked by Scamp, and Faith sprang at St John's boots. She yelped as he kicked her aside. Scamp's tongue was rasping on Adam's cut

157

cheek and eye. In her excitement she nipped St John's ear.

Cursing the dog, St John jammed his knee into Adam's stomach. There was a yelp from Scamp as the dog received a kick from St John. The impetus of St John's attack on both his brother and the dog momentarily put him off balance. Even through his pain, Adam reacted with the sharpened instinct for survival learned in countless brawls in dockyard taverns around the world. His lithe body jerked, he twisted aside and his fist ground into St John's nose. At the same moment he brought a foot up to encounter St John's hip and kick him away. Adam rolled and came up swaying to his feet and breathing heavily.

St John lay groaning on the stableyard cobbles and the two dogs began jumping over him, barking and licking him at the same time. 'Get those blasted dogs off me!' he yelled.

Adam called the dogs off. Jasper Fraddon was leaning on a pitchfork watching them. He had seen too many fights between them to be unduly perturbed. 'Now you've got that out the way, p'haps you best get yourselves cleaned up at the pump. If Mistress Elspeth catches sight of you there'll be hell to pay. If yer father were here, he'd bang ye heads together like he did when you fought as nippers.'

'Had enough, St John?' Adam challenged.

'Go to hell.' St John pushed himself up to a sitting position. His face was bloodied and his nose dripping. His shirt was ripped and his breeches were smeared with horse dung.

Adam looked as bad, and though the sleeve on his jacket was torn, his breeches were only marked by dirt. He marched past St John into the stable. Scamp followed him, pausing briefly to cock his leg and spray St John's boot.

Inside the stable, the familiar smell of horses, straw, and leather from the tack room as he saddled Solomon did nothing to calm Adam's mood. It was bleak, darkened by his anger at St John. All St John could think of was his own selfish needs. Adam had hoped that they could work together before his father returned, to sort out some kind of plan to ease the estate and yard expenses. St John would now reject any suggestion coming from him.

Adam led his gelding into the yard and mounted him to ride out at a canter, whistling to Scamp to join him. Once he reached open land, he gave the horse his head as they galloped towards the moor. He did not halt until he came to the ancient Druid standing stone where he and Senara had first made love. He dismounted and threw himself on the warm grass and leant his back against the lichen-garlanded edifice. His hopes of spending most of his leave with Senara had been dashed.

He flexed his bruised and bleeding knuckles, regretting that he had not given St John a sounder trouncing. The responsibility his father had placed on him weighed heavily. He did not trust St John. They would be at loggerheads over every minor cutback. He cursed St John's selfishness. Adam had argued with his father to stop him selling any of the Trevowan land. Even

159

though he would never inherit the estate, it was too precious to him to see any of it lost. He had finally persuaded Edward to sell the mineral rights to Sir Henry Traherne. That sale would not be sufficient to clear all the loans on the estate, but Adam had vowed to make up the shortfall by chasing their own debtors for payment.

That was just the start of the work ahead of him. During the next week he would be working long hours in the yard, pushing the men to increase their production. He also needed to obtain early payment on the next instalments due on the vessels they were building. That would mean travelling to St Ives for some of the money.

He watched a kestrel hovering in the sky over a rabbit warren and it suddenly swooped on silent wings to take in its claws a weasel, which had also been searching for prey.

Would he strike with the sureness and success of the kestrel, or blunder into danger like the weasel? He reflected with trepidation. The man who owed the most was Thadeous Lanyon. Money was also owed on the revenue cutter, but the navy were notoriously slow payers. Adam doubted that any demands or pleas by him would speed their payment.

Without Amelia's income the family would have trouble meeting their financial commitments. At least young Richard's fortune was not entirely lost and his future remained secure. But that could not assist the Lovedays. Uncle Charles, as the executor of Richard's father's will, had signed away the rents on the properties for the next five years, to repay a loan which he had

160

needed for reinvestment to try to recover some of Amelia's losses. It had been a complicated arrangement – which amounted to Richard still owning the properties, which could not be sold or mortgaged until he was twenty-one, but there would be no rent money available for five years.

It was a financial disaster. Aunt Margaret was virtually penniless – though none of this had been revealed to her. So much depended on Thomas, and the sacrifices he must make to salvage both the bank's reputation and the Mercer and Loveday money.

Adam walked to a nearby stream and, using his stock, washed the blood from his face and hands. He would bear the marks of his fight with his brother for some days, but he did not regret it. It had strengthened his resolve to ease the burdens carried by his father. Whilst Edward remained in London, Adam must be the linchpin to save the yard. He would also be the devil's advocate when he told the family the extent of the sacrifices yet to be made by each of them.

At least when Adam arrived at the yard there was the reassuring sound of hammers and saws at work. Forty men were dotted along the cradle scaffoldings and another eight in the carpentry sheds.

He climbed the scaffolding around Thadeous Lanyon's cutter and was joined by Ben Mumford. The curved beams which ensured the drainage of the deck were almost covered in planking and the central hatch was completed. Adam nodded in satisfaction to see the smaller deck at the stern well under construction.

'Mr Lanyon was round here again last week eager for its completion,' Ben announced. 'She could be ready for launching in a week. It would mean putting all the men to work on her. Otherwise she'll be another month before we can launch her.'

That was welcome news, but Adam kept his emotions guarded. He did not want Mumford to know how close they were to bankruptcy. 'If Lanyon is in such a hurry, he can pay for the privilege. Once she's launched there is still a month's work to be done on the masts and fittings.'

'Lanyon bain't one to part easily with his hard-earned cash.' Mumford shook his head. 'Neither is he known to be a patient man. Especially now he sees himself as a person of standing and substance. He'll have to wait his turn.'

'Is the naval cutter on schedule for completion?' Adam enquired.

Ben shrugged. 'We've lost some time with the weather lately, and the last delivery of timber was late, which didn't help. But she'll be finished on time, Cap'n.'

Adam looked across at the second hull. The workmen had made good progress while he had been in London. The four pulleys were in place at the corners of the scaffolding, and the piles of planks cut to the right size and shape which had been stacked besides its ribs were all but depleted. Next week she could be caulked.

'I will talk to Lanyon. It could be possible to reschedule the work on his cutter, if he makes it worth our while.'

'Why the rush?' Mumford scratched his bald head.

'We need the space to lay down another keel as soon as possible. With the books so full we could lose trade if there is too long a wait for delivery,' Adam prevaricated. What concerned him most was that the sooner a new keel was laid, the sooner they would be paid the first instalment by the owner.

Adam spent the morning checking the stock lists and the columns of figures in the ledgers. At least they had enough materials in the yard to keep them going for another three months. If he could get some extra money out of Lanyon they could weather the first crisis.

It was an easy matter to visit Sir Henry and arrange the sale of mineral rights, but he had to delay his visit to Lanyon until he no longer looked like a fairground pugilist. He needed to win the smugglers' banker's respect, not face ridicule for his appearance. Time was not wasted for he drew up a list of all money owing to them and spent every daylight hour in the yard, working as hard as any of the shipwrights and carpenters to lead by example and urge them to complete the next stage of work. He had thought to spend his night with Senara, but she was not at the cottage, having taken her pots into Liskeard to sell, and would be away for three days.

'Just as well she will not see your face, Cap'n,' Leah scolded him. 'Senara does not hold with violence. And you'd best use this cream of hers which will get rid of the worst of the swelling and

163

bruising before she returns.'

As soon as his shaving mirror told him he again looked presentable, Adam called on Lanyon at his shop. It was the only shop selling general merchandise in Penruan, and its shelves were piled high with cheap linen and woollen materials, food and ironware. There were sacks of flour, oats, and salt on the floor and barrels of salted pork and beef. The villagers rarely ate fresh meat unless they raised the animals themselves. Their diet consisted mostly of the fish they caught, and the vegetables they grew. In another corner of the shop hung dried hams, and on a marble slab some cheeses, though these were a luxury to many of the villagers, purchased only after a good catch or a smuggling run.

Hester Lanyon looked sullen behind the counter. 'Can I help you, Cap'n Loveday?'

'It is your husband I would speak with, Mrs Lanyon.'

'Get out of here, woman,' Lanyon brusquely ordered, 'and lock the shop door. I've business with Captain Loveday and I don't want interruptions.'

The barrel-shaped figure of Thadeous Lanyon sat at his desk on a platform to the rear of the shop, working over his ledgers. He was dressed in a sober brown linsey-woolsey jacket and breeches, and there were ink stains on his wig where he had pushed it back to scratch his head. Hester bolted the door and disappeared into the back room. There was a slump to her shoulders and she looked far from happy for a woman so recently wed.

Lanyon carefully placed his quill in the inkwell, then barked out without bothering to answer Adam's greeting, 'When will my cutter be finished?'

'She is on schedule to be launched in a month.'

'A month is lost time to me.' Lanyon strutted across the floor in his agitation. 'Why not sooner? I need her now.'

He jabbed an ink-blackened finger at Adam's chest and Adam sidestepped to avoid its contact.

'We have other commitments at the yard, and schedules to maintain. Extra work on one vessel delays the progress of another,' Adam explained. He had to handle Lanyon carefully, If he got a whiff of their financial problems, Lanyon would exploit the situation. 'I believe that my father has explained this to you. We shall meet our delivery date.'

'You're building a damned revenue cutter, so I heard,' Lanyon scowled. 'Is she as fast as my ship?'

'They are both built to the same lines, but they can out-run any other coastal vessel.'

Lanyon thrust his fat neck forward, his bulbous eyes blinking rapidly. 'How long before this revenue cutter is finisher?'

'Two months after yours.'

'And if mine were finished earlier? It would be nearly four months before the revenue cutter was at sea.'

Adam drew himself to his full height and clasped his hands behind his back in an imposing stance. 'It is not our policy to favour one vessel above another.'

'If I'd known you'd be building a sister-ship for the navy, I'd have taken my custom elsewhere.' Lanyon sucked in his thin lips. 'There's a dozen or more yards hereabouts who would be more obliging in their delivery time.'

'Yes, but would they have built you so fast a vessel? The cutter is the finest in her class. She will out-sail any other revenue ship afloat. That is why you commissioned her.'

'Damn your insolence, Loveday,' Lanyon bellowed. 'That's why I need her now!' Lanyon paced for several moments. 'Your father is in London, I believe. When is he back?'

'Family commitments and business will keep him there for upwards of a month.'

'So you're in charge of the yard. You have the say of what work is done and what bain't. I'm a reasonable man, I would expect to pay for preferential treatment, Captain Loveday.'

'I can do nothing which will endanger the reputation of the yard.' Adam's manner remained stiff. 'However, last winter was hard and the men are eager to work double shifts to safeguard their families against the possible hardships of this winter. It may be possible to deliver earlier.'

'At what extra cost?'

Adam named the price. Lanyon turned puce and blew out his cheeks. 'That is extortionate.'

Adam eyed him forthrightly. 'We are both businessmen. It is nothing compared to the profits you will make if the ship is finished early. However, I am happy to stay with the original completion date.' Adam turned to leave. 'Good day, Mr Lanyon.'

'Wait! You are too hasty.' Lanyon puffed out his barrel chest. 'I want that ship for use in less than a month.'

'Then I will accept a half of the agreed payment now as a token of goodwill,' Adam insisted.

'The devil you will. I've never heard such–'

'It is not unrealistic in the circumstances.' Adam remained firm.

Lanyon's face contorted as he struggled to master his temper. His bluster had made no impression on Adam and he was not used to being thwarted. Gradually the colour drained from his face and his breathing became even, but there remained a malevolent glitter in his protruding eyes.

'There's one further requirement.' Lanyon took a sheet of vellum from his desk with dimensions written on it. 'I want below decks changed to accommodate this. The door must be hidden and the room's existence undetectable to any revenue officer who may board her. I want the work done in secret. I've heard you're a passable carpenter yourself, Captain Loveday. There's no need for anyone else to know about this room. What will it cost?'

Adam guessed it was a storeroom for the most expensive of the smuggled contraband. Should the cutter be boarded by a revenue ship, its most valuable cargo need not be jettisoned as was the usual case when avoiding arrest. A smuggler had to be caught with the goods on board. 'It would be an exclusive feature and to make it complete undetectable a fair estimate would be another hundred guineas.'

'Why don't you set yourself up as a highway robber at such prices?' A spray of spittle issued from Lanyon's mouth and his angry flush deepened.

Adam chose to laugh instead of taking offence. Lanyon would pay up. He needed the ship and its secret room too much. He bowed curtly. 'Deliver the money to Mariner's House and the work will begin at once, Mr Lanyon. Good day to you; it has been a pleasure doing business.'

Lanyon cursed the Lovedays long and loud when Adam left. 'They won't get the better of me.' He shook his fist and turned to see the terrified face of his wife in the doorway. 'No one gets the better of me, do they, Hester?'

He gave a cruel bark of laughter and, going over to her, viciously pinched his wife's breast. 'Get in the back room; I need a bit of comforting after dealing with Loveday.' He relocked the shop door.

'Can you not wait until we get home, Thadeous? What about the customers?' Someone was banging on the door for admittance even now.

Thadeous lunged at her. 'My needs are greater than theirs. They'll be back. Where else they gonna get what they need?'

Hester held her hands in front of her to ward him off. 'You bain't gonna hurt me again, are you, Thadeous? I didn't do nothing to make you angry.'

The ring on his finger cut her cheek as he laid in to her, and with a terrified shriek she cowered on the floor. 'You questioned me, did you not?

168

You sought to withhold my rights from me, did you not? I'll teach you.' He threw himself on her, his pleasure sated only when she was sobbing in pain.

He got up and adjusted his clothing. 'Now get back home and make sure my dinner bain't ruined like it was last night, or you'll get another beating. Useless slut.'

Hester slipped out the back door of the shop, too ashamed to face any of the customers waiting for the main door to be opened. Thadeous treated her worse than a whore.

'Dear God, help me,' Hester groaned as she limped to her home on the top of the coombe. Its impressive eight-room structure of limewashed brick no longer enthralled her. It was a prison and a torture chamber. She had been such a fool to be tempted by Lanyon's lies.

For months she had been wooed and courted by Lanyon with such lavish devotion and gifts that he had turned her head. He had vowed to shower her with riches and her every pleasure would be pandered to. 'Women are to be, revered, worshipped and adorned,' had been the words constantly on his lips while he wooed her. In contrast Harry had taken her for granted and never bought her gifts.

Within a week of marriage, she had seen that his vanity would bedeck her in velvets and jewels, his pride salved at stealing her from a Sawle. He revered his word only as absolute law. A beating cowed her to his bestial mastery, while his twisted mind worshipped only his perverted lust, which must be appeased by his demands upon her cringing body.

She was sobbing as she entered the unwelcoming kitchen in her home. Yesterday had been washing day and it had rained. The sheets and Thadeous's shirts hung damply from a line across the hearth. Her husband hated seeing the washing indoors, but it was too late for them to dry outside now. And she ached too much to struggle with the sheets against the wind. The last maid had been dismissed for being too slow and lazy. The miserly Lanyon now insisted that it was his wife's duties to clean the house, cook, and serve in the shop.

She collapsed on a wooden chair and sank her head into her hands. 'Oh, Harry, what a fool I was. I can't bear this misery. What I would not give to be with you now.'

Chapter Nine

Senara waited outside the schoolhouse in the Loveday yard to take Bridie home. She stroked Wilful's nose as the donkey nuzzled the pocket of her gown, where she usually carried a titbit for him. The cob-built schoolhouse with its slate roof was a single-room building, which abutted the cottage where the new schoolmaster, Gideon Meadows, lived.

Bridie appeared happy to attend school, but it concerned Senara that she was shunned by the other children and had made no friends. She also worried that the children taunted Bridie for all that her sister had denied it. Bridie loved her school work and had surprised both Leah and Senara by the rapid pace she had learned to read and master her numbers. She would chatter all evening of the countries she had learned about and the strange animals like giraffes and elephants which fired her imagination.

'Do such creatures really exist?' she asked with wide-eyed wonder. 'If only I could see them. They be a wondrous sight for certain.'

'I saw an elephant once,' Leah said. 'He was part of a travelling show which came to Redruth Fair one time. Big as our cottage he be, with a great dangling nose like a person's arm which reached to the ground. It were a fearsome sight.'

Bridie related more of the tales of foreign lands, and Senara experienced a growing envy at her sister's education. She had missed so much growing up with the gypsies. Bridie had taught Senara all she had learned, but Senara hungered for further education. Her lack of it was another barrier between her and Adam. He was educated and had sailed the world, gaining a vast knowledge of places and things she had not even heard of.

The schoolhouse door opened and the children ran out: boisterous, shouting and jostling each other in their exuberance after being cooped up so long. Bridie as always was last. She hobbled slowly, her elfin face turned up to Gideon Meadows as she bombarded the schoolmaster with an endless stream of questions about a king called Henry.

'Did he really have *six* wives? And did he really cut off the heads of two of them? Won't he go to hell? Yet you said he made himself Head of the Church. And he was fat and ugly, wasn't he?'

'He was a golden handsome youth and the pride of the kingdom,' Gideon Meadows patiently explained. 'But he wrongly used his power to destroy any who opposed his wishes. Great men who were once his friends lost their lives on the scaffold. We have a better system of government now, although there is still need for reform, in the opinion of many.'

'I don't think I like kings if they cut off their wives' and friends' heads,' Bridie shuddered. She looked up and saw Senara waiting. 'Senara, did you know kings can cut off people's heads?'

'I expect a king can do anything he pleases,' Senara replied. 'Though a good king, or any person in a position of power, should have the welfare of others at heart to be a good ruler.'

'That is an interesting theory, Miss Polglase.' Gideon Meadows turned pale piercing eyes upon her.

His eyes were the colour of the sky in a twilight haze, bright with intelligence and, to her surprise, humour. In her experience schoolmasters were rather like parsons: too serious, rather pompous and with a swollen air of self-importance. Mr Meadows was different. He was tall and thin as a sapling, with cropped brown hair which tended to sprout around his head like dandelion seed. This was his first teaching job since leaving university, and Senara had often seen him striding across the moor, or along the

172

seashore, searching for flower or rock specimens.

Senara was discomfited. 'I would not presume to contradict your teaching, Mr Meadows. It was merely an observation.'

'It shows you to be an idealist, Miss Polglase.' The humour again sparkled in his eyes.

Her hand covered her mouth in horror. 'People have been thrown in prison labelled as such. I mean no harm, sir.'

'You take my words amiss. I find such sentiments refreshing. Your pardon if I alarmed you, Miss Polglase.'

She was cross with herself for speaking so openly, when too often she had seen the persecution it could bring. He had an open honest face but his expression was now pinched with concern that he had offended her.

Scamp and Charity barked from the direction of the foundry. 'Go and play with Scamp for a moment, Bridie. I would like a word with Mr Meadows.'

Bridie hobbled away to call to the dogs. Senara cleared her throat. 'Have you a moment, Mr Meadows? I am worried about Bridie.'

'Yes, of course, come inside.' They entered the schoolroom with its rows of benches, and trestle tables which were used as desks. There were two hand-drawn maps on the walls which caught Senara's attention.

At her interest, he said, 'This is a map of Great Britain. Here is Cornwall sticking out like a finger in the west. The other map is of the known world.'

Senara studied them in wonder. 'So many

173

countries and so much water. I did not realise there would be more sea than land.'

She turned back to the schoolmaster, embarrassed at her ignorance. 'Bridie loves her lessons, but she has made no friends. Do the children taunt her? She would not speak of it if they did.'

'I do not permit them to call her names.' Gideon Meadows looked affronted. 'But I cannot force them to make friends with her. It is a pity. She is a bright child – indeed, my best pupil.'

Senara nodded satisfied. 'You will tell me if she is plagued by the others? Our mother did not want her to attend school: she feared how cruel children can be towards one who is not as they are. But I would not have her ignorant.'

She wandered around the schoolroom where there were more sketches of wild flowers and birds with their names printed beside them. She also noticed the thick layer of dust along the bookshelf and the cobwebs collecting in the corners. There were also some mouse droppings on the floor.

'Do you not employ a servant to look after the schoolhouse or yourself?'

'My salary does not extend to such an extravagance.'

'It cannot be easy for a man living alone.' Senara took a further look around the room which for her held so many treasures and unknown knowledge. As she walked to the door she hesitated, not wishing to appear presumptuous. 'Mr Meadows, if I were to clean the schoolroom and your cottage, would you consider repaying me by private tuition? I cannot read, though I practise writing my letters every day with Bridie's help.'

He looked taken aback, but soon recovered. 'I would be delighted. Shall we say two hours twice a week to begin with? Once your work is done I shall begin your lessons.'

She nodded, overcome with joy at the world he was about to open up to her.

Gideon Meadows smiled. 'Then it is agreed. Admirable.' His thin face flushed with excitement. 'I shall enjoy your company. I know so few people in the district. The villagers seem wary of my profession, though Reverend Joshua Loveday has called on me. A remarkable man for a parson. Not what you would expect. Do you attend his services, Miss Polglase?'

'I am not much of a churchgoer, Mr Meadows. I feel closer to any divine spirit within a forest or upon a seashore. God's presence is everywhere, is it not?'

'Well, yes, I suppose no clergyman could argue with that. Except they would see themselves as the shepherd of your soul, and without proper guidance, we are all but lost sinners.'

Senara was unsure whether he was serious or mocking. Religion was a subject she preferred not to discuss. It was too volatile a topic. His gaze swept over her and there was interest as well as admiration in his eyes.

Senara had seen that look in a man's eyes too often not to feel wary of it. But her desire for knowledge was too fierce to heed her misgivings.

She thanked him and her step was light as she left the schoolhouse.

Adam arrived at the yard from visiting Sir Henry Traherne, and his spirits lifted to see Wilful tethered by the schoolhouse. Angel, the mastiff, was panting as he lay in the shade by the donkey. At seeing Adam, he rose to amble towards him. Twin strings of saliva hung from his mouth and when the mastiff shook his scarred head, Adam sidestepped to avoid the flying drool. He ruffled the ragged ears hoping that Angel's presence meant that Senara was in the yard, having come to collect Bridie from school. But school would have finished a half-hour past.

He heard barking and saw Scamp and Charity running circles around Bridie, who was throwing sticks for them. At that moment Senara appeared in the doorway of the schoolhouse accompanied by the new teacher.

It was the first time Adam had seen Gideon Meadows. Not only the ten children living within the hamlet which had sprung up around the yard to house its workers attended the school, but another dozen or so came from nearby farms.

'Mr Meadows!' He held out his hand. 'Adam Loveday at your service. May I welcome you to our community.' He tipped his tricorn to Senara and wished that they did not have to be so discreet in public. 'Good day, Miss Polglase.'

She curtsied but when she looked as though she would leave, he said quickly, 'That cut on Scamp's side which you tended last week seems to have become infected again. I was wondering if you would mind looking at it.'

'Certainly, Captain Loveday. Though from here Scamp looks in fine shape.' She watched the dog leap in the air to catch a stick which Bridie had thrown. 'But I would not see an animal suffer.' She walked towards Mariner's House and it was an effort for Adam to drag his gaze from her graceful figure.

Gideon Meadows' own gaze lingered, following Senara's progress, and then he bowed to Adam. 'Captain Loveday, it is an honour to serve here. Though it is unusual, is it not, to have a village spring up within a shipwright's yard?'

'It has evolved over the years.'

'Yet the village has no name. I have overheard talk that the Methodists want to put up a chapel.'

Adam frowned. 'I have nothing against the Methodists but I doubt my father would wish for a chapel on our land. Most of the villagers attend Trewenna church as we fall within its parish. This is not a village despite its size. We have no resident squire or parson. Since the expansion of the dry dock, when more cottages were built, the locals began calling it Trevowan Hard after the family house and estate.'

Impatient to rejoin Senara, whom he had not seen since his return from London, Adam left the schoolmaster. There was something about the man he did not take to, and it was not just because he had seen the interest in his eyes when Gideon Meadows watched Senara.

It was past midnight when the sound of a cane rapping on the door of the bank startled Thomas from sleep. He lifted his head from his arms which rested on the thick ledgers open on his desk. The candles had burned low and cast eerie shadows in the oak-panelled room.

The energetic pounding persisted. Fear gripped him that the beadles had come to arrest him for debt. With a shaking hand he pushed his fingers through his blond hair and stretched his arms to ease the ache from his shoulders.

'Thomas, dear fellow!' Lucien Greene shouted. 'Open the door. I will not have you become a hermit. It is too vexing for my constitution.'

The relief that it was his friend was over-whelming. Thomas had seen little of Lucien in recent weeks and had missed his company. He had avoided his former haunts of coffee – and playhouses, every moment absorbed with the problems overshadowing the bank. If one more prestigious customer withdrew their money, he would not be able to meet their demands and he would be declared bankrupt.

The last month had been a battle of wits, with rumours rife about his father's death, and that the bank was in trouble. Fortunately, many of the investors were families who had banked with the Mercers since his grandfather's time. Until this last year of disastrous investments, Charles Mercer had made vast profits for his customers. The Mercer name stood for trust and prosperity in the City, and Thomas had been able to convince many of their customers that the bank was sound.

Yet confidence had waned in their reputation, and lesser mortals feared for their savings. They judged Thomas as untested and too young to handle the responsibility of their investments, and they had withdrawn their savings.

Each night Thomas returned home exhausted. He had lost weight, and the effort to appear charming and solicitous to men who defamed his father's name was taking a toll on his health. Twice this week, when the honour of his father was questioned, he came close to challenging a client to a duel. Without Edward's intercession and pacification, such a duel would have poured oil on the flames of the scandal, and all would have been lost.

So many interviews, so much forced joviality, politeness and enthusiastic assurances were an exacting regime. And still bankruptcy loomed, and with it, the humiliation and squalor of a debtors' prison. Such an event would crush his mother's pride and she would be reduced to penury. That prospect alarmed him even more than the threat of prison.

Such fears took the shape of demons to haunt his sleep. They haunted him – tall as siege towers with dragon's fire for breath; their scaly claws raked to pluck out his heart and their wings beat the air as their long teeth snapped about his head. Each night he woke sweating and shaking with terror. Each morning he rose more haggard, but more determined for Mercer's Bank to rise like the Phoenix from the ashes.

The pounding on the door continued. Now it was Japhet demanding, 'Thomas, must I break this door down?'

Thomas hoisted up the sash window of the office on the first floor. The street was in darkness except for an occasional lantern burning on the corner of a house. There was one on the corner of the bank, lit each night by the lamplighter. Lucien and Japhet stepped back from the door into its pale pool of light.

'There you are!' Lucien cried as he stared up at Thomas. 'My dear fellow, you look like the ghost of woebegone servitude in a second-rate play. Get yourself down here. The night is still young. Time you shed your mantle of martyrdom and rejoined our merry band.'

Further along the street another window was thrown open. 'What's that damned racket? An honest man needs his sleep.'

'Good sir, an honest man should be rogering his lady wife at this time of night,' Japhet quipped, his voice thickened by an evening of drinking.

'Insolent knave,' the irate gentleman persisted. 'I'll call the watch. You damned Mohocks run amok in the City of a night. Drunken lechers to a man. Banging on doors, yelling obscenities at Godfearing folk, and shaming the devil with your lewdness. It is not to be borne!' He then proceeded to yell, 'Watchman! Watchman! To me. Thieves and murderers are afoot. Watchman!'

At the first of the neighbour's cries Thomas sped down the oak staircase leading from his office and through the rows of clerks' desks where the everyday transactions in the bank were performed. The client ledgers were neatly stacked on rows of shelves behind locked glass doors.

He unbolted the bank door and pulled his cousin and friend inside. 'Am I not in enough trouble without you rousing the watch and getting us arrested?'

The sound of the running feet of the watch clattered around the corner as the bank door was shut and rebolted.

'Is that any way to greet us?' Japhet grumbled. 'I gave up the chance of bedding the most delightful actress because I was worried about you. Fine way to repay me, I must say.'

Outside they could hear the neighbour still shouting his complaints to the watch. But there was no knock on the door.

Thomas leaned against it. 'Let us hope the watch will not pursue the complaint.'

They were standing in darkness with only the palest flicker of light from the outside lantern penetrating the fanlight above the door.

'Get your jacket, Thomas,' Lucien demanded. 'I will not have you become a hermit. Damn me, but if I haven't missed you, my dear fellow.'

'And I you,' Thomas let out a heartfelt groan. 'But I have some more figures to go through. There is another cursed meeting tomorrow with Father's lawyers. The creditors will wait no longer for their money.'

'Then what better reason is there than to make merry tonight, while you can?' Japhet reasoned. 'The gaming houses beckon. I won two hundred guineas last night and I shall loan you fifty. Who knows? You may make your fortune! Or at least enough to pay off your most pressing creditors.'

Thomas shook his head. 'You are well intentioned, Japhet, but I am not a gambler. I have seen too many men lose everything on the turn of a card. And in truth I am in no mood for frivolous pursuits.'

Lucien had found a candle and lit it from his tinderbox. The flames illuminated his figure dressed in an emerald and gold striped cutaway tail coat with a high collar which touched his ears. He wore leaf-green breeches and a lavender brocade waistcoat. A lace handkerchief fluttered in his fingers with his extravagant hand gestures.

'My dear fellow, I will not listen to such melodrama. This simply will not do.'

'My friend, I am poor company and I serve you ill by my neglect.'

'Nay, say not that.' Lucien was appalled. 'Your suffering is my suffering, don't you know? I would not see you so melancholy.'

'I am heartened by your presence tonight.' Thomas spread his arms to include Japhet, who was lounging against the wall, looking bored and impatient. 'I am surprised to see you, Japhet. I did not think that you and Lucien would frequent the same haunts.'

'Now he takes me for a moron,' Japhet said with a dry laugh. 'We met at the Garrick. I had just made this assignation with ... well, never mind who with ... though she was Venus personified. Lucien was with another party and asked how you were. I felt guilty I had made myself so scarce to avoid returning to Cornwall. Rum thing for me to do. Thought it time I put things right with my cousin.'

'You have done more than I expected. One learns who one's true friends are. I thank you both. Come back to the house with me now,

182

Japhet. It will please Uncle Edward that you have returned. He will still be up. He refuses to retire when he knows I am at the bank. Besides...' he drew a laboured breath, 'I have come to a decision and I would have you both there to discuss it.'

Thomas was glad of the darkness, for he could not bear to see Lucien's expression when he announced, 'I have decided I must marry. Meredith Lascalles of Lascalles Bank is eager for a merger and has been pestering Papa for a year or more. He is ambitious to raise the prestige of his own bank, which is not favoured by the nobles and gentry in the city. He wants the Mercer clientele.'

'Why did Uncle Charles not enter into this partnership?' Japhet asked. 'It would have saved him from financial disaster.'

Thomas fought against a rush of guilt. 'There was another condition Lascalles insisted upon – that not only the banks merge but also our families. I was expected to wed one of his daughters. It was the cause of my last row with Father. It was why I left the bank.' Guilt threatened to overwhelm him and his voice broke in anguish. 'If only Father had told me the true circumstances ... that so much was at stake. I would not have failed him in my duty. That is why I must make this sacrifice now to save the bank and my father's reputation.'

Lucien had remained rigid as a stone obelisk throughout Thomas's speech. Suddenly he became animated, his handkerchief waving erratically. 'It simply must be done. And you must look on the bright side, my dear fellow. Painful as all this is, you are experiencing the traumas, passions and emotions all playwrights must live through to ever achieve their full greatness with the written word. When you again take up your pen, your work will be so heart-rendingly divine, so poignant, so utterly exquisite, that the theatres will be clamouring to put on your plays.'

Aware that Lucien was using flippancy to hide his true feelings. Thomas persisted, 'You really do not mind, that I must marry?'

'I shall be devastated, consumed by jealousy, and shall endure the company of the trollop like a spear carried in my side. Indeed, I dare say my future poems will be of great tragedies, and heroic love conquering all adversities. I shall be acclaimed by luminaries, while in silence I nurse my broken heart.' He gave a shaky laugh. 'It must be done, my dear fellow. And the best made of it.'

'Then I shall call on Lascalles tomorrow,' declared Thomas.

Japhet gave a low whistle, breaking the tension with levity. 'Aunt Margaret will be furious she is not in London to take part in the culmination of all her years of matchmaking.'

St John was enjoying the freedom of not having his father present at Trevowan. The womenfolk were absorbed in helping Aunt Margaret through her grief, and had no interest in his movements. He met with Harry and Clem Sawle in the Dolphin one evening after it was closed. They sat in the candlelit taproom drinking French cognac.

184

A travelling pedlar was staying the night at the inn before moving on, and they had to wait until he had retired for the night before talking of their plans.

They made an incongruous trio with St John in a ruffled shirt, green velvet jacket and waistcoat, nankeen trousers and riding boots, and Harry and Clem in their rough fishermen's shirts and trousers and cumbersome laced work boots. Both Harry and Clem had several days' growth of beard while St John was immaculate and clean-shaven.

Clem was in a jubilant mood. 'This run will set me up after my marriage. The widow Keziah Warren be selling her farm, and we be setting up home in the old Pasmore place back of Penruan coombe.'

'It will cost you a fortune to make it habitable,' Harry observed. 'Old Ma Pasmore were the last to live there and she died seven years ago.'

'The roof is sound except over one back room,' Clem said. 'There be four other bedrooms so that be no problem. Kezzy be set on having it put in order. She be bringing all her furniture, and some livestock. She do make the finest cheese from her goat's milk. Sells it to emporiums in Truro and Bodmin, as well as in the markets.'

Reuban was lolling back on a settle in the corner, his eyes squinting blearily in the dim candlelight. 'That be a house to rival Lanyon's new mansion when it be put right. Always thought you, as my eldest, would live here at the Dolphin and take it over when I'm gone.'

'Don't reckon to be at the beck and call of my

185

fellow man all day,' Clem said with a hearty laugh. 'Nor be a fisherman, freezing and sodden in stormy seas, and all for a pittance. I got a tidy nest egg put by, and what with Kezzy being comfortable off, we shall set it to good use.'

'See yourself as a gentleman then, do you, Clem?' Reuban had a nasty gleam in his eye. 'What you say about that, Sal?'

His wife had entered to hand each of the men a slice of bread and a wedge of cheese for their supper.

Sal was pale. She knew Reuban was referring to the circumstances of Clem's birth. She had been pregnant by a naval officer when she married Reuban. It had been her secret but Clem had been too big to be a seven-month child. Though Reuban had not challenged her, she knew he had brooded on it. She did not want Clem learning about his birth now in such a way.

'Clem always had it in him to better himself. You were a good example, Reuban.'

Reuban cackled malignantly. 'I could tell Clem a thing or two which would shake him,' he mumbled into his quart of ale.

Clem ignored Reuban's drunken ramblings. 'Mark can run the Dolphin. He likes the work, never having taken to fishing. Unless Harry wants to be an innkeeper.'

Harry, well in his cups, sniggered drunkenly. 'I got grander plans for myself. The Sawle brothers be a force to be reckoned with. Always have been. And now there'll be no stopping us.'

''Tis madness to cross Lanyon,' Reuban warned.

'You're getting soft in your old age.' Clem eyed the old man with a jaundiced eye. 'No one gets the better of the Sawles: you taught us that.'

Reuban nodded, took a long swig of ale and slumped back with his eyes closed. Within moments, rasping snores interspersed his sons' conversation.

Clem sat forward, his voice lowered although there was no one but the conspirators present. 'I've been keeping watch on Lanyon's place. He had a visitor last night in the pilchard sheds. I crept round the back and heard them arranging for the landing to take place tomorrow night east of Pencarrow Head.'

'That's some distance away.' St John looked doubtful. 'Are you sure you heard right?'

'Lanyon never lands a cargo too near to Penruan these days,' Clem replied. 'That way no suspicion falls on himself. Better still, he's using tubmen from Polperro and Looe, so there's no chance of having to fight with men from Penruan. It's to be distributed through Launceston.'

'That at least is something,' St John said, 'but I'm still not happy about us using the Jowetts. They are brutal and unpredictable. We don't want any killings.'

'There won't be.' Clem was dismissive of St John's fears. 'Now is everything clear as to the distribution of the cargo? Three men from Okehampton, Tiverton and Exeter be meeting us on Holne Moor on Dartmoor. They will distribute it for us. It will mean riding all night. I don't trust the Jowetts enough to stow the cargo on Bodmin – too close to their home ground for comfort. They are capable of double-crossing us and selling it for themselves.'

'I cannot be away from Trevowan so long without suspicion.' St John felt his panic rising. 'You said it would be just one night.'

'Plans were changed,' Clem delighted in informing St John. 'You are either in with us, or not.'

'Since it was my idea,' St John challenged, 'I am in with you, of course. It will mean making further arrangements for myself.'

He could feel panic swirling in his gut. The Jowetts made him uneasy. Their mindless lust for violence could be disastrous. Yet the alternative, losing face to Meriel's brothers, would be humiliating. Meriel would never forgive him if he backed out. Without this money he would also lose the respect of his gambling friends for there were several IOUs still outstanding.

He resented any curtailment of his pleasure. Life was unjust. He had fumed when he'd received a letter from his father demanding a report on the income from the harvest which must be used on estate business. Did he not now have callouses on his hands from working like a farmhand so that he could enjoy the profits of a rich harvest? Those profits had now been taken from him. It was so unfair. God rot Uncle Charles! Life had been easy when Father married Amelia and all their financial troubles seemed behind them.

He was frightened by what the future could hold: a life without gaming, entertainments and sporting with his wealthy friends. And had not

Father also hinted that the Dower House would be closed until their fortunes improved? Meriel would not tolerate that. She had been more adamant than ever that smuggling would solve their problems. She had refused to share his bed until he had agreed to attend this meeting tonight.

'See that you plan well, St John,' Clem warned, incensing St John further.

'We all have to protect ourselves,' Harry added when he saw St John bristle with affront. 'I'm taking the lugger out on the morning tide up to the River Fowey and will moor her out of sight. That way Lanyon will think we be away fishing. We will all meet as arranged on the Launceston road. Be there an hour before dark.'

Harry rubbed his hands together and winked at St John. 'Lanyon has had this coming a long time.'

St John agreed.

Tomorrow he would have his own revenge upon Thadeous Lanyon and it would also make him a rich man. The anticipation bolstered his courage so that he felt invincible.

Chapter Ten

At the prospect of riches soon to come their way Meriel was in a buoyant mood during an afternoon visit to Lady Traherne. Traherne Hall was a square, red-brick mansion with long casement windows, each with a carved pediment. Meriel was shown into the dome-roofed conservatory, with its urns of exotic flowers. Roslyn, dressed all in white muslin, with a deep frilled underskirt and the overskirt pulled back over her hips, was reclining on a day bed whose side hangings of fine silk were draped to look like an oriental pavilion. Beside her was a wall fountain, the water flowing from the mouths of entwined fishes.

'I am so weary,' Roslyn complained as soon as Meriel arrived. 'Mama has taken to her bed in high dudgeon over some trivial incident. She will not acknowledge that I am mistress here, and that she has no right to interfere in my decisions. She lives at the Hall upon Henry's sufferance. And Gwendolyn is just as vexing. She has been gone since mid-morning on one of her rides. With Henry attending to both his mine and estate matters, I have been left to my own devices.'

Even Roslyn's irritable mood could not dampen Meriel's spirits, though she was annoyed when Hannah Rabson, Japhet's sister from High Tor Farm, was announced.

Roslyn instantly lost her ennui. 'Hannah, my dear friend. How wonderful for you to call. Just when I am in need of diversion. Meriel does her best, but you are so wickedly witty. It is a joy to see you. It has been too long.'

'We have been busy with the harvest,' Hannah explained.

Meriel swallowed the insult with difficulty, feeling out of place and excluded by these childhood friends. Hannah had arrived with her son Davey, and daughters, Abigail and Florence. The three children were sent to the nursery to play with the Traherne children. Meriel had no liking for the vivacious, dark-haired beauty who was as irrepressible as her elder brother, Japhet. Whenever Hannah entered a room, laughter soon followed, everyone's attention and conversation gravitating around her. That irked Meriel, who envied Hannah's easy and infectious wit.

The Rabsons lived in genteel poverty in an ancient granite farmhouse with worn and faded furniture. A beautiful woman like Hannah could have done far better for herself than a farmer. There was a decided odour of the cow shed on her. Meriel despised Hannah for not aiming higher in marriage. No matter that Oswald Rabson adored his wife, and Hannah seemed content in her marriage. Hannah's idyllic love had made her little better than a drudge, with only one servant and two labourers to help on the farm.

A flare of anger burned through Meriel. If she was not careful, St John and she could find themselves similarly impoverished. Thank God St John had given in to her demands to join the smugglers. She had no intention of allowing the Dower House to be closed, and she was determined to reinstate the number of servants from the profits earned from the trade. Edward Loveday could rant all he liked if he disapproved of how St John provided for his family. It had taken her three years to be accepted by the local gentry, and she refused to give up her fine clothes, jewels and attendance of lavish entertainments. And she certainly would not surrender her status because of Edward Loveday's ethics on law-breaking.

Meriel was confident that she could manipulate St John to her wishes. He was as loath to give up his pleasures as she was. Yet he needed her strength to make him thwart his father's wishes.

She ran an appreciative finger over the rich taffeta of her gown and moved her hand so that the aquamarine ring sparkled in a ray of sunlight. Hannah's presence reinforced Meriel's determination to endure none of the cutbacks Edward intended. Meriel thought Hannah a fool to accept her lot when her beauty could have won her a life of comfort and ease. For all the woman's genteel birth, she was plainly attired. The hem of her dress had been turned at least twice, its colours fading after four years of wear. Neither did Hannah wear any jewellery except a simple gold cross and her wedding ring. A murrain had wiped out half of the Rabson dairy herd last spring, and the cows which survived had all aborted their calves. Each year the Rabson family sank deeper into debt. And Oswald was too highly principled to become involved with the smuggling trade.

Not that you could guess their troubles from Hannah's manner. She spoke excitedly, relating an incident on the farm that morning which made her Ladyship laugh. Then she mentioned that she had earlier called at Trevowan.

'It is good to see Aunt Margaret looking more

192

restored in health,' Hannah continued. 'Amelia has been a comfort to her, but then they are old friends.'

Roslyn lost her haughty countenance in Hannah's presence. 'You are looking well, Hannah, but you should take more care of your hands and keep the sun from your face. A gentlewoman must protect her pale complexion at all times.'

'I am a farmer's wife. Such things are not important.'

'Then I insist you take this lotion I had especially prepared by my apothecary in Truro. It will whiten your hands and face.'

'And likely leave me raddled as though from the pox. There is lead and mercury in some of those creams. Japhet brought Mama and me some concoction from Senara Polglase. It works very well.' Hannah paced the conservatory, pausing to smell each of the brightly coloured exotic blooms. There was always so much vibrant energy about her, which Meriel found disturbing.

'Well, if you are too headstrong to take some friendly advice, Hannah,' Roslyn sucked in her thin lips to a prim line, 'I wonder why I waste my time. I have been trying to teach Meriel the rudiments of whist when she visits.' Her tone was at its most condescending. 'It is a simple enough game, I would have thought. But she has no head for it.'

The criticism stung. Meriel had won three tricks from Roslyn on the last occasion and she was certain that the woman had cheated to win two of the other tricks by voicing some obscure rule when Meriel had made to trump Roslyn's king and queen.

Meriel caught an exchange of glances between the two women and Lady Traherne raised her brows as though despairing of Meriel's aptitude.

'Meriel, my dear, would you ring the bell to summon the maid,' ordered Lady Traherne. 'We will take tea now that Hannah is here.'

Meriel kept her head high as she walked to the table where the silver bell was out of Roslyn's reach. Inwardly she was fuming. Lady Traherne always set her these tasks, and seemed to delight in making Meriel wait upon her.

Hannah, who had finished her inspection of the plants, finally sat opposite Lady Traherne and enquired after the health of her friend's children.

'They grow so fast,' Roslyn said proudly. 'Roger is a serious child but Millicent, even at two, is in to everything.'

'And how is Rowena?' Hannah turned to Meriel as she returned to her seat. 'Mama was saying how well she copes with her arm.'

Again Meriel's hackles rose; to find fault with Rowena was to find fault with herself. 'Everyone says she has the Loveday wit and charm. And I scarce notice her arm is crippled for she is so dextrous with her other hand. Besides, there is some movement in the left arm now.'

'That is wonderful news,' Hannah said. 'But you have not brought her with you. She should mix more with her cousins and neighbours.'

The tone was friendly but Meriel took her words as criticism and replied stiffly, 'Rowena is a diversion for Aunt Margaret, who dotes on her.'

'Children are a great comfort at such distressing times,' Lady Traherne observed. 'She is a sweet child.'

'Meriel, you should bring her to the farm so that Rowena can play with Abigail and Florence,' Hannah insisted. 'Elspeth was saying that Senara Polglase's remedies have greatly helped Rowena.'

'Talking of whom,' Lady Traherne leaned forward, 'Adam is still seeing her. I would have thought he would have found someone more appropriate – though he is very discreet, and I have heard no gossip of the Polglase woman and other men.'

'Are you saying that Senara Polglase is Adam's mistress?' Meriel almost choked on her ire. 'I have heard nothing from the family.'

Hannah regarded her with a lift of her dark brow. 'It may not have been openly discussed, but it has been going on since she saved Adam's life that night he was shot.'

'So long!' Meriel could not hide her shock and her stomach churned with nausea. Jealousy consumed her. She had thought her feelings for Adam long buried, and now they rose up to mock her. She had never liked Senara. The woman's beauty and serenity made Meriel distrustful of her. Also, Meriel had resented the way Elspeth praised the woman's remedies. It was Senara who had saved Rowena's life after the difficult birth, and corrected the dislocated knee joint, though she could do little to help her arm. But for Adam to be in love for her put Senara in a very different light. Meriel lost any sense of gratitude as her hatred flared.

'I do hope for the family's sake this is a passing infatuation.' Lady Traherne's voice was heavy with disapproval. 'One understands that a man like Adam will enjoy the pleasures of such a woman, especially after what happened in France. To be jilted by his cousin, Lisette, was too deplorable.'

'And had everything to do with her brother, Etienne's, greed in wanting to link his family with the nobility,' Hannah stoutly defended Adam's honour and name. 'Lisette adored Adam.'

'She was a childish creature for such a man of worldly experience,' Lady Traherne offered. 'I doubt that they could have been happy.'

'That we will never know.' Hannah frowned and leaned forward to confide. 'Adam deserves his happiness. Japhet is convinced that Adam is set upon wedding Senara Polglase.'

Lady Traherne threw up her hands in dismay. 'I pray it will come to naught. It would be most unsuitable.'

Sensitive about her own parentage, Meriel stood up. 'It is time for me to take my leave, Lady Traherne.' She had listened without interrupting, hoping to hear more of this liaison, but now her head was reeling at this news of Adam's mistress.

The maid had arrived with the tea tray and an array of tiny cakes. Lady Traherne snapped, 'Sit down, Meriel. Tea is served now. I will not hear of you leaving.' She poured a cup. 'Pass this to Hannah.'

Meriel could bear no more. 'Hannah is nearer to your Ladyship than myself. I may remain a tavern-keeper's daughter in your eyes, but I am no servant.'

The cup banged down on to the table and Lady Traherne looked sweetly innocent. 'Oh, I have offended you. You silly goose to think I meant to imply anything about your own marriage. It is just that it would not do for Adam to wed the Polglase woman. They say she is half gypsy. I could never contemplate receiving her.' The cup was again lifted and Roslyn looked from Meriel to Hannah, indicating that Meriel should serve her friend with the tea.

Meriel did not move. Hannah rose and took the cup from her friend and strolled to the window while she sipped it. Lady Traherne's mouth turned down, showing her displeasure as she poured Meriel's cup in silence. When she handed it to Meriel, it was with an accompanying salvo: 'The lower classes simply do not know how to conduct themselves, even those who think to better themselves once they have acquired money. Take that Lanyon fellow. He may own a goodly part of Penruan but his wife was serving in the shop yesterday with a bruised cheek and barely able to stand behind the counter. She was doubled over in pain, according to my maid Nancy.'

'Lanyon is known as a bully,' Hannah replied. 'One can only feel sorry for his wife.'

'You are too generous, Hannah. The whole village is saying she has got what she deserved. Did she not jilt your own brother, Meriel, to marry that odious man?'

'You are well informed about village gossip,

197

Lady Traherne,' Meriel replied, 'especially since you profess these people are so far beneath you. Thank you for the tea, but I will not stay while you insult the people I grew up amongst. Good day to you both.'

She swept grandly from the room through an open door which led on to the garden, and was a quicker way out than walking all through the house. Her temper soared as she heard Hannah laugh. Were they mocking her?

'You have met your match with that young lady, Ros,' Hannah said. 'Really, it is too bad of you to use her as you do.'

Meriel was too angry to be soothed by Hannah's words. She ordered a servant to have her mare brought from the stable and her riding whip thwacked against her gloved hand with impatience at the enforced wait. Even the gardens at Traherne Hall were opulent, with high topiary hedges, walled enclosures and dozens of Italian marble statues in arbours or along walkways. That Roslyn should have so much made Meriel even more angry. She hated her sometimes.

'And what has put such a pretty little thing as yourself in a taking, Meriel?' The male voice startled her and she turned to see Sir Henry approaching.

He had been standing in the shadows of the courtyard, unnoticed by her, giving instructions to the gardener. He dismissed the man and bowed to Meriel. 'I warrant Ros is being disagreeable.'

'Good day, Sir Henry. What makes you think that aught is amiss?' She hated to be so transparent to anyone. She prided herself on her duplicity, and ability to keep her emotions guarded from others. 'I am waiting for my mare and the groom is slow.'

'Which is my good fortune. The mare can wait. Walk a pace with me. It is long since you have graced our home when I am not upon business at the mine.' He took her hand and raised it to his lips, but at the last moment twisted it so that his mouth pressed against the bare flesh of her wrist above her glove. His russet hair had a natural curl which refused to be tamed, and several tendrils had escaped from his queue. There was also a twinkle in his blue eyes. Dressed simply in waistcoat and breeches on the warm day, he was more approachable than usual. 'You were missed at the soirée here last weekend. Your beauty lights up such gatherings.'

'Shame on you, Sir Henry.' Meriel smiled into his face with its light dusting of freckles. His looks were distinguished rather than handsome. He was tall and willowy thin, though there was a sturdiness to his shoulders and thigh muscles which revealed a deceptive strength. The admiration in his eyes, which were appraising her figure, increased her heart rate. It appeased her vanity, for she was still smarting at the news that Adam had found love with another.

The admiration of a wealthy and titled man was a balm to her wounded pride. Sir Henry had been trying to seduce her for over a year, and she revelled in the power she held over him – skilfully keeping him interested, whilst holding him at bay. To flirt with Sir Henry and encourage his atten-

199

tions was also a way to repay Roslyn for all the spiteful comments Meriel was forced to endure.

Her smile was pure enticement, though she coyly lowered her lashes. 'Sir Henry, you know the family is in mourning. It is cruel of you to remind us that we must shut ourselves away from any entertainments.'

'But you are here now. The rose arbour is at its most spectacular at this time of year. I am sure Roslyn has neglected to show it to you.' He circled her waist with his arm and began to propel her to the secluded arbour.

She spun away from him, laughed and wagged her finger at him. 'You are incorrigible, Sir Henry. You showed me the rose arbour on my last visit. And, as I remember, you tried to kiss me. I will not fall for such a ploy again.'

'How can a woman with such beauty be so heartless? St John is the luckiest of devils.'

'And you are one of the wickedest. You would endanger my reputation which I value most highly. Ah, here is my mare. It has been a pleasure talking to you, Sir Henry.'

He waved aside the groom and as he lifted her on to the saddle he ran his hand along her thigh. 'You will not always escape me so easily, Meriel. I am resolved that one day you shall be mine.'

She covered his hand, which still remained on her thigh. 'Were I to take you seriously I would be unable to visit Traherne Hall again, Sir Henry.'

After the shock of learning of Adam's involvement with Senara Polglase, and Roslyn's spite, even Sir Henry's flirting did not appease Meriel for long. She wanted revenge on both Adam's mistress and Lady Traherne for the pain they had caused her. How dare Lady Traherne treat her like a common servant, and constantly gibe at her lowly background? But how to effect revenge without it being obvious that she was the perpetrator presented a problem.

Meriel knew she could not afford to lose her hard-won standing in the community by openly reviling Senara Polglase. Neither could she risk losing Lady Traherne's goodwill. But the time would come when both women would regret crossing Meriel Loveday.

There was a meadow and coppice between the Traherne land and Trevowan, and as Meriel approached the trees, she was hailed by Gwendolyn, Lady Traherne's sister, also riding.

Gwendolyn was completely different from her haughty sister. She was considered by many to be plain and dowdy, yet she was not unattractive when she lost her shyness and became animated. To Lady Druce's consternation, Gwendolyn had twice refused offers of marriage from men deemed suitable by her mother. Gwendolyn had always been kind to Meriel, but they had not become friends. Meriel had preferred to cultivate Roslyn for the acceptance within society that Lady Traherne could bring to her.

'Meriel, I did not realise that you were to visit today, or I would have been at home,' Gwendolyn apologised as they brought their mares to a standstill.

'I received an unexpected invitation from Lady Traherne.'

'Oh, a summons was it?' Gwendolyn said. 'Ros

has been in a fearful mood all week. I expect she was awful to you. She needed someone to take it out on. That's why I escaped.'

'Hannah arrived just as I was leaving.'

'That will cheer Ros.'

Gwendolyn's sympathetic glance added fuel to Meriel's anger. She hated being pitied.

'Roslyn can be unfeeling and cruel at times. Do not let her upset you,' Gwendolyn added. 'How is Mrs Mercer? I know I should visit, but I never know how to deal with people's grief.'

'Elspeth and Amelia are very supportive and Cecily visits every day, even if she can manage only an hour. She has so many duties at Trewenna. Elspeth sends over the pony and trap so that she can visit easily.'

'I heard that Adam has returned from London. Yet he has not called at the house.'

'He is busy at the yard.' Meriel was curt, for her anger at his involvement with another woman again threatened to surface. Her mood was communicated to her mare, who began to circle in a restless manner which took all Meriel's skill to control.

'And Thomas must be finding everything so difficult.' Gwendolyn frowned when they again faced each other. 'Had he not left the bank? He read me some of his poetry on his last visit to Cornwall. It was very profound. Rather like Milton.'

'Edward remains in London to help Thomas with some legal matters. It has become very dull at Trevowan with no men to liven the company.'

Gwendolyn bowed her head and stroked the neck of her grey mare. 'And Japhet? Is he still in

London with Edward?'

Meriel bit back a tart reply at seeing the colour rise in the woman's cheeks. Her curiosity was roused. 'Hannah would know better than I what mischief her brother is up to.' When the blush stained Gwendolyn's cheeks with a raspberry hue, she added, 'You have a special interest in our cousin, do you not?'

For a moment Gwendolyn looked mortified, and her blush became even darker. 'Is it so obvious? Mama will be furious. She thinks he is feckless. And if Hannah were to know, how could I face her?'

To Meriel's consternation tears sparkled on Gwendolyn's lashes. The horses fidgeted and with an idea forming, Meriel commented, 'Japhet is a handsome devil, and has the charm to match. Let us dismount so we can talk at our ease.'

Meriel slid to the ground and tethered her mare to a fence post at the edge of the meadow. There was an empty stone cow trough nearby and she perched on its rim and waited for Gwendolyn to join her.

'Is Japhet the reason why you refused Mr Pascal's offer of marriage last autumn? Pascal was considered a good match. He was a lawyer and would inherit his father's practice, which is one of the largest in Truro.'

'Mr Pascal was more interested in the family name than myself.' Gwendolyn sat beside Meriel. 'I will not be a piece of property to be bartered. On my last birthday I came into my own inheritance. I do not need a husband to support me. If it were not for Mother's insistence that we live at

203

the Hall, I would be content in a house in Bodmin. But Mama will not hear of it. She takes to her bed should I even suggest it. I do not know how I can stand this life much longer.'

'So Japhet was not the reason you refused Pascal?' Meriel persisted.

Gwendolyn played with the fringed hem of her riding gloves. 'Yes he was. How could I consider marrying one man, when I have been in love with another for as long as I can remember?'

That struck an uncomfortable chord with Meriel who had been in love with Adam since she was a child. It made her chin jut at a stubborn single. 'It is a fortunate woman who wins her choice of husband.'

'Then I would rather remain unwed. Mama must accept that. I have tried to be an obedient daughter, but I cannot look upon another man and compare him favourably with Japhet.' Gwendolyn sighed, but having begun her confidence seemed unable to stop. 'I know Japhet's faults. He is an adventurer and his reputation is, well – somewhat notorious. But I live only for some word or sight of him.' Gwendolyn wiped the tears from her eyes. 'I am sorry to burden you with this. Promise you will tell no one. I have kept it a secret so long. If Japhet knew, I would die of shame.'

'Japhet should be proud you have such regard for him,' Meriel insisted, to ally herself with Gwendolyn. To further the match would annoy Lady Traherne, for once she had been infatuated with Japhet and had set her cap at him. He had ignored her.

Meriel took Gwendolyn's hand and squeezed it to comfort her. 'Japhet would be fortunate indeed to have you as his wife.' She allowed some irony to creep in. 'Of course, your money would be an attraction to him. He is in need of a wife with a fortune for he has none.'

'I would surrender my pride for him,' Gwendolyn sniffed. 'I love him so much.'

'More than the blackguard deserves. You must know that Japhet will run through your fortune in a year or so. He has no money, nor a profession to support a wife – other than gambling and horse-trading, which is hardly respectable.'

'I do not care.' Gwendolyn became impassioned. There was a glow to her face which brought forth her inner beauty. She could be attractive if she was not such a dowd. Her chestnut hair was thick and luxurious, but she tied it back in an unbecoming chignon. She would look so much better with it fashioned into soft curls around her face and left to drape over her shoulders.

Gwendolyn gripped Meriel's hands with such vigour she had to control a wince of pain. 'Meriel, I would rather live in poverty with the man I love than in grandeur with one whom I despise. Look at Hannah! She is happy with Oswald. I can give Japhet so much.'

'Do not romanticise poverty.' Meriel was stern, stung to honesty by the deprivations of her own childhood. 'There is no joy in dirt and squalor. Nor in having to slave from dawn to dusk merely to survive. Take a close look at the fishwives who are your age. They are bowed in body, their eyes hard from fighting to survive and they look so old. They are also disease-ridden, and half starved from lack of nourishing food. And they were brought up to expect nothing more. With respect, Gwendolyn, you would not last a year in such poverty.'

'I do not care,' Gwendolyn cried with gathering passion. 'Oh, say you will help me, Meriel. You see Japhet more than I. Just to be in his company more often would mean so much. I have not the beauty to attract him in other ways.' She gave a shaky laugh. 'See, I have no shame. I have unburdened myself upon you. I am resigned to being an old maid and know that I must content myself with seeing him when I can.'

Meriel considered her for a long moment. 'If this is really what you want, then I shall endeavour to help you. Any meetings with Japhet must appear as though by chance. I shall inform you of his visits to Trevowan when I can, so that you can call upon us.' Meriel's eyes sparkled as an idea struck her. 'I have the perfect ploy. You must show an active interest in Cecily Loveday's work at Trewenna. Offer to help her in her work with the poor. That way you will know all Japhet's movements, and have a natural excuse to call at the Rectory if he is there.'

Gwendolyn looked uncertain. 'Is that not too obvious?'

Meriel laughed. 'You have a lot to learn about getting your own way. It is about making people believe that what you want is what they also want for themselves.'

At Gwendolyn's puzzled expression, she

206

elaborated. 'Cecily is desperate for help, and is always trying to raise money for the poor. You have your own income. Why not follow Elspeth's example and devote time and money to the poor and needy? To achieve this you will visit Margaret Mercer at Trevowan tomorrow when Cecily will be there, and veer the conversation round to your idea.'

'I could not do that,' Gwendolyn looked horrified. 'I am hopeless in company.'

'Then I will attend with you and draw you in to the conversation. Cecily will be the one to suggest that you help her. It will be easy.'

'I am sure to make a fool of myself.'

'Yet you will visit Trevowan with me on the morrow?' When Gwendolyn hesitated, Meriel urged, 'Will it not be worth it to be in closer proximity to Japhet's family? Cecily would like nothing better than for you to wed Japhet. She would see you as his redeemer.'

'I would not dare to hope for so much.'

'But I do,' Meriel insisted. 'I can see this working.'

Gwendolyn giggled and flung her arms around Meriel. 'You are a true friend. I am so grateful. I will do anything for you.'

'So long as this remains our secret,' Meriel felt it expedient to state. 'Roslyn had a fancy at one time for Japhet. If she learns of our plan, she is bound to stop you seeing him. Also I would not like to lose her friendship because I have helped you.'

'Of course,' Gwendolyn agreed. 'I, too, would prefer that no one else knew, for despite your faith, I doubt anything will come of it.'

Meriel smiled. 'Then if you truly wish to gain Japhet's attention, you must appear less dowdy. Start by arranging your hair in a more flattering fashion. How Amelia wears hers would suit you, with ringlets down your back. You have a trim figure but you hide it. Make more of your breasts. Wear a corset which pushes them higher, and I have noticed you have slender ankles yet you wear thick stockings. Wear fine silk and do not be afraid to lift your skirts a little higher to display them.'

'I could not be so brazen.'

'Then Japhet will not notice you.'

Gwendolyn sighed. 'I suppose you are right.'

Meriel put her head on one side and studied Gwendolyn. 'Men are very susceptible to these things and they work if you want to gain their attention. It is not so hard.'

'What else can I do?' Gwendolyn had caught Meriel's enthusiasm and sounded eager.

'Flattery. Praise Japhet. Make him laugh. You have a turn of phrase which has St John roaring with laughter on many occasions. Wit will be appreciated by Japhet, and make him notice you. And you must persevere to overcome your shyness, for a man such as Japhet will have known only the boldest of women.'

Gwendolyn put her hands to her mouth. 'You make it sound so easy but I could never achieve so much.'

'I have always believed that if you want something badly enough you will get it,' Meriel advised. 'And faint hearts win no battles.'

Chapter Eleven

'Thomas, do you want me to accompany you to Mr Lascalles?' Edward asked at seeing how pale and nervous his nephew had become as he prepared to leave the house in the Strand for the interview.

'Thank you for the offer, sir, but as head of Mercer's Bank, I must be seen to be at ease and in control of this meeting.'

'Then I wish you well.'

Edward watched his nephew drive away in the Loveday coach. Thomas had made the right choice, but they needed a minor miracle to save the bank from collapse, and Lascalles was no fool. It would not be an easy meeting for Thomas.

Thomas Mercer's feelings echoed those of his uncle as he approached the Lascalles' house near Hyde Park. He had sent a footman earlier with a message to Meredith Lascalles at his bank to request a meeting. Lascalles had replied that he would receive Thomas at his house at seven and would be happy for him to dine with his family before they discussed business. The invitation was reassuring. Even so, Thomas's unease remained, for so much depended upon the outcome. Whatever transpired his life would be irrevocably changed.

He had dressed with care in a navy cutaway tail

coat. His breeches were cream and his waistcoat pale yellow. The outfit was more restrained than what once had been his usual attire, but it fitted his role as an eminent banker.

The Lascalles' house was a red-brick, four-storey Queen Anne building with a Dutch-style gable. Thomas was shown up to the first-floor saloon by a maid, and he was disconcerted to discover that he was not the only guest present. There were two middle-aged couples of sober bearing, and Sir Absalom Grimshaw. That was an encounter he had not envisioned. He considered Sir Absalom an enemy after the trouble he had caused. Yet he could hardly cut him dead in his host's house.

'Welcome, Mr Mercer.' Meredith Lascalles came forward from where he'd been standing by the fireplace. He was a corpulent man with a florid face, heavy jowls and fleshy, hooded eyes. His wig had three rolls of tight curls over his ears, and a long plait between his shoulders.

Also present was Mrs Lascalles and three of the banker's daughters: Arabella, the eldest, in her early twenties and with a sour expression; apple-cheeked and buxom Charlotte; and a giggling Virginia, who at sixteen had just finished attending her ladies' academy.

None of the daughters attracted Thomas. All were round as barrels, with heavy-lidded, sly and calculating eyes, and the large hooked nose of their father. Thomas felt a welling of panic. He could not go through with this.

'Your pardon, Mr Lascalles,' Thomas shifted uncomfortably, 'I had not expected this to be a social gathering. I am in mourning and, out of respect to my father's memory, I feel I should retire. Perhaps I could call upon you at your bank one afternoon next week.'

'Nonsense, you are here now,' Lascalles effused, but there was a brittle gleam in his eyes which Thomas did not find encouraging. 'What is the harm in staying? Apart from Sir Absalom, whom you know, this is a family gathering to which you are welcome. Permit me to introduce my cousin Frederick Lascalles and his wife, Anne, and my wife's brother Walter Rochford.'

'With respect, I really do feel I should leave.' Thomas backed towards the door.

Throughout the introductions Virginia had been giggling in a high-pitched fashion. It sounded like a rusty nail drawn across a writing slate, and set his teeth on edge.

Charlotte Lascalles fluttered her fan across her breasts, which were as large as cabbages. Her unpowdered brown hair was frizzed beneath a gauze mobcap, which unbecomingly emphasised her rosy, fleshy cheeks. 'Oh, that would be too bad of you, Mr Mercer,' she simpered. 'It is always a pleasure to have the company of a young man at our dining table, especially when that man is so handsome. We would be quite devastated if you were to leave.'

She smiled, revealing stained teeth which showed signs of decay. That her parents had not reprimanded their daughter's forwardness added to Thomas's discomfort. There was a hungry look in Charlotte's eyes as she gazed at him. This was a woman desperate for a husband, and the thought was terrifying.

The haughty features of Arabella Lascalles softened into a patronising smile, her eyes rapacious as a Gorgon, which sent shivers through Thomas. He could almost hear the mythological snakes around her head hissing, when she spoke: 'Mr Mercer, you simply could not be so cruel as to disappoint us.'

Sweat trickled down Thomas's neck and his cravat felt so tight that it would choke him.

'He looks fit to bolt like a filly at her first fence,' Sir Absalom Grimshaw sneered. 'Reckon he came here with a begging bowl in his hand, Lascalles. I told you Mercer's Bank was heading for a fall. You were well out of any dealings with them.'

'That is slander, sir.' Thomas's hand instinctively went to where his dress sword would have rested at his side, but he had decided that the purpose of his visit this evening made such a weapon inappropriate. He checked his temper. He needed Lascalles' goodwill, and insulting a guest in his house would surely lose it. He stood stiff-backed with pride. 'Sir Absalom, without foundation you slur my father's name and the reputation of our bank. Yet you received every penny of your money when you withdrew your custom. Malicious slander can ruin a bank and I do not propose to allow that to happen. You will apologise, or I shall be forced to consult my lawyer, and the good name of my father will be defended in court.'

'Your tone is offensive, young man,' Fredrick Lascalles decreed. 'You are a guest in my cousin's house.'

Meredith Lascalles stood with his hand holding the front edge of his dress coat. 'I believe Mr Mercer has a point. Since his father was so recently and tragically killed, his anger is understandable.'

'I speak as I find.' Sir Absalom remained undeterred.

Thomas bowed to Meredith Lascalles. 'With respect to your good self, sir, I find it impossible to dine at the same table as a man who maligns the reputation of our bank. Good evening, gentlemen. Ladies.'

He marched to the door and Meredith Lascalles followed him onto the landing.

'The matter was most regrettable, Mr Mercer. Sir Absalom has recently opened an account with us. I had not realised that there was ill feeling between you. Come into my study. It will be a while before we dine, and my wife will keep my guests entertained.'

Thomas wanted to flee the house and the nightmare which was engulfing him, but since Lascalles had been so profuse in his apology he could not politely decline, and allowed Lascalles to guide him into a small anteroom. What struck him about the room was the absence of books. His father's study was lined with them. This was Spartan, without any adornment or even a painting to give it character.

Lascalles gestured for Thomas to be seated on one of the two high-backed leather chairs. From a table containing a silver tray and brandy decanter, Lascalles filled two glasses, handing one to Thomas.

Abruptly his manner changed and his tone hardened. 'Mr Mercer, I was surprised to receive your note. Curiosity prompted me to invite you this evening.'

'I shall come straight to the point, sir.' Thomas wanted the ordeal over. 'You were considering a merger of our banks, sir. It is my intention to honour all obligations which my father had entered into.'

'Ah, but that was some months ago,' Lascalles rapped out, his blank expression giving no hint of his reaction.

'Then you are no longer in favour of the proposition, sir?' Thomas forced out through a dry throat.

Lascalles tapped his podgy fingers together under his chin. 'You were the reason our negotiations failed. Why should I now entrust the good name of my bank in this venture? Charles Mercer was respected in the City. You are untried and untested. Indeed, I go as far as to say that you failed the first test when you left the bank. That of duty.'

'I had my reasons.'

'Why do you now want this merger?' Lascalles fired out. 'Are the rumours true that the bank is in trouble?'

Thomas now knew how a mouse felt when it was being taunted by a cat. He retaliated with vigour. He might have the disadvantage but he would never kowtow to any man. His stare was proud and forthright.

'I seek to honour the wishes of my father. I also believe the merger serves both our interests. It is true that some of our customers may regard my lack of years and inexperience as a problem. A senior partner of your reputation would reassure them. I was privy to all my father's dealings over the past eight years and he taught me well. We have a very prestigious clientele, including several eminent politicians and courtiers. These remain loyal to us and bring prestige to any banker who becomes my partner.'

'For now they are loyal. But for how long?' Lascalles plied his questions with the ruthlessness of a grand inquisitor. 'Mercer's Bank was Charles Mercer. You have as good as admitted that you are not his match. You have lost customers since his death.'

'Only scaremongers such as Sir Absalom. I have the utmost faith in my abilities. Father taught me well. I have assured our customers that Mercer's Bank will continue its former traditions.'

Meredith Lascalles pursed his lips. 'Yet you have overdue dividends to be met. Why is that?'

The scathing tone caused Thomas's ire to rise. He mastered it with difficulty and in a calm voice explained, 'There are certain legal criteria to be met upon my father's death which have caused some delay.' Thomas's shirt was sticking to his shoulders and he fought against the urge to wipe his sweating palms on his breeches.

'It is clear to me that Mercer's Bank is only viable with Lascalles money behind it. I wonder at your audacity in approaching me, sir.' Outrage now flashed in Lascalles' eyes. 'You not only walked out on your responsibilities to your father, but on the negotiations to marry a

215

daughter of mine.'

Thomas sprang to his feet. To marry the Gorgon or one of her sisters was too awful a fate to contemplate. Yet the alternative was the Marshalsea Debtors' Prison. For himself debtors' prison was the lesser evil, but how could he so fail his mother and family? Again, it took all his control to overcome his anger.

'Mr Lascalles, when my father wanted this match between our families, I had not felt myself ready for marriage. I believed Papa had many years ahead of him. Now I see my duty clearly.'

'Do you indeed, sir?' Meredith Lascalles snorted and rose to face Thomas. He no longer hid his antagonism. 'I think you showed your true feelings in this matter when you left the bank. I am now in negotiations with another banker. And as to the matter of a match with a daughter of mine, I do not think I care for them to be allied with a playwright. You have a reputation of mixing with such low orders of fellows, who are little better than vagabonds and miscreants. I bid you good evening, Mr Mercer.'

Thomas was shaking with anger as he left the anteroom. Lascalles and Grimshaw were in league together. This would be all round the City tomorrow, and the bank would lose more credibility. He had failed. And failed in the most miserable manner possible.

On the landing he collided with a woman who had her head immersed in a book as she walked. The book went flying from her hands. Recovering his manners, Thomas retrieved it and curtly handed it to her. He assumed that she was the fourth of Lascalles' daughters.

'Why, it is Mr Mercer!' The woman's eyes widened with pleasure. She blocked his exit and unless he pushed rudely past her, Thomas was forced to cool his heels until she moved. 'It is an honour to meet you, sir. I was at Lady Braithwaite's soirée two months ago when she prevailed upon you to read your work. I was so moved by the words of your sonnets. I scan the papers daily in anticipation that a play of yours will be performed. *The Politician's Paradise* was wickedly satirising.'

'You saw *The Politician's Paradise?* It was performed for only two weeks. It was deemed too subversive because of the political unrest in France.' Thomas was astonished she was so complimentary.

'I adored it. I believe that you are to dine with us. You will recite something afterwards, I hope. Otherwise I shall be made to play the pianoforte for our guests, and my talent is mediocre. It is exciting to have a real poet–'

'Georganna, why are you not with our guests in the saloon?' Lascalles thundered as he emerged from the anteroom.

'I was ordered to have the maid redress my hair. I was reading and lost track of the time, which was why I was late in changing for dinner.'

'No good will come to you with your nose permanently stuck in a book, young lady,' Lascalles snapped. 'Off to your room or dinner will be delayed.'

Georganna smiled at Thomas. Her hair was falling down at the back but she was

217

unconcerned. 'We must talk of your work later. I hope I shall be sitting near you at the table.'

'Mr Mercer is leaving, Georganna. Now to your room lest I become impatient that you keep our guests waiting.'

'But you cannot go, Mr Mercer. To have a real playwright in our home is–'

'You are insolent. Go to your room at once,' Lascalles bellowed. 'And since you did not deign to appear acceptably attired, you may stay in your room and forgo dinner.'

Thomas bowed to Georganna, who continued to bar his way. Although plain, her animation made her almost attractive. Neither did she have her sisters' plumpness. She was slim almost to the point of being gaunt, and was as tall as an average man.

She moved aside and as Thomas descended the stairs to leave, Lascalles rejoined his guests in the saloon.

'Mr Mercer,' a hoarse whisper reached Thomas from above. He ignored it, impatient to be out of this nightmare situation.

'Mr Mercer, oh, please, do not go. I have been trying everywhere to obtain a copy of the pamphlet of your poems, but find they are out of print.'

'You also know of my pamphlet!' Thomas was so stunned that he paused on the stairs. 'Only a hundred were printed and they received scant acclaim.'

She hurried down the stairs and as she lifted her skirts Thomas saw that she had removed her shoes so as not to make a noise. 'I wish you were not leaving. Would it be presumptuous to ask if you have copies of your pamphlet to sell?'

To be free of her he said, 'I would gladly give you one. I am quite overwhelmed, Miss Lascalles.'

'Georganna! What the devil are you doing?' Meredith Lascalles stuck his head over the banister rail. 'This disobedience is too much. You will be confined to your room all day tomorrow to ponder upon the value of obedience.' He glared at Thomas. 'I thought you had left, Mr Mercer.'

Thomas strode from the house, glad to breathe the smoke-filled air of the city. He now had to face Uncle Edward with his failure. He was halfway down the Strand when he decided to send Georganna a copy of his poems. He had few enough admirers of his work, and she had faced her father's wrath and earned a greater punishment by expressing her interest.

Thomas could not face Uncle Edward yet; and since he himself was not expected back for another two hours he ordered the coachman to take him to Lucien's rooms at the back of the Haymarket. He needed diverting to distract him from his failure.

Chapter Twelve

St John was short-tempered with nerves as he waited for the day to pass for him to join the Sawle brothers. Once he even snapped at Rowena, who was playing with Richard's dog,

219

Faith. The dog had got into the Dower House and jumped up on to the cushions of the settle with muddy paws. Meriel hated any animals in the house and would be furious. He had turfed the dog out and confined the tearful Rowena to the nursery.

Meriel, on her return from Traherne Hall, had been in high spirits. She had dismissed the paw marks, calling on Rachel Glasson to sponge away the mess.

Rachel was slow to answer her summons and when she did appear the maid's expression was sullen.

'Is there anything amiss, Rachel?' St John asked. 'You have been less than diligent in your duties all day. Are you unwell?'

'Bain't nothing wrong with me. 'Tis Tilda I fear for. Gone, she has.' The maid stared at Meriel. 'She's been wronged by your folk.'

Meriel regarded her through narrowed eyes. Rachel was plainer than her sister, scarecrow thin, her mouth often sullen as though she had a grudge against the world. Meriel had chosen her for her looks, for a pretty maid might have tempted St John to indiscretion. Rachel was hard-working, and usually amenable enough since she had formed an attachment to one of the farm workers. 'If working here does not suit you, Rachel, we can replace you. I have no need of a discontented maidservant.'

Since working for the Lovedays was better paid and more pleasant than toiling in Lanyon's pilchard sheds, Rachel lost her defiance. With downcast eyes, she amended, 'I didn't mean nothing, Mistress Loveday.'

'I do not want your sister's name mentioned in this house, neither will you gossip about her to the other servants. Tilda left the Dolphin Inn under unfortunate circumstances, but she only had herself to blame. Get those marks cleaned off the furniture and ensure that Rowena is ready to accompany me to the family house in an hour.'

Rachel curtsied and left the room. Meriel sauntered around the parlour, humming to herself.

'You are in a good mood, my love,' St John remarked.

'And why should I not be? I have passed a delightful afternoon; Gwendolyn is such a dear woman. I am thinking of inviting her over more often.'

'I am glad that you have made another friend. I have always liked Gwendolyn. Her sweet nature is overshadowed by her shyness.'

'And how has your day been, my dear?' Meriel enquired. 'How fortunate that Edward remains in London – it will be easy for you to get away this evening.'

'I leave in an hour. I have told the family that I am dining with friends in St Austell and will be staying overnight. I do not want Fraddon reporting to Father that Prince was not in the stable one night. Especially if there is any trouble tonight.'

'There will be no trouble. You will have surprise to your advantage.' Meriel dismissed his fears. 'Harry and Clem do not take unnecessary risks.'

'But the Jowetts do!'

'Promise me that you will take care,' Meriel said, putting her arm round him. 'I am very proud of you.'

'I do this for you. God knows if it is not an act of madness.' He kissed her brusquely and felt her body stiffen in his arms. Suddenly he thrust her from him. 'Have you any care for me at all, madam? I risk my life this night to satisfy your craving for riches, and you give me not even a parting kiss.'

She laughed and hugged him, her eyes overbright. 'How can you doubt my fervour? My darling, I shall not sleep this night, fearing for your safety.' She kissed him ardently, only drawing back as his lips parted in response. 'You have a long ride ahead. Good luck and fortune be with you.'

With that he knew he must be content. Meriel bedevilled him, and yet he never knew what to make of her moods.

He was a mile on the Fowey road and his nerves were taut as a pulley rope. The sound of galloping hoofs behind him made him glance over his shoulder. Clem Sawle was drawing level.

'We'll ride together, Loveday.'

'I thought we were to travel separately. What if we are seen and word gets back to Lanyon?'

'Getting nervous?' Clem jeered. 'That's why I be here. I want you beside me after the last time. Harry has gone ahead.'

'We add to the risk of detection if we ride together.' St John glowered, resenting both Clem's presence and knowing it was because Clem did not wholly trust him. 'We are not known as friends.'

'But are we not brothers in marriage?' Clem laughed maliciously. 'Is it so unnatural if we ride together?'

'We hardly move in the same circles.' St John gave way to his outrage. 'I am supposed to be dining with friends.'

'So we met on the road. But who is to see us? Few will be abroad so late in the evening.'

St John conceded with ill grace. Clem, with his brutish masculinity, had a way of making him feel inadequate. He could never feel comfortable in the company of the rough smugglers, and not for the first time wondered if he had been mad to allow Meriel's greed to get him involved.

Adam had finished work at the yard earlier than usual. The men had worked until dusk to meet the new launch dates. Lanyon had given him a draft on his bank for half of the moneys owed and the rest would be paid next week. He had hinted that a consignment was due, the proceeds of which would pay the final instalment on the cutter.

With the money from Lanyon's first draft deposited in their Truro bank, Adam had been able to pay the business's most pressing creditors. Lanyon's payment next week would be in time to meet the interest on the loan and they were not due again for three months. It was a breathing space, but it would still be a struggle to meet the men's wages. Drastic measures were still needed to keep the yard and estate solvent and provide an income.

It had been over a week since he had visited Senara. A week where he had haggled with merchants, pressed owners for further payments, pushed the shipwrights and labourers to the limits of their strength to get Lanyon's ship ready for launch, and he had worked manually from dawn until dusk whenever he could in the yard. His head throbbed from juggling figures and payments and, although physically tired, he had missed Senara too sorely to spend another night away from her. If only she would put an end to his misery and wed him. He would have all he had ever dreamed of in this life.

He rode through a wood and as the trees thinned by the road, he saw St John and Clem Sawle riding together. Puzzled, he reined in. St John was looking ill at ease and Clem surly. They made incongruous companions. Twice, St John glanced around. There was a furtiveness about his manner which alerted Adam even though they appeared to be riding together amicably. That suddenly changed. There was an angry exchange between them and St John brought his whip down on Prince's quarters and sped off. Clem swore and gave chase.

The incident disturbed Adam. Clem had no love for St John. His brother could be in danger. Reluctantly, Adam turned Solomon from the direction of Senara's cottage and followed the two riders on the winding road. Only their heads were visible above the high hedgerows, and whenever St John turned in the saddle, Adam crouched over Solomon's neck to avoid detection. Even so, he kept a discreet distance and on

224

straight sections of the road concealed himself in the long shadows from the hedgerows.

St John had slowed his horse and Clem had caught him up. Their manner now looked companionable, but Adam was not convinced that St John was in no danger. Clem was notorious for his brutality. Several times St John glanced back along the track, causing Adam to halt Solomon and press the horse deeper into the shadows.

They continued past Nancarrow Head for a mile or so, the long blue-tinged shadows of dusk changing the contours of rocks and land. To Adam's surprise they turned inland. The terrain here was wild, with few villages and only scattered farms. It would be dark soon and Adam had no lantern with him to light his path. He glanced up at the sky. There were a few purple and apricot clouds marking the sunset. Higher in the sky the moon was full. At least he would have some vision when darkness settled over the undulating hills and valleys. It was then he saw two men walking through the gorse ahead and three more in a distant field all travelling in the direction St John and Clem were taking. Such a gathering meant only one thing on a night like this. Free traders.

So what the devil was St John doing involved with them? Since Clem was present, Adam assumed that Meriel had something to do with it. And how long had his brother been involved with such men? It was madness. St John was motivated by greed, for Adam doubted he was in this to raise money to pay off their father's loans.

Or was he? Adam wondered if he was not doing

his brother a disservice. Had St John finally learned to face up to his responsibilities, even in this risky and haphazard manner? There was no question that men like Thadeous Lanyon were making fortunes from the trade.

For a moment Adam applauded his brother's initiative, for he had not believed St John had such an adventurous spirit. Three other riders approached and Adam experienced another shock. Even from this distance, it was easy to recognise the thick-set figures of the Jowett men.

Adam's favourable appraisal of his brother turned to fear. The Sawles were brutal enough, but to be involved with the Jowetts was lunacy. Adam suspected that the Jowetts were behind a band of wreckers, setting false lights in the winter storms to lure ships on to the treacherous rocks. Any survivors from the shipwreck were ignored, some probably killed so that they could not identify those plundering the cargo. It was the most abhorrent and diabolical of crimes.

The Jowetts' presence sickened Adam. The old scar from a bullet wound ached in his shoulder. There had been speculation that the Jowetts had been behind the attack upon himself which had left him for dead. But no proof was found, nor a motive. When Adam had been shot and knocked unconscious, Solomon had bolted across the moor with Adam's foot still caught in the stirrup. It had been a miracle he had survived. And he would not have done if Senara had not been on the moor that night and seen Solomon, now free of his rider, sweating and shivering with terror. Angel had followed Solomon's scent and found

Adam unconscious and near death.

Now, seeing St John, the Sawles and the Jowetts working together sent a chill shiver through Adam's body. At the time of his attack the rivalry between him and St John had been intense. St John had learned that his twin was to inherit the yard. Was St John involved in that attack in some way? Meriel had been scathing in her hatred for him at that time. She was capable of putting St John up to paying the Jowetts to give him a beating. Had they planned his death?

The thought was harrowing. Did St John really hate him that much? He could not believe that his brother would want him dead. Yet his death would mean St John would inherit the shipyard...

Adam wiped a shaking hand across his face and glared at his twin. His suspicions aroused, his blood turned icy at the thought of such betrayal. No, St John might be a selfish bastard, but he did have a sense of honour. He would not stoop to murder, but he could have been swayed by Meriel and paid the Jowetts to attack him. Adam had underestimated St John – and Meriel's influence over him. They had been rivals for too long for any deep affection to develop between them, and now Adam knew that they would only ever tolerate each other while their father was alive.

Adam started out of his bitter reflection and stood in the stirrups, the better to scan the landscape. There was now no sign of the smugglers: they had gone to ground like rabbits in a warren. Ahead of him was the slope of a granite tor. The rocks loomed dark and menacing as a hobgoblin's fortress. The hairs on the back of his neck prickled. What could so many men be doing so far inland? There was no river inlet for boats to land their cargo.

It was still an hour before dark. All his senses were alerted to danger. Something dastardly was afoot, of that he was certain. And his fool of a twin was involved in it. He tethered Solomon amongst some tall gorse which would conceal him and removed the pistol, with which he always travelled since his attack, from his saddle holster. He crouched low and edged forward to spy on the track ahead.

A rustle behind him made him swing round and bring up the pistol. Before he could pull back the safety catch a pistol was pressed against the side of his head. A man with a black mask covering his upper face was silhouetted against the sky.

'Damn me, Adam! What the devil are you doing here?' Harry Sawle declared. 'You were nearly food for the fishes.'

Harry did not lower his pistol and Adam was aware that any man deemed a spy by such a gang, would be killed and thrown into the sea. Two other masked men whom Adam did not recognise had moved behind him to prevent his escape.

'I can't let you go,' Harry warned. 'There be too much at stake.'

Adam lowered his pistol. He had no wish to kill Harry and, since they had known each other since childhood, assumed Harry was of a like mind. But with the other two men present, Adam knew his situation was perilous.

'I followed St John and Clem. They were arguing and I thought my brother might be in some danger.'

'You be the one in danger,' Harry said with a shake of his head, the pistol still pointed at Adam. 'Will you join us? I can see no other way out of this.'

Adam was trapped. Even so, he noted the anxious glances towards the granite rocks of the other men. 'I seem to have no choice.' He pushed his pistol into the waistband of his breeches. 'But what do I join you in? You are too far inland to be landing a cargo.'

Harry relaxed and nodded to his companions. 'This man can be trusted.' He uncocked his pistol and pushed it into an inside pocket of his coat. 'We are to ambush Lanyon's haul. Our information is that his goods will be landed on the coast and the pack ponies will pass this way. We shall relieve him of the responsibility of distributing the goods and, of course, the profits.'

'This is madness!' Adam could not believe the recklessness of the plan. Or the consequences they would face. Lanyon was not a man to cross lightly. And Lanyon's profits from *this* haul were to pay for *Sea Sprite* to be finished. The yard needed that money. Damn St John and his greed! Adam was furious. Not only would the yard lose the money it badly needed but he was forced to be a part of the escapade. Did ever fate mock a man more? He could wring St John and Harry's necks for planning this. But if St John thought he was going to keep any of the profits for himself, he was in for a shock. Adam was determined that at least St John's share would be handed over to their father.

But there would be difficulties to overcome with Lanyon, and further contention to get him to raise a loan for the *Sea Sprite*. If Lanyon decided to wait for the profits from another cargo, then all the bargaining and work Adam had done in recent weeks to save the yard would be in vain.

Harry's eyes glittered with malice in the fading light, the last of the sun's red rays reflecting in his pupils so that they glowed like a demon's. 'Lanyon's got it coming. He be too fond of getting above himself. He thought he could make a fool of Harry Sawle.'

'So this is to do with revenge?' Adam's anger increased. 'I can understand your motives, but how is St John involved?'

Harry grinned. 'That be a long story and for St John to tell. Suffice, St John had a heavy investment in the trade a few years back. Lanyon disliked the competition and informed on us to the excise men. We lost both ship and cargo. St John has decided it is time Lanyon paid for his treachery.'

'So what is the Jowetts' part in this?'

'You be asking a lot of questions,' Harry snarled.

'The Jowetts are trouble, unpredictable and capable of murder. I would have thought that was the last thing you needed.'

'Since we couldn't use anyone from Penruan, who would have divided loyalties, the Jowetts provided the men. They've been told there's to be no killing. Most of the smugglers will have dispersed to their homes by the time they reach here. There'll be just the ones leading the pack ponies.'

'And do you not fear recognition?'

'Not on this run. The tubmen are from Looe. Apart from our masks, we'll blacken our faces with charcoal.' With his free hand Harry pulled a strip of black cloth from his pocket and held out the mask to Adam. He hesitated to take it, but could see no way out of this dilemma.

'It be the only way, Adam,' Harry said, pushing the mask into his hands.

Adam nodded and tied the mask behind his head and adjusted the eye sockets. 'I will be a presence amongst you, but I want nothing to do with moving the cargo.'

'Then you'll be missing out on a cut of the profits.'

'I have nothing against smuggling in general,' he answered in a low voice, which would not reach Harry's companions, 'but this cargo belongs to Lanyon. And the right and wrongs of his dealings with you and St John have nothing to do with me. Stealing is not smuggling.'

'And if there's a fight?' Harry challenged. 'What side be you on then?'

This was the issue Adam had greatest difficulty coming to terms with. 'If attacked I will retaliate, and if another amongst our gang is outnumbered and in danger, I would help him. I can commit to no more.'

'That be enough. I've never known you

abandon a friend in need, whether their cause be just or not.'

A cry of a seagull carried to them and was repeated twice.

'That be the signal that the lugger be sighted and is heading to the beach. We've a long wait until the ponies pass this way. My men have moved your horse to put it with the others.'

Adam followed Harry. His two companions had disappeared during the last exchanges to join Clem and the Jowetts.

'Happen you'd best make yourself known to your brother, Adam,' Harry advised. 'He bain't gonna like this.'

Adam saw St John sitting behind an outcrop of rock, fingering a dagger. He crawled towards him. 'There is much to be explained when this night is over, St John. I hope your motives were to help Father meet his debts.'

St John's head shot upwards and behind his mask his eyes bulged with shock. 'The devil! How did you get here? Were you spying on me?'

'Sssh!' an angry whisper came from Clem. 'Adam will be in charge of the prisoners. They're to be tied up and left. You'll be needing that rope.' He pointed to several coils on the ground.

Adam picked it up as Clem added, 'Keep out of sight. There'll be no talking. Sounds carry. Don't fail us, Cap'n Loveday, or you'll pay the consequences.'

Adam ignored the threat and hid behind an egg-shaped boulder. The last crimson rays of the sun disappeared over the horizon and darkness descended. The tor hid the men well but the terrain would be rough when they began fighting. It did not take long before the dampness of the evening dew on the grass seeped into his clothing. Adam had counted sixteen men. Were the odds in their favour or against it?

St John joined Adam and whispered with venom, 'Do not think you will have any of my share of the profits.'

St John moved away before Adam could answer and he saw his brother sidle up to Harry, his manner angry. Harry gestured St John to keep silence.

The incongruity of the situation was absurd, Adam thought. He should be with Senara, warm in her loving embrace, the pressures of the day eased from his mind by her tender hands. Instead he was caught up in this madness, shivering in damp clothing as part of an ambush.

The waiting seemed endless. The smell of the distant sea carried on the wind, mingling with the sharper scents of the heather and gorse. A half-hour stretched to an hour. Cramp attacked his calves and Adam gritted his teeth as he flexed his foot to ease the agony. To take his mind from the cold, Adam stared at the stars, locating the constellations of Orion and Andromeda, both old friends during his long night watches at sea.

Whenever an owl hooted, or a dog fox barked, Adam tensed, anticipating it as a warning call-sign. Still no figures appeared. From the arc of the moon across the sky Adam reckoned two hours had passed. If the smugglers did not arrive soon, his limbs would be numb with cold and useless. Intermittent shufflings from the others told him they suffered similarly.

At last the jingle of harness could be heard from the direction of the coast. From his hiding place Adam saw the Jowett men edge forward, eager to be the first to attack. The outline of a wagon and a score of pack ponies became visible in the moonlight. Some of the ponies had kegs strapped to their backs, others had two large wicker panniers that must be holding packages of tea or silk. He counted eight men to their sixteen. Adam checked the rope which was cut into lengths to bind the smugglers' arms and feet.

The men trudged with their heads bowed. Some would be miners who had already worked a long shift before walking to the coast. They would be tired and, Adam hoped, easy to overcome. He had no taste for bloodshed this night.

Suddenly the Jowetts rose up like dark, demonic spectres against the night sky, and launched themselves with cudgels raised at the leading ponies. Four more men emerged from the boulders to strike down the two smugglers straggling at the rear.

Adam watched as St John and the others ran into the affray. After their initial surprise, the smugglers shouted and cursed. Cudgels and fists slammed dully into bodies. Yells of pain and surprise were replaced by angry shouts and curses. The pack ponies reared in panic and men broke away from the fighting to stop them bolting. Smugglers and assailants jostled in a macabre mêlée and, such was the confusion, some of the men must have been fighting their own companions.

With the lengths of rope he'd slung over his shoulder, Adam tied the arms and feet of two unconscious smugglers, then struggled with a third, who was still conscious. Adam was forced to knock him out, punching his chin hard.

Who fired the first shot Adam was not certain. Others immediately followed. Adam cursed. There was no restraining the ambushers.

'I want them tied up, not shot.' St John's voice rose above the mêlée.

'Bastards! You'll rot in hell for this infamy,' a furious smuggler shouted. 'Kill 'em.'

Two more pistol shots had Adam running to a fallen man who was being attacked by Emmanuel Jowett. Jowett kicked the prone man in the head and three times in the ribs before Adam pulled him away. 'That's enough.'

Emmanuel Jowett swung at Adam. 'I don't take orders from you.'

'There are four pack ponies escaping across that field,' Adam diverted him. 'Do you want to lose them?'

Emmanuel Jowett swore profanely. 'To me, brothers,' he yelled, and set off with Gabriel and Ezekiel in pursuit.

Not for the first time Adam reflected that such godly names acted with such evil intent. He tied up the unconscious man attacked by Emmanuel, checking that after such a vicious assault he was still alive. Thankfully he was.

The fighting was abating. A man broke away to run in the direction of Looe. 'We bain't paid enough to be killed,' he shouted as he fled. 'Get away while you can, men.'

Two others followed him. The fighting was over in minutes. Adam, sweating from his exertions, tied up the last of the smugglers. Not all remained unconscious. Two kicked and cursed him as they fought to be free of their bonds. Two men remained on the ground and as Adam approached he recognised St John bending over Harry Sawle.

'He's been shot in the back,' St John said. 'He's not looking too good. Help me get him on his horse.'

St John heaved Harry upright and the man groaned in pain. Adam hooked Harry's arm over his own shoulder while St John took the other. They staggered under Harry's weight to drag him to where their three horses were tethered. The other members of their gang had disappeared with the pack ponies and wagon. Getting Harry on the horse was not easy and Adam threw the rope he was still carrying on the ground. Finally they managed to drape Harry on his stomach over his saddle. A dark patch of blood was spreading across his jerkin.

'I'll lead his horse,' St John gasped. 'Clem has gone with the cargo to a hiding place. There's nothing more to do here. The smugglers will come back to release their friends.'

'Harry should be tied on his horse.' Adam bent to pick up the rope. As he did so another shot rang out. There was a brief flash of orange from the direction the fleeing smugglers had taken, and then St John fell forward against Harry's back.

Alarm pumped through Adam. He put his arm around his brother, fearful that he was dead. St John groaned and when he put his hand to his shoulder, it came away covered with blood. He stared at it dumbly. Adam pulled back his jacket and shirt and saw the hole with the bullet still lodged within. 'It is not serious,' he lied, to reassure his brother, as they had several miles to ride.

'Damn, what a mess! How am I to hide this from Father?' St John's voice was shaky.

'We will worry about that later,' Adam stated. 'Your wound needs dressing and so does Harry's.'

'Chegwidden will blab. I'll not trust him nor any doctor who knows our family.'

'We will go to Senara. She will tend you.' To him it was the obvious choice, though he knew she would not be happy dealing with two patients with bullet wounds. She was too aware of how a doctor could persecute her if her treatment failed. But in this he could see no other choice and he had faith in Senara's skills.

'I'm not one of Elspeth's damned mares,' St John flared.

'She saved my life, if you remember,' Adam reminded him. His earlier rage returned at his suspicion that St John had been involved in the Jowetts' almost killing him. He stared at his wounded twin, who would die if the bullet was not removed, and felt that justice had been served. The brutality of the Jowetts tonight had caused the smugglers to fire on them. Adam was not a vengeful man and would not see St John's life put at risk.

St John did not answer. His head was bowed as he tried to pull himself on to Prince's back. The reminder of how Adam had nearly died when he had paid the Jowetts to ambush him and give him a thrashing, filled him with guilt. He had been relieved that Senara had saved Adam. But it was that guilt which made it harder to accept Adam's help now. He wanted no reminders of his part in that vicious attack on Adam.

But when Adam cupped his hands to give him a leg up, St John accepted ungraciously and settled in the saddle, his shoulders hunched. 'You'd best lead Harry's horse. This has turned out badly for us.'

'You knew the consequences when you got into this,' Adam lost patience with his twin. 'You have made an enemy of Lanyon and he is a dangerous man to cross.'

'No one recognised us,' St John snapped, and pulled off his mask.

'And what of your injury? Lanyon will be suspicious of that. And there is Harry in God knows what state of health.'

'I do not need a lecture from you.' St John turned his horse away. 'I suppose we had better see this woman of yours. I hope she can keep her mouth shut.'

Adam swung on to Solomon's back, removed both his and Harry's masks, and took up the other mount's reins. When he caught up with his brother, Adam accused, 'Perhaps if *your* woman had kept her mouth shut, we would not be in this mess. Meriel was behind this, wasn't she?'

St John did not answer. He did not need to. The pale moonlight revealed the guilt and anguish on his face.

Chapter Thirteen

The Polglases' cottage was in darkness when the riders entered the clearing. Harry was unconscious and St John was slumped over Prince's neck, weary from exhaustion and loss of blood.

When Angel and Charity set up a chorus of barking, Adam hurried to the door, tapped on it and announced himself.

From inside the dogs were ordered to be quiet. The door opened to reveal Senara in her nightgown with a shawl tied around her shoulders, her brown hair hung over her shoulder in a single plait.

She smiled in welcome, then saw his dishevelled state and gasped, 'Is something amiss? I had a strange dream. There were men fighting.'

'I need your help.' He whispered so that Leah would not hear him. Senara's mother would think that he had come to visit Senara and hopefully would be unaware that it was the early hours of the morning. 'There *was* fighting – of a sort. St John and Harry Sawle have been shot. Harry is unconscious and St John has lost a lot of blood.'

'Why did you bring them here?' She sounded nervous and put her hand to her throat.

239

'Chegwidden is your physician. It would not be fair on Ma and Bridie if I treated them.'

'They were with smugglers and the fight was between rival gangs. No one must suspect that they were involved.'

When she still looked worried, he reassured her. 'They wore masks so no one could recognise them. There is no danger to you or your family.'

She sighed. 'Then I will do what I can. Take them to the stable. I will tend them there. Get the men settled while I collect what I need.'

St John had slid from Prince but was clinging to the pommel of the saddle. 'Lord, I am weak as a child. Are you sure this woman knows what she is doing? Meriel will be worrying if I do not return.'

'Then Meriel can worry. The bullet is still in your shoulder and must be taken out as soon as possible.' Adam supported St John as his brother stumbled to the stable. There Adam eased his twin to a sitting position on the straw and took Wilful and Harriet outside to be penned in the fenced paddock.

Harry Sawle was still unconscious and Adam heaved him over his shoulder. His legs buckled under the thickset fisherman's weight as he staggered to the stable and placed him beside St John.

'Why have we been stuck out here?' St John complained, eyeing a pile of Wilful's droppings with disdain. The straw had been laid fresh that morning and he moved to find a place away from where the donkey had been standing.

'There is no room in the cottage and it would

be best if Senara's young sister did not learn of your presence. Not that Bridie is one to tell tales, but it is safer if she knows nothing.'

Senara had changed into a green woollen dress and carried a lantern, a bowl, and a basket filled with pots and bandages. She held the bowl out to Adam. 'Fill this with water from the stream.'

Placing the lantern on a post hook above her head, she peeled back St John's blood-soaked shirt and studied his wound. 'That bullet must come out.'

'Have you the skill?' St John drew back from her.

'I once took a bullet out of a dog when some so-called gentleman shot it for sport,' she replied. 'The dog survived.'

She moved to Harry to examine him. When Adam returned with the water, her face was strained in the lantern light as she looked up at him. 'The bullet has passed through his side. If it has ruptured the spleen or intestine I will not be able to save him. He should see a surgeon.'

'Do what you can.'

'I shall need more light. My mother is awake and is heating some water. I had to tell her what has happened. I shall also need a knife heated in the fire to cauterise your brother's wound.'

'You're not putting a hot blade to my flesh,' St John yelped.

'It depends on how easily the bullet comes out. It is the quickest way for it to heal.'

St John stared at her in horror, and she added more gently. 'I have herbs which will dull your pain.'

St John grimaced. 'I want a proper physician.' He swayed to his feet. 'I shall demand Chegwidden attends me.'

'And what excuse will you give him for receiving a pistol wound on the night everyone will soon learn that Lanyon was robbed?' Adam flared.

'I will say it was a lark at the gaming tables which went wrong.'

'A feeble ruse and too easily questioned,' Adam pursued. 'Simon Chegwidden has taken over the practice and he has been paying a lot of attention to Annie Moyle, Hester's sister. He is rather too closely linked with Lanyon for comfort.'

'But what does this woman know of bullet wounds?' St John's voice rose in panic. 'For heaven's sake, she tended a dog! I could die.'

'Brace yourself, man,' Adam snapped. 'You will not die. It is Harry who is in danger, not yourself.'

'I don't suppose the wench has any brandy to dull the pain.' St John remained antagonistic. 'Oh, the irony of it. A hundred kegs of the stuff was part of tonight's booty.'

'My herbs are more potent than brandy, Mr Loveday,' Senara declared, 'but the operation will be painful.'

St John glowered at Adam. 'I suppose you are relishing this.'

Adam was offended. 'I take no pleasure in seeing you and Harry in pain. You knew what you were risking.'

'Will you two stop bickering like starlings!' Senara did not bother to control her exasperation. 'I do not complain at being dragged from my bed, after I have this day walked to St Austell and back to sell my pots in the market. What skills I have in healing are freely given, but you are more stubborn than Wilful, my donkey. If you do not want my help you may leave without it, Mr Loveday.'

She moved to Harry's unconscious figure, efficient and in charge. 'Adam, would you remove Mr Sawle's jerkin. You may have to cut off his shirt.' Ignoring St John, she began to mix some herbs in a bowl.

Leah arrived with a kettle of hot water. 'Will you be wanting more, Senara?' She glanced at the two men, then turned her stare on Adam. 'I suppose you had no choice in this, he being your brother, but I'd rather you'd not brought them here. Will they be gone by daylight?'

'I do not know, Ma,' Senara answered. 'Harry Sawle is seriously wounded.'

Leah bowed her head. 'I'll keep the kettle on the fire. Let me know if there is anything I can do.'

Adam took her hand. 'Thank you, Leah. Perhaps it would be best if Bridie was kept away. I will fetch the water if more is needed.'

Senara bent over Harry and with infinite care she cleaned around the wound, then gestured for Adam to turn Harry on to his side. The wound where the bullet had left the body was large and ragged. She bathed it tenderly, but her voice was thick with concern. 'He really should see a doctor. I do not know if I am skilled enough to deal with this. There is a great risk of infection

243

and if the intestine or spleen has been damaged...'

'Do what you can,' Adam urged. 'We cannot risk a doctor informing on the authorities. You may as well know the truth. They were part of a gang who ambushed a cargo belonging to Thadeous Lanyon.'

Senara shook her head. 'Do not tell me any more. I prefer not to know.'

St John shifted on the straw and demanded, 'Can I not have some of those herbs, woman? The pain is past bearing.'

'I will not have you talking to Senara in that tone,' Adam rounded on him. 'She cannot work on both of you at once. Harry is the more seriously wounded.'

Senara continued to clean Harry's wound. 'I do fear infection. It would help if he had bathed more regularly. The wound must drain of any accumulating pus, so I cannot cauterise it or even risk stitching it together. It will need regular attention.'

St John again complained that he was in pain and in need of her attention. To silence him, Senara thrust a jug of herbs mixed with warm water at him. 'Take a few sips; it will ease your pain.'

She worked for half an hour. Once Harry's wound was clean she took up a phial containing the distilled essence of several herbs which had prevented infection in animal wounds, and measured six drops into a cup of water. This she tipped over the injury to aid its cleansing. Then, spreading some dried herbs which had been steeped in hot water on to a wad of moss, she packed it against the open wounds, and bound his ribs with a bandage made from a threadbare sheet.

Adam went out to see to the horses. He tethered them in the wood a short distance from the clearing.

Senara put her hand to Harry's brow. There was yet no sign of a fever. Perhaps he had been lucky and no internal organs were damaged. If the fever had not appeared by morning, he would likely survive. By the time Senara had finished tending Harry, St John was asleep in the straw and snoring.

'The fool drank all the brew,' Senara nodded in St John's direction when Adam joined her. 'He was supposed to sip it. It was poppy juice. Still, at least he is quiet, and it will make it easier to remove the bullet.'

She made Adam hold his brother down as she prodded with a bodkin to remove the round pistol ball. Just as it was near the surface St John cried out and his body jerked. Senara lost her hold on the bullet and had to begin again.

'You must keep him still,' she ordered, 'or I will never get it out.'

For some moments Adam struggled as St John, in his drugged stupor, hit out against an unseen attacker. Senara's gown was sticking to her body with sweat when she finally eased the bullet from the wound. She wiped her brow with her sleeve. 'It will have to be cauterised if it is to heal quickly.'

Adam went to get the heated knife from the

cottage. While Senara waited, she again used the herb essence from the phial to cleanse the wound. St John winced but remained asleep. When Adam returned holding the knife before him, its tip glowed red in the dark.

Senara braced herself to touch the hot blade to the flesh. There was a sizzle and the stench of seared flesh. St John screamed and flung out his arm. He caught Senara a glancing blow to her eye with his elbow, before Adam managed to subdue him. When his brother was quiet Adam called to Senara, who had been flung back on to the straw.

'Did he hurt you?'

She gave a shaky laugh. 'He lashed out like a mule but I am fine. Though I will have a black eye come the morrow.'

'Not much of a payment after all you have done, my darling.' Adam put his hand to her cheek as she scooped a fingerful of balm on to a cotton pad and placed it over St John's wound, then bound it. 'You must be exhausted, Senara.'

'Your brother will be able to travel in an hour or so once the effects of the poppy juice wear off. Though he will have a thick head from it all day.'

Senara studied both her patients. The colour was returning to St John's cheeks and his mouth had dropped open as he began to snore. She stared for a long moment at Harry. His sun-weathered face was tinged with an unhealthy grey and a sheen of sweat covered his brow. 'Harry Sawle will need regular attention for some days. If it is not possible for a doctor to attend, then I suppose he must stay here. But I do not like putting Bridie in a position where she may have to lie. A man as powerful as Thadeous Lanyon will have his spies searching for any injured men to punish for the theft of his cargo. Any who have helped them will not escape his wrath.'

'Then I must get him back to the Dolphin. I will not have you in danger.'

Senara straightened and stared out of the barn door in silence. Adam went to her and put his arms round her waist.

'I am sorry: I should not have brought them here.'

'You had no choice.' She sighed and bent her head. 'Too many people know of my knowledge with herbs. That is what I wished to avoid. It leads to trouble. A woman from Penruan sought me out. She was pregnant and wanted to be rid of the child. I sent her away, but once people start to believe that I will help them in such matters, there will eventually come a time when that knowledge will be used against me.'

'Surely you exaggerate. People who cannot afford to pay a physician are grateful for what you do,' Adam reassured.

'Not all. Some believe I have other powers. They make impossible demands, and turn nasty if I do not help them.'

'Are you sure you are not being over-fanciful, my love?'

Her stare was scornful. 'To be asked to prepare love potions or to rid a woman of an unwanted child are not fanciful notions. I have faced these situations before. A man may look too long upon me when I am selling my pots and his wife will become jealous. Then the rumours begin that I have overlooked a cow whose milk has dried up. That someone who refused to buy a pot of mine has sickened. That is but one step before someone charges me as a witch. The animals I love and have saved will be declared my familiars.'

'No one could ever think that of you, my darling.' Adam drew her into his arms. 'Perhaps in the last century that would have been the case, but surely not now?'

Senara pulled the neckline of her gown low on her shoulder. Even in the pale light Adam saw the jagged raised flesh. He had questioned her about it in the past and she had been evasive about its cause.

'This is a scar I carry from the time I was stoned by a parson's wife, who raised the village against me. That was because her son tried to rape me and I fought him off, scratching his face in defence of my virtue. You do not know what fear and superstition can do to people. When I lived with my gypsy grandmother her tales of persecution would make any civilised man turn away in disgust. Except sometimes it would be the educated bigots who could stir up so much evil and hatred against my people.'

Her eyes misted and she swallowed against a welling pain. 'My father was accused of stealing a horse and was hanged. He was innocent, the horse was later found on the moor. His gypsy blood was enough to condemn him. My step-brother was set upon and put in the stocks when

248

he went to a village to buy flour. They accused him of poaching but he had no game on him that day. Then they beat him almost to death as a lesson to our tribe to stay away from that village.'

'I did not know that you had a stepbrother. You have never spoken of him.'

'Caleph is several years older than I. He fell out with Leah when she wanted to leave the tribe after my father was hanged. I have only seen him once since then, at one of the fairs. Leah has been talking about resolving their differences. She was always fond of Caleph.'

It was rare for Senara to talk about that side of her life and Adam could feel the tension in her body. Senara did not lie or exaggerate. It made him suddenly fear for her.

'I will get Harry back to the Dolphin tonight. His family and St John will be sworn to secrecy about the help they received from you. How can we ever repay you for all you have done?'

Senara put her arms around his neck. She shook back her waist-length hair and smiled. 'Our sanctuary here has been turned into an infirmary, but my patients will not wake for some hours. We have so little time together, my love.'

'I had planned to spend the evening and entire night with you,' Adam grinned, leading her towards the hay loft, 'but after your journey to St Austell, you must be exhausted.'

She kissed him. 'I could be persuaded that the night holds greater enticement than sleep.'

Their time together was all too short. Their lovemaking was at first frenzied because of the dangers which had coloured the night, and then it became poignant, as every moment was treasured. Adam eventually drew back from Senara's embrace.

'It is but an hour to dawn. I must get St John back to Trevowan before the servants are about. There will be many to speculate upon his injury.' He rolled away from her and pulled on his breeches and shirt.

'There should be no complications,' Senara replied. 'I will give St John a balm to ease the discomfort. I will be at the yard two days next week when I clean Mr Meadows' cottage. I can inspect your brother's wound at Mariner's House if he wishes.'

'How long have you been working for the schoolteacher?' Adam voiced his displeasure. 'Why will you not allow me to give you money? I do not wish for you to be any man's servant.'

Senara pulled on her clothes. That she was annoyed showed in her terse movements. 'I am not his servant for he does not pay me. I perform a service and he repays me by two sessions of schooling. The arrangement suits us both.'

'Then I will pay him to tutor you,' Adam ground out. 'I am proud of you for wanting to gain an education. But why are you so stubborn about taking my money?'

'I do not want your money, Adam.' She was defiant as she laced the front of her bodice. 'It is important to me to do this on my own. I hate being illiterate and uneducated.'

'You are an intelligent woman, Senara. You know so much about healing with plants and have a rare understanding of animals. You also have as great a knowledge of the stars as I, which I learned as a midshipman to navigate at night.'

'It is not enough.' She became passionate in her entreaty. 'I want to be able to read. You have taught me so much when you speak of your voyages: about the countries you visit, the people and their customs, where they live and the strange and exotic animals you see. But I want to know so much more. I want to know about history, about the world of the ancient Greeks and Romans. Why the great stones on Salisbury Plain were built.'

'You are a stubborn, independent woman,' he conceded. 'That is what I admire about you. Yet that independence also shuts me out. It would give me so much pleasure to be able to provide for all your needs, yet you will not let me.'

'I would be worthy of you, Adam,' she placated and stretched up on her toes to kiss his mouth. Before he could say any more, she reminded him, 'Now it is time for you to leave, or you will not reach Trevowan before it is light.'

'It would be so much easier if you married me, Senara.'

'Easier for you, my love. But not for me.' She broke from him and nimbly descended the ladder to the lower floor of the stable.

St John was still asleep, but when she put her hand to Harry's brow to check for a fever, his eyes flickered open. He made to sit up with a start and moaned in pain. 'Where am I? What happened? Ow, I hurt like the devil.'

Adam knelt beside him. 'You are in a safe place. You were shot and we could not risk taking you

251

to a doctor. Senara has tended you.'

Harry was gazing up at Senara. 'So I have been ministered to by an angel.'

'She saved your life,' Adam explained.

'I thought you only treated horses,' Harry joked.

'Horses make better patients,' replied Senara.

'She is not only beautiful, but witty.' He winked at Adam. 'So gossip is right and she is your doxy. You always did have good taste. Take care when you are away at sea, Adam. All women are faithless.'

Adam angrily defended Senara's reputation. 'Not all women play a man false as did Hester, Harry.'

'Do they not?' Harry's cynicism scythed the air. 'Look at Meriel. She was in love with you for years yet married St John. And from the way she treats that besotted fool, I would not be surprised if it is you she loves still.'

'Your wound has addled your wits, man,' Adam snorted in disgust. Even so, he cast a wary eye towards the sleeping St John and was relieved that his brother had not overheard. He also glanced at Senara. Harry was a womaniser and had often been unfaithful to Hester. Was he deliberately making mischief between Senara and himself, so as to try to seduce her?

'Meriel means nothing to me,' Adam was gruff in his response. 'And you should mind your tongue. She has been faithful to St John.'

'She meant something once, did she not?' Harry goaded.

'A long time ago and it was before St John

courted her. Do not tar all women with the same brush, Harry. Hester wronged you.'

Harry cast an insolent gaze at Senara. 'It is unwise to neglect a beautiful woman, Adam.'

'I have done what I can for your brother and this man, Adam.' Senara sounded distant and icy. 'I shall be in Penruan in two days selling my pots; his mother can summon me to the inn to inspect my wares. That will not arouse suspicion in the village. I will explain to her how to use the herbs and change the poultice.'

Senara then ignored Harry and carried the lantern to St John's side. She lifted the poultice to inspect the wound. With a wince, St John stirred and woke. His lips were white with pain and suddenly he sneezed violently from the dust rising from the straw as he moved. With a groan he put his hand to his aching head. 'What was in that devil's brew I drank?'

'I told you to sip it.' Senara chided. 'You drank the lot. But it will do you no harm. Your shoulder will heal, but you must rest it. Unfortunately, a sling would make your injury too conspicuous, but you must not use your arm for at least a week.'

'How am I to keep this from my family?' He made to sit up and grimaced. 'What a mess. I hope the profits will be worth it. Adam, you are not going to tell Father, are you?'

Adam felt his anger rise. 'Then you did not intend to repay Father's debts by this venture?'

'I receive a pittance for managing the estate. Am I not entitled to money of my own?' The sullenness on St John's face changed as he saw

253

the fury in Adam's eyes. 'Of course I would have offered some to Father. But I am in partnership with Clem and Harry. I need capital for the next run.'

Adam made to grab at his brother, then remembered his wound and held himself back. His impotent rage was scalding. 'Damn you for a worthless cur. Your greed will be the ruin of us. You are right to fear Father's anger. I knew you were selfish but this is the limit, St John. You would bring disgrace to our name. And your injury will not be easy to conceal. At least vindicate yourself by helping the family for a change, instead of bleeding our resources dry.'

St John's face twisted with outrage and the years of jealousy and resentment burst forth. 'Me bleed the family dry? That is rich coming from you. When have you ever suffered hardship? You have the yard, which should have been mine. You have your own ship, which is making a profit from its voyages. You should be working in the yard, if it is in trouble, not playing the adventurer on the high seas.'

'My legacy paid for *Pegasus*. What happened to yours? Did you gamble it away? For you would not have been at this work tonight if you had the means to support the lifestyle your wife insists upon.'

St John cringed back as Adam towered over him.

Senara stepped between them. 'Stop this. Settle your quarrels elsewhere and not here. You will wake my mother and sister with your shouting.'

'Senara is right,' Adam bristled. 'But I expect

254

you to pay over a considerable part of last night's profits to Father. He will be proud that you have worked to aid the estate and forgive you much.'

'And if I do not, I suppose you will tell him,' St John raged and, with his good hand, brushed the clinging straw from his breeches.

'That will be between you and your conscience. Your work this night has served us ill. That cargo was Lanyon's means of paying us what he owes. Without his money we will have to take drastic measures to pay our debts.'

'Debts on the yard. Why should I suffer for what you will one day inherit?'

Senara saw the dangerous glint in Adam's eyes and pushed him away from his brother. 'Calm down. He is not worth it. Has your family not troubles enough without you fighting and causing your father more pain?'

Adam marched out of the stable to collect the horses.

Harry swayed when he was in the saddle but managed to sit up straight.

Senara stood by his horse. 'That wound must not be neglected.'

Harry's head drooped as he struggled against his pain. Grudgingly he replied, 'You did right by me this night, Miss Polglase. I be obliged to you.'

St John did not look at Adam as he walked to Prince's side. After a failed attempt to mount unaided, he allowed Adam to cup his hands and give him a leg up into the saddle. Senara pressed a small bag of herbs into his hands. 'Sprinkle these in some wine if the pain becomes too much. I will be at Trevowan Hard on Thursday if your wound needs tending.'

'You have been kind, Miss Polglase.' There was arrogance and condescension in his voice which unaccountably sent a shiver through her.

Before Senara fully considered her words, she said, 'Adam does not deserve your anger. He deserves better from you. You have much to atone for.'

There was fear in St John's eyes as he regarded her. Her words had touched something unpleasant within him. His sarcasm lashed her, though he was careful to keep his tone low so as not to reach Adam. 'When has a gypsy woman seen fit to judge her betters? Take care of what you speak.'

The threat was no idle one, but Senara did not flinch at it. She had been drawn against her better judgement to help a man in need. Would it one day be turned against her? She did not trust St John.

Chapter Fourteen

'This was your doing, madam,' Adam accused Meriel in a harsh whisper when he arrived at the Dower House with his injured brother. He had thrown pebbles up at Meriel's bedroom window to wake her and not the servants. He had also stopped her lighting a candle.

Dawn was brightening the sky and the fields and trees were veiled by a thick mist. It had cloaked their journey and kept them hidden from curious eyes.

Adam staggered into the parlour supporting St John, who was weak and unsteady on his feet.

Meriel was in her nightrobe, her golden hair loose about her shoulders. She put a hand to her mouth in horror as she gazed at her husband, who was deathly white after the ride. Adam lowered St John into a chair and rounded on her.

'He has been shot. And so has your brother Harry, who is more seriously hurt. I have to get him back to the Dolphin before the villagers stir. St John cannot risk being seen injured, or word will reach Lanyon and then I would fear for the consequences. It was a hare-brained scheme. Fortunately no one was killed.'

Meriel knelt at her husband's side and St John rallied his strength to smile at her. 'We succeeded. The goods are ours. It was a good night's work.'

'It was lunacy,' Adam snapped.

'But you are wounded, my love,' Meriel fussed. 'Some brandy will sustain you.' She glared at Adam. 'How is it that you are here? What was your part in it?'

'Consider yourselves fortunate that I did become involved, or Harry would be dead.' Adam remained stiff with censure. It was the first time he had been in the Dower House since Meriel became its mistress. The room was overcrowded with ornate furniture and ornaments, many of which had once graced Trevowan. He turned to go. 'Is not all this enough to satisfy your aspirations of grandeur, madam?'

Meriel blanched at his contempt, but before she could reply St John pushed himself upright in the chair.

'Adam, do you intend to tell Father?' he demanded. 'You have risked the family good name for your own selfish ends. It is time to redeem yourself.'

St John scowled. 'You stole the yard from me. You sort out its debts.'

Adam grabbed St John's stock as his temper erupted. 'You selfish idiot. The yard is what will save Trevowan.' He shoved St John back in the chair. 'If you have a shred of decency you will offer Father your share of the money. Or you may find that there will be no Trevowan for you to inherit.'

St John and Meriel glared mutinously at him. Adam lost patience with their greed. 'At least allow some vestige of honour to be redeemed out of this débâcle and be worthy of the name you carry.' He marched out of the house.

Meriel ran past him to Harry's horse. She was horrified to see him drooped forward over the pommel. He struggled upright at her approach.

'Harry, how serious is your wound? Are you fit to ride?'

'I'll live,' he muttered. 'We taught Lanyon the lesson he deserved.'

The frailness of his voice alarmed her. 'I'll come to the inn tomorrow and see how you fare. I am so sorry you were shot. Was it St John's fault?'

'St John proved himself this night. His own wound was through trying to help me. Treat him

258

fairly, Meriel. Don't betray his love. He's done right by you.'

Indignant at his lecture, she forgot her fears for his health and flounced away, throwing back over her shoulder, 'Losing Hester has made you mean, Harry. How dare you compare me to that strumpet?'

Harry gave a bitter laugh. Meriel had no remorse. He had expected some compassion from her, at least. Women were all the same, in his opinion – selfish and intent only on their own needs. No woman would ever get the better of him again.

Once inside the house, Meriel questioned her husband. 'Is it as bad as Adam says about the family money?'

'Adam would not exaggerate over such a matter.'

Her lovely face twisted with fury. 'But you cannot hand over all your share. It is your means to continue in the trade and prosper. It is so unfair.'

'Unfair!' St John raged, then remembered the need not to rouse Rachel Glasson from her sleep, and lowered his voice. 'I risked my life tonight to provide you with the riches you crave. Adam is right, though it sticks in my throat to say it. Papa needs the money more than we do. We cannot risk losing the shipyard and Trevowan.'

Used to St John's devotion and adulation Meriel was shocked at the loathing in his regard. All her plans to achieve grandeur had been cruelly stripped away again this night. The disappointment was intense, but to alienate St

John would be to court disaster.

'It is unfair how you have suffered, my love,' Meriel corrected. 'Your wound appals me. You sacrificed so much, and were so courageous and brave. Harry told me you were wounded trying to save him.'

'Everything must appear as normal,' St John insisted as she helped him to their bedchamber. 'No one must suspect that I have been injured.'

When a white-faced Rachel Glasson appeared on the landing, Meriel ordered her back to bed. 'The master has returned in his cups after an evening with his friends. He is not to be disturbed in the morning by Rowena or yourself.' Meriel stood in front of St John to shield him from the maid and she hoped that in the dark Rachel would not notice that St John was in his working clothes and not the elegant attire he would wear when visiting friends.

Rachel went back to her room and Meriel assisted St John to the bed and removed his boots. He was pale and weak.

'How far can we trust Rachel?' St John groaned. 'Especially after what happened to Tilda?'

Meriel chewed her lip. 'We will have to be careful. The girl bears a grudge against my family. She must not suspect that you have been injured. Do you think you can keep it from her? The wound must be painful.'

St John put a hand to his aching shoulder. 'I must go about my work as normal.' His brow creased in pain and he drew the pouch of herbs from his pocket Senara had given him. 'The

Polglase woman said these are to be brewed into a tisane twice a day. They will ease the pain and fight off any infection.'

Meriel was intrigued that Senara Polglase had done so much for her husband and brother. Now that she had learned Senara Polglase was Adam's mistress, she wanted to know what kind of woman had won Adam's love.

'Make sure you do nothing strenuous for the next few days, St John. I shall visit the Dolphin to discover how Harry fares.' Her conscience nudged her that she had lost her temper with her wounded brother. But Harry should not have been so mean.

'You will do no such thing.' St John grabbed her wrist and pulled her close to him. 'You will keep to your normal routine. Lanyon is no fool. He will suspect any behaviour that is out of the normal. You must be extra careful because you are Harry's sister.'

'You are running from ghosts when there are none. Why should Lanyon suspect us?'

At her wilful expression, St John lost patience with his wife. 'In this you will obey me, madam. I am weary of you disregarding my wishes.'

He had never used that tone with her before and she did not like it. The night with the smugglers had changed him. He was putting family duty before his own interests, and that could mean that her own hold over him was slipping. It must be rectified.

She changed the subject. 'Do you intend to give your father all the money from tonight's work?'

St John rubbed his chin. 'The haul was a

sizeable one. Depending on how much money is involved, I can win Father's favour by offering him two-thirds. That should leave me enough to continue free trading.'

After three hours' sleep St John began his work. He instructed Dan and Ned Holman to repair a fence. Tomorrow they were to summon their families to help with the potato crop. It would be torture for him to work in the field but he had no choice. The herbs Senara had prepared helped the pain, but his movements were sluggish. Elspeth, out for her morning ride, saw him.

'Lay off the brandy, nephew,' she ordered. 'Too much indulgence pickles the brains and sours the liver. It was the ruin of cousin Hector. He fell in a millpond and drowned.'

To be lectured on the appearance of a hangover was better than for Elspeth to suspect the real reason for his pallor. The effort of acting normally when he was in pain was debilitating. He escaped back to the Dower House before midday.

Meriel was not there. In defiance of St John's wishes she had sent Rachel Glasson with a basket of apples from the orchard, to be distributed by Cecily Loveday to the poor of Trewenna. The maid would be gone for most of the day. Meriel had taken Rowena on her pony to Penruan.

There she went straight to the cottage of Joseph Roche, the cobbler. He worked in his front room and the door was always open. The cottage was tiny and smelled of leather and fish stew. There was a pile of leather skins on the floor in the corner. On a rough bench were wooden boxes of nails and brass or tin aiglets, which fastened on the end of the laces. Joseph Roche was short and bandy-legged, with the top of his head a shiny pink dome and long wisps of greying hair hanging like a curtain from his ears to, his shoulders.

'Mistress Loveday! 'Tis not often you grace my threshold.'

'Rowena's shoes are too small. She needs a new pair of black leather and also some red satin slippers. Do you have some of the material left from last time?'

The shoes provided her with a legitimate excuse to be in Penruan. Usually Roche made and repaired shoes for the fishermen's families and stout work boots for the miners. But he was a skilled shoemaker and in the past had made some fine shoes for Rowena.

'There is enough.'

'I love my red slippers, Mr Roche,' Rowena beamed at him. She had no shyness. 'Do you have fairies and pixies to help you make your shoes?'

He chuckled. 'Only these old and wrinkled hands, little one.' He patted Rowena's dark ringlets. 'This one will break a few hearts when she is older, Mistress Loveday. Now I be needing to measure the young lady's feet for a new last. It won't take long. Will you be wanting silver buckles on her shoes?'

'Of course! Rowena always has the best.' Meriel was annoyed the man even thought it necessary to ask.

Rowena sat on a stool and asked about the types and uses of the tools hanging around the walls. When she saw the row of wooden lasts, each labelled with a person's name, she wanted to know who they belonged to.

'Rowena, that is enough of your questions.' Meriel was impatient at her daughter's chatter. She turned as another customer entered the room.

Ginny Rundle sat on a stool inside the door, her large bulk overspilled around it. 'I'll rest my feet while you tend to Mistress Loveday, Joe. Don't you mind me. Have you heard of the goings-on last night?'

Joseph Roche gave a snort. He worked on regular smuggling runs as a tubman. 'I heard. Rum doings by all accounts. A fight between two gangs and the cargo stolen. Bain't heard the likes of that afore. And hope never to again. There be enough trouble with the excise and revenue men without gangs turning on one another.'

'What do you make of it, Meriel?' prompted Ginny Rundle.

'What the free traders get up to is their affair. There have been fights in the past.'

'Between the revenue men and the tubmen, aye,' Ginny persisted. 'They say this were between two rival gangs. Must be a new gang. There's been some angry words in the village. What do your pa or brothers think about it?'

'I would not know. I see little of them,' Meriel strove to remain calm, 'though I had intended to call on Ma later this morning. Rowena needed new shoes. Children shoot up like saplings. All her petticoats and dresses are getting short. I will also have to buy some lace to lengthen them.'

'So you be calling at Lanyon's shop then?' Ginny eyed her with sly cunning.

'I shall have to. I have no time to journey to Truro this month. St John is busy on the estate with his father still in London.'

'They say it were Lanyon's cargo.' Ginny sucked in her lips. 'The man certainly left Penruan in a fury this morning. Reckon there be some, not far from here, who have no reason to love that man. Some who have a reputation for violence.'

'Who would that be, Ginny? I reckon every family in Penruan is in debt to Thadeous Lanyon in some form or other.'

'Not all of them had their woman stole from them. Your Harry has rarely been sober since the wedding.'

A sliver of fear touched Meriel's spine. Gossip like that must be avoided. She gave a brittle laugh. 'Harry is known for using his fists, not his brains. He has always liked his ale.'

Ginny snorted. 'The Sawles be hard men, not liking any who thinks they could get the better of them.'

'They would be flattered that they have that reputation. Mistress Rundle. Though what has that to do with last night?'

Ginny Rundle folded her arms across her barrel stomach. 'The Sawles were free traders long afore Lanyon came to the village.' She made it sound like an accusation.

'And your husband has worked with Clem and

Harry on many runs from Guernsey. It has been profitable for all concerned.'

Joseph Roche had finished measuring Rowena's feet and there was a warning in his glance as his regarded Ginny Rundle. 'Don't reckon the Sawles be involved. What need have they to steal another man's cargo?'

'I weren't implying that they had,' Ginny retorted. 'I was just saying–'

'And some things are better left unsaid,' Roche reminded her.

Meriel took her daughter's hand. 'Please deliver the shoes and slippers to Trevowan in two days, Mr Roche.'

She left the cobbler's cottage, satisfied at Roche's reaction to Ginny's gossip. Roche had the respect of the Penruan men and had no liking for Lanyon, who had begun to stock a range of secondhand work boots in his shop. He would quash any of the rumours of the type voiced by Ginny Rundle.

For a moment she was giddy with surging emotions. They had bested Lanyon and made a fortune into the bargain. And it had been her idea. She felt omnipotent. Had she not, a lowly tavernkeeper's daughter, by her own cunning and designs risen high?

And she could aspire to so much more.

Chapter Fifteen

A perverse need to view the opposition took Meriel to Lanyon's shop. It was an unprepossessing building converted from two cottages, built of granite and slate with lichen yellowing the northern walls, and situated at the centre of the quay. Today the drying sheds were deserted of women, but the smell of rank fish lingered in the air. Several fishermen were working on the quay, repairing nets and lobster pots. From the number of luggers bobbing in the shallow water of the falling tide, it looked as though few fishermen had sailed that morning.

The water lapped in muddy waves around the hulls, and black and rust swathes of kelp and seaweed draped over the lower rocks of the harbour wall. Overhead the sky was patchworked with thickening clouds.

Meriel paused to speak with one cadaverous-faced fisherman. 'Is that not typical? I cannot see my brothers' lugger, yet most of the fleet did not sail with the morning tide.' She had to raise her voice above the screech of gulls.

'Clem and Harry went out yesterday morning,' the man replied. 'The catch has been poor all week. Happen they went further afield.' He watched her slyly. 'Or happen they had other business.'

Meriel ignored the comment though it made

267

her uneasy. When Clem was contacted and returned with the fishing lugger, she hoped it would be with a full catch to allay the villagers' suspicions.

Her step was less jaunty when she entered Lanyon's shop. It was gloomy inside and the shutter was over the window at the far end where Lanyon usually sat with his ledgers. At first Meriel thought the place was deserted, for Lanyon always insisted that a customer was attended to as soon as they entered the premises. If they left without a purchase, the servants felt the wrath of his tongue.

'Is there no one to serve me?' Meriel demanded.

A soft sob greeted her remark and, from behind an assortment of wicker baskets on the counter a woman appeared, her head bowed so that Meriel would not see her face.

'How can I help you?' Hester's voice was barely audible.

Meriel was tempted to have the woman running from one end of the shop to the other bringing out goods for her inspection, but her obvious misery halted her.

'I thought Lanyon paid Annie Warne to serve in the shop. Or is his wife cheaper labour?'

'How can I help you, Meriel?' The lack of fight in Hester's tone surprised Meriel.

'Mistress Loveday, if you please. I need ribbons for Rowena's hair and your best lace to lengthen her gowns and petticoats.'

Three trays were brought out from under the counter and throughout Hester kept in the shadows.

Meriel picked over some pink and yellow ribbons. 'These will do, but they are nothing special. I have just come from Roche the cobbler. There's talk of some gang ambushing a run last night. Did you hear that, Mistress Lanyon? Gossip is that your husband owned the cargo.'

'I know nothing of Thadeous's business. I serve in the shop occasionally, that is all.'

'Ginny Rundle says your husband was in a rare, taking and has left Penruan. If the gossip is true, he must have lost a lot of money.'

'You know more about my husband's concerns than myself.' The voice remained dull. It was so unlike Hester, who had always been fiery.

Hester and Meriel had long been adversaries and it was strange that Hester did not stand in the light. The memory of Meriel's last visit to the Penruan church caused her anger to erupt, sour as bile. 'Does Lanyon make you happy, Hester? I give you that your husband holds a position of importance in Penruan. But how do you stand him touching you ... after Harry?'

Preparing herself for a cannonade of retaliation from Hester, Meriel was astounded when the woman suddenly fainted on the floor.

'Rowena, sit over there and do not touch anything.'

Meriel went behind the counter and, seeing a jug of water, threw it over Hester's face. The act was satisfying, but as Hester came round and pushed herself into a sitting position, Meriel saw the livid bruises on the woman's arm where her full sleeve had fallen back.

Her antagonism mellowed as she realised how

269

nearly that could have been her fate, when Reuban had planned to marry her to Lanyon. 'Hester, couldn't you tell the man was a monster? He beats you, doesn't he?'

'No, no, it was an accident...' Her too-ready protest ended in a sob.

Meriel did not believe her. 'Lanyon has had two wives afore you. Both young and dead within five years. The last one rarely left the house and when she did, it was usually with a black eye.'

'Go on, gloat.'

'We've never been friends, but I don't like to see any woman treated thus.'

'I hate him.' A night of pain and terror had made her vulnerable and her tears splashed on to her bodice. 'He promised me so much. Was so attentive and charming for so long. Always giving me gifts. Then Harry was betraying me by seeing a dairymaid. I was angry. There were always other women with Harry. I couldn't take it any more.'

'But to marry Lanyon...'

'It was to get back at Harry,' Hester wailed. 'Lanyon overheard Harry and me quarrelling. I was so mad with Harry. Lanyon said I would live like a queen. That he would never play me false.'

'And you believed him. Oh, Hester.'

Hester dragged her fingers through her hair. 'He got a special licence and took me to Truro and bought me a half-dozen fine dresses. Anything I wanted I could have, providing I wed him. I was not thinking straight. Harry had hurt me with his other women so many times.'

'But he loved *you*. Not the others.' Meriel shook

her head in exasperation at Hester's foolishness.

Hester groaned and, holding her head in her hands, began to rock back and forth. Meriel bolted the shop door. Rowena was amusing herself lining up a row of wooden clothes pegs around the edge of a sack of flour.

'Come now, don't let anyone else see you in this state.' She helped Hester to her feet. Hester grabbed hold of the counter, her body slumped in a gesture of misery. 'I don't know how I can go on.'

'Harry will hate me for saying this. He still loves you. He will do anything for you. No, don't start crying again.'

Hester raised her head and Meriel saw the hope floating in her eyes. 'You do not have to suffer this way, Hester. Harry does still love you.'

'What use is that?' Hester eyed her suspiciously.

'I know we have never been friends, but I was lucky to escape Lanyon's clutches. You chose this life, whether out of anger or greed – what does it matter. Do you deserve the way he treats you?'

'There is no pleasing the man. This is my punishment. I knew what Harry was like. I should've forgiven him. I miss him so much.'

Meriel had often heard Harry bragging to Clem of Hester's passionate nature. They had been lovers for years. 'Then tell Harry how you feel. He can save you from this marriage.'

Hester's mouth gaped with horror. 'Lanyon would kill us.'

'Harry is his match.'

She could see that Hester was wavering. 'Lanyon is often away on business. You would not be

271

the first wife to take a lover.'

Meriel did not pursue the matter further. She had seen her chance to help Harry get his revenge on Lanyon. The rest was up to them.

Adam was walking towards Lanyon's shop to present the bill for payment of the fitments, when he saw Meriel leaving. What was the minx up to? No doubt playing with fire, if he knew Meriel. Was the woman mad?

She looked pleased with herself. He was too far away to hail her and proceeded to the shop.

'Cap'n Loveday,' Hester was flustered and remained in the dark behind the piled-up goods. 'My husband is away today.'

'Then be so kind as to give him this.' Adam laid an invoice on the counter and frowned at seeing the discoloration of her face. Any sympathy he had felt about the wrong done to Lanyon last night vanished, though it was a pity that his wife had to bear the brunt of the man's anger.

'Kindly inform your husband that as soon as his payment for the fitments is received, work will resume on the cutter. Good day, Mistress Lanyon.' He tipped his tricorn to her and left.

Sal was in the middle of an argument with Reuban when Meriel walked into the kitchen of the Dolphin. As usual her parents were quarrelling over their sons.

'You fuss too much, woman,' Reuban shouted. 'They can look after themselves.'

'They bring nothing but trouble to my door. I've had enough of it. They'll end up in prison, or

272

with a knife in their guts. Why can't they be content with the profits from the inn and their fishing?'

Reuban's joints ached from the rheumatism which tortured him. Always short-tempered, he was now more belligerent than ever. He had been drinking since he learned that Harry had been shot. He swayed to his feet, his wispy chest-length beard matted from last night's vomit. His shirt was splattered with beer stains and stank of stale sweat. Sal turned away from him in disgust.

Reuban jabbed a finger into her back. 'Them boys do all right. Quit moaning, woman. I've work to do since Clem bain't here.'

'Then it will be the first time in weeks since you did more than drink the profits. And get yourself cleaned up. You stink worse than the pilchard sheds.'

He made a swipe at her, but Sal avoided his blow and Reuban, caught off balance, jarred his hip against the kitchen table. His face contorted in pain and he made another grab for his wife, fumbling with his belt to give her a beating. 'Less of your impudence, woman. Bain't I provided for you?'

'Leave Ma alone, Pa,' Meriel demanded.

Reuban scowled at her, unimpressed by her fashionable shepherdess-style blue gown and velvet pelisse she had worn to show off to the villagers. 'Miss Hoity-toity come to visit, has she? Brought your old man some baccy, or an ounce or two of snuff to ease his suffering, have you?'

'I brought Ma some lavender soap. Though from the looks of you, you could be using it.

273

Reuban Sawle used to be someone in this village. You've become a drunken joke, Pa.'

'Why you–' Reuban smashed an empty bottle on the counter and waved it in front of her face. 'I bain't so drunk I can't ruin your pretty face. Then where would you be, daughter? Thrown out on the scrap-heap. You think yourself so high and mighty, but that man of yours wouldn't have wed you if we hadn't forced him.' He passed the bottle in front of her face, making her step back, his all-but-toothless smile evil. 'Your looks trapped him but all you gave St John Loveday were a daughter. A man needs sons. Specially a man of property. You bain't produced them, have you? How long are the Lovedays gonna tolerate a tavern-wench in the family who can't give them an heir?'

Meriel backed further from her father. He had spoken her worst fears. 'At least I've made something of my life. You've ended up a useless drunk.'

She side-stepped as the bottle was thrown at her. It smashed in pieces against the wall an inch from her head.

'Bitch!' Reuban spat. 'Get out of my sight. You be an unnatural daughter and an unnatural wife.'

Sal pushed Meriel towards the kitchen. 'Why do you always manage to rile him?' When she saw Rowena staring at the scene with wide, horrified eyes, she lost her temper. 'Now the lass be scared. Bain't you got no sense?'

'How is it I'm always in the wrong?' Meriel snapped. She banged the tablets of soap on to the table. 'They're for you, though I wonder why I

274

bother. I came to see Harry. How is he?'

The moods in the Sawle household had always been volatile, rising and waning from one moment to the next.

'There be no sign of a fever. At least for that I can be grateful.' Sal shook her head. 'He be too weak to rise from his bed. Why they need to get into these scrapes is beyond me. They make a good living as fishermen. Ay, they will never be rich, but unless the catch is poor, neither will they starve. There be such a taking in the village over that affray last night. The village men are up in arms that a gang would ambush the tubmen. Lanyon is threatening to find out who the rogues were and tie them to stakes in a cove to be drowned at high tide. There's been such justice before.'

Meriel shivered as it dawned on her how much danger her plan had put her family in.

'Lanyon is getting above himself. His pew is an affront to the Lovedays,' Meriel countered.

'Lanyon has always been a businessman. And any bad feeling from him was because of you, madam. If you'd wed Lanyon, he'd not have set the excise men on Clem and your husband's cargo. Neither would he have wed that slut Hester to slight Harry.'

'Don't set the blame on me,' Meriel fumed. 'I wanted nothing to do with Thadeous Lanyon and I told Pa so. His greed began this, not me.'

Sal slumped down on her rocker by the hearth. 'The trade is dangerous enough without making enemies in your own village. If it ever gets out that Harry and Clem–'

Meriel lost patience with her mother's complaints. 'I'm going up to see Harry. Keep an eye on Rowena.' Meriel ran up the stairs to her brother's bedroom, eager to tell him of her conversation with Hester.

Harry was asleep but woke when she sat on the end of his bed. He did not look pleased to see her. There was a yellowish stain on the bandage round his naked torso.

She poured out her news about Hester and saw his eyes darken with anger, then glow with a purposeful light.

'Why are you telling me this?' Harry sounded guarded.

'Because I know you still care for Hester. What she did was wrong. But you have been unhappy and...' She shrugged and plucked at the frayed corner of the blanket covering his bed. 'I thought you would be interested, that is all.'

'You up to something, Meriel?'

'No, Harry, truly not. I feel guilty about snapping at you last night. I was worried about you and St John. Your injuries gave me a terrible scare. You know what a wasp I am when I get upset.'

He did not answer but, from his thoughtful frown, he was clearly considering her words. It was enough. This was too good an opportunity for Harry to get his revenge on Lanyon for him to ignore.

Adam had stabled Solomon at the Dolphin while he completed his errands in the village and intended to enquire of Harry's health before he left Penruan. Because it had been getting light he had carried Harry to his bed, and had stayed only briefly to inform Sal of his condition.

He had no wish to encounter Meriel, whom he assumed was visiting her family, and decided to ride back to Trevowan Hard. Sal was feeding the hens in the yard on his return to the inn and waylaid him.

'Come take a sup of ale with us, Cap'n Loveday.'

'How is Harry?' He dropped his voice as a precaution against being overheard.

'He'd like a word with you. He be fretful and wanted to send Mark to contact Clem and your brother.' Sal shook her head. 'I bain't having Mark be mixed up in this. It be bad enough two of my boys are involved.'

'I have no wish to be further involved, Sal. It is a sorry business.'

'I reckon you saved my Harry's life. I be that grateful to you, Cap'n.'

He put his hand on her shoulder. Sal looked old and tired, so different from the energetic woman of a few years ago. He had a fondness for her, for during his childhood he had often played with Clem and Harry and she had mothered the child starved of female kindness. 'I will talk to Harry, but I will not promise anything. Though our job is far from over to prevent any suspicion falling on our families.'

On entering the kitchen he discovered Rowena playing with Sal's box of darning wools. Meriel was not in the room.

'Uncle Adam.' Rowena ran towards him and he

caught her up in his arms.

'What have you been up to this morning?'

'Mama has brought me ribbons and lace and new shoes and red slippers.'

'Your mama has been busy.' He continued to hold her when Meriel appeared from the stairwell. 'Is it wise to be seen in Penruan today?' he addressed her.

'Am I to deny my daughter's needs?' Meriel countered. 'Surely to avoid the village would give equal rise to gossip.'

'And by visiting Lanyon's shop are you not taking that to extremes?'

'He was not there. He left the village this morning in high dudgeon.' She grinned. 'A pity he will never know who dealt the blow to him, for then he would learn that his position in Penruan is not as strong as he believes.'

'You had better pray he *does not* learn, or even suspect. He is a dangerous enemy.'

Meriel tipped her head to one side and the glitter in her eyes made the hairs on Adam's neck prickle. 'Ah, but is he a match for the Sawles?'

'Pride goeth before a fall, Meriel. The Sawles are not invincible. Harry could have died last night. Does that not teach you anything?'

She laughed at his words of caution. He lowered Rowena to the ground and saw that Sal was watching him with an odd expression.

'Surely, *you* can see that this is madness, Sal?'

Sal was deep in thought and took a moment to recover. There was terseness in her voice. 'Sometimes I see too much.' She picked up a wooden pail and went out to the water pump in the yard.

'Harry wanted a word with me,' Adam said, moving past Meriel to the stairs.

When he had left the kitchen, Sal banged down the filled bucket and rounded on Meriel, keeping her voice low. 'The child is his, isn't she? You have but to see them together to notice the resemblance.'

Meriel paled. 'Don't be daft, Ma. Rowena gets her colouring from St John's mother.' Meriel remained defiant. 'Everyone comments on it.'

'Then they see only what they wish to see. God help you when the truth breaks. You bain't as clever as you think, my girl.'

Chapter Sixteen

A week after the meeting with Meredith Lascalles, Thomas was on the brink of despair. The repayments to customers who had withdrawn their money had been made by the sale of some of the family's paintings, silver and the diamond and ruby necklace which had belonged to his grandmother. There was little money left. If another run was made on the bank he would be unable to meet the customers' demands.

No longer able to keep such events from his mother, Thomas had written to her at Trevowan, explaining something of their financial situation. He had agreed with Edward that it was better to reveal their position gradually than to expose her to the shock of how Charles had been on the point of ruin.

'In six months you could recoup some of the losses,' Edward had advised. 'The shock of Charles's death is enough for Margaret to contend with at this time.'

'We have to survive those months first.' The quarterly interest payments due on the loans the bank had earlier made to customers kept them running on a daily basis. But Thomas knew they were surviving on a knife edge. He could not eat or sleep.

Without Edward, who encouraged and supported him in so many ways, he could not have coped. So often it all seemed hopeless.

One thing he constantly worried about. 'We need to attract new investors, then I will have some capital to speculate with. But how?' he often said to his uncle.

The safest investments for his customers always yielded the lowest profits. But after the disastrous chances his father had undertaken, Thomas was loath to take the higher-risk-but-greater-profit road. In the month since his father's death, Thomas had studied all the investments his father had made in the last ten years. He had compiled lists of those which had done well and those to be avoided. The chief clerk had been with the bank for twenty years and Thomas consulted him, but he was a man of natural caution, and his advice would not give them the returns they needed.

It was Edward who urged him to take a middle road.

'You have to take some risks, Thomas.' Edward was with his nephew in the study after another long evening of going over the books. 'New customers will raise confidence in the bank in others. To attract them you need to pay a higher interest on their money.'

'And what if I cannot meet those rates when the interest becomes due?'

'Then you are in the same position that you are now. It is a chance you must take. At least you would have done all you can.'

'But I would have to sell the last of our valuables to raise the money. And there is no guarantee I will succeed with investments when Papa failed.'

'It is a risk, but I believe a necessary one,' Edward confirmed. 'Charles resorted to desperate measures and was unlucky. You will be more circumspect. It is also as well to remember that appearances are everything. You must be seen more in the coffee-houses with influential customers.'

Thomas was not convinced. 'How can I risk selling more of our possessions? These matters cannot be kept secret and all confidence in the bank will be lost.'

'Not if Japhet sells them. Charles was a great collector of art. He has paintings by Canaletto, Gainsborough, Hogarth and several of the Dutch masters who are so popular. They should raise enough to meet your present needs.' At Thomas's frown Edward pressed on. 'Charles always saw them as investments for your children. The creditors have been waiting too long and cannot be fobbed off with talk of legal hold-ups any longer. The average fop may owe half the tradesmen of London, but not the owner of a bank.'

'The sale of the remaining silver should cover the creditors' bills,' Thomas sighed heavily. 'If the paintings raise enough to meet the mortgage loan on this house which is due next month, there still will not be enough left to invest lavishly.' He paced the room in a despondent fashion. 'Mama adores the paintings. There will be nothing of value left for her to come home to.'

'Your mother is a practical woman,' Edward reasoned. 'She would pawn all her jewellery without a second thought to save the bank and the Mercer name.'

'I trust it will never come to that. I insisted her jewellery, apart from the diamond necklace, was taken to Trevowan. I had nightmares that a creditor would demand them in payment of his bills.'

Edward was confident. 'Do as we have planned and you should gain six months' breathing space and hopefully attract new customers. We are far from beaten, Thomas.'

'I do not want to sell so much without Mama knowing. A letter would be a cruel way of informing her. Perhaps I should spend a day or so in Cornwall.'

Edward shook his head. 'It would look bad for you to leave the City. It would be seen as flight. I will go. Adam has kept me informed of his successes in obtaining money owed to the yard, but Amelia must be told of our financial situation. I will return to London in two weeks.'

Japhet enjoyed his adopted role of country squire as he approached art dealers and silversmiths to sell the paintings and silver. He haggled as virulently as any Lombard to gain the best prices. At the end of the week, all had been sold and the money transferred to Mercer's Bank from an account Japhet had temporarily opened at Coutts.

He returned to the Strand expecting to find Thomas in high spirits. Instead his cousin was slumped in a chair in a darkened room. There were bright squares on the wallpaper where the paintings had once hung. The silver and Sèvres china from the sideboard were gone and so was the large crystal and gilt chandelier, and also the Persian rugs from the floor.

'The dining room is the same,' Thomas said forlornly. 'The house is as gloomy as a tomb. How can Mama ever bear to live here again? Everything of value has been sold except for Mama's harpsichord, which was her wedding present from Papa, and some things in her bedchamber which she cherished.'

'Why have you sold so much?' Japhet thought his cousin had gone to extremes in the last week.

Thomas rubbed his hand across his face. 'Lord Radford has closed his account at the bank. How else could I meet his demand for money? He had been convalescing in the country and had not heard of Papa's death until last week.' Thomas gave a bitter laugh. 'At least Radford had the grace to look shame-faced when I handed him the bank draft. I told him he would not get a better interest rate elsewhere, as once all legal matters were settled next month, our rate would be a full one per cent above any other London bank.'

'Did that not tempt him to keep his money with you?' Japhet asked.

'Alas, no. But he did say if the interest remained at such a figure in six months, he might reconsider his decision.'

Japhet had been down on his own luck so many times and bounced back that he refused to allow his cousin to be downhearted. 'So today was a setback. What good to mope here? Uncle Edward insists that appearances are important. You must be seen about town, Tom, and not looking as though you carry the weight of the world on your shoulders.'

'I am sorry if my circumstances are affecting your social life, Japhet.'

'You mistake me,' Japhet amended at Thomas's sarcasm. 'Take a look in the mirror. You are drawn and haggard. This is not the image you can afford to portray.'

'Spare me a lecture.' Thomas crossed to the marble fireplace and rested his hands on the mantel, his body slumped as he stared into the empty hearth. 'I do not know how I can go on like this. Everything I try turns to ashes. Radford was the last straw. There is scant money to invest to build for the future.'

'Then rewrite your future, man! Good Lord, you are a playwright. Create the world you wish to portray. Did not that playwright fellow

Johnson write, "All the world's a stage and all the players people on it"?'

'It was Shakespeare, and that is a loose interpretation of his great words.'

'There you are! Good advice! Create your own stage. Write your own part.' Japhet's face lit with inspiration. 'Yes, that is the very solution. Write yourself a part as the sought-after banker. You've enough friends as actors to play investors at the coffee-houses.'

Thomas looked at Japhet as though he had just escaped from Bedlam. 'What are you talking about?'

Japhet laughed. 'Let the world believe Mercer's Bank is attracting new investors, and the investors you need will be attracted to the bank.'

'Is that not deceitful?' Thomas was wary.

Japhet shrugged. 'People believe what they want to believe. There is nothing more powerful than the appearance of success, or failure. Which do you prefer?'

'I am sure Uncle Edward would not approve.'

Japhet flashed a wicked smile. 'Uncle Edward will not be in London for at least ten days.'

When Thomas remained unenthusiastic, Japhet changed tack and lounged back in his chair. 'Moping here solves nothing. Tonight cheer yourself at Vauxhall Gardens. Lucy Greene is giving a recital of his poetry.'

'I wish you would not call him Lucy. His name is Lucien,' Thomas snapped.

Japhet bit back a caustic comment on Lucien's sexuality which Thomas would not appreciate. In the light of the single candle Thomas looked awful. His eyes were darkly circled and his cheeks hollow. All the vigour and joy of life had gone out of him.

'This will not do, Tom,' Japhet leapt to his feet. 'Desperate measures are needed to save the bank. Do you doubt you can give your investors the return they seek from their money?'

'I have every faith that I can.'

'Then what is the problem in using your natural cunning to attract those investors in the first place? Come, we will go to Vauxhall which will dispel your melancholy and inspire you to write the scenarios to be enacted in the coffee-houses.'

'In which case I would be better employed writing tonight instead of cavorting at the pleasure gardens.'

'But the right frame of mind is all-important.' Japhet would not be daunted. 'And besides, Lucien will be delighted if you attend his recital. You have seen so little of him lately.'

A flicker of exasperation crossed Thomas's face. 'I am in mourning. You cannot have for-gotten that, even if you choose to be flippant about the wreckage of my life.'

'Melodrama does not suit you.' Japhet refused to be defeated. 'A fit of the vapours is wearisome enough in a woman, but in you ... quite frankly, dear coz, it is positively indecent. Since most respectable citizens visit the pleasure gardens masked, we shall go incognito.'

Thomas stared around the pillaged room and shuddered.

Japhet lost patience. His cousin was usually as

irrepressible as himself. 'If one is setting oneself up as a martyr, Tom, then should not one do so with style and aplomb? As I see it, you can either go to hell miserable, or you can go to hell happy.'

Thomas's head shot up and he glared at Japhet, who continued to taunt him. 'As my dear reverend father says in times of crises, "A man has a duty to nourish the soul."' Japhet chuckled. 'And Papa would be the first to remind you that the Bible says, "A man hath no better thing under the sun, than to eat, and to drink, and to be merry." Vauxhall Gardens is the very place.'

Suddenly Thomas's mood changed. 'Then let us both go to hell happy, cousin. A month of Puritan restraint and anguish has solved nothing.'

'That sounds like a true Loveday talking,' Japhet responded, slapping him on the back.

They walked to the river and took a wherry to Vauxhall stairs, where they waited in line with other revellers to enter the grounds. The sound of music and the twitter of roosting starlings in the tree-lined walkways greeted them, together with the drone of human voices.

Japhet had visited Ranelagh Gardens but not Vauxhall. The grand scale of the place amazed him. The pleasure gardens were lit by hundreds of lamps and coloured Chinese lanterns. The Grand Walk colonnaded by trees stretched the entire length of the gardens. This was traversed by the South Walk, over which soared triumphal arches aglitter with lights. Everywhere the design of its interior was on a gothic scale. There were picturesque ruins, rural fantasies, Chinese and

Greek temples. Wherever you walked you were never far from music. A small orchestra played in an oriental-looking edifice and quartets were hidden in discreet alcoves.

Away from the main walks were secluded dark walkways. From the sound of female giggles, Japhet assumed that these were favourite trysting places for those seeking privacy. It boded well for his plans to seduce a willing wench later in the evening.

Aware of his duty to keep his cousin company, Japhet curbed his appetite for conquest. 'We should dine before we begin drinking in earnest.'

They approached the supper booths built in a semi-circle around a raised grandstand. The music of Handel serenaded the diners.

'Lady Middlewich has reserved three adjoining dining booths,' Japhet said. 'Lucien is to recite his poem "The Perils of a Parson's Wife" for their pleasure.'

The carefree atmosphere of the pleasure gardens had lifted Thomas's spirits. 'That is Lucien's bawdiest piece and one I trust your dear mother never hears. Lucien's parson's wife has more amorous adventures than Defoe's Moll Flanders.'

They saw Lucien Greene seated at the back of one of Lady Middlewich's boxes, sipping from a glass of wine. With his Adonis looks he had drawn the attention of four buxom women. He flirted outrageously with each, making them squeal with laughter, but there was about him an air of boredom. He looked up to see Thomas and his relief was obvious. He abandoned the ladies to join the cousins.

'A man may have to sing for his supper on these occasions, but sometimes one feels too much is expected of one.' He rolled his eyes heavenwards. 'Have you ever seen such harpies as those who descended upon me? I am so glad you have come, my dear fellow. You are in need of entertainment, Tom. And just in time for my recital. I can see Lady M summoning me to begin.' Then he raised a finely plucked eyebrow and winked at Japhet. 'Unless it is this young buck who has caught her attention. Lady M has a voracious appetite and a prodigious fortune.'

Japhet glanced in her Ladyship's direction and habit made him perform an elegant bow. She was as raddled as a crone, which even her thick-powdered face and patches could not hide.

All the supper booths were full, but Thomas and Japhet leaned against a decorated pillar close enough for them to hear Lucien's recital. The laughter from the booths caused many of the revellers to pause in their eating or strolling to listen, and soon they were surrounded by an appreciative crowd.

Japhet, ever restless for the pursuit of a new conquest, scanned the audience. Yet from time to time even his gaze was diverted from a pretty face by the splendour of the supper boxes themselves. Here, reality was suspended, the booths decorated like Greek temples, Eastern palaces, or fairy grottos. Paintings of Bacchus and other ancient gods adorned some, others depicted the hunting field, cockfights, or even scenes from popular plays. Everything was designed for the customers' pleasure, within a setting of hedonism.

Japhet licked his lips in anticipation. A constant flow of beauties paraded before him, distracting him from Lucien's recital. Masked, well-born ladies sauntered behind bold, vivacious actresses, and courtesans strolled on the arms of their wealthy paramours. Parties of young men and women were in high spirits as they hurried past, intent on discovering other illuminated tableaux of strange and exotic fantasies.

Japhet was interrupted in his contemplation by Thomas's hand on his arm. His reply was instinctive for his cousin's words had not registered as Japhet smiled into the eyes of a raven-haired beauty. 'Yes, Tom, Lucien was superb. Now that beautiful woman in the pink gown in the next group, I've a mind to–'

'Lucien has not finished,' Thomas declared. 'The Lascalles are in the third booth on the right. After the way Meredith Lascalles treated me, I do not trust my temper in their proximity. Will you tell Lucien I will meet him by the grand cascade?' Without waiting for Japhet to respond, he marched away.

The strain was indeed getting to his cousin, Japhet noted as he studied the Lascalles' booth. A tall woman in green was sidling to the door and disappeared from sight. Japhet lost interest and scanned the crowd for the raven-haired woman, who had earlier captured his attention. She was watching him, her masked eyes bold above a fluttering fan. He was about to introduce himself when he remembered his message for Lucien.

To an enrapt audience Lucien strolled along

the front of the three booths hired by Lady Middlewich. Japhet turned back to the woman who had attracted him. She was with a party of a dozen men and women who had paused to listen to the poet. Japhet always used brazen tactics when in pursuit of a woman, and sauntered towards her.

'Dear Lady,' he took her hand and bowed graciously, 'such an age since I last had the pleasure of your company. And I see you are an admirer of Lucien Greene. He is a friend of mine. You must allow me to introduce him to you.'

'You are bold, sir. I do not recall–'

'When last it was we met,' he swiftly parried. Her eyes were sparkling with interest and he knew she was putting up a token resistance in front of her friends. Her voice was cultured and though she wore no jewels her gown was of silk embroidered with pearls. Clearly she was a woman of wealth and position. He bowed again. 'Japhet Loveday at your service, dear lady. It was that ball. Now who held it? One attends so many. Was it Lady Helena or the Duchess of–' He broke off and then gave an exclamation. 'I am sure now it was not a ball but at the theatre.'

She left him waiting in suspense for endless seconds whilst continuing to hold his stare. A gallant in the party stepped forward.

'Maria, is this gentleman annoying you?'

She smiled at Japhet. 'Far from it, Giles. Mr Loveday is vastly entertaining. Though I am mortified that he cannot remember where we met. Or that it was just a month ago at Drury Lane when Sheridan's *The School for Scandal* was playing.'

Japhet flashed his most provocative smile. 'How could I forget Sheridan's masterpiece, but my eyes were dazzled by your beauty. Do I importune, for I hear that Lucien has finished his recital? May I introduce you?'

She placed her hand in his. 'You may indeed, Mr Loveday. But then I must return to my friends.'

Japhet hid his disappointment that he could not immediately whisk her away.

Her laugh was warm and enticing. 'I confess, Mr Loveday, I have never heard of Mr Greene until this evening. And since we have never met, I am intrigued at your charade.'

He put his hand to his heart. 'Have we indeed not met before? Then you must be the lady who haunts my dreams. Such perfection of beauty is unforgettable. What is your name, dear angel of my dreams, that I may have it carved upon my heart?'

'Maria Jameson, sir. But I fear a heart such as yours has many names carved upon it.'

Japhet looked aghast. 'How deeply you wrong me, dear lady. There is room in my heart for but one lady – yourself. Can you not leave your friends? I will escort you safely back to your home.'

'I fear my husband would not approve, sir,' she reproved sternly, but her eyes remained inviting. 'He is elderly and an invalid and has entrusted me to the care of this party of friends.'

'Then I am distraught. How may I see you again?'

She glanced at her companions before replying,

'I ride in Hyde Park every morning.'

He raised her fingers to his lips and knew his conquest was made.

Thomas walked fast to dispel his anger. As he entered one of the dark walks he became aware of someone calling his name. He was in no mood for company, especially as the voice was female.

'Mr Mercer, could I speak with you?' The voice was now directly behind him.

He turned with reluctance and could not at first place the tall, masked woman. 'How may I be of service, madam?'

'Oh, you do not recognise me.' She became agitated in her disappointment and laughed nervously. Then removing her mask, she announced, 'I am Georganna Lascalles. I wished to thank you for the book of your poems which you sent to me.'

Thomas had forgotten the incident. He was surprised that after one brief meeting and with himself now wearing a mask, she should remember him. 'It was my pleasure, Miss Lascalles. Think nothing of it.'

'But I do so admire your work. I was enchanted.'

'I doubt your father would approve.'

At his note of censure she lowered her eyes, her voice hesitant. 'I was appalled at the way you were treated by him. But Meredith Lascalles is not my father. He is my guardian.' Her head tilted back and with defiance and pride, she added, 'My father was Jonathan Lascalles. You may have known him as the playwright Jonathan London.'

Thomas's interest was aroused. Jonathan London had been murdered more than a dozen years ago in a tavern fight. 'Mr London was a talented playwright.'

'Thank you. I am proud to be his daughter, but my uncle will not have his name mentioned in the house. He never approved of him. That is why he was so rude to you and angry when you refused to marry one of his daughters. He was affronted that you preferred to be a playwright.' She again hung her head and looked flustered. 'I thought you were owed an explanation. Now I must return. There will be a hue and cry when I am missed.'

Thomas was strangely touched by her honesty. 'I pray you will not be in trouble on my account, Miss Lascalles. Let me escort you to your dining booth. The gardens are not safe for a lone woman.'

She replaced her mask and laughed. 'What gallant will trouble themselves with me when there are so many beauties to attract their eye?'

'You underrate yourself, Miss Lascalles.' The compliment was sincere. She was not pretty, but she was a remarkable woman in many ways. It had taken spirit to risk her uncle's displeasure to seek him out. That she was the daughter of Jonathan London, a playwright he had always admired, made her quite exceptional to his way of thinking.

As they entered the central walk, the grand cascade was fully illuminated. Georganna gasped. 'Is that not an outrageous splendour?'

294

The cascade was a towering grotto with statues of real and mythological sea creatures amid rainbow-coloured fountains. Thomas thought it rather gaudy and tasteless, a tableau to appeal to the simple taste of the masses.

'Outrageous indeed, Miss Lascalles,' he agreed with irony.

'Then you too think it is rather tawdry.' Her eyes lit with mischief. 'My cousins were enraptured. Vauxhall has its place, but I would rather spend an evening at the playhouse. But my uncle disapproves. I shall enjoy the fireworks later. They are always spectacular.'

The pair were close to the supper booths and could see the Lascalles' booth filled with guests.

Thomas halted. 'I will leave you here, Miss Lascalles. I doubt your uncle would appreciate you being in my company.'

'Convention forces my uncle to keep me under his control.' She sighed. 'One day I will brave the censure and set myself up in a house and live alone, though I shall be cut off from polite society by such rebellion.' She curtsied to him. 'It has been a pleasure to speak with someone who is part of my father's world.'

Then with her head down and with unladylike haste she ran to the side entrance of the booth. Thomas watched her passage to ensure she was not accosted, and then followed her progress until she was seated at the back of the booth.

It was the most astonishing encounter, and he did not quite know what to make of it.

Chapter Seventeen

The fox jumped into the water of a fast-flowing stream. His coat was streaked with sweat and the cool water eased the cuts on his pads where he had sped over jagged rocks in his quest for survival. The earth rumbled and vibrated from the pounding of over a hundred horses' hoofs, their riders bent upon his destruction. There had been a brief respite as the hounds lost his trail, then they had given excited tongue as they found his scent and the pursuit continued.

He followed the course of the stream for some distance. The banks were steep and lined with trees, but these thinned towards the vast expanse of the moor. Behind him he could hear the hounds baying. An overhanging branch, thick as a tree trunk, was some feet above him. He leapt on to it, crawling on his belly along its length, then bounded on to a granite boulder, and clambered down between a cleft to peer back across the moor. The hounds were whimpering and running in circles, tumbling over themselves to find his scent. The huntsmen were blowing on their horns, and in the far distance the straggling riders caught up with the hounds.

It had been a long run covering over eight miles of meadow and woodland. The dog fox panted hard: wily, amber eyes bright; heart thundering against the pain of exhausted lungs. His pink tongue lolled through sharp white teeth revealed by his open jaw. He studied his enemies and looked as though he was grinning. The hounds were frantic to rediscover his scent, but they failed. The huntsman blew his horn, and the pack veered away in search of easier prey. The dog fox shook himself and yawned. He was the victor. It was the ninth time he had outwitted the hounds.

Elspeth cursed the hounds for losing the scent, yet the fox had led them a fine chase. It was an overcast November day, with the clouds a murky canopy above the bare branches of the trees. The ground was firm enough for a headlong gallop, though it broke up beneath the horses' hoofs, clods of earth flying up to splatter over the riders and their mounts. Elspeth was exhilarated. The pain in her hip had been blotted out in the thrill of the chase, but now as the riders waited for the hounds to give tongue the pain flared at every prance by Bracken. Elspeth lifted a hip flask to her lips, the wine laced with a pain-killing potion prepared by Senara. Squire Penwithick drew level on his grey hunter. He was sweating and covered in mud.

'Good sport, Elspeth! The best this season!'

'The day is not over yet. There's another couple of hours before the light begins to fail.'

The squire shook his head. 'I am for home. These old bones of mine cannot take too much pounding. You still ride as fearlessly as you did as a young woman.'

She laughed, pleased at his compliment. In the saddle she felt like a young woman again. She had no patience with balls or polite society; it was on the hunting field that she came alive. Hunting was her passion. Her mares never failed her, each one bold of heart with a courage to match her own. She looked round now for the stable lad from Trevowan who should have been following the hunt at a sedate pace, and leading her second mare, Griselda. She saw him and changed horses.

'Mind you take good care of Bracken,' she warned as he led her tired mare away. Now seated on Griselda, who was fresh and eager for the chase to begin, Elspeth became impatient with the hounds.

The cry went up, there was a blast of horns and they were off. Elspeth veered away from the press of less intrepid riders milling on the edge of the wood. She knew the country well from her years of experience. If the fox broke from the covert and headed across the moor towards the Druid stone as they usually did, she would be up with the hounds from the start. The smell of peat and trampled heather rose from the ground. Elspeth smelt the tang of leather and the lathery sweat as Griselda lengthened her stride. The wind fanned Elspeth's face, heightening the glow on her cheeks, and her body swayed in unison with the horse, the rhythm more exhilarating than a lover's embrace.

She could not contain a shout of joy. The excitement channelled through her like a mill race. Here she was in command, her own mistress, her ill temper and sharpness banished. The hunt fired her blood. The chase stirred passion in a heart guarded and sterile. She rode as recklessly and fearlessly as a man. The Loveday wildness, which was erased in all other areas of her life, now reigned supreme. This was her life, her fulfilment, her reason for being. Her five beloved mares were her most prized possessions – they were her children, more precious than life itself – for without them she was but half alive, a shell drained of emotion.

'There you have all the facts, Margaret. I am so sorry.' Edward had arrived at Trevowan at midday and taken his sister to his study to tell her in private the true state of her financial affairs.

Margaret sat in silence, her back ramrod straight. Although he had not expected her to succumb to hysterics, his sister's composure was disconcerting. Her pallor was accentuated by her mourning black, and after several moments of silence a shuddering breath tore through her.

'I suspected all was not well. Why did Charles not tell me, or stop me entertaining? There was no need for the new carriage to be purchased last year.' Her tone hardened. 'I am not one of those stupid women who demand every creature comfort at the expense of financial stability.'

'Appearances are everything in the banking world,' Edward reasoned. 'And Charles would have wished to spare you unnecessary worry.'

Her eyes flashed with a dangerous light. 'I thought I was his helpmeet, his confidante. This is what hurts.'

Edward placed a hand on her arm, and felt the tension in the muscles. 'Charles was a proud man. He would not have wanted to admit to you

299

that his judgement had failed him.'

'Then at least he should have told you. You have lost your money and Amelia has lost her income. Thank God Richard is protected by the trust fund. How does it affect you? You had heavy loans on the shipyard.' The pain was heavy in her voice and she pressed a beringed hand to her temple. She had lost weight and her cheeks were hollow beneath the rice powder and rouge of her make-up. Her hair was elegantly coiled but there was more grey in it since Charles's death. 'How could he do that to you? You were more than his brother by marriage. You were his friend.'

'He took desperate measures. If they had paid off we would have been applauding him for the good fortune that he had brought to us.'

'Instead, we are all ruined.'

'No. Thomas is fighting to save the bank. You should be proud of him. And the Lovedays will survive. It may be the worst financial crisis we have had to overcome – I doubt it will be the last.'

'But this was none of your doing.' Margaret blinked against welling tears, and her throat worked as she struggled to speak. 'You have lost so much. You have been so kind and worked so hard through this crisis, Edward. And it is far from over.'

'You must not worry about us. Adam has drummed up the next advances due on the ships. We shall slowly recoup our losses.'

'Adam too has suffered.' Margaret did not look convinced by her brother's cautious optimism. 'Should he not have put to sea in *Pegasus?* He cannot afford to lose out on a voyage.'

'Adam hired an able captain. He is content to fulfil his duty in the yard this winter.' Edward did not say that *Pegasus* had sailed only half laden because one of Adam's investors had backed out. The profit would be slim from her voyage.

Margaret blinked rapidly to dispel a betraying tear. Edward was glad to see that her old strength and resilience were returning. 'I am so ashamed. I can live with the loss of my own money, but so many of our friends and acquaintances will have suffered enormous losses. I do not think I can face them.'

'There is no need. You are welcome at Trevowan for as long as you wish to stay. And I believe that Thomas will find a way through. He has changed. He is taking his responsibilities seriously.'

'I knew that his playwrighting was just a phase – part of his Loveday blood which flouts convention, if you will.'

Edward did not contradict her. His long talks with Thomas had shown him that, while his nephew wanted to save the family reputation and bank, he had no intention of running the bank. Once it was stable he intended a merger or a sellout. He had been insistent that his future lay in the theatre, not the world of banking.

'From what you have told me...' Margaret faltered and again struggled to regain her composure. 'Charles was not murdered, was he? He killed himself because he could not face the people he had brought to ruin.'

Edward avoided her forthright stare. He

301

nodded. 'There was no sign of any blows to his body. He died by drowning.'

Margaret hung her head. 'Poor Charles. My poor, distraught, darling–'

Her voice broke and she held out her arms to her brother. Edward drew her close. The woman he had always known to be so strong, so in control, began to shake, then agonised sobs rent her body. She clung to him with her face pressed in to his chest.

'You must not feel any shame.' He stroked her hair. 'We are here to help you, Maggie. Mourn Charles, for he was a good man, but not any loss sustained by us.'

When the torrent finally subsided, she sniffed and wiped her eyes. Her grip was strong as she took his hand in her own. 'Can we beat this? It is a huge burden that Thomas carries. You were right to instruct him to sell what he can. Silver, paintings, jewellery are but superficial trappings of wealth. I can live without them. My needs are small. I can live as easily in a small cottage in the country as London.'

'It will not come to that. This is your home for as long as you need it.'

She managed a watery smile. 'You mean well, Edward, and have spared me much humiliation by insisting that I leave London. But I cannot abandon Thomas. He has need of me. I should be there supporting him.'

'In this I must oppose you, Margaret. Your presence at this time will put more strain upon him. I have promised to return in a few days. I came to Cornwall to speak with you about these matters. A letter would have been too brutal.'

'But Amelia has need of you here. She does not complain but her pregnancy saps much of her strength.'

That was a blow Edward was not expecting and his fear for his wife's health overwhelmed him. 'Is Chegwidden concerned that all is not well with her or the child?'

'No, indeed not,' Margaret hastened to reassure. 'Dr Chegwidden insists all is well but has ordered that Amelia rests every afternoon and does not exert herself. All this worry over finances cannot be good for her. I pray it will not cause her any harm.'

'Amelia's concern will be for you and Thomas. But of course the family must now be told of the severity of our circumstances. I had instructed Adam to say little until my return.'

Margaret hesitated as though unwilling to place another burden on his shoulders. 'There have been arguments between Adam and St John. And St John has been acting strangely these last few days.'

Edward sighed. 'I will talk to St John next. I do not want any ill feeling between my sons while I am in London.'

St John appeared in his study before Edward even had to summon him. He held a casket and placed it on the battered Jacobean table Edward used as a desk. 'Adam told me of our financial troubles. This should help.'

Edward studied him with scepticism and flipped back the lid of the casket. His eyes

303

widened in surprise. 'There must be three hundred pounds here. Where has it come from? Gambling?'

St John raised a brow and flushed, but did not take offence. 'A venture. A very successful one, as it happened. It should help you meet some of the loan payments, I believe.'

'Indeed,' Edward was impressed. 'This is most generous, St John.'

'I do have a regard for my future inheritance, sir.'

Edward spread his hands wide. 'Where did this money come from?'

St John hesitated to answer and Edward noticed that he appeared to be favouring one arm. 'Have you injured yourself in some way?'

'The venture was not without its dangers,' St John evaded. To tell his father the true story could not be done without also informing him of the vendetta against Lanyon and his own earlier involvement with the smugglers. Edward would demand to know how he had then raised the money for that venture. He was not about to admit that he had taken some old Loveday silver from the attic and pawned it to finance his share. Better to let his father believe it had been a smuggling run. If Edward learned of the ambush on Lanyon's cargo, he doubted his father would link the two events. At least he prayed not. Edward would never countenance robbery, no matter what the reason.

'St John, have you become involved with smugglers?' Edward accused.

'I invested some of my legacy in free trading. It

has paid off. I know you do not approve, which is why I have kept it from you.'

'Indeed, I do not approve. It is madness.'

St John held his glare. 'The trade is profitable. I am not the first of our family to have replenished our coffers from the trade.'

Edward shook his head. 'Not in my or your grandfather's time.'

'And we have never been so close to losing everything.'

Father and son glared at each other across the desk. Edward on the attack, St John defensive and outraged that his sacrifice had earned him only censure.

'Are the Sawles involved in this?' Edward demanded. 'I suppose this is the cause of your quarrels with Adam. Did your wound make him suspicious? Did he make you pay over this money?'

'Either you want the money, or you do not.' St John's temper erupted. He had forfeited the money with ill grace and Meriel had been sulking all day over the amount he intended to offer his father. He had seen it as a noble gesture and had not expected this ridicule. 'I cannot live on the pittance I receive. I have my own household to maintain.'

'The expenses of which have been met by the estate,' Edward reminded him.

'I am of age, sir. My life is mine to do with as I will. I offered you this money with good intent.'

Edward had spoken out of fear for his son. He nodded and sighed. 'It is appreciated, though not its source. I would not see you endanger yourself.

It is a violent trade. And you were wounded. How did that happen?'

'We were fired upon by the excise officers. It is but a scratch.' St John turned away at this further lie. 'If the money will help you, sir, I hope you will take it.'

Despite his reservations, Edward revised his opinion about St John. He had always thought his older son lacked the adventuresome spirit he admired in Adam. It took courage to engage in the free trade but, although the rewards were high, the consequences could be dire.

'We do need this money. That does not mean I approve of your dealings with free traders. We have had a good harvest this year, due largely to your efforts. Honest toil is the more valiant labour. When I return to London I trust there will be no more quarrelling with your brother. A family is strong only in unity. Do you agree?'

'Yes, sir.'

'Good, for I shall need your co-operation. These are difficult times for us. Expenditure must be drastically cut.'

'I understand that but I have the means to support my family. We do not wish for the Dower House to be closed.'

'I can pay for none of its expenses,' Edward warned. 'Even your allowance will have to be cut.'

'You will not have to sell any land, will you?' Since his fight with Adam, St John feared that his inheritance would be lost.

'Not this year, but unless our financial situation improves, I may have to. As yet I do not want to cause speculation that the yard is in trouble. We could lose custom. Any changes made on the estate will be explained as innovative ideas on your part. The land itself must yield more profit. Two more fields will be put to the plough. The dairy herd will have to go. The bull will fetch a good price and, with some of the money from the sale of the herd, I shall increase the sheep stock which is less labour intensive.'

'But we will need more labourers to work the land.' St John was antagonistic. 'I work like a slave as it is.'

'As shall we all to overcome this,' Edward insisted. 'There's workmen enough with the Holman, Nance and Tonkin families living in tied cottages. I shall spend more time on the estate while Adam is at the yard.' He regarded St John sternly. 'And it is time your wife showed her capabilities. Four dozen bantams should lay well and provide enough eggs for the market. There's land behind the Dower House to build the coops. If she does not agree then I will close the Dower House, whether you can afford to maintain it or not.'

'I do not see the need for my wife to work, sir,' St John answered stiffly.

'But I do.'

'And will Amelia and Aunt Elspeth be dirtying their hands with menial work?' St John shouted.

'That is enough of your insolence!' Edward dismissed his son.

On reflection St John considered that he had got off lightly. He had no intention of quitting the trade. Meriel would just have to comply with their father's wishes.

The next interview Edward had to face was with Amelia. She had spoken to Margaret while he had been with St John and when she entered his study she put her arms around him. 'We will get through this.'

'Are you aware how bad our situation is, my love?'

She nodded. 'Margaret explained. She is distraught that I have lost so much. She feels our friendship has been betrayed, which is nonsense. Charles did not set out to ruin us.'

'At least Richard's trust fund could not be touched.' Edward studied his wife, fearful that the shock might harm her or the baby in some way. 'There will be no income from your properties for some years. Once the naval frigate is completed, the loan can be paid off on the yard. This time next year, it will be showing a profit. We are not destitute. But there is the mortgage interest to be met on the house apart from the loans on the yard.'

Though she looked strained and pale, there was fervour in her eyes. 'We have each other, my love. My main concern was for Richard, but it is many years before he comes of age. I am only concerned that Richard's school fees to Winchester can be met, for it was his father's wish that Richard attend his old school. I have emerald and diamond necklaces which can be sold.'

He took her hands. 'That will help but I fear will be nowhere near enough to cover every-thing.'

Edward led her to a chair and leaned against his desk opposite her. Did he worry about her unnecessarily? Amelia's auburn hair had a luxuriant shine to it and her skin was clear and blooming, her eyes bright and sparkling. Her pregnancy was beginning to show and her fuller figure suited her. His heart was heavy. 'I fear I have failed you, my love.'

'No, Edward, never that.' Her eyes were bright with fear as she stared at him. Amelia had been at her wits' end dreading what this meeting would bring. It had brought to bear her worst fears, but somehow with Edward beside her, she found the strength to be strong.

'I want to do what is best,' she offered. 'I have an idea to have some of the lawn dug up behind the stables and plant a fruit bed: raspberries, red- and blackcurrants which can be preserved. I can also keep bees. My father did when I was a child and I used to help him. We could have a dozen hives and sell the honey at market.'

He was amazed at her versatility. 'Amelia, I could not expect so much from you. For Meriel it is different. She was born to such work.'

'Please let me do this. I shall enjoy it.' She was putting on a brave face for she had been shocked at how haggard Edward looked. Suddenly all her fears for their future threatened to overwhelm her. Her hands shook. 'I know you are trying to spare me, but I can see how tense and worried you are, my love. I am not some useless appendage. I am not afraid of a little hardship.'

Then her courage deserted her and tears rolled down her cheek. Edward gathered her in his arms and kissed her hair, holding her close. 'I have been so worried. And I missed you so much,' she sobbed. 'Now when I must be strong for you, I am so weak.'

He murmured words of endearment and encouragement. She dabbed at her eyes and then there was a hard jab from inside her stomach followed by another. She gasped. Then cried out, 'The baby is kicking me! Oh, Edward, I was so frightened all was not well with it.'

She took his hand and placed it over her stomach. 'See how hard your child kicks me? It is a sign. I feel it. All will be well, both with our child and for ourselves.'

Edward was about to leave his study when he heard Elspeth's cane tapping on the marble floor of the hall. This would be another difficult meeting, but he must get it over with.

He opened the door of his study and saw Elspeth flushed from the hunt. Her riding habit was splashed with mud and several splodges were on her cheek. Although she was limping badly she looked jubilant.

'Edward, you are back! About time too. We drew a fox in Four Acre Wood and he gave us a fine chase across the moor. That old rascal got away but we drew another. Fine sport indeed! You should hunt more yourself, brother. You are looking too peaky by far.'

When he did not reply but stood rigid, his manner guarded, she felt her first twinge of unease. It prompted her to bluster, 'Now, what is all this about Charles's bank and the cutbacks we have to follow here?'

'Come into my study, Elspeth.'

The exhilaration from her ride drained from her. Edward was looking strained, his manner too serious for her comfort. For Elspeth, the best form of defence had always been attack. 'Matters not too good, then? I have gathered together all my jewellery. I want you to have it. It is to be sold. My mares cost a great deal to feed and I will not have them a burden on you.'

'It will not be as simple as that, Elspeth.' Edward looked distraught and fidgeted with the inkwell on his desk. 'This is so hard to say. I can never repay you for the years you were mistress here, managing the house without complaint and in the most efficient manner.'

'I will not sell any of my mares. Edward?' she confronted him with a stony-faced hauteur which masked her inner quaking and the icy pincers gripping her heart.

'I am afraid you must. It is not just their upkeep. They are valuable animals. You may keep one of them. The others will be sold to meet some of our debts.'

Her lip trembled and she shook her head in emphatic denial. 'No! You cannot ask so much. They are everything to me.'

'I know your sacrifice will be hard.'

His voice came to her from a great distance. Edward could not be asking this of her.

'They are not the only horses we must sell. Amelia's carriage horses will go and her carriage. Japhet has given me the name of a reputable horse-dealer who will be arriving next week.'

311

'But my darlings cannot be sold off to just anyone. I could not sleep at night fearing that they will be ill-treated.' Tears dripped from her eyes. The stalwart armour which shielded her emotions had been chipped away, leaving her pain raw and exposed. 'You cannot mean to treat me so shabbily, Edward. Please! Not my mares! Do not make me sell the mares.'

Edward groaned and put his hand on his sister's shoulder. She shook it off and glared at him, her eyes piercing in their intensity and accusation. Her pain flowed out of her, buffeting him in waves before she slumped in the chair in utter despair. He could have coped with it better if Elspeth had railed at him as he had expected. This was so unlike her; he knew how deeply she must be hurting. Edward hated to cause her so much misery and forced himself to remain firm. 'If there was any other way, I would not ask you to sacrifice so much. Perhaps you could keep two of them, but the rest must go.'

'But not to any horse-dealer.' Some of her spirit returned. She shuddered and her knuckles whitened over the handle of her cane as she faced him. The pain was still in her eyes but so was a brittle glint of determination. 'I will sell my mares myself to owners whom I know will care for them.'

'Will that not be more painful for you?'

She glared at him as though he was a fool. 'What could be more painful than losing my darlings? At least this way I will know that they will be well cared for.'

'I am sorry, Elspeth.'

She stood up and when he stepped forward to take her in his arms, she avoided his touch. With only two horses she would not be able to hunt so often, for she could be invited to join three or four hunts a week. Her body stiff with the effort needed to hold her emotions and tears in check, she walked in silence from the room.

Edward sank down on to the chair Elspeth had vacated and dropped his head into his hands. Anger raked through his entrails and heart, vicious as talons. In London he had had to be strong for Thomas's sake, and facing his family now he could not let emotion distract him from what must be done, however painful, to survive this financial disaster. But he was furious at Charles for causing all this heartache to the people he loved, and also for bringing him so close to ruin. Trevowan was a large estate and house which gobbled up money to maintain it. They had never been immensely wealthy like some of their aristocratic neighbours, but for generations the Lovedays had worked hard to build up their position in society. Charles's recklessness with their money had undermined the foundations of his home and business. The cutbacks and sale of possessions that he'd planned would do little more than paper over the cracks. A few months ago Edward had felt that his life and the future of his estate and yard were rising to a greater eminence. Charles had destroyed all that. His fist slammed into his open palm in an outward expression of anger.

He got up and poured himself a large brandy. He would also have to reduce greatly the allowance he paid to his brother, Joshua, to supplement his meagre stipend. That would cause Joshua and Cecily some hardship, but at least now that Japhet, Hannah and Peter had left home, Joshua no longer had to support his children. The warming liquid soothed his frayed nerves and took the pain from his frustration.

Although the loans on the shipyard were crippling the family now, the expansion and the increased work attracted by Adam's innovative designs would be their salvation. Once they overcame this present crisis, Edward could gradually begin to restore all that had been sacrificed and lost.

The final payment on Lanyon's cutter had not been paid. Adam was angry. Since the loss of the cargo, Lanyon was having difficulty raising the money. St John had made the grand gesture of handing over a sizeable portion of his profits from that night to their father, but it did not match the money owed by Lanyon. Adam needed that money to meet expenses. Today he ordered that work be stopped on the cutter, and had sent Seth Wakeley's eldest lad, Timmy, to Penruan with a note informing Lanyon that no further work would be done until the money was received.

He was by the dry dock supervising the refloating of a merchant brig whose hull had been scraped and repainted, the lower planks recaulked with oakum and sealed with lead. The gates of the dry dock had been opened earlier, allowing the dock to fill with the incoming tide.

314

Ropes were rowed across to the opposite bank of the inlet and attached to the winch which would pull the merchant brig in to mid-channel. The owner's skeleton crew were already on board to sail the brig back to Falmouth. The owner was an old customer with four merchant ships, but one of his vessels had been lost at sea in the last year and he had asked for an extension on the payment of the brig until his next ship docked in two months. Adam had agreed, but the delay was causing further problems.

Clem and Harry Sawle's fishing lugger was the next vessel to be overhauled in the dry dock. Harry's recovery from his wounds was slow, and Adam had agreed to do the work ahead of other orders, as the Sawles needed an excuse why Harry was not at sea with the rest of the fleet. At least Clem had paid in advance for the work.

Adam snapped the ledger shut with suppressed fury. The next payment due from an owner was not payable for two months. He still had to meet the men's wages. Also the stores in the Ship kiddleywink needed replenishing.

The last landlord had died two years ago. To add to his investments in Trevowan Hard, Adam had restocked the kiddleywink with a greater range of groceries and necessities. It saved the families now living there from making the long journey to Penruan for provisions. A new landlord, Toby Jansen, had been bosun on Uncle William's frigate, HMS *Neptune*, until he had lost an eye and an arm during a run-in with pirates off the coast of Malta. Jansen had served with William for fifteen years and on his discharge

315

from the navy, William had written to Edward asking if there was any work suitable for the bosun in the yard. Toby Jansen and his wife, Prudence, worked hard to make a success of the inn, grateful that Toby had been given a chance to earn an honest living with such a disability.

St John had jeered at the appointment. 'How can the yard be a success while you employ cripples? You've already that carpenter who has a wooden leg.'

'Seth Wakeley may have lost the use of a leg but he is skilled with his hands,' Adam had answered. 'Seth now has his son, Timmy, and Jojo Tonkin from Trevowan as his apprentices, and is teaching them his trade. That is good for the yard. And Prudence Jansen is as much a driving force within the Ship as Sal Sawle is at the Dolphin.'

Adam had never regretted accepting his father's advice to employ Toby Jansen. The Ship kiddley-wink had proved a good investment and another room had been built on to it to accommodate the extra stock. They also attracted customers from the local farms and Trewenna.

The expansion of the Ship kiddleywink had meant loss of business for Thadeous Lanyon, which had added to the ill feeling between the two families. It had been a surprise when Lanyon came to Edward Loveday for an order for the cutter. But since they were the only yard at that time producing such a vessel, Lanyon must have swallowed his pride to commission the Lovedays to build it.

Adam had spent hours juggling the repayment of bills. If Lanyon defaulted on this payment, the men would have to be put on half-pay.

This was a side of the business from which he received no satisfaction. When a man was laid off, his family could starve. The lessons of the last weeks had taught Adam a great deal about the financial acumen and need of careful scheduling to run an efficient and profitable yard. It had been invaluable training, for the overheads of a shipyard were immense. When Adam inherited the yard, he would not have the income from the Trevowan estate to help support it during any time of crisis.

A sudden sleet storm had the men running for their oilskins; it meant that the work would progress even more slowly. On his way back to the yard office, Adam was hailed by Timmy Wakeley. The boy was drenched and Adam ushered him in to the warmth. 'Stand by the fire, lad, and tell me what Mr Lanyon said when you delivered my message.'

Timmy rolled his eyes. 'Mr Lanyon said you were to go immediately to the shop to discuss the matter.'

'Did he indeed?' Adam said, his own temper sliding. 'Go home, Timmy, and get those wet clothes off.'

When the boy ran out Adam stared at the rain streaming down the window pane. Who the devil did Lanyon think he was, summoning him like a lackey? The terms of his note were clear. Work would resume on the cutter as soon as the money was paid. Lanyon could damn well come to him if there was a problem.

Adam knew he was being unreasonable, for

with any other customer, he would not hesitate to renegotiate terms. But he suspected that Lanyon would demand the release of the vessel without the final payment being made. And Lanyon would then delay that payment for as long as possible. Let Lanyon wait.

Adam was too angry to be reasonable. If the money had not arrived in a week he would visit the smuggler's banker then. No matter how much he needed the money, he refused to go grovelling to Thadeous Lanyon. All the while the cutter remained at the yard, Lanyon could not use it to outrun the revenue men. Lanyon was capable of raising a loan. Let him pay the exorbitant interest rates charged on those moneys. He had charged high enough rates himself when others were desperate for funds.

Chapter Eighteen

Nothing happened in Penruan that was not chewed over or gossiped about. What else was there to do to relieve the boredom of the long winter months, when rough seas prevented the fishing fleet setting sail? During the past month Lanyon had provided great amusement for the villagers at his anger over Adam Loveday's refusal to release his cutter. There was an underlying battle of wills between Lanyon and the Lovedays. Lanyon was obviously seeking to usurp their position of supremacy within the village. Many had toasted Adam's stand when Lanyon finally paid his dues to the yard and took possession of this new ship.

The tension between Lanyon and the Sawles was also mounting. Clem and Harry, who was still drinking heavily, openly ridiculed Lanyon for his new pretensions.

To confirm his superiority, Lanyon took to parading Hester in her finery through the village in their new carriage. Gossip thrived, for few in Penruan were overfond of either the Sawles or Lanyon, both of whom had inflicted their own brand of fear on most of the villagers, the Sawles through physical pain to any who dared cross them; Thadeous Lanyon by causing financial strain to their meagre pockets with his high interest rates on any credit given in his shops.

When both families brought a strange woman into the community, the gossip intensified. Strangers were always viewed with suspicion, especially in a village where a man's wanderings on a moonlit night were the subject of secrecy. Strangers were avoided and treated as outcasts. That two should arrive within a week of each other caused both speculation and concern.

After a business trip, Lanyon returned with Phyllis Tamblin, a shy waif, fifteen years old, hired as a housemaid. She had pretty delicate features, doleful brown eyes and sandy hair. Many jeered that Phyllis Tamblin's slight build made her a poor choice for the heavy work of a maid.

'With her pretty looks she'll be more than a housemaid in that employ,' Clem sniggered in

319

the taproom of the Dolphin.

Barney Rundle swigged back his beer. 'If she be a maid now she won't be a maid for long. Not the way Lanyon can't keep his hands off the women.'

'I would have thought Hester were woman enough for him,' Joseph Roche added, but looked over his shoulder to check that Harry was not around.

Clem glowered at him and Joseph made a great show of ordering both Barney and Clem a drink.

'That baggage Hester will get what she deserves out of that marriage,' Clem announced, 'and I doubt it will bring her happiness. Harry were well shot of the scheming trollop.'

A week later Clem drew up at the Dolphin in a farm wagon which was laden with furniture, a fierce-looking billy goat tied behind. It butted the tailgate as soon as the wagon stopped. Beside Clem sat an Amazon of a woman. He lifted her down and took her through to the full taproom.

'This be Keziah, my wife. You'll bid her welcome and accept her amongst us.'

Sal put down the tankard she was filling at the bar to regard the woman. Keziah was a strapping, large-boned woman in her mid-twenties and was only a handbreadth under two yards high. Her wiry shoulder-length hair, the colour of amber, was worn contrary to fashion; and to Sal's mind, contrary to decency, as it hung loose and uncovered.

'This then be the farmer's widow you've been seeing, son. It would have been nice to be at your wedding.'

'Kezzy wanted it kept simple. No fuss,' Clem stated. 'We wed over Polgarra. The farm were sold up and we'll be living here for a time.'

'You be welcome, Keziah,' Sal said. Further speech was cut short at a braying and sudden scattering of men from round the door. Sal screamed, seeing the devil himself rearing up on his hind legs and his horns glinting in the candlelight.

Someone grabbed a stool and raised it above their head to strike the avenging demon.

Keziah grabbed hold of the man and flung him to one side. 'What do you think you be at, man? That be my goat, Baltasar. A prize billy he be. Sired dozens of kids.'

'I thought it were Satan himself,' Sal groaned. A lantern hanging from a beam swung erratically, where it had been knocked in the scuffle. It threw shadows over her round face, still showing signs of shock. 'Get that beast out of here. A pub bain't no place for such an animal.'

Baltasar continued to butt and charge the men. Three had leapt up on to benches and two had run outside. The goat was between the door and the rest of the drinkers' and several were trying to squeeze behind the bar out of the way of his horns.

Keziah elbowed her way through. 'Quit that yelling. You be frightening Baltasar.' She made a mewing noise and caught at the rope around the goat's neck, which had been chewed through. Then taking an apple from her pocket, she fed him and scratched his forehead until the beast quietened. 'He be quite tame. Don't like strangers, though. Like most people, I guess.' She pulled on the rope and led the goat outside and he followed as obediently as any trained dog.

'Well, I be...' Barney Rundle wiped his sweating brow as he climbed down from the bench he had leapt on. 'Evil-looking bugger, bain't it?'

Sal laughed, recovering her wits. 'That were some way to introduce your bride, Clem. She'll have made an impression in the village.'

When Keziah reappeared, Sal ushered her through to the kitchen. 'You must be parched. I've got some tea saved. Let me brew you some.'

'Never touch the stuff. But I'll have a quart of your fine ale. Used to make my own cider, but a quart of ale will serve me a treat.'

Sal fetched the ale from the bar and Reuban ambled into the kitchen after her.

'It be time our Clem were wed,' Sal said. 'You be a comely wench. Strong-minded too. Got a tidy sum from the sale of your farm, I suppose?'

'Aye, some. I be putting some of it to use in Penruan.' Keziah had a piercing blue stare which held a trace of amusement at Sal's question. 'We be buying a cottage on the side of the coombe with two fields behind it. I shall breed the goats and sell their produce as I did afore.'

'That be Blackthorn Cottage, the old Pasmore place. There be a lot of work to do on it,' Sal advised. 'Been empty for years. It be a fair climb up from the harbour.'

'That do suit me fine. I know village folk – get uppity about strangers. I be happy to keep my distance.'

'The woods behind the cottage got a reputation

for being haunted,' Barney Rundle took pleasure in informing her. He was still shaking from the fright Baltasar had given him.

'Those woods would make a good place to hide contraband. Such places be the haunt of smugglers not ghosts. I reckon Baltasar be a match for either if they trespass on my land.'

Within a month Clem and she had moved into Blackthorn Cottage. Keziah dressed better than most women in the village, but without the ostentation adopted by Hester Lanyon. She had a long, bouncing stride, in her lace-up boots, which set her large breasts quivering with each step.

When she walked through the village she greeted everyone with a cheery welcome, taking no offence if they refused to reply. Often she was seen leading Baltasar, and his presence made the villagers give her a wide berth. The wariness of the villagers amused Keziah. 'You'll get used to me soon enough, my lovelies,' she would call after them with a throaty laugh.

Once the fields behind Blackthorn Cottage were fenced, Keziah left the village for two days and returned herding a dozen nanny goats through the street. 'These be my beauties,' she called to any who stared at her. 'Wait till you taste the cheeses I make from their milk.'

'You can keep it,' Ginny Rundle sneered. 'Sour-tasting stuff.'

'Not *my* cheese, my lovely,' Keziah chirped. 'Can't make it fast enough for the grand folk taking the waters in Bath. I do have a customer has it sent regular on the mail coach to his shop there. Bain't that just something?'

Ginny Rundle shook her head, not sure what to make of Keziah Sawle. Neither, if they were asked, did anyone else in the village. Except Sal who, though she kept her opinions to herself, reckoned that Clem had finally met his match with Keziah. Whether that created a marriage made in heaven, or a marriage made in hell, only time would tell.

Since the arrival of Phyllis Tamblin, Hester's life had become even more unbearable. Thadeous, not satisfied with bedding the new maid, had suggested that she join them in their marriage bed. His attentions were vile enough, but the perversion he suggested was too much to endure. So far, Hester's protests had been honoured, but Thadeous had become more surly, and his demands on her more brutal. She suffered in silence. Her only escape from her misery was by creating a fantasy world in which Harry rescued her.

She began to watch her former lover from afar. She had noted the recent change in Harry. He was thinner and had lost the bold swagger she had so adored. Was it true what Meriel had told her? Did Harry still love her? It gave her hope.

Hester scanned the harbour from the shop window. Thadeous insisted that she spend more time there and had dismissed the shop girl. As the daughter of George Moyle, the chandler, Hester was used to shop work, but that work had been shared between the family, as were the household duties between her sister, Annie, and herself. Thadeous never served a customer unless they were either important or pretty. Hester was treated as no better than a skivvy.

The fishing fleet had returned two hours ago and although it was almost dark Harry was still on his lugger doing some repair work on the sail rigging. She kept returning to the window to stare with longing at his broad-shouldered figure as he worked. The sun caught his blond hair, whipping it around his bronzed face, and her heart ached to gather him to her breast. She had been such a fool. How she missed him – yearned for him.

The need to see him became overwhelming. Thadeous had gone to the Gun to collect the takings from the landlord. He always stayed for a drink and was not expected back at the house for an hour. Rebellion stirred in Hester and with it a deeper need. She would close the shop early.

With a shawl covering her red hair and pulled low over her face, Hester waited by the quay. She could hear movement on Harry's boat, but there were other fishermen stowing their nets and she did not wish their meeting observed.

She was shivering with cold when Harry finally appeared. It was dark now. The moon was obscured by heavy cloud and only the faint lights behind shuttered windows brought any illumination to the village. When she saw Harry jump on the quay, she called softly to him. Harry paused, then walked on. The quay was deserted but she remained in the shadows.

'Please, Harry, don't walk away. I must speak with you. I be sorry for what I did. It was madness and I be paying for it.'

'You made me a laughing stock,' Harry ground out. He stood in front of her with his arms folded. 'A man would have paid dearly for that.'

'I be paying, Harry.' She moved forward to stand close to him. 'I be in torment. I allowed my temper to override my reason. I was hurt when you were seeing that dairymaid. Lanyon promised me so much. I never meant to wed him. I flirted with him to make you jealous. Then I sort of got caught up in events, and did not see how I could back down.'

He did not speak, neither did he move away, giving her the courage to continue.

'I love you, Harry. I always have. I'm so miserable.' She began to sob and swayed against him.

Harry caught her in his arms and pulled her into an alley between the pilchard sheds. 'You know what Lanyon will do if he finds you with me?'

'I don't care. I love you. I can't live if you continue to hate me.'

Desperation swept over her and Hester began to kiss him. When he did not pull away, her passion cast restraint aside. Her fingers tore at his clothing, her tongue and lips hungry for the taste of him. Only Harry could cleanse her of the corruption which Lanyon inflicted upon her.

His response was as ardent as she desired. He pulled two buttons from her bodice in his eagerness to free her breasts and then his hands hoisted her skirts to her waist and he thrust her back against the wall to enter her. She clung to him in the throes of passion. 'Oh, Harry, what a fool I've been. There's never been no one like you. Do you still love me?'

He did not answer, but the force of his kisses plunged them both into another passionate frenzy. When finally they drew apart, Hester's body glowed and she felt alive as she had not done since she married Lanyon. 'What are we to do, Harry?'

'Bide our time, sweetheart. Bide our time.'

'But I can't stay with Lanyon.'

'You must till I can settle the score with him.'

'Why can't we run away? We could start a new life.' Fear shivered through her voice.

'That is a woman's way,' he scoffed. 'Not mine. Lanyon wronged me. He must pay. Penruan is *my* home. He be the usurper.'

Hester wrapped her shawl tight around her, and was frightened by his words. 'Lanyon is powerful. How can you strike at him and not end up in gaol?'

'It will take time.' He remained adamant.

Hester backed away from him. 'Do you not care how I must suffer at his hands? His touch is repellent.'

'For that alone I could kill him. But I'd be the first the law suspected. If we are to have any life together, we must triumph over him.'

The seeds Meriel had sown in his mind during the week he had been bedridden had taken root. The pain he still suffered from his wound was a constant reminder of his hatred for Thadeous Lanyon.

He looked over her head to take in all Lanyon's

property throughout the village: the pilchard sheds, the shop, the Gun Inn – all shadowy forms against the hill of the coombe. Those were the visible assets. There was also his wealth, the new cutter and his hold over the smuggling trade in this part of the country. Hester, as the widow of the owner of all this, would bring her new husband the realisation of a dream. It would be the ultimate revenge.

But in this Harry knew he must tread carefully. It would take time to arrange Lanyon's death without any suspicion falling upon himself. In the meantime he could enjoy Hester and savour making a cuckold of his enemy.

Every day Thomas spent two hours in one of a few chosen coffee-houses in London. These establishments were a favourite meeting place for businessmen and gentry. Here men of like interests could discuss business affairs, politics and the news of the day. Thomas had followed Japhet's idea of writing scenarios for his acting friends to play the parts of investors. During his first visit many of the bankers and businessmen present regarded him suspiciously. Thomas had greeted them warmly and exchanged a few pleasantries.

'Thought you would be closeted in your bank, Mercer, trying to balance your books,' Meredith Lascalles jeered, and there was a peal of laughter from his companions.

Thomas ignored it and sat in a booth in a quiet corner. He was nervous and aware that he must not overplay his hand. The atmosphere was more congenial and refined than in a tavern. Each time, the ruse enacted by his friends was different. On that first occasion he had simply had a blackamoor dressed in livery with a crest badge on his sleeve, which indicated that he belonged to a nobleman, enter the coffee-house.

The actor had demanded haughtily, 'Is Mr Thomas Mercer present?'

Thomas had not immediately responded, allowing the blackamoor's entrance to have greater effect. He'd remained engrossed in reading a newssheet.

'I was informed that Mr Mercer, the banker, would be here,' the actor had declared even louder as he strode through the groups of men gathered around the tables. 'Her Grace is most insistent that she meet with him today to discuss a new business proposition before she leaves for the country. Has anyone seen Mr Mercer, if he is not here?'

'Mercer is over there,' Lascalles had grudgingly offered, 'but her Grace would do better to take her business elsewhere.' Lascalles had squinted to make out the crest on the actor's sleeve, desperate to see which ducal house he belonged to, but the blackamoor had twitched his winter cloak over his arm so that it was not easily discernible. 'May I offer my services?'

The actor had looked Lascalles up and down. 'And who may you be, sir?'

'Meredith Lascalles. Our bank is–'

'Not of the same class of clientele as Mercer's, I believe. Her Grace insisted that Mr Mercer attend her. The Countess of Hetherington recommended his bank.'

Thomas had stood up as the liveried black-amoor scanned the room. 'I am Thomas Mercer. How may I be of service to her Grace?'

The servant had delivered a letter to him, which Thomas had opened and read. 'I would not keep her Grace waiting. I shall attend her at once.' He'd strode from the coffee-house, aware of several astonished faces watching him.

On other occasions he had asked his friends to dress as wealthy businessmen and they had spent an hour or more speaking of investments. The disguised actor, on leaving, would be effusive.

'I could not seek a better investment, sir! You came most highly recommended. I see I shall not be disappointed.'

Gradually, as other scenarios were played out, the bankers themselves began to approach Thomas and discuss current investments and dividends.

'You seem to be doing very well,' one of his rivals commented. 'There were some unpleasant rumours when your father died.'

'All false.' Thomas allowed his anger to show. 'My father's name was smeared when he was unable to defend himself.'

'Glad to hear it. If one bank fails it can cause panic in the City and others will go down.'

Thomas hoped that the reputation of Mercer's Bank was beginning to recover, but new customers were slow in approaching him. Then he had the idea of attracting the French *émigrés*. Each week more appeared in London, many of them with part of their fortunes intact. Today

Thomas had chosen a coffee-house popular with the *émigrés*. He had mixed with some on other visits, commiserating with them on their misfortunes, and mentioning his kinship with the Rivieres in Paris.

'Claude Riviere, when he was alive, had extensive contacts in England. We were proud to be his London bankers,' he pointed out. Thomas knew that foreign countrymen in an alien land tended to band together. If he could attract a few of the wealthier *émigrés* to bank with him, others would follow.

Thomas glanced round the coffee-house and was satisfied to see many of the tables crowded with Frenchmen. After leaving Cambridge University he had spent a year travelling through France and Italy before he took up a position at the bank. He could speak fluent French, which would be an asset, for many of the bankers needed an interpreter.

The coffee-house was situated in a busy alleyway close to St. Paul's and Cheapside. The interior, as with so many of them, was dingy, and lit candles dripped wax from their sconces on the walls. The level of voices could be deafening at times during heated debates, and the two serving-maids were kept busy by constant demands for refreshment or food.

Thomas looked up as a shadow passed over his table. An elderly man stood before him in an old-fashioned periwig with gold lace edging his tricorn hat, and his fingers adorned with a half-dozen rings with stones as large as nutmegs.

'Monsieur Mercer, I am the Comte de Beauville,' he announced in a booming, heavily accented voice. 'I have been in your country since one week. My countrymen tell me that you are friend of the *émigrés*, and that it is to your bank I must entrust the care of my money.' He snapped his fingers and two footmen stepped forward to place a large casket on to the table. 'Here is my money. Twenty thousand gold Louis. You count it and give me a receipt, *oui?* Your bank can deal with the goldsmiths for me. Goldsmiths are rogues: I do not deal with such fellows. You will obtain the best price for my money? I think this will be so.'

Thomas bit his lip to stop himself smiling. Under the wig, grey bushy eyebrows and skilfully applied make-up to age a young face, Thomas recognised Lucien. From the sparkle in his friend's eyes, it was evident he was enjoying himself.

'My dear Comte, I cannot possibly count your money here. Have your servants take it to my bank. That is where I do business. And certainly I will obtain the best price from the goldsmith for you.'

'*Mon Dieu!*' Lucien executed an imperial wave as he turned to take in his surroundings. 'I thought it most odd that a man who has such a formidable reputation in the City should conduct his business here. This is where my friends said you would be found. I do not know your English ways.'

Everyone in the coffee-house was watching them. Thomas stood up, his face flushed at Lucien's outrageous manner, fearing that his friend had gone too far. A glance at some of the businessmen showed him that they were amused, for the French *émigrés* were often a source of ridicule in the City, with their foreign manners and habits. Yet their manners were no more affected than some English nobles.

Lucien waved his arms to dismiss the servants. 'Away. Make haste. Take that to Mercer's Bank. I have much to do this day.' He turned his back to the customers in the coffee-house and winked at Thomas.

Thomas bowed to him. 'I shall meet you at Mercer's Bank in half an hour and we will discuss your business in private.'

As Lucien strode imperiously towards the street, several bankers clamoured around him, beseeching him not to make so hasty a decision and that the doors of their bank would be open to him. He put up his hands and gave a theatrical shudder. '*Mon Dieu,* you bay around me like the *canaille* of Paris who have driven me from my beloved country. Be gone, *canaille!* Be gone! Monsieur Mercer is a man of integrity and dignity. My business is with him.'

Lucien swept out to the street and snapped his fingers to summon a sedan chair to convey him to Mercer's Bank. As Thomas hurried to follow him, three *émigrés* called him across to their table.

'You have many of our countrymen banking with you, is that not so?' a thin-faced Frenchman asked.

'That is so, monsieur.'

'Then I too think it is appropriate that I discuss

my financial position with you.'

'I shall be delighted. I am free at four this afternoon, if that is convenient.'

An appointment was made and one other of the men at the table made an appointment with him for the next morning.

As Thomas progressed towards the street, he saw Sir Absalom Grimshaw glaring at him from the window seat of the coffee-house. Thomas paused, tipped his high beaver hat to the baronet, and bowed, unable to resist a gibe: 'Good day, Sir Absalom! A fine day, is it not?' He was not referring to the weather for it was overcast.

The baronet grunted. 'I might be paying your bank a visit myself, Mercer. Happen I was hasty in withdrawing my cash. What interest rate are you offering?'

'Our interest is higher than that of any of our competitors if you wish to lodge a set sum with us for a period of no less than two years. There are also other favourable rates and investments for you to consider.'

Sir Absalom glowered at him, his greed battling against his suspicions that Mercer's Bank was still unsound. In recent weeks it had been the talk of the coffee-houses how popular Thomas Mercer was proving with investors. 'Happen I'll think it over. I'll discuss it with you tomorrow at ten.'

'Be so kind as to make it at midday. I have other appointments until then. Your servant, sir.' He bowed to Sir Absalom and, although he hated the man for the rumours he had spread about the bank and his father, Thomas was in no position

334

to turn down a customer with his amount of money to invest. Besides, Sir Absalom was a gossip and if he returned as a bank customer many others could follow.

For the first time since he had taken over the bank, Thomas felt the burden lighten on his shoulders. Thanks to Japhet, his ruse had paid off. The stuffy, snobbish bankers had been hoodwinked by a group of actors whom men like Lascalles despised.

Chapter Nineteen

It was an autumn and winter of contentment for Senara. She had not expected Adam to be home for so long, although she regretted the troubles which had instigated it. Edward Loveday had returned to Cornwall, and Senara hoped that there would be less pressure upon Adam. This was the first night she had agreed to stay at Mariner's House.

She hummed to herself as she swept and dusted Gideon Meadows' living rooms. The furniture was basic: a wooden settle and a table with a single wooden chair in the main room, and a bed and chest in the bedroom.

The four months of schooling had opened her mind to so many wonders. She could read now with ease, and write in a fluent copperplate script. The intricacies of mathematics were often a struggle for her, but she was determined to master them also. When she had discovered the world of the ancient Greeks, she had been intrigued by their culture and mythology. Tales of the oracle at Delphi particularly fascinated her, for she had never questioned her own intuition which gave her glimpses of the future. Though her visions often proved true, they were not something she could summon at will, and were particularly evasive concerning her own future.

Adam was increasingly persistent that they marry before his next voyage in the spring. She told herself she was foolish to refuse, but always she held back from accepting. They had never been happier together and she missed him desperately when two or three days passed without them meeting.

Gideon Meadows sauntered into the room. He had been out when she'd arrived. 'Good day, Senara.' There was a faint smell of ale on his breath. The school was closed over Christmas and he had obviously been in the Ship kiddleywink. 'Do you wish a lesson when your work is finished?'

'If it is convenient.'

'But it will be dark when you walk back to your home.'

'I have no fear of the dark. It so often feels like a friend.' She did not tell him that she was going to Adam's house, for they were discreet about their relationship, though many suspected that she and Adam were lovers.

'Then let us begin now. Your work looks to be done.' He scanned the rows of books on the shelves in the recess by the fireplace. 'History, geography or mathematics?'

'Not mathematics today.'

He nodded. 'We will start on the wars between the houses of York and Lancaster in the medieval period. They were a power struggle between the rivals for the throne.'

'Must history only be about wars and the nobility? What about the ordinary people? Their suffering was often the greater. The men were so much flesh and bone to be ordered into battle and viciously mown down. The women had to raise families, bring in the harvests and often fend off marauders. Why are they not proclaimed the heroes and heroines, instead of some unfeeling prince who only cares about his own importance and accumulation of land?'

Gideon Meadows looked disapproving. 'The fate of kings affects us all. Consider what is happening in France at this present time.'

Senara saw a stream of tableaux like paintings in her mind, each more horrific than the last. She put her hand over her heart. 'So many deaths. They have a huge cutting blade mounted on a scaffold. God help their King and Queen.' She shut her eyes and shuddered as she saw the regal heads falling into baskets.

'My dear, Senara, you look ghastly. Are you ill? What were you saying about a scaffold?'

She shook her head. 'It was nothing. Could I have some water?'

When he returned with a horn cup she sipped from it, and the nausea which had been churning her stomach subsided. 'There will be much suffering ahead for the people of France.'

Gideon smiled in a patronising way. 'There have been many civil wars and it does look as though the troubles in France could go that way. One expects a woman to see only the suffering and not the greater events which shape the future.'

She stood up. 'I fear I cannot stay for a lesson after all.' She was disturbed by what she had seen and his attitude had angered her.

'But our history lesson has barely begun.' Gideon was at her side. There was a disturbing glitter in his eyes and his thin face looked tense. She could smell the ale on his breath and suppressed the urge to flee.

'Was it something I said or did? I would not offend you, Senara.' He reached out a hand to take hers and she backed away. 'Indeed the opposite. I hold you in the most revered regard. I would save you from the sin in which you have fallen.'

Senara stared at him with a mixture of horror and incredulity. The teacher was always so contained in his manner. He was an ardent Methodist, walking several miles each Sunday to the chapel recently built at Polmasryn. Uncomfortable, she retreated and took down her cloak from the peg on the wall. As she tied it, she suddenly found herself enfolded in his arms, his lips pressed against her neck.

'I must save you, Senara. You must not spend your life in sin. The yard knows of your liaison with Captain Loveday. He wrongs you, but I will make amends. Marry me! I will save you from lust and sin.'

Senara wrenched herself from his hold. 'Love is not a sin. There is little enough of it in this cruel world. Or tolerance – as wars so aptly prove.' She ran from the schoolhouse, knowing she would never return.

Minutes later she was in Adam's arms and her scudding heart had calmed.

'Hold me, Adam.'

'What is wrong, my love?'

'Nothing,' she dismissed her fears. 'I have missed you. That is all.'

In his arms and beneath the onslaught of his kisses, the horrors she had seen for the future of France faded. She offered up a prayer that Adam would not be drawn into the death and destruction which awaited that land. But even as she prayed, cold fingers clutched her heart.

Japhet was the next to arrive back in Cornwall and was in time to dissuade Aunt Margaret from returning to London.

'The roads were all but impassable in places,' Japhet advised. 'My horse was hock-deep in mud at times. If the journey can be made at all, it will take over two weeks. Also the inns are smoky and unsavoury at this time of year.'

Edward was insistent. 'You must stay until the spring. It is better for you and better for Thomas. He would be worried about you travelling.'

'I suppose you are right.'

Margaret sat next to Japhet in the winter parlour. A fire crackled and roared in the grate as the logs glowed red. Japhet stretched out his long legs, enjoying the warmth after so many days chilled to the marrow on horseback.

'How is Thomas?' Aunt Margaret asked eagerly. 'I feel that I should be there to support him at this difficult time.'

'Thomas is well. He works long hours and has shut up the London house to save money, and stays with Lucien. Lucien makes sure he is eating properly and has been very supportive.'

'Why must it be Lucien Greene he spends so much time with? I do not like the man,' Margaret sniffed. 'He is a bad influence on Thomas. What Thomas needs is a wife. A good woman with money behind her. If I was in London I could–'

'Thomas does not need to be pushed into marriage,' Edward reasoned. 'He is aware of his duty.'

'But a wealthy wife would solve so many problems,' Margaret persisted. 'It would also give Thomas stability. It is time he settled down.'

'He does meet women.' Japhet had seen the determined set to Aunt Margaret's lips. It warned him that she could take it in her head to leave the next morning for London and begin her matchmaking plans for her son. He felt obliged to spare Thomas that.

'Who?' Margaret fired at him.

'Well, there is the Lascalles woman. She has been at the playhouse on a few occasions.'

Margaret's eyes lit up. 'That is wonderful news. Was it Charlotte? She would make the best match. She is rather insipid but has a pleasing enough disposition. The eldest, Arabella, is so sour-faced and has no sense of humour. But I suppose the youngest, Virginia, would be acceptable.'

'It was none of those,' Japhet corrected. 'It was Georganna Lascalles.'

'But that is no good. She is Meredith Lascalles' ward. He will insist one of his daughters is chosen if there is to be a merger.' Her eyes flashed with impatience and she rose with a determined air. 'This will not do. I must go back to London, Edward. I cannot allow–'

'Margaret, Thomas will not thank you for your interference.' Edward was stern.

Japhet saw his mistake and tried to placate his aunt. 'Aunt Margaret, next season is the time for you to select a wife for Thomas. There will be all those eager mamas parading their daughters on the marriage market.'

'Do not be so cynical, Japhet,' Aunt Margaret rapped his knuckles with her fan.

'Then consider that Thomas is at present too busy to go a-wooing.' Japhet had suffered at her passion for introducing him to prospective brides and he lost patience with her need to interfere. 'Thomas has enough to deal with. He is concentrating all his energies on the bank until the spring.'

'That is why I should be in London,' Margaret fretted. 'I should not have let you persuade me to stay for so long, Elspeth. If I had left last month the roads might have been passable.'

Elspeth snorted in disapproval. Little seemed to please her, now that three of her mares had been sold. 'And what could you do in London, except interfere with Thomas's work? He would have to give up any free time from his troubles at the bank, to ensure that you have company. You

341

would also pressurise him to wed this Lascalles wench, or some other woman with your match-making. And inevitably you will quarrel. Do you not think Thomas has enough to contend with? It is better this way.'

Margaret looked outraged. 'How dare you imply such a thing? Do you think I do not know what is best for my son?'

'A mother's idea of a grown son's needs is scarcely the same as the son's idea,' Japhet was stung to reply.

Amelia had just entered the parlour, looking fresh after her afternoon nap. Her hands were folded across her swollen stomach. 'Elspeth and Japhet do have a point, Margaret. Thomas would be worrying about your health and whether you were lonely or unhappy. It would distract him from his work.'

'And it is our pleasure to have you at Trevowan for the first Christmas in nearly a quarter of a century,' Edward placated.

Against her better judgement Margaret spread her hands in surrender. 'I pray I do not live to regret this decision.'

The atmosphere in the room remained tense and Japhet made his excuses to leave. 'I still have five miles to travel to Trewenna, where I shall stay until after the festivities.'

Edward studied his nephew. Japhet looked haggard from the long journey but was in good spirits. 'Cecily will be delighted to see you. I was surprised that you did not stay the winter in London.'

Japhet shrugged. He had left London reluctantly because he had too many debts, and had escaped arrest by constables sent by an irate innkeeper over an unpaid bill. He had made his escape through the gable window of the inn and had fled across the rooftops as the constables banged on his door. It had meant leaving behind most of his clothes and possessions, but fortunately his Arab mare, Sheba, had been at the farrier's for reshoeing, or she would have been taken to settle his account.

The landlord's daughter, whom Japhet had bedded several times, had saved his clothes and some of his valuables when her father ordered them to be taken and sold. She sent word to him, they had met, and she had tearfully begged to go with him.

Grateful for her help, Japhet had kissed her with passion. 'Without money I cannot support you. I will return soon, I promise. I am for ever in your debt, my sweet.'

He kissed away her tears and although his promise would be forgotten, he had meant it sincerely at the time.

With scant funds, Japhet had stayed in the poorest inns on the journey to Cornwall. Yesterday in Bodmin, he had relieved a merchant of his purse containing three pounds.

Winter was a poor time to replenish his finances, and he was resigned to spending the next two months at Trewenna Rectory. It would be a dreary winter and he hoped there would be some diversion to distract him from the boredom of life at his parents'.

December gales had lashed the coast for more than two weeks. The winds whipped the slate-coloured sea, sending waves to crash on to the granite rocks and rise up high as church spires. They pounded against the harbour wall, and tossed the moored vessels about like driftwood. Four of the fishing luggers had been ripped from their moorings and smashed against the rocks. The Sawle vessel had so far been spared, but every fisherman kept an anxious eye on the sky and sea, praying for calm.

The village huddled against the protective rocks of the coombe, but its streets were awash from the downpour. Tiles had come loose and fences blown down. Few ventured abroad. It was a battle to put one foot in front of the other in the wind. By mid-afternoon, the waves of the rising tide were flooding the quay, some even reaching the steps of the lower cottages. The square before the church was filled with ankle-deep water.

Sacks filled with sand had been piled around the door of the Dolphin and so far had prevented the inn flooding. Trade was poor and Reuban was disgruntled. He was bored without customers to serve and drink with. Sal was busy cleaning in the kitchen. Clem had moved into his own cottage and preferred the company of his wife to that of his father. He had not been near the Dolphin for days. Harry was God knows where, but likely up to no good, for he had become close-mouthed and secretive of late. Mark, his youngest son, Reuban dismissed with a scowl. The boy was a disappointment to him. He had always been quieter than Clem or Harry, taking after Sal in

344

his gentle temperament. Mark had spurned any involvement with the smugglers; that made him weak in Reuban's eyes, and he never lost a chance to goad Mark. Now his youngest son had also disappeared without saying where he was going.

As the wind howled down the chimney, gusting smoke back into the taproom, even Mark's company would have been welcome. Reuban swigged back another pint of ale, his tenth since midday. The barrel was now empty and another needed to be broached.

He went down in the cellar and rolled the new barrel on its side. His unsteady gait and pain from the rheumaticky joints in his hip and hands made hauling it up to the taproom impossible. When he lost his balance and jarred his hip against another barrel, he cursed Mark, who was supposed to have moved the barrel.

'Bain't never here these days. Bloody useless, he is.' Reuban's temper rose, fuelled by his inability to perform a task he had once done with ease. Increasing age did not sit well on him. He no longer felt he carried the same standing in the village. Clem had already taken over the free trading. Reuban did not like relinquishing the power he had once wielded, even to his son. Harry was just as bad. He never heeded anything Reuban said,

'Don't do nothing I say, those boys,' he mumbled. 'I bain't standing for it. I bain't so old I can't teach them who is still master here.'

He staggered in to the kitchen. 'Where's Mark? He needs his hide lifting, leaving his jobs half done. I'll teach him when he gets back.'

Sal looked up from scrubbing the flagstones, her hands reddened and chapped from the water. 'I heard him whistling in the stable. He's just got back.'

Reuban unbuckled his belt. 'I'll teach him.'

'No, Reuban,' Sal screamed. 'Leave him be. He can move the cask now.' He lashed out and the belt caught the side of her face.

Suddenly Reuban's arm was caught and twisted up behind his back. 'Leave Ma alone. I be sick of your bullying. Hit Ma again and I'll give you the whipping you deserve.'

Mark was breathing heavily. His slouch hat had come off in the struggle, wet tendrils of hair dripped over his face and water ran from his oilskin cape. His wiry figure was tense with anger and he bore a black eye from where Reuban had lashed out at him yesterday. Until now he had never retaliated.

'Damn and blast you for an unnatural son,' Reuban yelped, his swollen joints tortured by his son's hold. He kicked out and caught Mark's shin with his heavy boots.

Mark maintained his grip until Sal had heaved herself upright and retreated to the far end of the kitchen. 'Let him go, Mark. I don't want fighting.'

'I won't stand by and let Pa beat you, Ma. I've had enough. I'm seventeen, old enough to decide what I want. I'm leaving the inn. I want to work with horses. I'm gonna get work as a groom.'

'The devil you will,' Reuban snarled. 'This be your home and this be where you work.'

'Not any more. You used to be someone in this village. Now you are a drunken bully and I want nothing to do with you.' He looked across at Sal. His boyish face was flushed and he was close to tears. 'I'm sorry, Ma.'

Sal shook her head. 'So am I, son. But you always did have a fondness of horses and a groom bain't such a bad life.'

'You knew this was coming,' Reuban made another swipe at Sal. When Mark flung himself at his father, Reuban picked up a stool and brought it down on Mark's head.

Mark fell to the floor, blood running from the side of his temple into the puddles of water on the washed flagstones. He was stunned and had trouble rising to his feet.

Sal screamed, 'Get out, Reuban. Mark will do what he has to do. He be a man now.'

Reuban tossed aside the stool and glared down at his son. 'He'll do as I say.' He gave Mark a parting kick in the ribs. 'That'll teach the ungrateful whelp who is his master. Reuban Sawle is still a man to be reckoned with.' He limped into the taproom, swearing and muttering to himself, 'Ay, no one gets the better of Reuban Sawle ... no one...'

Sal paid no heed to the occasional crash as she bathed Mark's wound. He pushed her hand away.

'I can't stay, Ma. I hate him and the way he treats you. I've never wanted this life. I want to work with horses. It were for Clem or Harry to take over here, not me.'

Sal nodded. 'Where do you intend to work?'

'I heard Squire Penwithick were looking for a new groom. He's got himself two new hunters and old Dan be getting on in years. That's where I've been and he's given me the job.'

'The squire be a good man to work for.' Sal hid her sadness at losing her favourite son. 'And that will mean living at the manor. It be for the best. At least it's not too far away. You come and see your old ma when you can.'

There was a crash from the taproom and Sal frowned. Reuban could kick the furniture and curse all he liked as long as he stayed out of her way. His temper and moods were becoming worse, and she rarely had the strength to fight him.

'No one gets the better of Reuban Sawle,' a slurred shout came from the taproom.

Sal groaned in despair. 'He's drinking again. Go and stay with Clem tonight.'

'No, Ma. I'll not leave you on your own with him in that mood. If I'm not here, he'll take it out on you. I'll not run from my home because of that bully. I'll leave with pride in the morning.'

She pushed a lock of his sandy hair back from his brow. 'I be proud of you, son. You've never given me no cause for worry like the others. Get away from here while you can. Now get those wet clothes off, or you'll be starting work at the manor with a fever.'

He went upstairs to change. Sal wandered into the taproom. It was deserted.

'Reuban!'

She shrugged when there was no answer. 'Drunken sod has passed out. He can stay where

348

he's fallen and sleep off his foul temper. Serve the surly bugger right.' Sal went back to scrubbing her kitchen floor. Then, with a shake of her head, she threw the dirty water out into the yard and waddled back to the taproom. Last week when Reuban had passed out he'd knocked a stool over so it had fallen into the flames and nearly set the inn on fire.

There was no sign of him. Nor when she shouted down in to the cellar nor up the stairs to their bedchamber. She peered out through the rain trickling down the small window.

'Needs his head examined if he's gone out in this.'

Reuban was looking for Harry. He resented the way Harry ignored his orders. He had taught Mark his place and now it was Harry's turn. He weaved his way to the quay, too drunk to pay any attention to the rain. There was no sign of Harry or his boat. Reuban's legs were stiff from the cold and he limped painfully back to the Dolphin, cursing his sons with each step. A violent gust of wind knocked him sideways, lifting his long beard so that it smeared over his eyes. He collided with the corner of the church lych-gate and with a grunt sank down on to its seat.

A rumbling of wheels had him squinting through the growing darkness. When his bleary gaze settled on Lanyon's new carriage, something snapped inside him. Lanyon now saw himself as the most important man in Penruan. Lanyon had humiliated Harry by stealing his bride. Lanyon was in charge of the smugglers where once

Reuban had ruled.

Reuban lurched to his feet and in the fading light lumbered over the slippery, flooded cobbles towards the carriage. He shouted abuse and raised his fist in the air.

Briefly he saw Lanyon's pale face in the carriage window. The man looked frightened. And so he should. Reuban Sawle was still a man to be reckoned with. He threw himself at the door to wrench it open.

Drink marred his judgement of distance; encroaching age and half-crippled bones betrayed him. His boots slithered on the ground, his fingers touched the side of the carriage and then his body twisted and he fell. Agony sawed through him as the carriage wheels ran over his legs, crushing them.

Meriel reached the Dolphin Inn an hour later. A message sent to her by the Reverend Mr Snell said that her father had met with an accident and was not expected to last the night. St John accompanied her.

When they entered the kitchen it was empty. There was a light shining from the taproom. Reuban lay on the counter, which had served as an operating table. The floor was still wet from Sal scouring it to remove the blood. A lantern hung on a beam above Reuban's head. His face was the same colour as the sheet which covered his chest and his beard had been laid over the blankets to spread to his navel.

On first sight Meriel assumed he was dead. Sal, Harry, Mark, Clem and Keziah were seated in frozen silence around him.

'I came as soon as I heard.' Meriel went to her father's side. The flesh on his face seemed to have shrunk on to his bones, the eye sockets deeply shadowed. 'Has he gone?'

Sal took her hand. 'He be still alive. Barely. Chegwidden don't reckon he'll last the night.'

'It be best if he didn't,' Clem groaned. 'Pa wouldn't want to be a cripple. He'd be like one of those freaks at the Midsummer Fair.'

It was only then that Meriel realised how short her father's body looked. Both his legs had been cut off above the knees. She gagged and turned away to battle against the nausea rising from her stomach.

'Dear God. What happened, Ma? Mr Snell sent word of an accident.'

'He walked in front of Lanyon's coach, so Lanyon said,' Harry ground out. 'Lanyon reckons his driver could not avoid him. Lanyon's got to answer for this.'

'Harry, I don't want to talk like that,' Sal insisted. 'Your pa were drunk. Lanyon did right by him. Told us what happened and got two men to carry him here. He sent his driver to fetch Chegwidden and he said he'd meet his bill.'

'But he weren't sorry about what happened,' Clem raged. 'Inside the man were gloating. And how do we know it were an accident? How do we know he didn't see Pa drunk and run him down?'

Mr Snell, who had been standing in the corner praying in a low voice, glared at Harry. 'Such talk is not befitting at a deathbed. Our Lord teaches us forgiveness. You should be praying for your

351

father's recovery, not raising your voice in condemnation of another.'

Clem let out an enraged bellow. 'It's obvious whose side you're on. Lanyon paid a fortune for that fancy pew of his and no doubt paid you for the privilege. He's always first to leave at the end of a service, and tosses a gold coin in the collection plate so everyone will see how generous he is. Pa bain't been inside your church for years. So what you doing here with your preaching and pontificating?'

'Mr Snell is here because I sent for him.' Sal slapped Clem's arm, then turned to the minister, who was visibly shaking. 'Pay no heed to Clem. It's been a shock, Mr Snell.'

'I meant every word.' Clem made a grab at the parson's stock. 'Pa wouldn't want you here. He didn't believe in your God.'

'Then all the more reason that his soul must be saved.' Mr Snell stood his ground, his Bible clutched before him.

Keziah stepped between the two men. 'I bain't much of a churchgoer myself, but you done your bit to save the old man's soul, parson. Happen it be better if you were to leave now.'

Mr Snell opened his mouth to protest, then seeing the fury on Clem's face snapped it shut. He turned to Sal, his expression one of pained commiseration. 'My prayers will be with you and your husband this night, Mistress Sawle.'

Sal nodded, and St John escorted him to the door.

'Is Reuban really likely to die?' St John asked the vicar. 'He's always been such a tough old cove.'

'It is in the Lord's hands. Young Chegwidden has performed many such amputations in the navy. Some survive, but Reuban is not a young man.'

'It were my fault,' Mark said, holding his head in his hands. 'I shouldn't have goaded him. He got so angry.'

Meriel reached out to Mark's shoulder and could feel him trembling. 'All you did was stand up to his bullying.'

'Reuban couldn't take losing his hold on the family and village. He couldn't bear not being cock of the roost.' Sal wiped a tear from her eye. 'The rest were the drink. It's always been a curse on him. It's what makes him violent.'

She stared into the flames of the fire, her voice nostalgic. 'He weren't always so mean. When we first met he was a commanding figure. He had such a proud upright strut to his walk a woman had to notice him. And he were big and handsome, bold and daring. Saved enough from his smuggling to buy the Dolphin. That were no mean achievement. We never went without.'

The family had their own memories of Reuban. The others were less charitable than Sal. They remained with Reuban through the night. As the first rays of dawn were lighting the horizon, the old man stirred. And then he began to scream in agony even when Sal administered the opiate prepared by the doctor. Finally the large dose of the drug took effect and his eyelids drooped, then in a lucid moment flickered open to stare at Clem.

'See Lanyon pays,' he said in a hoarse rasp

353

before sliding back into unconsciousness.

Harry and Clem were all for dragging Thadeous Lanyon from his bed and ending the man's life. Meriel and Keziah grabbed Clem, and Sal and St John restrained Harry.

'There will be no talk of vengeance,' Sal shouted. 'Bad blood brought this about. It be time it ended. I want your word, boys. The likes of Lanyon bain't worth swinging from a gibbet over.'

To appease their mother Harry and Clem agreed, but as their glances held over their father's figure, they each saw the vow of vengeance in the other's eyes.

That Reuban did not die, but began a long and painful road to recovery, cursing Lanyon with every laboured breath, did not alter the brothers' vow. They wanted their father well enough to savour their final triumph over their enemy.

Chapter Twenty

With Japhet back in Cornwall, Gwendolyn Druce was determined to capture his attention and his heart. Twice she visited Cecily Loveday at Trewenna Rectory to help dispense extra food to the poor amongst the parishioners. Each time Japhet was absent. She could barely contain her disappointment. After her second failure she visited Meriel before returning to Traherne Hall.

'It is so unfair that I missed him again,' she groaned.

Meriel was ironing one of Rowena's dresses on the kitchen table. The heat from the cooking range and the iron had reddened her face. With only one maid, much of the housework fell to her and she was displeased that Gwendolyn's visit had caught her at her labours. She ordered Rachel to continue with the ironing after she had served refreshments for their guest. Somewhat flustered, Meriel greeted Gwendolyn, who had been taken to the parlour. Not that Gwendolyn seemed to notice Meriel's distress, she was too upset.

'Japhet had been gone less than half an hour,' Gwendolyn went on. 'I did not even meet with him on the road. He has been back two weeks. I have had only one glimpse of him, and that at a distance.'

'Calm yourself,' Meriel advised. 'Japhet will be at the Christmas festivities here and at the ball to be held at Traherne Hall. Have I not arranged that you dine at Trevowan with our family?'

'But they are another ten days away!' Gwendolyn was agitated in her distress. 'So many wasted days. It is months since I last spoke with him. But he will not notice me. I am too plain. Too ordinary.'

'You do yourself a disservice.' She hid her irritation at Gwendolyn's fading confidence. 'You have blossomed in recent months. Japhet can take his pick from any number of standard beauties, but you are not only attractive, you also have the wit and humour he admires.'

'But it is the beautiful women he will be drawn to.'

Rachel arrived with a tray of Madeira, and cinnamon biscuits baked by Winnie Fraddon and sent over from Trevowan House. Meriel waited until Rachel left and she could hear her working in the kitchen before she continued. Rachel was a gossip and Meriel did not want the intrigue she was involved in with Gwendolyn to be the talk of the district.

'You have made the best of your most striking feature – your hair,' Meriel said. 'The new style is becoming. Your clothes with the tighter corset, which cinches in your waist and accentuates your bust and hips, will not fail to attract him. Especially if you dare to wear a lower décolletage.'

Gwendolyn blushed. 'Mama will have an apoplexy if I discard my fichu.'

'And with luck so will Japhet,' Meriel grinned. 'That is our aim, is it not? He will not fail to be entranced.'

Gwendolyn was not reassured. 'He has known me so long. I will be the same old Gwendolyn to him: tongue-tied and foolish as any schoolgirl in his company. And I shall blush like an idiot every time he looks at me.'

She paused and looked uncertain. 'I was wondering ... oh, this sounds so silly ... but Senara Polglase has a knowledge of herbs, doesn't she? Do you think she knows how to make a love potion?'

'What a fascinating idea,' Meriel mused. Senara was a bane to her now she knew of Adam's relationship with the woman. Meriel had long meant to satisfy her curiosity about where Adam's mistress lived. Encouraging Gwendolyn to visit her would be the perfect chance. 'It is such a fine day. It will be good to get out of the house. There is time to ride to her cottage today,' Meriel decided. 'I shall accompany you.'

'Oh, but I did not really mean–' Gwendolyn became flustered. 'I mean, I do not think I should. It was a foolish idea.'

'You want Japhet, do you not?'

'Yes,' Gwendolyn sighed. 'But...'

'Then wait until I change into my riding habit. I will be quick.'

Meriel hurried upstairs, calling to Rachel Glasson to help her with the laces of her gown.

'Mama, you are going riding? Can I come with you?' Rowena pleaded.

'No, my sweet. Not today.'

'But I want to. No one takes me riding now. Papa is too busy. Aunt Elspeth has hurt her hip again and Grandma Amelia does not like to ride any more. Please, Mama.'

There was a long silence from Meriel while Rowena continued to plead. Finally she replied, 'Perhaps you should be with us. Dress quickly. You must be ready by the time Jasper Fraddon has saddled the horses.'

Gwendolyn was pacing the parlour when Meriel and Rowena appeared in matching red military-style riding habits. 'It is better if Rowena is with us,' Meriel explained. 'Senara Polglase can examine her arm, and we will have an excuse for our visit.'

'Are we doing the right thing?' Gwendolyn still needed convincing.

Meriel smiled. 'It will be amusing to see where this woman lives. Aren't you curious about someone who surrounds herself with so much mystery, and hides herself away?'

Gwendolyn found Meriel impossible to dissuade and though increasingly certain that her idea had been a preposterous one, in half an hour she found herself outside the Polglase cottage.

Meriel cast a disdainful eye upon her surroundings. The dwelling looked to have no more than two rooms and she regarded it as little better than a peasant's hut. The fresh lime-washed walls, new thatch and tidy vegetable and herb garden went unnoticed.

At the sound of their approach a hideous apparition appeared at the door.

'That's Angel,' Rowena informed them. 'He was injured when his last owner made him fight bulls.'

The dog growled and in fear Meriel ordered Rowena to remain on her pony. 'Is anyone at home?' Meriel called, annoyed that Senara had not appeared on their arrival.

'I was not expecting visitors.' The cool voice behind them held no welcome.

Meriel turned in her saddle to see Senara framed in the doorway of the stable. She held a fox cub in her arms.

'I am Meriel Loveday. This is Gwendolyn Druce. You know Rowena.'

Senara smiled at the girl, but her expression was again blank as she regarded the two women.

358

A dark brow lifted in query.

The insolence of the woman enraged Meriel but she managed to control it. 'Rowena has been complaining of pains in her arm. Dr Chegwidden is useless. You have helped her in the past. Would you kindly examine her and see if anything can be done?'

'Mistress Loveday, with respect is it not time that Rowena saw a doctor from London, who would have greater knowledge than Dr Chegwidden?' Senara remained guarded.

'That is our intention next spring. I would not have her suffer in the meantime, if it can be avoided.'

Senara lifted the cub up to show Rowena. Its back leg was bandaged. 'She was injured in a rabbit snare. Isn't she lovely?'

'Can I stroke her?' Rowena asked in wonder.

'Of course, but move slowly so that you do not frighten her.'

'She is so lovely.' Rowena frowned. There was a greenish tinge to her blue eyes which were bright with intelligence and questioning. 'Great-Aunt Elspeth hunts foxes. She says they are vermin. Why have you saved her life?'

'Because it has a right to live and I would not see any animal suffer for want of kindness and care.'

'Then is it wrong for Aunt Elspeth to hunt them?'

'That is her choice – as you must one day choose. Once man so hunted man for pleasure. Fortunately, that is now considered barbaric. We have not yet extended such chivalry to animals. I

359

will put the cub back in her cage and then I will tend to you.'

Senara disappeared into the stable. Meriel dismounted and lifted Rowena from her pony. She gripped her daughter's hand and looked nervously at Angel, who continued to growl.

'The dog will not harm you,' Senara said, reappearing. 'Come inside, Rowena.' She led Rowena into the cottage without a word to the others. They paused by Angel. 'He likes little girls; you can stroke him.'

Rowena put her arms around him and kissed the mastiff's head. Angel regarded her solemnly out of his one eye, and as the girl passed into the cottage, licked her long dark ringlets with his immense tongue, leaving a wet patch on her scarlet hair ribbon.

Meriel shuddered and her face flamed with anger that Senara had not invited them into the dwelling. It had been a deliberate slight.

'Where does your arm hurt you?' Senara lifted Rowena on to the table and began to undo the jacket of her habit.

The arm, which had been damaged at birth, was thin and wasted. Rowena pointed to the shoulder. 'Am I like the fox cub? Can you make it better?'

'I cannot promise so much. The fox cub will always limp. It is for you to be brave and help your arm to become strong.' Senara moved the arm gently in a circle. 'Do you try to use your arm as much as possible?'

Rowena shook her head. 'Aunt Elspeth makes me. But it hurts.'

'That could be a good thing. It could mean that the arm is getting stronger. You are a brave girl. You want your arm to be strong, don't you?'

Rowena nodded and smiled at Meriel, who had flounced into the cottage uninvited. Gwendolyn hesitated by the door.

Meriel took in the details of the room: the drying herbs hanging from the rafters, potter's wheel and sheaf of wicker canes to make baskets showed how the women made their money. On the floor were rag rugs, and a rocking chair covered in a patchwork quilt was by the hearth. A besom stood by the window – the broomstick of witches. Was this woman a witch or enchantress to have so entranced Adam?

'How is the child?' Gwendolyn said, feeling awkward at the silence.

'There does seem to be some improvement. But she needs to be encouraged to use her arm more and build up its strength. I can give you a balm to be rubbed on as Rowena says it pains her.'

She took a large pottery jar from a shelf and scooped several ladles of thick green salve into a smaller pot.

'I wanted to thank you for saving Harry's life,' Meriel said. 'I have brought you this brooch.' She laid a gaudily painted tin brooch on the table. One of the young fishermen from Penruan had bought it for her years ago.

'I have no use for jewellery.' Senara stared hard at Meriel.

'I suppose you are waiting for Adam to shower you with gold and diamonds?'

Senara turned away without answering and

361

replaced the jar on the shelf. 'If there is nothing else, I will bid you good day. There is no charge for the balm and Rowena may keep the pot once it is empty.'

'I did not come here for charity,' Meriel fumed, and placed a handful of silver on the table.

'I do not accept money.' Senara pushed it back to her.

Meriel ignored her and Gwendolyn, surprised at Meriel's rudeness, interrupted. 'I, too, have come for a reason. I was wondering if you could sell me a love potion.'

Senara's face whitened. 'You have made a mistake.'

'Oh, I did not mean to offend,' Gwendolyn hastily amended, 'but I thought, well, you have such a knowledge of herbs and things ... and with your gypsy blood...'

Senara stared at her with her green eyes flashing, then all at once she relaxed. 'No, you did not mean harm, but there is harm in what you ask. An attractive woman such as yourself, who has a fortune to command, has no need of love potions.'

'But the man I love hardly knows that I exist.'

Again Senara studied her and reached out and took her hand, turning it over to study the palm. 'You will marry and I see many children.'

'Who will I marry?' Gwendolyn could not stop herself asking.

Senara shrugged. 'It is someone you already know.' She dropped her hand and stood back. Whirling round in pleasure, Gwendolyn danced outside.

Meriel, who had been incensed at Senara's attitude, was torn between ridiculing Senara's fortune-telling, and the need to know her own future. She held out her hand. 'Will I too have many children?'

Senara glanced at her hand and took a step back. 'We both know that is in God's hands. I have told your friend what she wanted to hear.'

'I think you see, but will not tell me.' Her lips curled with malice. 'Gypsies read palms.'

'I do not engage in the tricks of a fairground. You, more than most women, know that we can create our own futures.'

'What has that to do with children? If I can create my own future as you seem to think, then give me a potion which will make me breed. Help me to conceive a son.'

'That must be in your hands, not mine. I can ease pain and cure a few simple ills. What you ask is beyond my powers.'

'Oh, I doubt that it is,' Meriel spat, 'but you won't help me. A son would dispossess Adam, would he not? That is why you will not help me.'

'There is no potion to make a woman conceive. Rowena's birth was difficult. Could it be that you find it difficult to be as loving towards your husband as he would wish?'

Meriel was breathing heavily and her stare was malignant.

Senara shivered, feeling the coldness which was at the core of this woman. She regarded Meriel serenely though her heart pumped with fear. 'You know that Adam's child will inherit Trevowan.' Senara spoke the words before she was aware of what she was saying, and only now did her gaze slide towards Rowena, who was staring in amazement at the barn owl asleep on the roof rafters. A shudder of intuition she would rather not have to acknowledge passed through her. The child bore an uncanny resemblance to Adam.

Meriel backed away, visibly shaken. She had seen the way Senara looked at Rowena. Had the woman guessed the truth – that Rowena was Adam's child? She had guarded her secret well, fearing the consequences from either of the twins if they were to learn the truth. 'I shall have a son. I must have a son.' Her heart was also pounding and she was frightened. Senara knew more than she was saying. Meriel forced a brittle laugh. 'You are a charlatan. Sell your fortunes in a fairground, for that is where they belong. You should be put in the stocks for your skulduggery and lies.'

'Do not judge others on your own merits,' Senara addressed Meriel's departing figure.

Meriel paused by the door and looked back over her shoulder. Senara felt the room grow cold with menace. Angel growled and moved protectively towards his mistress. Meriel's lips curled back as she stared around the cottage with its bunches of drying herbs hanging from the beams. The barn owl awoke and flapped its wings.

Meriel sneered, 'A witch's lair with her familiars, if ever there was one.'

'They are injured animals whose lives I saved, no more.'

'But what of your potions? Clearly you have

bewitched Adam Loveday. Why else should he risk the censure of his family for such as you?'

'I have no more cast a spell upon Adam than you did upon St John.' Senara managed to hold the malicious glare without flinching. It was a moment of supreme danger, born of superstition and ignorance, and one she had run away from many times in the past. She would not allow this scheming woman to rob her of happiness. Her voice was low and confident. 'Do not blame me because you love one man and wed another. It does not take special powers to see that, for it is betrayed in your manner and guilt. Love your husband more and you may find that you achieve all that you desire.'

'How dare you imply any such thing?'

'And how dare you name me witch when all I have ever done is help your family,' Senara fumed. 'Your words are offensive. But then you vent your jealousy for the love you feel I have stolen from you. That love was freely given long after you had chosen your husband and a new life.'

'Do you think a gypsy whore holds any interest to me?' Meriel was scornful, her defensive tone covering her guilt. She grabbed at Rowena's hand and dragged the girl outside with a violence which made Senara wince. Rowena still managed to wave to Senara and pat Angel as she passed. Her smile was so like Adam's it made Senara's heart ache.

Gwendolyn was still spinning in a carefree dance. 'Do you think it was Japhet she meant? It was, was it not? I will marry Japhet. She has the sight and knows these things.'

'It is all a game, Gwendolyn,' Meriel snapped. 'It is but an afternoon's entertainment. You do not believe all that nonsense.'

When the two women and child had ridden out of the clearing, Senara swept up the money Meriel had left behind. She took it to the stream and threw it into the water and offered a silent prayer to the Lady – the ancient one, whose spirit lived in all water, giving life to both land and beast – to accept it as an offering for her protection. Then she drew a bucket of the clear water and sprinkled it around the cottage to cleanse it of the feeling of menace and evil which had invaded her home that afternoon.

When she finished she was trembling. She was no witch, but she knew the power of the old gods who had once been revered in this land. There was much that was good in the teachings of the Church. Yet too often she had been an object of bigotry instead of tolerance and compassion taught by their Saviour. The superstition she had been taught by her gypsy grandmother was different. She respected another's beliefs, but the land was too precious for the old ways to be forgotten. The ancient spirits of nature and the elements still had the power both to serve or to destroy man. Any family who gleaned a harvest from the land, or sea, was aware of that.

Out of respect for Margaret's mourning, the days of Christmas were spent quietly at Trevowan. When all the Lovedays gathered to dine on the Sunday following Christmas, after Joshua's

366

service, Meriel insisted that Gwendolyn join them as they left Trewenna church. The Trahernes had not attended the service.

'Just for an hour or so,' Gwendolyn agreed. 'Mama, Roslyn and Sir Henry are entertaining. Sir Henry's friend Sir Hugh Portman is staying with us and it would be rude not to be present.'

'Sir Hugh is dour company,' Hannah observed as she herded her three children into the farm wagon they used for transport.

'That is why I escaped to church. Sir Hugh's only interest is gaming, so making conversation can be difficult,' Gwendolyn observed, 'and Mama seems set to make a match between us, which fills me with horror. It will be an uncomfortable evening.'

'Sir Hugh would not be a suitable choice for you at all,' Margaret Mercer's own matchmaking skills made her observe. 'There must be far more eligible men to choose from.' A zealous light brightened her eyes and she whispered to Gwendolyn, 'Would not Adam be the perfect match? You have always got on so well.'

'Adam's heart is engaged elsewhere,' Meriel reminded Margaret Mercer.

'We will not go into the unsuitability of that liaison,' Margaret responded.

Meriel insinuated with feigned casualness, 'Of course, there is Japhet. Cecily despairs that he will ever wed.'

Margaret glanced at Adam and Japhet, who had both mounted their horses and were laughing together. 'Much as I adore Japhet, I doubt he would make any woman the perfect husband. I doubt marriage would curb his wildness.'

Margaret entered the Loveday carriage, and Meriel and Gwendolyn, who had ridden to church, walked to the mounting block. St John was in conversation with his father and Uncle Joshua. Seeing the women approaching, Japhet leapt from his saddle.

'Ladies, permit me to assist you.' He stooped before Meriel, his hands cupped for her to place her foot in. 'Such dainty feet and you are as light as a feather,' he teased. 'You are more beautiful each time I see you.'

She laughed, enjoying his flirting, but on this occasion wanted it directed towards Gwendolyn. This was a perfect opportunity to bring the two together and thereby spite Roslyn. 'Ah, but I am married and unavailable. Whereas Gwendolyn has truly blossomed into a rare loveliness, do you not agree?'

Japhet turned to Gwendolyn and was surprised to see how pretty she had become and how her figure was more shapely and rounded.

Gwendolyn blushed under his hazel gaze. 'Meriel is being kind. Her beauty outshines us all.'

'Do not be so modest, Gwen.' Meriel was sharp, which caused Gwendolyn's blush to deepen.

Japhet covered Gwendolyn's gloved hand with his own, his eyes bright with teasing. 'You do look different. Quite lovely. There is a glow about you. I reckon our Gwen has fallen in love. Who is the lucky devil, for it cannot be Sir Hugh?'

Gwendolyn's face flamed to strawberry and then drained to ashen. 'Japhet Loveday, I have never heard such nonsense,' she somehow managed to force out to cover her embarrassment.

'Why is it nonsense? I never could understand why you remain unwed. You must have had offers.'

'None I found acceptable.'

'I thought all women were desperate for marriage and children at any cost.'

His flippancy annoyed her. 'Many have no choice. They would be a burden on their families if they did not marry. I only live at Traherne Hall because Mother and Sir Henry insist. I would be content in a modest establishment of my own. I have a high value of my independence.'

Japhet gave a low whistle. 'You would scandalise the whole community by so flouting convention.'

'Quite so. Yet the trappings of propriety and convention can be onerous.' The way he was looking at her caused spirals of longing to shimmer through her body. Fearful that she would betray her emotions in some foolish way, she touched her heels to her mare's sides. 'Come, Meriel, the air is chilly. A gallop will warm us. Let us race the men back to Trevowan.' She set off at breakneck speed overtaking the Loveday carriage and Hannah and Oswald Rabson in their wagon.

Meriel declined to race, feeling it was undignified and knowing herself to be a barely competent horsewoman. Japhet took up the challenge and issued it to Adam, who followed him.

Hannah cheered Gwendolyn as she passed. 'You show the men, Gwen. Do not let them catch you.'

All three arrived at the stables of Trevowan together. Japhet leapt to the ground to lift Gwendolyn from the saddle. Both their faces were flushed from the ride. 'Now that riding would beat Aunt Elspeth into a cocked hat. I thought we would never catch you.'

'Celeste is a fine horse; her Arab blood matches that of your mare, Sheba.' Gwendolyn was stingingly aware of the touch of his hand through her riding habit. They were standing close enough so that she could feel the touch of his breath on her cheek. It was as potent as a caress and made her light-headed.

She turned away too quickly and stumbled against him. 'Oh! I am so careless. Forgive me.'

Japhet laughed and put his hand on her arm to steady her. He threw his reins to Jasper Fraddon to rub down Sheba. 'Only one thing beats a hard gallop to heat a man's blood, but I will not be so indiscreet to mention it.'

She slapped his arm and laughed. 'You are incorrigible! I pray you will never change, Japhet.'

He laughed too, and then frowned. 'Strange creatures, women. That is exactly what most women set out to do – change a fellow once they get their claws in him.'

Adam joined them as they walked to the house. 'I would think you drive most women to despair, Japhet. Women like stability and security in their husbands.'

'Ah, but it is very different with a lover. They want excitement.' Japhet grinned, his arm placed in casual familiarity around Gwendolyn's shoulders. 'Does that shock you, Gwen? It is cruel of me to tease.'

'I have known you too long to be shocked by anything you say, or do.'

'That sounds like a challenge!' His eyes sparkled with devilment.

'Perhaps it was,' she answered in a breathless voice, then feeling herself blush, turned away. The rest of the family had arrived and she walked off to greet them, leaving Japhet staring after her.

He grinned as he turned to Adam. 'I always thought of Gwen Druce as a dowdy little mouse. When did she change?'

When Gwendolyn made her excuses to leave two hours later, Japhet offered to accompany her. He was attentive and charming throughout their ride, but any hopes which had begun to dwell in her breast that he was interested in her, were dashed after she invited him to dine at Traherne Hall. Although he accepted, within ten minutes of meeting Sir Hugh they were planning an evening of cards and gambling. Roslyn insisted that they play whist and that Sir Henry make up the fourth. 'Some music would be soothing, Gwen,' she ordered her sister. 'Do play for us.'

Gwendolyn sat at the harpsichord for an hour, limiting herself to only an occasional glance at Japhet, who seemed to be winning most hands. He was in high spirits and if he caught her glance upon him, winked at her. Even such absent attention on his part could cause her heart to flap against her breastbone like the wings of a caged bird. He was so handsome, so apparently at ease in the opulent surroundings of Traherne Hall. No one on first meeting him would guess from his dress or manner that he was the son of a parson whose stipend barely covered the needs of his family. Beside his graceful manners it was Sir Hugh who looked like the bumbling yokel.

By the time she stopped playing, her mother, Lady Druce, was dozing by the fire. Gwendolyn picked up a book to read.

Sir Henry threw in his hand, having lost thirty guineas, and excused himself.

'You cannot break up the set, Henry,' Roslyn and Hugh both complained.

'I have an estate matter to deal with. Forgive me, Sir Hugh, Japhet. Gwendolyn will take my place. You may find your luck will now change, Japhet. She always beats Ros.'

'Do join us, Gwendolyn.' Sir Hugh squinted myopically at her. 'I am down thirty guineas to this rogue and intend to win it back.'

Gwendolyn took the seat vacated by Sir Henry, which was opposite Japhet.

'Am I about to lose all my winnings?' Japhet teased.

'That is in the luck of the cards,' she responded. She won several hands and then realised that Japhet needed his winnings tonight to support himself through the winter. She raised the stakes and played carelessly so that she ended by losing twenty guineas to him. He had won another thirty from Roslyn and twenty-five more from Sir Hugh.

When Japhet took his leave, he bowed over her hand and dropped twenty guineas into her palm. 'I have never seen a woman play with the skill you do, but you deliberately lost those last hands.'

'I was tired; my concentration wandered.'

He shook his head. 'I make my living gambling, Gwen, but from you I will only take what is fairly won. And there are more exciting games that I may yet challenge you to.'

The innuendo was seemingly ignored, though her heart gave a leap of anticipation. Was that a glint of admiration in his eyes? At his grin she lost her courage and parried, 'I have a great fondness for many games. Faro is a favourite, and I have an uncanny knack of calling the dice in hazard that can be embarrassing.'

'That is a gift indeed. I am intrigued. I will call upon you soon and you will show me this remarkable talent.' His gaze swept over her as he raised her hand to his lips. 'You are different, Gwen. Have you been hiding your light under a bushel and now would surprise us all?'

'That remains to be discovered.'

'Does it, by Jove?' There was a mischievous light in his eyes.

Shocked by her own boldness, she tried to withdraw her hand from his. He held it tight, his gaze speculative upon her face. Again he kissed her hand, his lips lingering upon her flesh. 'Good night, Gwen. Take care that you save me a dance at the ball.'

On the night of the Traherne Ball Gwendolyn

recklessly discarded her fichu. The Grand Saloon had been cleared of the heavier furniture to provide room for the dancing, and chairs lined the walls. The two crystal chandeliers ablaze with candles were reflected in the large casement windows with their backdrop of a clear starry night.

Japhet asked Gwendolyn for two dances in succession and flirted outrageously with her. Then the men began to drift into the gaming room and she was abandoned. An hour later when he emerged Japhet was smiling with pleasure. She was the first he asked to dance then, and when the music faded he led her out on to the terrace. Meriel saw them go and smiled. Lady Traherne glared at her sister's back and when she made to follow the couple, Meriel intervened to stop her.

On the terrace Gwendolyn was tinglingly aware of Japhet standing close behind her. She could feel the warmth of his breath on her neck and it set her heart capering with anticipation. Her heart was thundering so hard that she feared he must surely hear it. She tried to remember all the things Meriel had told her to say or do to make her irresistible to a man. She could remember nothing and, as the cold air nipped her arms and breasts in the low-cut gown, she was overcome with shyness. Her tongue seemed to swell in her throat, and even if she could think of something witty and fascinating to say, it would be impossible to utter it.

When Japhet's hand touched her shoulder she jumped violently.

'Do I frighten you so much?' Japhet said.

'Of course you do not frighten me. What a foolish goose you make me sound.' Blushing at the sophistication of her words, she turned to face him and again her throat locked. His face was in partial shadow, but he was studying her intently and there was a gleam in his eyes which took her breath away.

Slowly he smiled. 'It would grieve me if my presence frightened you. You are so different from how I remember.' He touched a ringlet of her hair which curled over her shoulder, and his hooded stare transfixed her. His finger skimmed lightly from her ringlet across the sensitive hollow in her shoulder and briefly across the bare skin above the rise of her breasts.

She caught her breath at the exquisite sensations his touch had aroused. Then he lowered his head and kissed her lips. It was a warm caressing kiss, light as a breeze but with the power to send a spiral of fire to the pit of her stomach. The strength of his arms bound her to him. The kiss deepened, his tongue parted the seam of her lips to tease the soft inner flesh. She surrendered to his mastery and the joy his lips evoked. When they broke apart she would have fallen, she felt so light-headed, if he had not laughed softly and held her close.

'What a surprising woman you are.' The huskiness of his voice showed the intensity of his emotion.

Gwendolyn languorously savoured the taste of him still in her mouth, and the scent of sandalwood on his skin and hair. The kiss was all she had dreamed it would be and more. Her hand rested lightly on his chest and she could feel the hard drum of his heart – a heartbeat which had quickened for her tonight.

'My sweet, Gwen, you are–'

'Gwendolyn!' Lady Druce's voice shattered the magic and intimacy they had shared. Japhet moved away from Gwendolyn and she stared dazedly at him, grief-stricken that she would never hear what he had meant to say, for she was certain that it was something special.

'Gwendolyn, you will catch your death out here.' Lady Druce was displeased at the dreamy expression on her daughter's face even if Japhet was standing several paces from her and looking blithely innocent. The coil of hair which had been dislodged from Gwendolyn's coiffure told a less innocent story. Her mother's voice was tart as she addressed Japhet. 'Cecily was asking if you would fetch her shawl for her, Japhet. She left it in the dining room.'

Japhet winked at Gwendolyn as he left the terrace but Lady Druce made certain that he did not spend another moment alone with her.

For the week following the ball Gwendolyn lived in anticipation of Japhet's visit. His kiss had been so filled with promise that it had fulfilled all her dreams. If only her mother had not come upon them when she did, who knows where that precious moment might have led?

She had dared to hope that Japhet was interested in her. When he raised her hand to his lips on their departure, he had whispered that he would call.

But he did not come. In desperation, she called at the Dower House.

'Did you not hear that he left four days ago for Truro?' Meriel announced. 'He won a hundred guineas from Sir Hugh. I warrant we will not see him again this winter unless his money runs out.'

Chapter Twenty-One

The incident with Meriel had affected Senara more than she cared to admit. It was obvious to her that Rowena was Adam's child but Adam was unaware of the fact, as were the rest of the family. Meriel would be furious that she had guessed her secret. It was also obvious that Meriel was still in love with Adam, or in love with him as much as the self-centred woman was capable of loving any man. Her hatred and hostility towards Senara had been palpable. Meriel was in a position to make life very unpleasant for the Polglase family. Senara knew better than to underestimate Meriel Loveday's ingenuity, or spite, if she felt herself crossed.

For the moment, Senara believed they were safe from Meriel's vindictiveness as Senara knew too much about Harry Sawle's secret life. Even so, she would remain on her guard.

Throughout the winter Senara was coerced by Adam to spend more nights at Mariner's House. They were discreet, with Senara leaving for her own cottage as soon as it was light, but inevitably the shipwrights and their wives learned of the relationship.

Senara forced herself to slide from beneath the warmth of the bedclothes on a chill, rain-lashed dawn. Adam was still asleep. The fire in the bedroom had burned low and she threw on a log and prodded it with the poker. The flames were sluggish, and without further kindling to ignite the embers it would take a long time for the log to warm the room. She was shivering as she began to pull on her petticoats in front of the fire.

Adam's arm snaked around her thigh, his voice drowsy. 'Are you mad, my love? Get back into bed. You cannot ride home in this weather.'

He pulled her down on top of him, his mouth seeking her neck as he began to caress her. 'I should leave,' she murmured against his kisses.

'Your body is like ice. I will warm you.' He wrapped the blankets around them, but it was the enticement of his mouth on her flesh which dissolved her resistance.

When they finally drew apart he still held her tight.

'I have to go, Adam.'

'There will be no work done in the yard until the rain stops. There is no need to rush away.'

'As owner and master here you may lie abed all you please. I have a living to earn. I have an order for jugs and storage pots to complete for a store in Fowey. It is my first order for them, and it must be delivered by the end of the week.'

'And how are you to get to Fowey?' Adam asked. 'Wilful does not like the heavy rains.'

'Wilful will earn his hay,' Senara sighed. 'With

the roads so bad in winter there are few outlets for my wares. The shopkeeper has also ordered a dozen of the wicker baskets which Leah and Bridie have been making all winter.'

'Then borrow the yard wagon and two of the horses for the day.'

Her face lit with pleasure. 'That will make it so much easier. If the pots and baskets sell as well in Fowey as they do at the fairs and markets, our financial worries will be over.'

'As they would be if you wed me, Senara.' He groaned and traced his fingers through her hair. Her obstinacy exasperated him. It was typical of Senara that she would not even ask for the loan of the wagon. 'Why do you continue to refuse me? It is stubbornness.'

She wrenched away from him and pulled her shift over her head. 'You know why. And do not spoil this wonderful time we have had together by a quarrel over my reasons.'

He had tried to be patient with her all winter, but the nights she stayed at Mariner's House only proved to him that she was the only woman he wanted to spend his life with. He rose on his knees to put his arms round her. 'You know I adore you. This is where you belong.'

'Your father does not think so. He does not approve. He does not like me staying here.'

'This is my house and I want you here. And I want you as my wife.' Adam tried to stop her dressing, but she stood up and donned her skirt.

'Your father will never agree. This has been a difficult winter for the yard and your family. You have worked hard to keep the yard solvent. A

379

winter of bad weather could bring ruin if your orders are late in completion.'

Adam acknowledged how precariously they had managed to meet this winter's wages and bills. 'The *Pegasus* is due to dock soon. There will be profits from the voyage.'

'Which should be used to invest in goods for the next one. And the sailors have to be paid, and provisions bought for the next voyage. There will be little to divert to the yard. Edward will expect you to marry a woman with a handsome dowry. Has he not already begun to hint at such?'

There had been several arguments with his father over the subject. Edward Loveday did not consider Senara a suitable bride.

Senara was hurrying past the schoolhouse when the door opened and Gideon Meadows stepped out. He was startled at her presence. Senara bade him a hasty 'Good day' and increased her pace.

Some of the shipwrights were already at work in the sheds and others were leaving their cottages. She wanted to be out of the yard as quickly as possible.

'Miss Polglase!' Meadows ran after her. The rain had lessened to a drizzle, but he wore no hat and it was dripping off his lank hair on to his nose. 'Please wait. I owe you an apology. My behaviour the other week was inexcusable.'

She nodded acknowledgement and started to walk away.

'Please hear me out.' He again ran in front of her.

She glanced along the row of cottages. It was

now daylight and many would be aware that she had spent the night with Adam. Gideon Meadows was drawing even more attention to her presence there.

'I would like you to accept your old job back. It is a shame that my conduct is the cause of you missing the education you wanted.'

'I am busy with my pots. I have no time to clean for you, Mr Meadows.'

'But what of your education? You were such an accomplished pupil. There is so much more I can teach you.'

There was a fervour in his eyes which Senara no longer trusted. 'I shall always be grateful for all that you taught me. I can study on my own from books.'

'Borrowed from Adam Loveday, I suppose.' Anger flushed his gaunt cheeks. 'Has he no regard to your reputation? What about when he tires of you, as a man like that will? You will be reviled.'

'I am half-gypsy. We are used to such intolerance.' She glanced over her shoulder, aware that two women had brought their rug mats outside to beat and were standing in their doorways watching them.

The teacher's face contorted in misery. 'Forgive my harsh tongue. I did not mean my words to sound so condemning. I wished to spare you pain.'

'Senara, is there a problem?' Adam came up behind them, his expression stern.

'There is no problem, Captain Loveday.' Senara held her head high and walked stiffly away.

Gideon Meadows shifted uncomfortably under Adam's searing gaze. 'Take care how you conduct yourself, Meadows, if you value your work in the school here.'

'I would do nothing to harm Miss Polglase,' he answered with a pious sneer. 'Others have less regard for her reputation. It is you who shame her by your conduct, Captain Loveday.'

Adam was tempted to dismiss the schoolmaster for his impudence. But he was not a man to take rash offence over another's honesty. He saw the haunted look in Meadows' eyes as he stared after Senara's figure.

'Miss Polglase is not a subject for discussion. She will be treated with the highest respect by everyone within the yard.'

'Not everyone will be so tolerant,' Gideon Meadows pointed out. 'Her reputation is lost and that can make a woman vulnerable.'

Adam did not need reminding. It was another reason why he wanted to marry Senara. He could not understand Senara's reasoning behind her refusal. That she loved him was indisputable. She had once said that it was the very depths of her love which enabled her to sacrifice her own happiness for him. She remained convinced that he would, and must, marry a woman of his own class. Nothing he said could change her mind. The complexities of a woman's mind were beyond his understanding. He could give her everything most women cherished: love, adoration, financial security far above anything she had so far known, and respectability.

He went into the carpentry shed and picked up

an adze and took his dissatisfaction out on the wood as he used more force than was necessary to plane it into shape.

It was now nearly a month since Hester had last seen Harry. The bad weather made it difficult to get away from the house and in winter Thadeous did little business outside of Penruan. She was desperately unhappy. Her meetings with Harry and their lovemaking had kept her sane. They gave her hope that one day her misery would end, and she would be free of the monster she had married. Where once laughter and frivolity had been second nature to her, now she was constantly in tears.

'You've a face like the inside of a used chamber pot, woman,' Thadeous scowled at her as he came into their bedchamber and tore back the bedhangings of their tester bed. He wore a nightcap and gown, his round face with its bulging eyes, his barrel-belly and skinny legs, making him look more like a malevolent toad than ever.

Hester suppressed a shiver of distaste. She was huddled under the bedclothes. Any show of revulsion brought out his basest cruelties.

'You're a sore disappointment, wife. Always moping and snivelling. You scare the customers away. And little pleasure I get from you in bed. You're a cold baggage and give no comfort to a lusty man.'

'I do try, Thadeous.' She stretched her quivering mouth into a hesitant smile. 'You hurt me sometimes. I cannot relax.'

'Hurt you? What nonsense! Useless bag of bones, that's what you are. All those fine dresses and jewellery I bought are wasted on you. Phyllis would look better in them.'

'Then all the village would know how you favour your whore over your wife.' A spark of her old fire emerged.

The force of his blow jarred her head against the carved headboard. Then he grabbed her wrist and hauled her to the floor. 'You mind your tongue. A man needs his pleasure. And little you give me.'

Her hand came up to protect her head against his blows. His heavy signet ring ripped the flesh on her cheek and nose, drawing blood. He threw himself down on top of her and ripped her nightgown in two in his haste to enter her. His hands were brutal and bruising as his excitement rose at her pain. He ground into her like a battering ram, ignoring her pleas to be more gentle.

Hester sobbed in pain when her husband got into bed, leaving her weak and shivering on the floor. When she found the strength to crawl under the covers, she inadvertently put her frozen leg against his warm flesh.

'Bitch!' He kicked out at her stomach and propelled her back on to the floor. Her head banged against the side of a chest and she lay still.

The pain which ripped through her brought Hester back to consciousness some time later. She screamed as agony tore through her stomach. Her body was icy and her teeth chattered with cold and shock.

'What's that row?' Thadeous lit a candle and peered down over the top of the mattress at her.

Hester's body arched and she clutched at her stomach in agony as the tiny foetus slid between her thighs on to the floorboards.

Thadeous bellowed in rage. 'Curse you, woman! That was my son you've just emptied from your belly. And I not even aware that I was a father.'

Phyllis Tamblin had been drawn by the cries and peered through the crack in the bedchamber door. Phyllis was slow-witted, and having been in an orphanage since the age of four had never known love, only abuse. She had been raped at ten by the orphanage beadle, then quickly learned that by showing eagerness for his attentions, she ate better than the others there. She enjoyed many comforts from Thadeous Lanyon for allowing him into her bed. But as she watched his rage now, she was frightened.

Thadeous saw her at the door. 'Get in here and clean up this mess,' he bellowed.

'Don't the mistress be needing the doctor?'

'She can bleed to death for all I care. That would have been my son. My son! Did ever a man suffer more than I? Four wives and still I have no son. Why did the stupid woman not tell me she was with child?' He began to claw at his clothes and hair like a wild man.

Phyllis sped down the stairs to get some cloths and water. She did not like the mistress, who had taken a dislike to her on her arrival, and often shouted at her for not doing her jobs properly.

But the sight of the blood which pooled on the floorboards beneath the woman was alarming. Hester was again unconscious.

Phyllis cleaned the mess as best she could. The smell of blood was everywhere and she could almost taste the despair which permeated the bedchamber. She felt it so often in the orphanage that to her it was as tangible as the heat of a log fire. She had not expected to find it in a respectable household. Though from what she had learned of Thadeous Lanyon and his activities there was little about the man which was respectable. She took care not to displease him.

It needed four journeys to the kitchen for fresh water to get the floor clean. The tiny human form had filled her with horror. Unable to touch it, she had thrown a towel over it and pushed it with her foot in to the corner of the room. Lanyon had long since dressed and disappeared.

Phyllis wiped the floor around the woman's naked figure. The task done, her slow mind focused on her mistress. Should she get Hester back into bed? The woman was too heavy for her to lift. Still it weren't right to leave her on the floor. Had the master gone for the doctor? He must have done.

Lanyon had not gone straight to Chegwidden's house. He was angrily pacing the empty drying sheds. Four wives and all useless. Hester had failed him. Let the bitch die and he would find himself another.

Gradually, as he paced, his mind became more

rational. After the death of his third wife. Bertha, following years of beating and ill-treatment from Lanyon, Chegwidden had asked some probing questions. In law a man may beat his wife with impunity, but to cause her death was another matter.

He had been ill-fated with his wives; all had disappointed him. The first, whom no one but himself knew about, had been a snivelling jade. He had sold her to a brothel to be rid of her before he moved to Penruan. He assumed that she was long dead – not that bigamy troubled him. The second, Clara, was weak. She had lapsed into a twilight world induced by constantly taking laudanum.

It had eventually killed her, but at least she had come to the marriage with a sizeable dowry which had enabled him to buy the shop and drying sheds. As for Bertha, she had died of a fever – that it had been induced by his beating which had ruptured her spleen he refused to acknowledge. That was why Chegwidden had been suspicious. Thadeous had insisted her bruises were caused by a fall down the stairs.

Chegwidden was too fond of his kegs of brandy left in an outhouse to take his suspicions to the magistrate. But his son could be another matter.

If Hester died, there could be more unpleasant questions raised. At least she had conceived a child which none of his other wives had managed. She could conceive another.

He banged impatiently on Chegwidden's door. The maid answered it, and declared that both doctors were still abed. Lanyon stormed into the house, shouting that the doctor attend his wife at once for she had miscarried and had fallen unconscious.

He then returned to the house and managed to get Hester into a clean nightdress and into bed before Simon Chegwidden arrived. When the doctor was shown to the room by Phyllis, Lanyon was kneeling beside Hester's unconscious figure, his hands clasped in prayer.

Simon Chegwidden was inexperienced in childbirth after his years as a naval surgeon. 'Was Ginny Rundle not summoned?'

'It happened so quickly,' Lanyon lied. 'My wife complained of an upset stomach. We thought it was the fish from last night's supper. Next I know, she'd got out of bed and had fallen on the floor. She was screaming in pain. The child came almost at once, before I realised what was happening.'

Simon Chegwidden checked Hester's pulse and found it weak, and her body was exceptionally cold. 'Get some hot bricks wrapped in cloths for her feet. Has there been excessive bleeding?'

Lanyon looked at Phyllis, who hovered by the door, her thumb stuck in her mouth and her eyes round with fear. 'Not that I am aware of,' she mumbled.

'How far advanced was your wife's pregnancy, Mr Lanyon?'

Unwilling to admit he had been ignorant of the event, Lanyon shrugged. 'It bain't delicate for a man and wife to talk about these things.'

'Where is the child? Have you disposed of it yet?'

Lanyon glanced nervously at Phyllis. She pointed to the corner Dr Chegwidden examined the foetus. 'Nothing wrong with its form. Did your wife have a fall to bring on the miscarriage?'

At that moment Hester groaned and opened her eyes. She stared incomprehensibly at Dr Chegwidden.

'I am afraid, Mistress Lanyon, that you have lost your baby,' he said. 'Did you have a fall which may have caused it?'

Hester closed her eyes, knowing that Thadeous had caused the miscarriage. What use to blame him? Pride made her hide her injuries from the customers in the shop, and it made her lie now. 'I tripped on the mat and caught my side on the corner of the chest there. I also banged my head.' The pain in her temple made her suspect that it was bruised.

'It was a nasty fall. You have cut your face as well. Why did you not send for Ginny Rundle? Did you not suspect you were losing the baby?'

Hester did not reply. She was feeling too ill to tell more lies.

Simon Chegwidden put his hand on Lanyon's shoulder. 'Sad business. Get some broth into her to help her to regain her strength. Best to get Ginny Rundle to attend her. She is knowledgeable in these matters. If she should bleed excessively, or run a fever, call me at once.'

'I want my sister, Annie,' Hester implored.

'Of course, my dear. I shall send for her,' Lanyon replied. 'Sleep now and rebuild your strength.'

After the doctor left, Lanyon returned to his

wife's room. 'Your sister may visit on one condition – that your family believe that you miscarried because of a fall. I have business associates throughout the shipping trade, and I can see your father's chandler's shop ruined if you speak out of turn.'

Hester knew he was capable of destroying her family. It was a threat he had used before when her father accused him of beating his daughter. But her father was a gentle man and no match for Thadeous's bullying, and he had not interfered again.

'Why did you not tell me you were with child?'

'I had only just begun to suspect. But covered in bruises I could hardly go to Chegwidden or Ginny Rundle for advice.'

'Yet again you have failed and displeased me, madam.' He walked from the bedroom, slamming the door behind him.

Hester turned her head into the pillow, too miserable even to cry. She had not told Lanyon of the child, because she knew it was not his. She was waiting to see Harry and tell him he was a father. Surely then, he would have taken her away from Lanyon. She had lost so much more than Harry's baby. She had lost her immediate chance to escape the misery of her marriage.

Chapter Twenty-Two

Rafe Edward Loveday was born on 21 February 1792. The speed of his birth took everyone by surprise. After a day of feeling vague discomfort, Amelia had complained of her first pain after rising from the supper table. Another struck within a few minutes, sending servants running for Ginny Rundle and the doctor. By the time her maid had helped her divest herself of her clothing and don a nightgown, the pains had intensified and an hour later the six-pound Rafe presented himself to the world with a lusty cry.

Edward, hearing it from the dining room, was stunned having mentally prepared himself for a long and tortuous wait. He took the stairs two at a time with the sprightliness of a man half his age. Ginny Rundle appeared on the landing, tears of joy streaming down her portly face.

'You've a son, sir. A bonny, healthy son.' She held the wrapped, red-faced bundle out for him to take.

Edward cradled the boy in his arms, his throat working with emotion. 'And Amelia. She is well?'

'And waiting impatiently for her husband to kiss her,' Amelia called from the bedchamber.

Edward hurried to her, still in shock from the suddenness of it all. 'It is our son who is the impatient one. He has robust lungs. And you look radiant, my love. No one would credit you had just given birth.'

'Flatterer! I feel I have run from here to Truro and been kicked by a mule all the way.' Amelia lay back on the pillows, with her auburn hair streaked with sweat against her brow. Her eyes were bright with happiness and Edward sat on the edge of the bed, holding his wife in the fold of one arm, and his new son in the other.

'I did not think it was possible to be this happy,' he said in a voice choked with emotion as he kissed Amelia. 'Thank God, you had an easy birth.'

Ginny Rundle snorted from the corner of the room where she was tidying away the soiled sheets. 'Only a man could make such a remark. There be no such thing as an easy birth.'

Edward laughed and kissed Amelia again. 'I did not mean to undermine your efforts, my love. I was in such fear of losing you, that this pregnancy has given me little joy until now. And now my cup runneth over.'

'And talking of cups,' Amelia lifted her son from Edward's arms, 'this one needs feeding and your family should be celebrating with your finest brandy and wine. I wish Richard was here to meet his new brother and not away at school. He was so thrilled. You must write to him at once, Edward.'

'At once, my love,' Edward marvelled at her euphoria so soon after her travail. 'Perhaps you should rest. St John and Adam have been summoned. There will be much rejoicing at Trevowan this night.'

Adam arrived ten minutes after Dr Simon

Chegwidden, who had pronounced the mother and child fit and well.

Ginny Rundle shook her head behind his pompous, preening manner. She muttered to Sarah Nance, the bailiff's wife, who had also been called in to help with the birth, 'Waste of time sending for him. He bain't arrived in time to deliver a babe yet. And I doubt he'd be capable. Poor Hester Lanyon near bled to death because he had not examined her properly. Lucky I was there or she'd be grave fodder, that's for sure.'

'Heard tell Hester looked right poorly. Is it true Lanyon beats her?'

Ginny touched her nose. 'I bain't one to spread gossip, but she had an evil bruise on her belly and her face were all cut which didn't come from no fall. Though Lanyon were right upset about losing the child. No doubting that.'

'He be desperate for an heir, that be for certain,' Sarah declared.

'Ah, but were the child his?' Ginny winked slyly. 'Lanyon bain't sired one afore on his wives and countless servants he's been involved with.'

'Talk like that could get you into trouble, Ginny,' Sarah warned, but her eyes were gleaming. 'Who do you reckon the father is?'

'I wouldn't want to be spreading gossip, would I?' Ginny scratched beneath her huge pendulous breasts and sniffed. 'But it don't take too much deduction, do it? Hester bain't happy in her marriage. And Harry Sawle's got the swagger back in his step lately.'

'That is dangerous talk, Ginny.' Sarah shook her head. 'And I for one won't be repeating it.

You're right about Harry Sawle, though.'

The family were in high spirits when Adam arrived from the yard. He stripped off his greatcoat and gauntlets and handed them to Jenna Biddick, his face reddened by the cold of the icy wind.

'Family all be in the peacock room, Cap'n,' Jenna informed him.

Edward came across the room with a glass of brandy for him. 'Amelia has given birth to a son. You have a brother, Adam. His name is Rafe.'

Adam gratefully downed the brandy, savouring its warmth. The high-banked fire and the light from a dozen candles chased the chill from his body. 'Congratulations, sir. Is it permitted that we see the latest member of our family? A brother. That is splendid.' He held his glass up and declared. 'To Rafe Loveday. Long may he live and prosper.'

Edward was beaming with pride and his gait was unsteady from the amount of celebrating and toasting of his new son's health he'd done. Adam had never seen his father drunk and he found it amusing.

Margaret patted the couch where she was seated for Adam to sit beside her. 'We are waiting for Rafe to finish taking his milk before he is presented to us. It is a joyous occasion. I am glad I was here to witness it. A birth in a family is always special. Especially after so much sadness.'

Adam squeezed her hand. Elspeth was holding her glass out for Edward to refill. She was looking flushed and excited.

'So we have another boy to run round the house yelling and shouting. The Lovedays always have a predominance of boys. We were outnumbered, were we not, Margaret? Another girl would have been nice. A companion for Rowena. But at least this time it is just the one boisterous male to terrorise the servants; that is, if he takes after the twins.'

Adam laughed. 'Were St John and I so dreadful?'

'Turned the place into Bedlam.' Aunt Elspeth regarded him over the top of her pince-nez. 'Pair of fiends, you two were.'

Edward saw Ginny Rundle approaching and hurried to meet her and take Rafe. 'Here is your brother. May I present you all to Rafe Edward Loveday!'

The family gathered round: Margaret and Elspeth both eager to hold their nephew, St John and Adam peering over their shoulders at their brother.

'He is tiny!' Adam exclaimed in amazement, never having seen a baby so young.

'Ugly little devil, isn't he?' St John said with a laugh. 'Then so was Rowena. She looked like a turtle without its shell. But she was two pounds heavier than this little chap.'

'Rowena was beautiful.' Meriel was indignant but did not attempt to hold Rafe.

'Come see your new brother, Meriel,' Margaret insisted.

Meriel regarded the child. 'He's a real carrot top. Got more of Amelia in him than a Loveday from the looks of it.' She stepped back before

395

Margaret could hand her the baby.

'And who pulled your corset laces too tight, young lady?' Elspeth glared at her.

It was obvious that Meriel was furious that Amelia had produced a son. Rafe Loveday would have a hold on the estate in the future, to a far greater extent than a daughter would have done. Meriel, in her hunger for riches, had to acknowledge that Rafe's arrival would further deplete St John's inheritance. It could even affect her future if St John died before her and she had not given him a son. On Rafe's birth, Edward had told the twins, he was to change his will. In his earlier will he had split the yard and estate between the twins, but it had been on the condition that the two assets remain separate on their deaths only if they both produced sons. Otherwise the estate and yard would revert to the eldest surviving grandson sired by the twins. Failing that, it would now go to Rafe. In any event Edward would certainly provide handsomely for his third son's future and that legacy to Rafe would affect the money from the estate left to St John. That clearly displeased the haughty madam.

The christening was set for the second Sunday in March and would be performed at Trewenna church. The Lovedays and many of the shipwrights and their families attended from the yard. Richard was brought back from his boarding school in Winchester. Word was sent to Japhet's latest address in Falmouth and his younger brother, Peter, attending a seminary to study for the priesthood, was also notified. Neither was expected to attend.

On the day of the christening a room adjoining the nursery at Trevowan was opened up for the children. Apart from Rowena there were Hannah's son and two daughters and the two Traherne children, all under the age of five.

The trek to church was made under a milky sky and a heavy frost tinselled the bare branches of trees, gorse and grass. Wrapped in fur cloaks, with foot and hand warmers filled with hot pebbles, the women in the carriages were snug enough. Not so the riders. The hard ground permitted a brisk canter which in some measure warmed their blood, but their faces beneath mufflers were reddened by cold. Flasks of brandy were frequently handed round between the men and many were tipsy upon entering the icy confines of Trewenna church.

Joshua Loveday kept his sermon short and the two hymns were sung with resounding force. The ice had to be broken on the font and Rafe Loveday screamed his displeasure as the freezing holy water was dribbled across his brow.

Once back at Trevowan with the fires banked high and more mulled wine to greet the guests, both bodies and the atmosphere thawed.

Neighbours who had braved the roads to attend the church service joined the Lovedays for the feast which had been prepared in Rafe's honour. The gathering was of eminent families: Squire Penwithick, his wife, Dorothy, his studious son, Lance, and Lance's wife, Alice; Lord Fetherington, the Honourable Percy and his cousin Adolphous who was staying with him; the Trahernes, Lady Druce and Gwendolyn. Also with squire Penwithick were three French *émigrés*: the ageing Comte and Comtesse Valpasseur and the middle-aged Baron Tournon.

Hannah sidled up to Adam. 'Meriel is not looking pleased. She will see Rafe as a rival to St John's inheritance.'

Adam frowned. 'Father will provide for the boy and we can but hope that Amelia's fortune will eventually be restored. She still has the properties in London, though, of course, we will receive no income from them for five years.' He nodded to Lady Traherne, who was looking bored and restless. 'Your friend also looks as though she is chewing lemons.'

'Ros is never happy. Henry has refused to allow her to redecorate the music room and winter parlour, or have the grounds landscaped. She wants a lake dug and fountains and a palisade of Italian marble. The mine is barely staying in credit with copper prices so low. I lose patience with her. She does not know what it is like to struggle to make ends meet.'

'Are things that dire on the farm? Oswald looks pale and is thinner.'

'He works too hard and he cannot shift the cough he has had all winter. The life of a farmer is never easy, but I would not change my home for all the grandeur of Traherne Hall. At least I have found contentment.'

'Not least a progeny of children. Florence is not eight months old and you are expecting again, so Aunt Cecily has informed us.'

Hannah gave a throaty laugh. 'It is those long cold winters on the farm. When the wind blows from the east, it finds every crack in the joists or timbers to blast through. The only warm place is under the blankets. Besides, I want a large family.'

She smiled at Gwendolyn Druce, who had joined them.

'Such a fine gathering of friends and family for the christening,' Gwendolyn remarked.

'But no Japhet to bring a blush to your cheeks,' Hannah teased.

Gwendolyn fanned herself energetically, agitated by the remark. 'Peter is also absent. Such a shame for Cecily; she sees so little of her sons.' She hurried off to join Meriel.

Adam lifted a questioning brow at his cousin. 'What was all that about?'

'Gwendolyn is infatuated with Japhet. She spends all her free time at the Rectory helping Mama with her charity work, and hoping that Japhet will return.'

'It is not like you to be so merciless in your teasing. Gwendolyn looked upset.'

'I only tease her because I think it would be an excellent match for Japhet. Japhet will have to marry for money if he is to make something of his life. Gwendolyn would be the perfect wife. She adores him and is not the type to try and change him – though whether that would be a good thing or not is debatable.'

'Japhet is not ready to settle down,' Adam advised. 'And any hint that you are matchmaking will set him to flight.'

She regarded him archly. 'And what of you? No sign of any intended bride to grace Mariner's House?'

He did not answer. That he did not respond to her banter made her put her hand on his arm and say softly, 'The family is concerned about your relationship with Senara Polglase. She is no light of love, is she, Adam? Do you mean to wed her?'

When he still did not reply, she felt it her duty to persist, 'Senara is a lovely woman in every way, but she could never be at ease amongst your friends here.'

'They accept Meriel,' he retaliated.

'She is accepted because of the Loveday name. She is not greatly liked. Only Gwendolyn has truly befriended her and then, given her infatuation with Japhet, her motives could be suspect. And what of Senara's gypsy blood? It is their nature to move from place to place. Will she not always be restless and chafing at the constraints of convention and propriety?'

'I believe I know Senara better than you do.' He spun on his heel and marched away.

Hannah put out a hand to detain him then, with a shrug, snatched it back. She had not meant her words to sound so condemning, but if Adam was planning to marry Senara Polglase, she doubted he would do so with his father's blessing.

Squire Penwithick hailed Adam. The corpulent squire was talking with Edward and Joshua, his loud voice booming as he drank freely of the Loveday brandy. Hannah had angered Adam by her words, striking too closely to the truth to settle comfortably with him.

Penwithick said, 'You must be missing life at sea. When is the *Pegasus* due to dock?'

'Early April. If the voyage has gone to plan.'

'Then she will sail again once her cargo is loaded? To what destination this time?'

'The old colonies, if we can fill her hold. I have not yet found a replacement investor and the profit on this voyage will not be large. I have not spent as much time as I should have with my agents over the new goods to be shipped.'

'It has been a difficult winter?'

Adam nodded.

'Do you sail this time, as Edward will be at the yard?'

'I expect so.' The decision was not settled. He had planned to captain the *Pegasus* for the first four or five years, but while the yard remained in crisis, he felt uneasy about not being in Cornwall to help.

'It is only right that Adam captains his ship next time,' Edward said. 'There is another month or so before a decision must be made.'

'But it is the adventure that drives you as well as the profit, is it not?' Squire Penwithick said with a chuckle. 'Young blades like Adam thrive on it. I have not forgotten the service he did for our government when he gained valuable information for us in France.' The squire shook his head. 'It is a country simmering for revolt.'

Squire Penwithick, as a Member of Parliament, had the ear of the Prime Minister, Mr Pitt. Penwithick was in contact with many men who worked for the British Government in France.

Edward stroked his chin. 'One would have hoped that after King Louis was restored to power last September and accepted the new constitution, all would be well.'

'There were riots in Paris in January,' Penwithick sighed. 'There are so many food shortages and the slave rebellion in the West Indies has brought a sugar shortage. The price of food is high. How can the poor eat? And a starving family will make even a placid man fight for his rights.'

'The poor in England are also suffering with the closure of many of the mines as copper prices are so low,' Adam said. 'But there have been no riots.'

'Miners are a hardy breed, used to deprivation,' Penwithick answered.

'And how is our King's health?' Edward asked.

'He has never fully recovered from his bout of madness. There are times when he totters on the edge of reality. The Prince of Wales does not help with his extravagances and fast set.'

'In London it was obvious that the King becomes more popular despite his frail health.'

'And long may he reign!' Penwithick raised his goblet. His wife, Dorothy, had joined them. She basked in her husband's glory and spoke little at gatherings. Her hair was heavily powdered and she left a faint dust cloud in the wake of her passage. She was much given to adorning herself with patches and today wore one in the shape of a peacock on her ample bosom.

'On the subject of France,' she said, 'I hear such dreadful stories from the émigrés we meet,

Edward. Have you heard from Louise Riviere? Did you not intend to bring her to England from the French convent when she had recovered from her seizure?'

'The last news was before Christmas,' Edward replied. 'It is over three years since she was struck down and her recovery has been slow. I fear I have neglected my duty to her.'

The squire shook his head in disagreement. 'No man could do more for his family than you, Edward. Obligations in France had to take second place. Louise does have a son to look after her.'

'A son whose only interests are those concerning himself,' Edward snapped. 'He has not visited Louise once in all the time she has been convalescing at the convent. She is also anxious about her daughter.'

'The girl whom Adam was betrothed to?' The squire cleared his throat. 'Rum do, that. The chit jilted him to run off with a French marquis, did she not?'

'I do not think Lisette had much choice over the marriage,' Edward corrected. 'Her brother was always against the match with Adam. It was her father who was eager that she marry Adam and be safe in England. He suspected that there would be trouble with the monarchy and constitution. How right he was. After he died, Etienne was set upon furthering the family fortunes, and married Lisette to the Marquis de Gramont.'

'But is this marriage legal? A betrothal is a binding contract and many consider that such an arrangement is as legal as a marriage.'

'With the troubles flaring up in France there was nothing at the time we could do to dispute it,' Edward declared. 'It would have caused a scandal, and Lisette's reputation would have been irreparably damaged. Our only concerns are that Lisette is at least happy with her nobleman, and safe from harm. With more *émigrés* arriving from France it does not bode well.'

'She was such a sweet young thing. So pretty,' Dorothy Penwithick said.

'It is a difficult situation any way you look at it,' Penwithick frowned.

'Putting aside the rights and wrongs of what has happened, Lisette is my niece,' Edward went on. 'Claude Riviere was also my friend. If you are able to learn anything about Lisette from any *émigrés*, we would appreciate it. These are worrying times.'

'My men shall make enquiries.'

Adam moved away to stare out of the window. Dark clouds were rolling in from across the sea. It was a long time since he had given much thought to Lisette. Mention of her troubled his conscience. Should he have done more to honour his vow to Uncle Claude, to ensure that she was safe? The marriage to the marquis had angered him, for he knew it was Etienne's doing. Etienne's greed had led him to sacrifice his sister. Adam could not believe that Lisette was happy with Gramont. The man was a cruel lecher, whose deviations had resulted in at least one death of a young prostitute in Paris.

He massaged his temple against a building

pressure. The thought of Lisette – so young at sixteen, and so sweet and so innocent, married to that monster – added to his sense of guilt. He had not loved Lisette, and had agreed to the marriage out of duty. Yet he had been fond of her.

That there had been no word of her was unnerving. After King Louis had been arrested in June last year when he had tried to flee the country, Adam had heard from *émigrés* that Etienne had dropped his pretension of loyalty to the crown to gain favour with the nobility. Etienne was now a known and active insurgent.

Perhaps it was time to bring Aunt Louise to England. *Pegasus* was due to dock in a month. After she was unloaded, she could be spared for a short voyage of ten days or so to bring Aunt Louise to England. He would discuss it with his father.

Chapter Twenty-Three

The frost held and with the mud on the roads frozen it would be possible to travel to London. Margaret Mercer left Cornwall three days after the christening, with only her maid, Josie, for company. Edward had wanted to accompany her, but she refused. Her brother had his own business to attend to in Cornwall and had spent too long away from it on her behalf.

Thomas's last letter to her had been encouraging. All creditors had been paid, and they had lost no further wealthy clients. Also some of the investments he had made had returned a substantial profit. They were not yet clear of financial problems, but the future was more stable. It would still mean a year or so of careful planning and reinvestment.

'I knew Thomas was capable of saving the bank,' Edward had said over breakfast on the day she left Trevowan. 'He has done his duty by his father. You must be proud of him.'

'I am. And I feel guilty that he has spent so much of this winter alone. I should have been there to help in any way I could. To entertain clients makes them more amiable to invest greater funds. That was Charles's policy.'

'And I am sure it is a sound one,' Edward had replied and then reminded her, 'but there was no money for entertainments. You must remember that to save the bank Thomas had to sell many of the paintings and items of value. The carriage and horses would also have been sold if they had not been with you in Cornwall.'

'None of those things are important. I shall follow Thomas's advice in such matters. Though I would have preferred to have heard that some heiress had taken his eye. It is the best solution to the stability of the bank, and high time that Thomas was married.'

Throughout the journey Margaret compiled a list of suitable brides for her son. Of course, she would have to review it once she reached London, for some might no longer be eligible. Heiresses did not linger for long on the marriage market.

Her plans of matchmaking helped the days of

the arduous journey to pass. By the time she reached London, Margaret had a shortlist of five. She was excited at the prospect of helping her son to select a bride.

Margaret arrived at the house at twilight. She was aching in every bone from the journey and chilled to the marrow. The house was in darkness, the door locked and the windows shuttered. It took several minutes of insistent banging for the elderly footman, Dillinger, to open the door. He was still shrugging himself into his livery jacket and fastening the buttons.

'Madam! We had no word you were returning.'

She walked past him into the shadowy hall. The gloom of the house was oppressive. Even the semi-darkness revealed the halfdozen paintings missing from the walls. Margaret felt a weight descend on her heart. There was an emptiness to the house, a tomb-like quality which was morbid.

She shuddered, disliking such fanciful thought. 'Fetch candles, light a fire in the drawing room and my bedroom, and I will require hot water for a bath and a hot meal as soon as possible.'

'Yes, madam.'

Margaret walked up the stairs to the first floor and entered the parlour. Her hand went to cover her heart as the shock hit her. Gone were the paintings, the delicate French furniture, the two Persian carpets, the silver, the large ormolu Louis Quatorze clock, and several ancient Chinese vases and the large gilt-framed Venetian mirror. What was left of the furniture was shrouded in dust-sheets.

'Madam,' Dillinger spoke from behind her,

'there is but myself and Mrs Dillinger left. Master Thomas paid off the other servants and closed up the house. He's been living with his friend Mr Greene. Shall I send word to him that you have returned?'

'Do that. Thomas was not expecting me until the end of the month. But first make up the fire in my bedchamber. Do not trouble with the one in the parlour. I will stay in my room to eat and retire early.'

To occupy herself and keep warm, she lit a double candlestick and inspected every room of the house. So many of the possessions she and Charles had chosen together had been sold. Despite her resolution an occasional tear ran down her cheek. Each missing object was like another part of Charles being taken from her.

Her inspection over she held her head high as she walked up the stairs to her bedchamber. The fire was burning brightly in the hearth and a porcelain hip bath had been placed before it. Within the room nothing had been changed, although the ornaments and gilded furniture would have sold for several hundred pounds.

Opposite her bed Thomas had hung the painting of Charles and herself with Thomas as a baby in her lap. It tore at her heart and she could no longer stop her tears. Grief poured from her. She had loved Charles deeply and there were still days when she could not believe that he had been taken from her. She could almost sense him in the room, trying to comfort her – telling her all would be well. But how could it be without him?

'Oh, my darling, how you must have suffered in

the last months. You were so strong, so honest... To be driven to take your life, your pain must have been unbearable. Yet I can see that your sense of honour would have demanded nothing less from you. You were never a coward.'

She continued to gaze at the portrait. Charles had not spoken a word of their troubles, not wishing to worry her. She put her fingers to her lips and then pressed them against the canvas figure of her husband. 'You were all that mattered to me, my darling. Nothing else was important. I hope that now you are at peace, and know how much I loved you.'

The soft tap on the door stiffened her spine. Margaret wiped her eyes and drew a shaky breath before turning to address Mary Dillinger. She was carrying a pail of hot water; her husband was behind her with two more. They were both in their sixties and had been with the family since before Margaret had married Charles. She was glad that Thomas had not needed to dismiss them.

'Our circumstances have changed, but I am sure as soon as it is practical, we shall be employing more staff to help with your duties. Josie will help where she can.'

There was a sniff of disapproval from the maid, who had just entered to unpack Margaret's trunks, which she chose to ignore.

'We don't mind the extra work,' Mary Dillinger replied. 'Though I ain't much of a cook. Mrs Howard always ran the kitchen. But I can rustle you up plain fare.'

'That will be adequate. I intend to live simply.'

Dillinger came forward. 'I sent a boy round to the bank and to Mr Greene's home for Master Thomas. There's been no reply.'

'Thomas will come when he can. I shall bathe now and be ready to receive him in half an hour.'

The couple left and returned with more pails of hot water until the bath was sufficiently full.

'No matter how late the hour,' Margaret instructed them, 'I will speak with my son when he arrives.'

Thomas did not return to the Strand that evening. When he received the message from Dillinger, he was dining with friends and drinking heavily after watching a play.

He swayed to his feet. 'Mama has returned. I must leave you, my friends. I cannot have my mother alone on her first night back in London.' He tripped over the leg of a table and would have fallen had not Lucien caught him.

'You cannot see your mother in this condition. Lud, she will think you are in your cups every night, and I know you have been as abstemious as a Puritan. 'Twas only that it is Gilbert's birthday that you joined us tonight. You must be sober, and the essence of the perfect banker, when you greet your mama.'

Thomas tried to protest, but after a dozen brandies and very little food, his legs would not obey his commands. He was carried back to Lucien's rooms and roused by Lucien's man-servant early the next morning. He presented himself to his mother, shaved and immaculately dressed, but red of eye and with a pounding headache.

Margaret was still abed and held out her arms for Thomas's embrace. 'You are so thin. So pale. You have not been eating properly. I knew I should not have stayed in Cornwall.'

'And you should have sent word you were returning so soon. The house would have been ready for you and more servants engaged. The place must have been a great shock to you. I would have prepared you. I am so sorry, Mama.'

'I approve of all you have done. What do I need with fripperies and the like? They are paltry compared to saving your father's reputation and that of the bank. You have done splendidly. But can we afford more staff at present?' She was instantly practical. 'I will not entertain if we no longer have the means.'

He shrugged. 'A cook is a necessity now you are living here, and another maid of all work. I would not deprive you of your comforts.'

She patted the bed for him to sit upon, and Josie appeared carrying two cups of chocolate for them to drink. Thomas sipped his with an inward grimace, preferring coffee in the mornings to the sweet confection.

'Tell me our present situation,' Margaret demanded. 'The truth, though, with no prevarication.'

He told her everything in detail, his manner sombre and strained. 'There is a list of everything that was sold, but I kept the silver tea service and second-best china so that you would not be ashamed to serve tea to your friends.' He gave a twisted half-smile which was apologetic.

Margaret again felt herself close to tears at his

411

thoughtfulness. She blinked the tears away, hating to be so weak. 'And you kept my room as it was, but are you sure enough funds were raised?'

He nodded. 'There have been many sacrifices. The house is half empty, but if the furniture is arranged in the small parlour and—'

'I will manage and make do, and hold my head high. If the bank had failed many people would have lost their savings. Do not talk of sacrifice. I am surprised you managed to keep the house.'

'It was heavily mortgaged and if my investments do not meet my expectations, then we will have no choice but to sell. But after the mortgage is repaid there would be little left.'

'It will not come to that, I am sure. Once you wed an heiress, our future will be settled.' She sensed his withdrawal from her and added, 'You cannot escape that duty, Thomas. Surely after all this time you have someone in mind?'

'I have been spending all my time at the bank with no time to socialise.'

'If you have not given thought to a bride, then I have.'

Thomas stood up. 'There is no need to discuss it now. I am expected at the bank. I have an important customer attending at eleven.'

'We will discuss it over supper this evening.' Margaret was undaunted.

Thomas fled the house. His mother would give him no peace until he chose a bride. The proposition was as inevitable as it was unsavoury.

Throughout March and April Meriel took on a

new role. That of peacemaker at the Dolphin Inn. Harry talked of nothing but achieving his revenge on Thadeous Lanyon, convinced that the smuggler's banker had run his father down on purpose.

'You cannot act against Lanyon in a way which will harm him and not risk suspicion falling upon you,' Meriel reasoned with her brother. 'All in Penruan know of your hatred for the man.'

'I can bide my time. But he will get what's coming to him.'

'Then bide your time long and well, brother.'

Reuban was propped on a truckle bed in the kitchen. He was a bad patient and a worse cripple. 'That bastard will pay. Damned useless I am with no legs.'

'Lanyon saved your life by bringing you into the inn and he paid Chegwidden's fees,' Sal insisted. 'There's been too much talk of revenge in this house.'

Reuban hawked and spat into the fire. 'Where's my ale? No one listens to me. Get my ale. If I had me legs back it would be a different story. Lanyon would suffer. Never you fear. What kind of sons have I got who don't repay that bastard in his own kind?'

Sal thrust a quart tankard in his hands. 'You'll get your sons hanged with your stupid talk. You were drunk that night. Too drunk to walk or think straight. It be your own stupid fault you were run down.'

Reuban lashed out at her but his fist hit air, and instead he rained curses on his family. Eventually exhausted by his ranting, and the drink which Sal had laced with poppy juice, he fell asleep.

Sal had lost three stones in weight and was looking old and wizened. 'I've taken about all I can stand. Listen to Meriel, Harry. Get your revenge by rivalling Lanyon with your smuggling if you must. Get your revenge by making the Dolphin a more popular drinking place than Lanyon's Gun. But I won't have the shame of having a cold-blooded murderer for a son.'

Harry sat hunched and glowering by the fire in the taproom. His mother knew little of the blackness of his or Clem's true character. Since they were young men they had been egged on by Reuban to rule by intimidation when necessary. More than one man had met his death because he had crossed the Sawles. There was still anger and bitterness in him at the way Hester had betrayed him. The sex he had with her did little to assuage it even though Hester was as passionate as he wished. He could not forgive her. Neither could he love her as once he had done. She had taken something from his manhood, destroyed the last residual softness and compassion. He was now a man driven with ambition and the need for revenge.

'After the taking of Lanyon's cargo there's many wondering whether you and Clem were involved,' Meriel added her opinion to that of her mother. 'Too many who know your ways are awaiting for you to act against Lanyon.' She bent low to whisper, 'Besides you are getting your revenge by striking at the man's pride through his wife. That were your child Hester lost, and Lanyon is mourning it for his own. Get another

414

one on her, and let him raise your bastard believing it is his. That must suffice for now.'

'Little chance of that while Hester is still abed after losing the child.' Harry scowled and glanced at Sal to check she had not heard. His mother's hearing was not as sharp as once it was.

'That is her way of avoiding her husband's attentions,' Meriel said. 'And with the weather so bad where would you be meeting her?'

The wind slammed against the window pane as though to emphasise her point. Sal coughed as smoke puffed back into the room from the chimney. She was gutting and skinning two rabbits Mark had shot and spoke to Harry over her shoulder. 'You've been cooped up too long with the winter storms. Get yourself out to sea with the fleet once the weather lets up and you won't be half so restless and ill-tempered.'

'St John is impatient for the next run to be made,' Meriel added. 'Have you decided if you will take your own lugger to Guernsey to run the goods, or get the Guernsey agents to supply and deliver?'

'More profit if we can use the lugger, but Clem reckons we should stick with distributing it once it has landed.' Harry gave a bitter laugh. 'Can't bear a night away from his marriage bed, the love-lorn fool. Never thought I'd see Clem so smitten.'

'He's happy with Keziah. She is a fine lass,' Sal defended. 'It's 'bout time he curbed his wilder ways. Wouldn't do you no harm either, Harry.'

Harry scowled and emptied his ale tankard. Meriel turned the conversation back to smuggling.

415

'St John expects a one-third share in the run. He's earned it after last time.'

Sal snorted and rounded on her daughter, jabbing the ladle she was using at her. 'Why do you want your man involved with the smugglers? It is madness. Edward Loveday will be furious. He used to turn a blind eye to such goings-on but that was before Adam was set upon by smugglers the other year and nearly died. He won't buy goods from the free traders now.'

'Little you know, Ma. He took St John's money from his last run to pay off some of Trevowan's debts.'

'And I expect gave his son a lecture for his pains and generosity,' Sal sniffed. 'Most of the men round here get involved in the trade because it keeps food in the bellies of their families after a poor pilchard season. You want St John involved because of greed. And you with more wealth and good-living at Trevowan than you deserve! You've not gone hungry since you wed St John, nor gone without fine clothes and fancy entertainments. Yet you won't be satisfied until you go too far, will you? Will you be satisfied when your husband and brothers rot in gaol because of your greed?'

Another week of storms brought a further halt to work in the yard. Violent winds had torn down one of the pulleys on the revenue cutter and had damaged some planking when it crashed against the ship's side. Throughout the winter more than seven weeks' work had been lost because of gales, storms and torrential rain. It had meant extend-

416

ing loans to meet what wages were to be paid. After Adam's hard work to keep the debts at bay, the yard was sliding back into financial trouble.

'It does not look too good, does it, sir?' he addressed Edward as they climbed down from the scaffolding after inspecting the damage.

It was still raining and apart from half a dozen men shaping timber in the shed, the only other work being carried out in the yard was the blacksmith hammering out nails in his forge. They skirted round the larger puddles as they approached the office.

Adam took off his oilskin and shook it, saying, 'I've drawn up new work schedules for the men once the weather permits them to work outside.'

Edward studied the schedules. He rubbed his chin and nodded his agreement.

'Winter is never a good time with gales and storms. This year has been more difficult than most. Having taken on so many extra men, it is hard to see them sitting idle and not earning.'

Adam stared out the window to the inlet running at full tide. A thick branch of a tree whirled like a top towards the River Fowey.

'*Pegasus* is overdue, is she not?' Edward had not removed his greatcoat and he pulled his chair closer to the fire.

'There has been no word from Bristol. I should have insisted she docked at Falmouth; it is easier to keep a check on her.'

'Bristol is a better dock to land the cotton in. I can spare you here, if you wish to travel to the port.'

Adam shrugged. The inactivity caused by the

417

bad weather vexed him. '*Pegasus* is only a week late. It is too soon to be concerned over her. But it would not go amiss to check with my agents on the goods bought and stored for the next voyage. It may be necessary to carry another merchant's goods to fill the hold, if she is not to lie up for weeks without a full cargo. That puts me in competition with shipping lines who have been in the business for years, and have established a reputation.'

'You have neglected your merchant investments by putting so much time into the yard. What of your investors?'

'As you know, one backed out after the first venture.' He paced the small room, irked by inactivity when so much needed to be done. 'The other investor is waiting to see how high the profits are before he commits himself again. They will not be good.' Adam had accepted the situation and remained philosophical. 'The yard is what is important. I knew it would not be easy to become a merchant adventurer.'

'Then go to Bristol,' Edward insisted. 'You may even run into your graceless cousin Japhet. Cecily has not heard from him in weeks and is worried.'

Adam shook his head and grinned. 'If Japhet is in trouble or out of funds, he would return home. If he is in gaol, he would contact you for bail or help. If he was injured we would have heard. While he has money to line his pockets and is pursuing a life of ease, there will be silence.'

'Aye, you are probably right. So will you go to Bristol?'

The prospect was tempting. There was much to be resolved with the *Pegasus* and her cargo. He would ride to Falmouth and then find a boat which would take him to Bristol. A more pleasurable thought struck him. He would persuade Senara to accompany him. They could have as long as two weeks in each other's company, and if he could break down her resistance he might yet even return to Mariner's House with her as his bride.

Chapter Twenty-Four

The late April weather was kind to them in Bristol. Senara had agreed to accompany Adam and had been a constant source of delight to him. Each day he marvelled at how easy she was to confide in and talk to. While her beauty never failed to excite him, Senara's lessons with Gideon Meadows had given her the knowledge of many subjects which had long fascinated him. She was the perfect companion and he was more in love with her than ever.

They had taken two rooms, a bedroom and parlour, in a terrace of Georgian houses habited by the merchants of the town.

'This is too grand,' Senara had protested. 'You should be saving your money to invest in the next cargo.'

'The inns in Bristol are far from respectable and the haunts of sailors and prostitutes.'

419

'There are respectable inns, Adam. I have lived in Bristol.'

'But these rooms are far more pleasant, are they not?' He had ignored her protests and the frown which had accompanied them. As a surprise for Senara, Adam had ordered a pale green cotton and also a lilac dimity gown for her, plus an Indian shawl of sage with a cream patterned border. They had been delivered on the fourth day after their arrival.

He returned to their rooms expecting to find her wearing one of them. Instead she was wearing her old dark green dress, the dresses and shawl still partially wrapped in the calico they had been delivered in.

'Do you not like the dresses?' he said with concern. 'They can be changed if the colour, or style, is not to your liking.'

'I do not want you to buy me things.'

'But it gives me pleasure.'

'It shows that what I already possess is not good enough for your standards. I shame you in my own clothes.'

'You could never shame me, Senara.' He went to take her in his arms but she evaded him. 'Why must you be so stubborn? I thought all women doted on pretty clothes. I thought the green and lilac were colours that you favoured. I took pains in my choice.'

His exasperation and hurt showed. It made her feel guilty, but she did not want Adam for the things he could buy her, but for himself. 'I will wear the clothes while in Bristol, for I have seen how the women frown at the shabbiness of my

420

dresses. But the new ones are not fitting for my work or life at the cottage. They are the dresses of a woman of leisure.'

'There would be little leisure time for any woman who was my wife. My income from the yard is just enough to live on and all my profits from *Pegasus*' voyages for some years will be ploughed back into future cargo.' He was half joking and half serious, his eyes sharp as he studied her reaction.

'Is there word of *Pegasus?*' She changed the subject.

'She docked this afternoon, which is why I am late returning. She was blown off course during storms but sustained no damage or loss of life.'

'That must be a relief to you. She is a fine vessel but there are always risks.' Senara picked up the lilac dress and smiled at Adam. 'I will dress especially for you this evening and we must celebrate.'

'We shall attend the playhouse, how is that? But I fear tomorrow I shall be away for most of the day checking the cargo lists with my agents.'

'I should like to attend the play.' As she turned to enter the bedroom, he caught her to him and was crushed in his arms.

'It's two hours before the play begins. Before you dress especially for me, I would have you first undressed. The more I am with you, Senara, the more I miss you when we are apart.'

She answered his kisses with fervour, for every moment they were together was becoming more precious to her, too. Yet when they were not together, she was restless and bored. If she ventured on to Bristol's streets, the sneering glances from the women in the neighbourhood emphasised her fears for her and Adam's future. Also they brought back memories of how her army captain had betrayed her in this town. Idleness did not sit well with her, and town life was stifling. She missed the freedom of the countryside and her work and animals around her.

The next week was busy for Adam. His own cargo for shipment would not fill one-third of the *Pegasus'* hold. There would be no profit in the next voyage if he did not fill her hold with goods from a merchant willing to pay for its passage. Competition was fierce. The merchants had their own ships or were under contract with established shipping owners to carry their goods.

Adam haunted the coffee-houses and port offices in search of business. That he was not a local man added to the merchants' suspicions, and he began to wonder if he would have to sail to Falmouth or Plymouth in search of a cargo.

Failure followed on failure, and he decided to sail to Falmouth in two days. His own goods remained in the warehouse in Bristol and that storage was costing him extra. If *Pegasus* was not to lie idle, it might be possible to do shorter runs for merchants trading with the Mediterranean ports.

Cargo was not his only problem. The captain he had engaged for the last voyage was also pressing him for a decision. He had the chance to sail on a ship out of Bristol at the end of the following week to the Spice Islands. The owner needed his acceptance by the next day. Reluctantly Adam released the captain from his employ. He was a good captain and Adam did not entrust the care of *Pegasus* lightly. It seemed the decision had been made for him that he must captain the *Pegasus* himself on her next voyage.

Adam had spent two hours that afternoon walking the length of every deck of *Pegasus* to inspect how she had weathered and borne the handling of the sailors on her voyage. He could not fault the cleanliness of her decks, though they were now scuffed by the marks of boots, and seasoned to a darker hue by the elements. The once-pale timbers below decks were also darkened from the smoke from lanterns. Pegasus had been the home to over forty men who had left their marks by dagger, restless hands and rough manners. She was no longer the fresh-faced child, scrubbed and shiny, but a seasoned campaigner in her prime.

He acknowledged the two sailors left on watch and walked down the gangplank, proud of the ship he had created, and of her performance. He paused a moment to gaze up at the white figurehead with its gilded hoofs rearing over the waves which would break beneath the bowsprit. The gilt had worn away in places and the paint was no longer fresh, but cracked and peeling. Even so, his heart lifted with pride.

The jangle of chains from the quayside drew his attention. At seeing a line of black slaves herded into a warehouse, his stomach clenched with anger. He despised the trade for when he was in the navy he had boarded a slaveship and seen the suffering of slaves on board who were treated worse than cattle. He had learned since that many of the slaves had been stolen from their villagers and sold by slavers to a life of misery, separated from their homeland and families. It was time England listened to the abolitionists and ended any connections with the trade in this country.

A hand suddenly descending on his shoulder made Adam spin round, his fist raised as though expecting an attacker.

Japhet grinned at him. 'I saw *Pegasus* had docked and hoped you would be near at hand. I've just got back to Bristol.'

'Where have you been?'

'Here and there. You know how it is.'

'No, I do not!' Adam grinned. 'I live a very staid life compared to you, cousin.'

'Now that I do not believe,' Japhet laughed. 'Where are you staying?'

'I've taken rooms. Come and eat with us. Senara is with me.'

Japhet gave a saucy whistle. 'And what is so staid about having the delectable Miss Polglase as your companion? I take it Uncle Edward is not in port?'

Adam ignored his taunts. I'm here to find a cargo to transport, but have had no luck. We sail to Falmouth in two days, and you are welcome to join us. Aunt Cecily worries that it is so long since she heard from you.'

'I am not sure of my plans. And Mama should know better than to worry. But I suppose it has been a while.' He shrugged. 'We must dine tonight and catch up on family news. Or will that rather preclude your lovely lady?'

'Senara will enjoy fresh company.'

If Senara felt any misgivings at being presented with the most rakish of the Loveday family and a man who had tried to pursue her, she did not show it.

'The lovely Senara, fairest woman in all Cornwall,' Japhet pronounced as he bowed over her hand and raised it to his lips. 'Were not Adam my friend and cousin, I would give him a run for his money to win you as my own.'

She parried his compliments and flirted with him in good humour. Several times, when Japhet's compliments became too effusive, Adam shot a warning glare at his cousin. Japhet's outrageous anecdotes made Senara's sides ache from laughing, but as the evening lengthened and she listened to their banter, sadness clouded her happiness. They spoke of a world she could never be comfortable in: a world of fops, of outrageous extravagances, reckless escapades, duels of honour, snobbery and a world where money ruled. Senara, who was content with the simple things in life, found these differences as frightening as they were incomprehensible. How could there be any future for Adam and herself?

It was an evening of merriment and several bottles of wine had been consumed. When Japhet took his leave, he was unsteady on his feet. He kissed her boldly on the cheek, announcing in a husky whisper, 'Adam clearly adores you. You are good for him. Beats me why you do not wed the smitten dolt.'

'They are kind words, sir, but it is the drink talking,' she corrected.

'Deadly serious business, marriage.' He waved a finger at her. 'Lord knows, I've done my best to avoid it.' His long finger tapped the end of his nose. 'But I know when a couple are meant for each other. Saw it straight away with my sister, Hannah, and her Oswald. It is there between you and Adam.'

To show support for Thomas, Margaret came out of deep mourning and took off her black gowns. Unable to afford a new wardrobe, she sewed black lace on to her paler gowns as a compromise. To show society that Mercer's Bank had recovered from its financial crisis, she planned a soirée for their leading clients and men of influence in the City. The crisis was far from over and the bank still in a precarious position.

'We have to look prosperous to attract rich clients,' she declared to a hesitant Thomas.

'But the house is bare of furniture,' he protested. 'Everyone will see our straitened circumstances. It will have an adverse effect.'

'Leave it to me. Lady Marsha is an old friend of mine, and has always been indebted to me for introducing her to Lord Hubert, whom she married two years ago. She will lend me what is needed. A few paintings and chairs will make all the difference. I shall call on her this afternoon. It will cost us little. I trust you did not completely ransack, or sell the wine from your father's cellar.'

'A quarter of it remains, the rest were sold.'

'It is adequate.' She threw her arms round Thomas and gave a hearty laugh. 'We will show London how formidable the Mercers can be. And I shall invite Lascalles. He will see that we prosper. If we are to consider a merger to improve the bank's security, then invitations must be sent to other bankers.'

'I am not sure that Lascalles should attend. There is ill feeling between us.'

'A banker must rise above such things, Thomas. Lascalles will be one of several bankers present. This is a display of strength to show to our detractors that the Mercers are still a force to be reckoned with.'

Thomas had not the heart to stop her plans. It would take his mother's mind from her grief and all she had lost. She was already at her desk writing the guest list, and another list of necessities to be borrowed to make the evening a success.

After so many struggles and setbacks Thomas did not have his mother's optimism. Yet as he had appreciated the help from Uncle Edward and even Japhet in his haphazard and careless way, he had learned that it did not do to underestimate the Lovedays when they put their minds to matters.

To Senara and Adam's surprise Japhet joined them on *Pegasus* an hour before she was to sail to Falmouth.

'I thought you could do with an extra hand, as you'd not be taking on a full crew to man an

427

empty ship,' he explained.

'I had planned to tack close to shore for most of the journey,' Adam replied, 'and have engaged only a skeleton crew. You are welcome.'

Japhet shrugged and went off to stow his luggage in the mate's cabin.

On docking at Falmouth, two hacks were hired for Japhet to escort Senara back to her cottage and then go to visit Trewenna Rectory. Adam would remain in Falmouth for four days and if no cargo was available would continue to Plymouth.

On the third day he secured a cargo bound for The Hague. The merchant's own ship had been shipwrecked off the Scilly Isles last week and he needed urgent passage. It would mean only two weeks at sea and would return a profit. Adam was to sail in four days. He sent word to Senara and to Trevowan to inform his family of his plans.

To Adam's surprise Squire Penwithick came on board the night before he was to sail.

'I was dining with your father when your messenger arrived,' he declared. 'Are you able to divert to Honfleur on your return? There is a group of nine *émigrés* wishing to leave France. They are not without funds and can pay for their passage. They will come aboard at night heavily disguised and you must be ready to sail at once.'

'Why do I suspect that these are no ordinary *émigrés?*'

'Their names are unimportant, but as you probably suspect they would be arrested if their identities were discovered. The Austrian war has been disastrous for France and the early defeats have pushed up prices and added to the food shortages. The reports I receive tell of fear and suspicion everywhere. The King is more unpopular than ever.'

Adam sighed. 'I will, of course, do what I can.'

The squire nodded in satisfaction. 'I knew you would not fail me. You will put in to Honfleur to take on fresh water and provisions. Your contact is a one-eyed innkeeper, Armand Reyneux at the Half Moon tavern off the waterfront. The mission is not without its dangers. Should the French become suspicious the harbour guns could be fired on you.'

Adam agreed to the venture. By the time he returned to England he might have accrued enough profits to fill the *Pegasus*' hold for her next voyage.

St John was jubilant. Two smuggling runs in late April and May had been successful. Tonight he was to meet Clem at the Dolphin to divide up the profits. A grudging respect had built up between St John and the Sawle brothers, though he remained wary of Clem, who was the more brutal.

Harry was late and when he entered the inn his swagger was pronounced. Clem grinned. 'You've been with Hester again. Good for you. Teach that bastard Lanyon a lesson that the Sawles won't be mocked.'

They were in the taproom after the last of the customers had left. Reuban was snoring, propped up on a settle by the fire.

'Let's get the old man carried up to his bed, before we settle things,' Harry suggested.

Clem shook his head. 'He'll not wake. Not after the amount of brandy he's knocked back.'

There was a rustle of silk and Meriel came in from the kitchen.

'Didn't expect you, sis,' Harry taunted. 'Slumming it, are you? Or eager to get your hands on the money from our last run?'

She ignored Harry's taunting and sat in a corner. 'Ma is asleep. She is worn out. I hope both of you are helping her to run the pub now that Mark is no longer here.'

'What time do I get?' Clem snorted. 'I've a wife now and am out every day with the fleet. It's been a good season for mackerel so far.'

'I do my bit.' Harry glared at her. 'Just 'cause you've risen too high to dirty your hands to help Ma don't mean to say others would see her burdened.'

Clem took out a money chest from its hiding place in a hole under a flagstone and counted its contents into three piles. 'I reckon we should invest half of this in the next run and build up our investment gradual like.'

'Why not put in three-quarters?' Harry suggested. 'We could have another run next month, and another five or six before the weather turns in October. To really make this pay next year we need to think about investing in one of the new cutters built in the Loveday yard. I've heard no revenue ship can get near them.'

'You run too fast, Harry,' Clem warned. 'We are a small set-up. It takes years to build up contacts.'

'I still say we need a fast vessel. It would do no

430

harm to keep an eye on the ship auctions. We could pick up a confiscated smuggling sloop cheap. One gang's loss is our gain.'

'Also we could risk losing everything, as I did before,' St John cautioned. 'I think we should progress slowly as Clem suggests.'

'Perhaps Meriel has too tight a hold on your purse strings,' Harry scowled. 'She can wait on her trinkets, can't she?'

'Greed is often a man's downfall,' Meriel snapped.

'I say we use two-thirds from these profits.' St John was angry at Meriel for undermining his negotiating power.

'Two-thirds,' nodded Clem in agreement.

'Ay, two thirds,' Harry compromised. 'And we use our lugger to get the cargo from Guernsey. That saves paying an agent.'

'I prefer that the Guernsey men land the goods,' Clem hedged.

'What is this I be hearing?' Keziah's voice boomed as she came in from the kitchen.

Clem started, clearly not expecting his wife to be present. 'It's business, m'dear.'

Keziah stood over the table, arms crossed over her chest, her gaze assessing the amount of money on the table. 'Unless you three have taken up highway robbery, there's only one business yields so much. And it bain't law-abiding.' Baltasar nuzzled past her skirts and sniffed the table top, searching for food.

'Get that damned goat out of here.' Harry pushed the hairy face aside and received a butt in the ribs.

Keziah turned on Meriel. 'Shame on you for encouraging them. Lawlessness bain't my way, Clem Sawle, as well you know. You said you made an honest living as a fisherman when you asked me to wed you. That be good enough for me.'

'I don't take orders from no woman, Kezzy,' Clem flared. 'This is business. Honest enough. We take care no one gets hurt and it brings benefit to many.'

'Don't give me that, husband. How can you stop anyone being hurt when the excise men turn their guns on you? Lawlessness is what it is, however you look at it. You know my views, Clem.' She walked out.

To everyone's astonishment Clem barely hesitated before he took after her. He caught up with Keziah's angry strides in the stableyard.

'This is business from long afore I met you, Kezzy. A man's gotta honour his obligations, bain't he?'

'Do as you think fit. I don't want a penny of that money in my home. And I don't want a man who says one thing and does another. Think well on your decision, husband.' She strode away.

Inside the taproom Reuban had stirred and gave a sinister cackle of laughter. 'That Kezzy is some woman.' For some reason he favoured his new daughter-in-law. 'Needs a clout now and then to keep her in line, though, like any woman. Especially our Meriel. Never knowed a creature so wilful or stubborn. Good hidin' now and then don't do no woman no 'arm and teaches her her place. Bide my words, St John.'

'You've always been too fond of your fists,'

Meriel shouted at him. 'You've made Ma's life a misery.'

'What's that about my life being a misery?' Sal lumbered into the taproom. 'You keep your opinions to yourself, my girl. You pa has done right by me. And there's a fair bit of misery come your husband's way from wedding you. So don't you come the high and mighty, madam.'

Meriel and Sal continued to squabble in the background as Clem reappeared. He was full of bluster on his return, but he did not commit himself to a date for the next run.

A week later he sought out Harry on their fishing lugger and told him he'd not be part of it.

'Gone soft now you're wed?' Harry scoffed. 'Never thought no woman would wear the trousers in your house.'

'Kezzy's got a bee in her bonnet about smuggling. Her brother were killed by smugglers, when he came upon them by accident one night crossing their land.' Clem shifted uncomfortably, unable to meet Harry's eye. 'If I cross her she won't have me in the house. Best let it ride this year. She's a grand woman in many ways.'

Harry shook his head. 'Got you under her thumb, has she?'

Clem's hand shot out and punched Harry in the face. 'I bain't under no one's thumb, nor bound to any man if I don't want to be.' The blow spun Harry backwards and, caught off balance, he fell over the side of the boat.

'I've used my savings to buy my own lugger,' Clem snarled. 'You can pay me for your half share in this one, when you've got the cash.'

Harry's yell of rage as he swam to the quay and hauled his dripping figure up the iron ladder was ignored by Clem, who strode purposefully away.

Throwing off a tentacle of kelp which clung to his hair, Harry shook his fist at his brother. He never thought he'd see the day that Clem turned respectable. Then he realised that his brother had offered him sole ownership of the lugger. Clem had always been reluctant to use their own craft to smuggle goods. Now was as good a time as any for a trip to Guernsey and the rewards would be all the greater.

Chapter Twenty-Five

The voyage to The Hague was without incident and the wind and weather favoured their journey. Two weeks after Adam had sailed from Falmouth, he was docked in Honfleur and had made contact with Armand Reyneux. The *émigrés* were to board that night and Adam would sail immediately.

The sailors were ordered to keep out of sight below decks. The ship was to appear as though the crew was on shore. The passengers, even the women, were to arrive disguised as sailors. As soon as they were aboard, the crew were to slip anchor. It was a quartermoon and to aid them a sea fog was obscuring the waterfront.

When two dinghies appeared out of the fog the French passengers were helped aboard. Throughout, Adam scanned the quay where an occasional light penetrated the fog. Sounds were muffled, distorting distance and space. Somewhere a sailor on watch played a penny whistle, there was the creak of timbers and anchor chains, the slap of water against hulls, and an occasional shout from below decks. The chill fog formed droplets on the lock of Adam's black hair which fell across his brow.

Wordlessly the *émigrés* climbed on board while Adam remained alert for any warning shout that they had been discovered. With the passengers aboard, the heavily greased anchor chain was raised and the sails unfurled. Adam ordered the sailors on board to be silent as an English voice could betray them.

Still the danger was far from past. There were several vessels riding at anchor in the harbour and these had to be negotiated around – no easy task in a fog where navigation lights were difficult to discern. As they made their way stealthily towards the sea, the bowsprit of a frigate entering the harbour loomed out of the mist, before the warning clang of its bell was sounded.

With his heart leaping to his mouth, Adam cursed and swung the wheel hard to starboard, his arm and shoulder muscles straining to hold the ship on its new course. He still dared not risk sounding his own bell in warning. He stared in dread as the frigate bore down on them like a battering ram. Her bowsprit could hole *Pegasus* and sink her.

Adam held his breath as *Pegasus* responded to the helm and veered away. The frigate was perilously close. Above him the last of the sailors climbed down from the rigging, and the creak of winch and pulley released the jib sail. It billowed in the wind and *Pegasus* gathered speed.

Still the fog-shrouded frigate filled their vision, lumbering like an ancient leviathan on a course of death and destruction. The French sailors were shouting in panic. Then with a sickening judder the two ships grazed sides at midships. Angry voices from the frigate were followed by sailors streaming on to her deck, their faces pale as spectres.

'Get below and check for any damage,' Adam ordered a sailor, praying that they had not been holed. The collision had not carried as much force as Adam had dreaded, and already the frigate was behind them. He remained apprehensive until they had passed the harbour mouth and were out to sea. Behind them no alarm had been raised and he relaxed when the sailor reported that there had been no damage to the hull. But they had been holed high above the water line on her gun deck and the wooden railing had been smashed.

At daylight Adam inspected the damage. They had been lucky and carpenters were put to work on makeshift repairs. *Pegasus* would need a week's work in the yard before he would put to sea in her again.

The *émigrés* proved more trouble than weathering the worst hurricane or fog hazard. They demanded better quarters, better food, and nothing suited them.

'We are a cargo ship,' Adam patiently explained. 'I have given up my cabin to two of the ladies, and the mate's cabin for another. The men must be satisfied with their hammocks.'

A storm halted their complaints as they all retired below decks, too ill except to lie on their hammocks and beds.

As they entered the English Channel, making for Lizard Point before tacking east to Plymouth, the most senior of their party came on deck. In his fifties, he had the bearing and manner of an aristocrat. The storm had cleared and the sky was a cobalt blue with only a few feathery clouds. Throughout the voyage, Adam had spoken to the passengers in their own language.

The Frenchman stared across the sea at the green hills of England now clearly visible. His hands clenched the ship's rail and his proud mouth was turned down with sadness. Adam sensed the man's anguish. His homeland was in turmoil. It could not be easy for a man of honour and property to condemn himself to exile.

'Good day, Monsieur,' Adam addressed him. 'With this stiff wind we should make Plymouth in two hours.'

The Frenchman nodded. 'I think you are not quite what is usual for a sea captain. You speak French like a native of Paris, and in your manner you are a gentleman, no?'

'My mother was French and I have often visited my relatives in Paris. My family are shipbuilders. In fact we built this ship.'

'She is a fine vessel. We have made good speed, I think. Your mother and her family must find what is happening in our beloved France most terrible.'

'There is much suffering for the French people,' Adam agreed, 'but I have not seen my relatives for almost three years. My uncle died and my aunt has retired to a convent.' He was about to close the subject when a tugging of guilt made him say, 'My cousin wed the Marquis de Gramont from the Auvergne. Have you by chance news of them?'

'Gramont?' The Frenchman stared imperiously at the shoreline. 'Your cousin did not marry wisely. The man is–' He broke off, then continued tersely, 'Your cousin, if she was spared, is now a widow, Captain.'

'So Gramont is dead! But how? Why do you say "if she was spared"?' Alarm tingled along Adam's spine.

'I heard that his château was burned by the peasants. The Marquis was not popular. He was mutilated and tortured.'

'Dear God, not Lisette!' Adam was horrified. She was so gentle. So young. 'And you have no idea what happened to his wife?'

The Frenchman was hesitant in answering, then added, 'Gramont was not a man I cared for, nor whose fate I had any interest in. I am sorry if this shocks you.'

'I knew something of Gramont's reputation, and my cousin did not wed him willingly.' Adam's face hardened at the memory of Lisette who had been forced to jilt him by her brother. How his cousin must have suffered. Etienne Riviere had a lot to answer for.

'The Marquise was not often seen in her husband's company,' the Frenchman continued.

'There were other estates which may not have been touched. But what nobleman is safe at the hands of these volatile rebels?' He tipped his hat to Adam and turned away to stroll the length of the deck.

That Gramont was dead Adam felt was the man's just deserts. But what of Lisette? Her fate could be too terrible to contemplate. The vision of her petite, innocent face, hardly more than a child when he had last seen her, made his knuckles whiten on the ship's rail.

He felt a stab of guilt that Lisette had been all but forgotten by their family. And what of Aunt Louise? With financial pressure easing at the yard, perhaps it was time that some investigations were made in France as to the welfare of the Riviere family.

When the *émigrés* alighted at Plymouth and were met by Squire Penwithick's agent, Adam decided to sail on to the Loveday yard.

Edward was waiting on the landing stage as he rowed ashore from the mid-river channel.

'From the looks of your ship, your voyage was not without event. How badly is she holed? What happened?'

Adam briefly explained their encounter with the frigate at Honfleur. They paused in their walk to Mariner's House to allow two horses pulling a tree trunk towards the saw pit to pass. 'Fortunately any repairs will be above the water line so she does not need to go in dry dock,' Adam added. 'But that is not what is important. I have learned that Lisette's husband has been murdered.'

Edward nodded. 'Squire Penwithick informed me of his death. He has no news of Lisette. We must pray she has escaped.'

'With no cargo to carry I can sail to France once *Pegasus* is repaired. I will persuade Aunt Louise to return with us.'

Edward looked strained as they entered Adam's living quarters. There was no fire alight as he had arrived unexpectedly and Leah had not been notified. However, fresh wood and kindling was in the hearth awaiting a taper.

'Would that the matter were so simple. Penwithick managed to get word to Louise. She refuses to leave the convent until she knows that Lisette is safe.'

'Then perhaps we should go to France to find Lisette, or at least learn her fate, sir?'

'And where would you begin? Has not the danger you faced at Honfleur proved how reckless such a venture would be?'

When Adam made to protest, Edward cut in, 'It is not possible. You do have a cargo. One of the Bristol merchants you contacted wrote to me. He wants you to collect a cargo of wines from Bilbao. But the main purpose of the voyage is for us to prove that *Pegasus* is the fastest for her class and size. He is interested in having two ships built for his own fleet. This is to be a test of her speed. Someone has been undercutting our prices and we have lost three orders for next year. If we do not get this order then half the shipwrights will have to be laid off.'

'Do you think it is safe to leave Aunt Louise in the convent?'

'I cannot believe that Etienne would completely abandon his mother, or Lisette. This remains a difficult time for our family. We must trust that the situation in France remains stable.'

Adam paced the room. 'The voyage should take no longer than two months.'

'We cannot afford not to take this chance,' Edward emphasised. 'Meanwhile Squire Penwithick has promised to have enquiries made about Lisette. If she is found she will be taken to the convent to be with her mother.'

Adam put aside his misgivings at the delay. The challenge to have *Pegasus* return from Bilbao faster than any vessel of her size would mean that future orders would be assured as word spread amongst merchants of her speed and reliability.

'When do I sail?'

'It should have been on the next tide for Bristol. I shall put the shipwrights to work on her immediately and rig up lanterns for them to work through the night. The merchant is impatient. With luck you could be in Bristol in four days.'

The challenge revived Adam's spirits. The short sojourn at sea after so many months at home had whetted his appetite for testing his skill against the elements and for adventure.

'Will you dine with us at Trevowan this night, Adam?' Edward asked.

'No. I shall pay my respects to the family once I have changed but leave before you dine. I had other plans for this evening.'

His father's manner changed to disapproval. 'This liaison of yours should not interfere with

441

family commitments. Richard is back from school and Elspeth will be affronted if you put your mistress before a reunion with your family.'

Adam knew his father frowned upon his relationship with Senara. There had been many such comments through the winter. It was why he had not yet broached with him the subject of marrying her. But he knew he could not indefinitely evade the issue. Once he had his father's blessing he was convinced that Senara would no longer refuse to wed him.

Margaret Mercer's soirée was all Thomas feared. His mother had invited an armada of prospective brides. There were several wealthy widows, all older than Thomas, and each with a desperate glint in their eyes to remarry which terrified him. There were also a half-dozen insipid unwed heiresses. His mother had presented a list of the women to him earlier with their expected dowry, or settlement, beside their name. He had been appalled at her mercenary approach and, seeing his horror, Margaret had been firm.

'You have dallied long enough, Tom. Marriage is a business arrangement. I had always hoped that you would wed a woman of some eminence but, with the scandal of your father's death, we must take what is on offer.'

Thomas knew his mother was right. It still did not make the decision palatable. None of the women on the list held any interest for him.

The guests were introduced and as he suffered the fervent gaze of widows and mamas, he felt his despair mounting. Meredith Lascalles was effusive in his greeting. While he had been waiting with the guests to file past their host and hostess, Lascalles had noted the value of the contents of the room, which was impressive as they had been loaned by Lady Marsha.

'Reports are that Mercer's Bank is doing well.' Lascalles' bluntness incensed Thomas.

'Our investors are happy with the new interest rates. Our reputation has carried us through the unjust speculation and scaremongering.'

Lascalles inclined his head and moved on, and Thomas found himself sweating under his high linen collar and stock. He bowed to Mrs Lascalles and her three daughters. His smile was less forced when it alighted upon Georganna at the rear of the family. Her manner was cooler than he expected after their strange encounter at Vauxhall. He had seen her twice since then at the playhouse and had returned her wave. Although she was with friends, and not her family, he had not visited her box.

'Thomas, you have not filled in any of the ladies' dance cards,' his mother hissed in his ear. 'That is most remiss of you. There will be an hour of dancing after the recital.'

'Miss Lascalles,' he bowed to Georganna, 'for which dance may I be permitted to lead you on to the floor? I am sure your card must be full.'

'Duty is onerous, is it not, Mr Mercer?' she said with sharpness. 'I have the fifth dance free.' She walked off without a backward glance.

'You could have chosen a more apt woman than Georganna Lascalles, Thomas. I expect you to dance with at least one of her sisters, also

Cecilia Fothergill, Viola Marwick and Lady Joan's niece.'

The greetings over, there was a half-hour to mingle with the guests before they would take their places for the recital. Thomas picked the other women to dance with and felt his duty done.

He missed Lucien's company. He would have made the evening bearable, but Margaret had thought it wise that he did not attend.

She had manipulated the presence of Charlotte Lascalles at Thomas's side during the recital. Thomas had no choice but to escort her to the music room. Mozart's music usually enthralled him, but Charlotte whispered and giggled throughout, which irritated him beyond measure. Restless, he glanced at the guests and saw Georganna listening with rapt attention. He caught her eye and smiled, then was forced to answer yet another inane question from Charlotte Lascalles.

The recital over, Margaret insisted that he take the wealthy widow, Viola Marwick, to the dining room where refreshments had been laid out. The woman was on the top of his mother's list, but her yellowed teeth and sour breath made him escape from her side at the first opportunity. He was feeling more nauseous by the minute at what was expected of him.

He found it easier to talk to the clients and found Lascalles twice had joined the group of men which surrounded him. Then the musicians began to tune their instruments, and Thomas dreaded the hour of dancing to come. The heat in the room was oppressive and the urge to get away was too strong to resist. He needed ten minutes alone to face the ordeal ahead.

He entered the library. A single candle burned in the corner by a high-backed chair which was turned towards the window. Intent upon relaxation, he filled a clay pipe with tobacco from an ivory humidor. Having left his tinderbox in his bedroom, he reached for the candle. His hand froze midway as the light fell upon the sleeping figure of Georganna Lascalles. A book was open in her lap and he saw it was of Donne's poems. There was such serenity upon her face that he envied her that peace and found himself smiling. She had kicked off her satin slippers to fold her legs under her in the chair. He could not imagine any of the other women present tonight behaving in such a way. Her natural and unaffected manner was refreshing. He replaced the candle and intended to leave so that she would not be disturbed.

As the light flickered across her face, she started and her eyes opened. They widened with shock at seeing him. The book fell to the floor and, flustered, she tried to straighten her legs and pull her skirts down over them.

'How unforgivably rude you must think me. The door was open and I was drawn to inspect the books. My manners shame me.' She stood up.

'I am always intrigued by what others read.' Thomas bent to retrieve the fallen book at the same time that she did, so that their hands and heads clashed.

With a laugh she rubbed her temple. 'Oh dear, I am always so clumsy.' At seeing his unlit pipe, she added, 'You have come here for some peace. I am depriving you of it.'

'Why cannot more women be as you? Most of those out there I find daunting. They are impossible to understand.'

'As men are to women. Is that not the mystery which makes the chemistry between them so profound?'

'I would not know.' Thomas frowned. 'Women are complex creatures. I thought that when we met earlier you were displeased with me in some way. Now you do not seem at all vexed by my company. Was it because I did not visit your box at the play?'

She did not meet his gaze. 'I did not expect you to. Your friends were more interesting than mine. You were enjoying their company and I suspect you have little time away from the bank. It was my uncle's manner which angered me earlier. I was embarrassed at his conduct.'

'You have an unusual perception of people and a consideration of their feelings. It is a worldly insight for a woman, who by her own admission, is bound to her family.'

She shook her head and laughed. 'It is the poets I read who are worldly. And I have much spare time for that. Yet you are a poet who makes music with words.'

'Oh, I say, that is going a bit far.' He flushed at the extravagance of her compliment.

She slid her feet into her slippers. 'As usual I am too forward. And I am keeping you from your

446

guests. My uncle will be displeased if you do not pay any attention to Charlotte. She was bought a new gown especially for this occasion.' She put her hand to her mouth and looked distressed. 'Now I have been indiscreet.'

The laughter disappeared from Thomas's eyes. 'I am suppose to choose a bride this night. I must away to woo an heiress.'

'You make it sound as though any heiress will do.'

He shrugged, but was uncomfortable that he had spoken so rashly. Even so, he added with a wry smile, 'Needs must, I fear. Now it is I who am indiscreet.' He attempted to jest but his voice was harsh.

'Then if it is any heiress you seek, you must find one who would not curb your talent as a playwright and poet.'

'That is not likely.' He backed towards the door, aware that he had said so much.

'Then marry me.'

She spoke so quietly Thomas judged he must have misheard her. 'I beg your pardon?'

'I said – marry me.' She kept her head bowed. 'I have a fortune and I would never stop you writing, or seeing your friends such as Lucien Greene. You have a special friendship with him, do you not?'

Thomas almost choked in astonishment. 'You are impertinent, madam.'

'I am trying to be honest. This is not easy to say. But it is too important not to be voiced.' She took a deep breath. 'At the risk of you despising me for my forwardness, I will say this before the chance is lost.'

He held up his hand. 'I think you have said enough.' Thomas did not know what to make of her outburst.

Georganna raised her eyes to meet his frowning stare and before her courage failed her, said in a breathless rush, 'I am very much my father's daughter. I love the theatre, yet my uncle forbids me to attend. I would surround myself with poets and writers, and instead am kept within a house which has no care for my feelings or interests.'

Thomas spread his hands. 'That must be awful for a woman with a lively and informed mind as yourself. I can understand why you wish to marry, but you know my circumstances...'

The music from the quartet drifted to them and Thomas knew he should be joining his partner for the first dance.

Georganna pressed her hands together in an impassioned plea. 'That is why I spoke. Please, hear me out. My uncle had no wish for me to wed, for I hold that which is too important to him. My father and uncle were equal partners in Lascalles Bank. My father left me his one-half share. If you wed Charlotte, Uncle Meredith could not match that with her dowry, and he will seek to gain the upper hand in any merger.'

Thomas sank down on to the arm of a chair. 'I find this hard to take in. I thought my mother was aware of every woman's dowry in London, down to the last pound. She had you marked for a small annuity.'

'It is not common knowledge. It would not suit my uncle's purposes, or until recently mine.' She dropped her gaze to the floor. 'You see, I have never wanted to marry. I can offer you my fortune, but it would be a marriage in name only.'

'Good heavens! This is even more extraordinary.'

Georganna blushed, but did not look up. 'I have a horror of childbirth. It is unnatural, but the thought of it fills me with abject terror.'

'I thought all women craved children.' Thomas scratched his head, not sure what to make of this conversation.

'Not I. When I was six I saw my mama bleed to death after a four-day labour and my sister born dead. Her screams haunt me still and the blood ... the blood was everywhere. I will give you my devotion as a good wife should. I will support you in your need to write, but I will never bear you a child. That is my condition.'

Thomas stared at her in amazement. Georganna fidgeted with the lace on her sleeve. 'I have shocked you. But how else could I explain? I believe that a marriage would serve both our needs. There is no reason why you should not become a sleeping partner in the bank, should we marry. My father was. And I have the greatest respect for your work. I would be honoured to be married to the man who will one day become as famous a playwright as my father. I also find your company stimulating and I hope that in time we will have a mutual respect and affection for each other.'

'How extraordinary.' Thomas stared at her incredulously.

Thomas's name was called and Georganna knew her chance was passing. 'I only ask that you consider my suggestion. Of course, my uncle has been so objectionable I would not blame you if you wanted nothing to do with our family.'

Thomas opened and closed his mouth several times before he was able to speak. 'This makes no sense. How can you wish to surrender your inheritance and have so little in return?'

'But I would be part of your circle. I will gain my freedom and live amongst playwrights and poets. I presume to think that in our own way we could find a measure of happiness.'

'I do not know what to say!' His head was whirling and he was still not certain that this was not some bizarre imagining.

Georganna squared her shoulders and put her head on one side. 'Forgive me. It was a foolish notion. I should not have been so forward.'

'No. You did right. But–'

The library door opened and Margaret Mercer was framed in the light. 'There you are, Thomas. What are you about, ignoring your guests? Mr Lascalles wishes to speak with you.'

He did not move or speak as each woman waited expectantly. Then his shoulders pulled back and his stance was imperious as he turned to regard his mother. He had been standing directly in front of Georganna, shielding her from his mother's view. 'I have need to speak with him.' He moved aside. 'Mama, Georganna Lascalles has just agreed to become my wife.'

'But Thomas, she is all but penniless!' Margaret cast a despairing look at Georganna. 'Not that she is not worthy. Georganna is a charming woman, but–'

'And she will be my wife.' Thomas took Georganna's hand and raised it to his lips. 'She is the answer to my prayers.'

Chapter Twenty-Six

The woman sat on the headland above Penruan. A rose and gold sunset laced the heavens and she watched the fishing fleet sail out of the harbour. The dozen luggers with their stained sails were no more than jagged peaks on the horizon as evening became eclipsed by night. It was a warm evening and the morrow would dawn clear and sunny. Tomorrow would be another day of hunger, where she must push her tired and emaciated body through the rituals of survival.

She clutched her bundle close to her breast and rocked to and fro. Gradually, the outline of the village became lost in shadows. Here and there candles and rush lights were lit, but most women would be already preparing for their beds. The dawn tide would bring the fleet home and fish would need to be sorted, gutted, dried or smoked – hours of back-breaking work for those fortunate enough to have employment.

For a long while the woman stared at the church tower in the centre of the village. She had been tempted to go there but it was long since she had felt God's presence in her life. In her sin, she felt God had abandoned her. The last time she had sought a night of shelter in the porch of a church, she had been woken by the parson beating her with a stick. He drove her from the village, screaming abuse that she was a vagrant and a trial to his parish. She had fallen and with no pride left had held out her palm for alms.

'In Christ's name have pity.'

He had thrown her two coppers which had bought her a small portion of bread: her first food in four days.

The village below her blurred, and the pangs of hunger clouded her senses. She named each of the occupants in the houses in the sing-song voice of a child: each had deserted her. Her gaze paused upon a cottage forbidding in its darkness. No mother there to welcome her. No father who cared.

Then her stare rested on the Dolphin Inn. She rose slowly, and stumbled in the darkness as it drew her like a lodestone. She remained outside the inn to stare into the dim interior through the tiny window panes. Old men were hunched over their quart pots, their faces yellow in the candlelight. Faces she knew, but none who would welcome her. The one she sought was not there. Neither had he been amongst the fishermen on the quay, for he stood out too easily in a crowd to pass unnoticed.

With a frown she scanned the houses lining the winding streets which rose along the side of the coombe. One house stood apart from the rest and she had heard that this was where he now lived. He and his woman. His wife. The word was

452

as corrosive as venom in her tortured mind. *She* should be his wife. She had more right. Had given him so much, yet had been cruelly spurned.

The woman dragged herself up the hill, her thoughts centred upon her purpose. This house was brightly lit within. She remembered how derelict the place had been and could not contain her jealousy at how much money must have been spent on the new roof and extra land. The stonework of the eight-room house had been limewashed and the door and windows painted black. It was as large as the Rectory of Penruan church. This was the house of a man of some standing in the community. She hawked and spat on a newly dug flowerbed. The villainous smuggler and son of an innkeeper had done well for himself, while she had lost everything.

Through a window, in what appeared to be a buttery, a large, handsome woman was working. The amber-haired woman was singing tunelessly as she worked and the woman watching was reassured by the strong features, which were unlined and showed humour and kindness.

The door next to the buttery was open and with one eye on the woman through the window, she edged forward and placed her bundle inside the door on the floor. As she began to back away, a horned demon sprang at her and struck her side. The devil had come to claim her soul for her wickedness. With a scream, she fled. Terror brought a surge of energy to carry her into the woods behind the cottage.

Keziah, on hearing the scream, stopped her

work and peered out of the window. Baltasar was charging across the back field. Keziah chuckled. 'That will teach that no-good fox to come sniffing round here. You give him what for, my lovely.'

She continued with her cheese-making until some time later a persistent mewling caught her attention. It was not one of the goats. The sounds grew louder and she wondered if Baltasar had wounded a stray cat. She wiped her hands and went to the door, carrying a candle with her. Baltasar was in the doorway sniffing a dark form.

'What have we here? A badger, is it?' Keziah was about to give it a prod with her boot, when a tiny hand thrust itself out of what Keziah now saw was a dark shawl.

Baltasar raised a hoof to prod the bundle. Keziah screamed and picked up one of Clem's boots by the door and threw it at the goat. Baltasar backed away, and a stream of urine spread on the floor to show his displeasure at his mistress's rough treatment.

'Get out of here, you dirty beast.' Keziah threw the other shoe. Baltasar grunted and trotted off with his head in the air. Keziah picked up the bundle. It was sodden round the middle but as the folds of the shawl fell back, the baby began to cry in earnest.

'Holy mother!' she groaned, too shocked to move. Then she let out a yell. 'Clem, get yourself in here. You bain't gonna believe what's been left on our doorstep.'

Clem was in an outhouse cleaning his rifle, for Keziah would not allow a gun in the house. He had not sailed with the fleet as he had only returned on the morning tide with a large catch after three days at sea. When he entered the passageway Keziah was staring down at a baby in her arms.

'Where the devil did that come from?'

'It were on the floor by the door. From the sound of it, it be hungry, poor mite.'

'That bain't be our concern. Best take it to the vicar's wife. Martha Snell deals with foundlings.'

'But is it a foundling, Clem?' Keziah had been inspecting the child and had walked over to a candle. 'I think your past has caught up with you, Clem Sawle. I be wanting an explanation.'

Keziah held out a scrap of paper with the poorly printed scrawl: 'He be Clem's.'

Clem backed away. 'I bain't owning to nothing. It bain't mine.' He knew Keziah's temper was awesome when she was roused. He expected her fury at any moment to descend on him.

'I bain't deaf to talk, Clem, and I bain't stupid. You'd been seeing the barmaid at the Dolphin. Some reckoned you'd wed the woman. Bert Glasson threw her out, so they say. Was she with child?'

Clem looked trapped and Keziah rounded on him. 'I want the truth, Clem. I won't stand for no lies. Not over such as this.'

'Tilda were with child. That don't mean to say it were mine. She were free with her favours. But she bain't been seen for months. No one knows where she went.'

'I reckon she were here tonight. And I reckon she believes this child is yours.'

455

'I still say you leave it with Martha Snell to deal with. Or there be Tilda's sister, Rachel, working at Trevowan. She is the one to bring up her sister's child. But how do we know it is Tilda's?'

Keziah stared hard at him. 'Who else would bring a baby to us? It were her. Poor woman must have been desperate.'

'How come we didn't see or hear her? Baltasar is usually better than any guard dog.'

'He has been out the back most of the evening. I did hear something about half an hour ago. Baltasar was chasing what I thought was a fox over towards the woods. Could have been the mother. Best you go and search for her.'

'And give her back her property.' He made to snatch at the child.

Keziah held the baby protectively against her chest. 'Go look for the mother. She may be in need of food and care. I don't put no blame on you for what was in your past before you wed me. 'Tis only Christian to see if she needs help.'

Clem slammed out of the house. His temper was soaring. He'd wring Tilda's neck with his bare hands if he got hold of her. How dare she dump her brat on his doorstep? Bloody woman would cause no end of trouble for his marriage. Keziah was too fine by half. Need care! Tilda, would need care all right, if he got his hands on her.

He searched for an hour and neither saw nor heard anything. His anger had dissolved as he tramped through the woods and now he felt only anxiety. His life had changed since he had met Keziah. He had never thought any woman could

456

affect him as she did. What if she threw him out? His bravado and bluster sank to his boots. He loved Keziah and did not want to face life without her.

He hesitated in the doorway. He would not beg, not even for Keziah, but he was ashamed at the pain this night must have caused her. To his surprise his wife was sitting in a rocking chair with a bowl of goat's milk and a rag, trying to get the child to drink.

'We'll have to find a wet nurse come morning. Goat's milk won't be no good for a baby.'

'You don't mean to keep it.'

'It be your son, Clem. And it be our duty to rear it. Would you see it abandoned in an orphanage? And what if I be barren? I were married for seven years to Walter, and I never conceived. Perhaps this is God's way of giving me a child.'

'But what of Tilda's family? The talk...' He shook his head. 'Could be a nasty business.'

'We'll say it is a child I took pity on in an orphanage. That will be an end to the matter.'

He was amazed at her generosity. When he asked her to wed him, Keziah had told him she feared she was barren. At the time he had wanted her and had no thought of children. But if this was his son...?

'And if Tilda comes back to claim him?' he pointed out.

'We'll deal with that if it happens. But a woman who abandons her child this way won't have done so lightly.'

Clem scratched his head. 'So you mean to keep him? I suppose you've already chosen a name.'

457

'Zack, after my father. Unless you object.'

Clem let out his breath. He was still stunned by the night's events and the way Keziah had handled them. 'I reckon if you be taking on the role of his ma, then you have the right to choose his name.'

Keziah grunted, her head bent low over the child as she encouraged it to suckle on the rag. 'And if I hear that you ever play me false now we're wed, Clem Sawle, I shall walk out that door taking this child with me. You will never see the two of us again.'

No one in the village mentioned having seen Tilda Glasson, though there was brief gossip at the suddenness of the arrival of the foundling in Clem and Keziah's home. His presence was only noted with the arrival of the wet nurse, Gilly, a young dairymaid. She had worked on Keziah's farm and become pregnant by a travelling labourer, who had mended some fences for Keziah last summer. Gilly's daughter was two months old and Gilly was grateful to be taken in to the Sawle household as wet nurse. She never gossiped about her charge or mistress.

Ten days after Zack had been baptized in Penruan church, Tilda Glasson's body was found raped and strangled on Bodmin Moor.

Senara was never short of tasks to be completed. There were always herbs to gather, preferably at dawn with the dew still on them. Then there were unguents to prepare, lavender and marigold soap to make, the vegetable plot to tend and animals

458

both sick and domestic to look after. That was without ensuring she had plenty of pottery to sell at market. It was a satisfying life in many ways. The pottery was selling so well that she had been able to buy many necessities for the cottage and the family never went short of food. Another task was to build up the woodpile for the winter. Since she had saved Harry Sawle's life, he came by once a week and spent an hour splitting logs and refused any payment.

Senara was grateful for Harry's help, but she took care to avoid being alone in his company. Twice he had cornered her in the barn and tried to press his attentions on her. Fortunately, for all his reputation as a womaniser, he had accepted her refusal.

'You're a beautiful woman, Senara,' he had said on his last attempt to kiss her. 'You can't blame a man for trying, especially with Adam away so often.'

'A woman alone can be content, Mr Sawle. There be no need for you to feel obligated for me tending you that night. I did it because Adam asked me. And I would not willingly see any creature suffer. I do not expect you to cut wood in repayment.'

Harry shrugged and grinned. 'Happen I be hoping you be feeling lonely one day when I call.'

She laughed. 'I never feel lonely. I am at peace with the woodland animals, and have Mother and Bridie for company.'

'Do you blame a man for trying?' Harry had come closer as he continued to flirt with her.

'A woman is flattered if a man tries to kiss her. She is offended when they persist, if she has made it plain such attention is unwanted.'

'Ah, but there be women who like to lead a man on. Adds to the excitement.'

The smile left her eyes. 'Then they are fools.'

'Some women say no, although they mean yes, because they like a bit of persuading so that they don't appear easy.'

'They are even bigger fools.' She turned to go and he grabbed her hand. She stood frozen, her eyes flashing with contempt. 'I am sure you have work of your own on your fishing lugger, Mr Sawle. There is no need for you to cut more wood for us.'

She was prepared for a struggle, aware that Leah was cleaning at Mariner's House and Bridie was at school. Angel rose from his sleep in the shade and padded towards them and growled. Her hand was dropped and Harry stepped back. 'Adam is a lucky man. There's many a married woman who would not be as loyal as you.'

He strode over to where the horse from the inn, used for pulling the wagon, was tethered, and rode away. Rachel Glasson watched him leave. She had been sent by Meriel to collect some balm for Rowena's arm. Rachel had never liked coming to the cottage. Senara disturbed her with her aloof manner. What Senara did with herbs was little short of witchcraft to Rachel's simple mind. And Senara had refused to help Tilda get rid of her unwanted child when Clem would not wed her. Rachel crossed herself to ward off evil. Everyone knew women like Senara could rid a woman of an unwanted child. Rachel had spent a tearful night with Tilda before her sister left the district. And now she was dead.

Anger mingled with her fear of this place. Tilda would still be in Penruan but for Senara. Tilda would still be alive. Hatred burned in Rachel. She had heard enough of the conversation with Harry Sawle to know that she had helped him in some way. Very likely she was Harry's whore, for Harry would not chop wood for a woman if he was not getting a reward for it. And Senara was Adam Loveday's mistress. What right had a witch to live, when Tilda, who had done nothing so terrible, had died in a horrendous manner?

Rachel wanted to run from the cottage, but knew that she would be dismissed if she returned to the Dower House without Rowena's balm.

Senara had gone into the cottage and was at the door holding out a jar as Rachel approached. 'I expect you have come for this. The last jar of Rowena's cream must have run out by now if it has been used every day.'

Rachel felt terror claw at her throat. She was a simple woman used to taking orders. Now she found she could not speak. Only a witch would know in advance why she had come here. She had not the intelligence to realise that Senara had made an obvious deduction at seeing the maid. Elspeth always sent a groom if she wanted something for herself or her mares.

Rachel snatched the jar from Senara and all but threw the coins at her in her fear and ran away.

Once on Trevowan land her fear ebbed, but not her hatred for Senara, whom she blamed for

Tilda's death. She sought out Meriel on her return.

'Your brother Harry were at the Polglase cottage,' she said slyly. 'Been seeing her, has he? Seemed like they were real friendly.'

Meriel looked up from sorting through a pile of Rowena's clothes and setting aside any in need of sewing. She frowned. 'How friendly?'

Rachel folded her arms across her chest. 'You know Harry and his women. Thought the Polglase woman be Adam Loveday's wench, Harry were chopping wood for her, and we both know he wouldn't be doing that because he needed the money.'

Meriel narrowed her eyes, seizing a chance to deride Senara. She was also furious that Harry was involved with her. 'What can one expect from a gypsy? Any man will be fair game. And Harry has money enough to be generous. The way she has kept Adam dangling round her, one wonders if she uses more than her natural charms over men.'

Rachel's jaw dropped. 'You don't think she slips them a love potion to enslave them? I've seen Gideon Meadows looking calf eyes at her, and he be a strict religious man so they say. She used to visit him regular when Captain Loveday had sailed to the colonies.'

Meriel did not answer. She wanted to stir up trouble for Senara and she knew that Rachel bore a grudge against her for not helping Tilda. She picked up the jar of balm and gave a theatrical shudder. 'Sometimes I wonder if I do right using this on Rowena. Elspeth swears by the woman's cures, but... How do we know what forces she uses?'

'That be right. Don't bear thinking about, do it?'

Meriel dismissed Rachel. A half-hour later she sent her into Penruan with a pair of boots to be repaired by Joseph Roche. Rachel liked to gossip. And what she had seen at the Polglase cottage, as well as her opinion of Senara, would soon be circulating in the village. If Harry's name was linked with Senara, it would detract from any suspicions that Harry was seeing Hester. Though what Hester would make of it, Meriel could only speculate. Hester had a spiteful temper when roused. The village women were forced to use Lanyon's shop as it was the only one in the village. Hester could do a lot of damage to Senara's reputation if she set her mind to it.

Meriel smiled. She would use Rachel and Hester to stir up trouble for Senara and no one could implicate herself.

Before Adam sailed to Bilbao, his stepbrother, Richard, plagued him relentlessly to be allowed to sail with him.

Amelia protested, but Richard was persistent, showing the force and determination of his character.

'Why can I not sail with Adam, Mama? It will be such an adventure to tell the chaps when I return to school.'

'But I see so little of you, my dear. The school holidays are precious to me,' Amelia replied. She was in the orchard with a fine net draped over a wide-brimmed hat as she examined the honey-combs in the dozen beehives.

'But, Mama, Adam is happy for me to go and Papa has agreed.'

Amelia replaced the thatched top of the beehive, satisfied that the bees were thriving and producing a good quality honey. She pushed back her veil to regard her son sternly. 'Edward would not agree to such a thing unless I had given my consent, Richard.'

He flushed but the eagerness in his expression was making it hard for her to deny him. 'Papa said I could go if you agreed, Mama. Adam had been at sea many times at my age. It would be so thrilling. Uncle Joshua said it would make a man of me.' Richard puffed out his chest. He had grown three inches in the last year and was now tall for his age. He had the blond hair of his father and, with a high brow and prominent cheekbones, was going to be a handsome man.

'And do not say I am too young, Mama,' Richard beseeched. 'Uncle William went to sea at ten and Adam was eleven. I am twelve. It is just for a few weeks. We will still have time together before I must return to Winchester.'

'There are so many dangers at sea, Richard,' Amelia protested. 'I will not rest for worrying about you.'

'But Adam is the best of captains. He will not let me come to any harm. Please, Mama. Adam sails tomorrow to Bristol to take on board the cargo. I have everything packed in an old sea chest we found in the attic.'

Under such merciless onslaught Amelia finally agreed.

Adam welcomed Richard on board with a grin. 'Stow your trunk below decks in my cabin where you can put up a hammock each night. It will be cramped but that is all part of seafaring life.'

Richard was delighted to be sharing with Adam and knew it was a special privilege. Adam had become his hero and Richard was determined to show he was as fearless as any man on this voyage.

They made Bilbao in good time and apart from the rough seas in the Bay of Biscay the voyage had been uneventful. To Adam's amusement Richard had taken to the life with ease, and had not even been seasick, which had been an embarrassing malaise he had suffered when his grandfather first took him on a voyage.

As they were to leave Bilbao, a merchantman, the *Henrietta*, bound for Bristol, was also to sail. Adam stood at the wheel, preferring to guide his ship through the crowded harbour and safely out to sea himself. His blue-green eyes squinted against the bright glare which rebounded off the water and threw long shadows from the rigging across the decks. 'Anchors aweigh. Unfurl the foresail, we shall ease her out gently.'

Adam looked up at the square-rigged sail catching the wind with a loud flap of canvas. He groaned at seeing Richard clambering along the yardarm amongst a half-dozen other sailors. His stepbrother had no fear of heights and spent hours every day up in the crow's-nest. The boy was nimble-footed, but Adam was aware of the

465

danger of falling and would have preferred his stepbrother to be less adventurous. Amelia would never forgive him if Richard was hurt.

'Present yourself on deck, Mr Allbright,' he ordered his stepbrother.

'Are we going to race that merchantman?' Richard said as he joined Adam on the poop deck and recovered his breath. 'We'll show them how fast a Loveday ship can make a passage.'

Adam grinned. 'If we can beat the *Henrietta* back to Bristol then we will have proved how fast Pegasus can be.'

'But the *Henrietta* has three masts and we only have two. They carry more sail than us.' Richard sounded disappointed.

'Look at her more closely. See how wide her hull is and how high she rides in the water. That will slow her.'

'Then you think we can beat her?'

'I am putting the reputation of the Loveday yard on it.'

An hour later Richard stood at the ship's rail and shouted in vexation. 'The *Henrietta* is pulling away from us. She's going to win.'

Adam ordered the spritsail and top mizzen sail unfurled. The wind was brisk and the sea relatively calm. *Pegasus* responded with the effortless ease and power of a greyhound chasing a rabbit. The sleek lines of the brigantine skimmed through the water but in these perfect sailing conditions the *Henrietta* could prove faster.

By the evening of the first day it was obvious that the captain of the *Henrietta* was equally

466

intent on beating them back to Bristol. Whenever the *Pegasus* drew nearer, there were frantic shouts and orders from the other ship.

At dawn the next day the *Henrietta* was a distant silhouette on the horizon but the wind had died. The duck-egg-blue sky was without cloud and the milky morning haze was fast dispersing. As the bell announcing the change of watch was rung, Adam came on deck and ordered the long boats lowered.

'Get the tow ropes attached. The men will row in the long boats closer to the coast. We will pick up the offshore wind while the merchantman languishes in the calm.'

With the long boats lowered Adam stripped off his jacket and joined his men, taking up the front oar. With twenty oarsmen in each boat, he set the pace, bending his back over the oar and pulling with powerful strokes. A sailor sang a shanty to help keep the rhythm.

The weight of the *Pegasus* strained against the ropes and each rower began to breathe heavily. Only the top sails were unfurled, otherwise, once the wind took hold, there would be no stopping the ship for the men to get back on board. Sweat glistened on the sailors' faces and soaked their shirts. By the end of an hour, Adam's muscles were shaking from the pain and effort to continue, and the broken blisters on his palms stung from the sea salt. His teeth were gritted, gleaming white against the bronze of his face, and each breath was agony, rasping through tortured lungs.

There was a shout from the ship and he

glanced over his shoulder. The top foresail was flapping, labouring like a fledgeling swan testing its wings. The fluttering stopped and the canvas became limp. A groan rose from the men. Then, as they watched, the canvas flickered: lifting, swelling and filling.

'Back on board, men,' Adam shouted as the brigantine began to overtake them. The anchor chain was lowered while the men climbed the ropes over her side and the long boats were hauled on deck. Before even the anchor was raised the sailors were climbing the ratlines in their bare feet and unfurling the lower sails, and the *Pegasus* was picking up speed.

'We will stay closer to the shore to keep the wind,' Adam told the first mate, 'and head out to sea once it strengthens.'

'Look, Cap'n,' Richard jumped up and down with excitement. 'The *Henrietta* is now behind us with no wind in her sails.'

Throughout the day Richard regaled anyone on deck with a running commentary on the position of the other ship, his browned face shining with excitement. The next morning the merchantman was spotted on a parallel course with some miles distance between them. By mid-afternoon they had more wind than they wanted. Black, billowing clouds had filled the sky and a sudden squall had blown up, bringing with it driving rain. The sea had turned dark as the waves heaved and rose around them.

Adam had handed the wheel to two men whose strength was needed to keep the ship on course. A heavy tarpaulin coat protected Adam from the worst of the elements. His eyes were reddened and sore from the salt and dousing spray as he peered through the gloom at the rearing then plunging fo'c'sle, its deck awash, then draining in gushing streams each time it rose and fell.

'Batten down the hatches,' Adam commanded as a wave crashed on to the deck amidship. *Pegasus* shuddered under the buffeting but Adam knew she had weathered fiercer storms in the Atlantic and Caribbean. Even so, it was not a time to be less than diligent. He was glad Richard was safe below decks. A wave could easily wash him overboard.

Adam was forced to hold on to the mizzen mast as he turned his back on the howling wind and tipped his head back to examine the rigging. A violent pitch of the ship threatened to hurl him to the deck and the muscles in his arm strained as he held himself upright. The rain lashed his face as he studied the masts and yards, the top sails now tightly reefed. The roar of the sea was deafening. His voice was hoarse from shouting orders above the demonic cacophony of the storm. The wind wailed through the rigging like a banshee and from the bowels of the ship rose the rhythmic clang of the pumps. The sailors aloft securing the last of the ropes were drenched to the skin, their hands and bare feet mottled with the cold.

The ship reared up and as the wave broke beneath its prow, it hung suspended in the air for sickening seconds before it dropped like a striking hawk back into the sea. Adam's stomach lurched, he lost his hold on the mizzen mast and his body was flung against the deck rail, bruising, and momentarily winding him. It was as he heaved himself upright that he saw Richard sliding the length of the deck in the foam of a retreating wave.

'Grab hold of something,' Adam yelled, though the words were torn from him and were scattered by the wind without reaching Richard. Adam leapt down the steps to the lower deck, staggering against the violent roll and pitch, his hands gripping the nettings to prevent himself being dragged over the side.

Richard had been thrown against a hatch and was partly wedged between that and the steps up to the half-deck. He had managed to fling an arm over the lowest step but his slender body was being tossed from side to side like driftwood. Another wave crashed on deck, smacking into Adam with the force of a battering ram. It rolled along the deck engulfing Richard's figure. A gut-wrenching fear smote Adam that his stepbrother would not have the strength to maintain his hold beneath that powerful onslaught. His own feet sliding on the deck, Adam advanced towards the steps. The other seamen were too busy with their own work and none appeared to have seen the danger to Richard.

His frantic search revealed no sign of Richard. Sick with terror, Adam screamed the boy's name.

In the poor light there was a movement from a pale object. It was a hand. Then another wave broke over them. Adam was thrown to the deck, sea water filling his mouth and nostrils. His flailing arms encountered a stout rope, hanging loose from the rigging. He twisted it round his arm as he continued to slide towards the side of the ship. The rope snapped taut, jarring Adam's arm but preventing him from being swept overboard. The receding water sucked at his body and he was blinded by sea splashing into his eyes. Then he felt the soft brush of another figure against his thigh. With his free arm he grabbed the form, and from its frailty knew it was Richard. The ship rolled, banging Adam hard against the mainmast, his muscles tearing as he clung on to his stepbrother.

Above the roar of sea he heard shouts around him.

'We got the lad, Cap'n,' a sailor yelled.

Another helped Adam to his feet as the ship continued to lurch and sway. Adam swung round to encounter a rough seaman holding Richard in his arms. There was a livid gash on the boy's temples, and his eyes were closed.

Heedless of the chilling rain and his own shivering body, Adam pressed his fingers to the boy's throat, terrified that there would be no pulse. It beat strongly and Adam braced himself against the mainmast.

'Get him to my cabin and summon the surgeon.'

Adam staggered after the seaman, weak from his exertions. There was a long rip in the tarpaulin sleeve of his coat where the rope had sliced through it from the force of the strain it had taken.

It took all of Adam's strength to reach the steps leading to his cabin, and so weak were his legs

471

that he all but slid down them. The sound of the storm was muffled, his passage unsteady as he ducked his head to avoid a swinging lantern and enter his cabin. Richard was laid on his bed and Adam turned to see the squat, bulldog figure of Brian Little, the ship's surgeon, enter.

'He's alive, thank God,' Adam said, easing Richard's jacket from his still, frozen body. He stepped back to allow Little to examine Richard and absently rubbed his arm which ached and was beginning to stiffen.

'Nasty cut to the head,' Little observed. 'That knocked him out. Nothing seems to be broken. Severe bruising to his ribs, legs and arms. Nothing that won't mend.'

'How can you be sure that his skull is not fractured?' Adam was shaken at how easily Richard could have died. He shrugged off his wet jacket and shirt, and from a cupboard pulled out two blankets to lay over the boy.

'It don't feel broken and his pulse is strong. Eyes bain't rolled back in his head neither.' The surgeon frowned as he looked at Adam. 'That arm of yours, won't be fit for much for some days.'

Adam glanced at the arm which had been clinging to the rope. It was turning purple from the biceps to the wrist and the elbow was swollen.

There was a groan from Richard, who rolled on his side and spewed up his lunch and stomach full of sea water over Adam's boots.

'There's gratitude for saving him,' Little said with a chuckle.

Richard lay back on the bunk as the ship continued to pitch. He held his head. 'W–what happened.'

'Cap'n saved your life, boy,' Brian Little snapped. 'What the devil were you doing on deck?' At a nod from Adam he left the cabin to continue his duties.

Adam changed into dry breeches and towered over the bunk as he slid one arm up a clean shirt. 'You disobeyed my orders and came on deck. Good God, lad, what possessed you? I told you of the dangers.'

Richard flinched at the sharpness in Adam's tone. 'I had to. You had called all hands on deck.'

'You must have known I did not mean you,' Adam raged, his anger driven by fear that Richard could have died.

Richard's lower lip trembled. His hair was plastered to his skull and the graze had a bruised lump as large as a chicken egg beneath it. The boy's eyes were wide with shock and his body was shivering. Even so there was defiance in his shaky voice: 'It would be a poor midshipman who stayed cowering below decks when the captain demanded action. You didn't stay below decks when there was a storm and you were my age.'

'I was in the navy and had no choice.'

'As I will be,' Richard declared, but blinked rapidly to dispel threatening tears. 'I intend to enlist as a midshipman when we get home.'

'How long do you think you will survive in the navy if you do not obey orders?'

Richard flinched again and then his stare fastened upon Adam's bruised and battered arm

473

as he eased the sleeve of his shirt over it. 'Oh, you've been hurt saving me.' The tears welled up and this time were unchecked. 'I am so sorry, Adam. I didn't think. I wanted to show you that I wasn't scared. I am sorry. Truly I am.'

Adam buttoned his shirt. 'You not only put your life at risk but those of others trying to save you. That is what is unforgivable.'

Richard hung his head. 'I can see that now. I am sorry.' Then his head came up and the defiance was back in his eyes. 'But I wasn't frightened. The storm was glorious. And more than anything I want to be a midshipman.'

Adam let out a surprised breath and hid a grin. He should be furious at the boy but Richard's courage was admirable. Most lads after such a fright would have been hysterical with fear. The sea was in the boy's blood as it had always been in his own.

'That will stir up a storm at Trevowan,' Adam replied. 'Amelia will not be pleased. And you should remember that fear is nothing to be ashamed of, Richard. It can sharpen the senses and keep a man alive. A captain who does not feel fear is a danger to his ship and to his men.'

Richard put a tentative hand to the swelling on his head. 'Mama will not agree to my joining the navy if she sees these bruises. Will they have gone by the time we reach home?'

'They should have, but let them be a warning to you. While you remain on my ship you will obey my orders, or next time I will take a slipper to your behind. For disobeying me you will stay below decks for three days.'

The roll of the ship was lessening and Adam pulled on his tarpaulin coat to return to the deck to ensure they were back on course.

'Thank you, Adam,' Richard said. 'You saved my life. And I am sorry about your arm. You were awfully brave. You will not tell Mama what happened? For then she would surely not allow me to join the navy. That I could not bear.'

Adam winked at him. 'It will be our secret, lad.'

Chapter Twenty-Seven

The voyage to Bilbao was completed by mid-July. After the storm there had been no sight of the *Henrietta*. Adam had no idea if she was ahead of or behind them. With a feeling of anguish he scanned the ships moored along the quay at Bristol. There was no sign of the merchantman.

'Have we beaten the *Henrietta?*' Richard said, standing on the gunwale for a better view of the docks. There was only the faintest of bruises on Richard's brow and the gash had almost healed.

'It seems that we have,' Adam grinned. He had taken off a sling protecting his arm only as they entered the River Severn. His arm had swollen and stiffened, and for a time the surgeon had feared that Adam had torn the ligaments, but it had proved no worse than a severe strain.

Mr Garrett, the owner of the cargo, was delighted at the speed of the voyage and the *Pegasus* was unloaded and about to sail to the

Loveday yard two days later when the *Henrietta* was sighted. Mr Garrett, who had been debating whether to commission a ship like the *Pegasus* to be built by the Lovedays or a larger vessel by a rival yard, came on board. He ordered the brigantine to be built as soon as possible, and he gave Adam a substantial down payment as a first instalment for materials and labour.

After mooring in the Fowey, Adam and Richard rode straight to Trevowan. As Adam approached the stables, he saw Aunt Elspeth in the paddock with Rowena on a Shetland pony and leading rein. He waved to them as he handed Solomon's reins to Jasper Fraddon.

'The master be in the stables examining Rex,' Jasper advised. 'His gelding has strained a tendon.'

'Where's Mama?' Richard demanded. 'I have so much to tell her of my voyage.'

'In the house, lad, or the nursery,' Fraddon offered.

Scamp appeared, to dance and yap around Adam's legs and demand his attention after his absence. Solomon had been ridden over to the yard stable two days ago in readiness for Adam's arrival. During his voyages his horse and dog stayed at Trevowan. Adam joined his father by Rex's stall. The horses had not long been mucked out and the stable smelled sweetly of fresh straw. There was still water in the cobbled runnels from the floor being washed.

Edward straightened from examining the gelding's fetlock. He stood in a ray of sunlight, with dust motes swirling around his head like fireflies. Edward patted the horse's bay rump. 'He pulled up lame on me. Rex is a good hunter. It does not look serious. How was your voyage, Adam?'

'A success. We returned two days earlier than the merchant's own ships had been capable of. He wants a ship built as soon as possible, though I told him it would not be ready for launch until next spring.'

'At last it seems the worst of our troubles are behind us,' Edward said as they walked back to the house. 'Margaret has written that Thomas is to wed Georganna Lascalles in the autumn.'

'Does that solve the problems at the bank?' Adam asked.

'Yes, for Georganna apparently inherited a half-share of Lascalles Bank from her father. Meredith Lascalles did not want it widely known, especially as in any merger he could lose the controlling interest. It appears that Lascalles and Mercer's will merge. And I believe that once all is running smoothly, Thomas intends to become a sleeping partner and will continue with his playwrighting. Also, Amelia's investments are beginning to recover. So the future is less uncertain.'

'That is wonderful news, after all Thomas and Aunt Margaret have been through...' He grinned with relief. A boulder seemed to have been lifted from his shoulders. He had not realised until this moment how greatly the pressure and fear of ruin had weighed his spirits. 'And the yard is no longer in danger of going under, is it?' The months of constant worry could not be instantly banished.

Edward shook his head and smiled. 'Much of that success is due to you. It had been a difficult year, but our debts are all but cleared. And I am aware that by not sailing to America, *Pegasus* has not given you the profit you needed to expand your own business as merchant-captain.'

'It will take many years to build such a concern and the yard is more important. It is where I see my future.' He laughed. 'I earned more this year than I would have done had I stayed in the navy on a lieutenant's pay.'

'I am glad you see it that way,' Edward said with pride. 'It is in terms of adversity that you discover a family's strengths and weaknesses. My sons have not disappointed me. St John has improved the livestock, increasing the flock of sheep, and an extra field was ploughed, which looks to be showing a good harvest of corn this year.'

'And you have your new son,' Elspeth reminded them all. She had joined them having completed Rowena's riding lesson and sent her niece back to the Dower House. 'Rafe thrives and is a joy to us all, as is Rowena.'

'We have come through a lot,' Edward acknowledged as they returned to the house. They found Amelia in the Green Saloon with Rafe asleep in her lap.

Amelia smiled down at her baby and then across at her husband. 'Richard looks so well from the voyage. He will talk of nothing else.'

Richard was sitting on the floor playing with Faith, who had rolled on her back. Elspeth turned her attention to him. 'I swear Richard has grown during his voyage.'

Richard jumped up and stood to attention, his manner unusually serious as he announced, 'It was the most thrilling experience of my life. I have decided to become a midshipman.'

'That is rather sudden, is it not?' Amelia looked alarmed.

'I am set upon it, Mama. Adam told me it can be a hard life, but I want to be a captain like Adam.'

'But it was decided that you were to go to university and study law when you are old enough.' Amelia looked at Edward hoping for his support.

'No, Mama. I would hate that. I love the sea.' He turned to Edward. 'You will not make me become a lawyer, sir? Is it not a tradition for the Lovedays to serve in His Majesty's navy? Uncle William docks soon. Could I not serve on HMS *Neptune* with him, as Adam did when he was a midshipman?'

'It is a month before William docks. Time enough to discuss your future thoroughly. I will not go against your mother's wishes.'

Richard flung himself at his mother's feet. 'You will not deny me this, will you, Mama?'

Amelia saw the glow of health in her son's face. Until he had come to Trevowan he had always been a sickly child. The sea did seem to agree with him. But it was a dangerous life. 'I will not make a decision about something so important without considering it. Be patient, Richard.'

He sprang up. 'That is as good as a yes, is it not, Mama? I am going to be a midshipman.' He ran out of the parlour with Faith barking and running after him.

'He does seem very set on the idea,' Edward said with a shrug.

'But he is so young.' Amelia protested.

'Many midshipmen start their naval life at nine. Richard will soon be thirteen.' Edward replied, but he was abstracted and walked over to the window. For several minutes he remained oblivious to the conversation, rubbing his chin, his expression serious.

'Is there anything wrong, sir?' Adam finally broke through his father's thoughts. 'You are not angered that I have encouraged Richard to defy his mother's wishes.'

'No. Clearly the boy is set upon naval life.' Edward sighed. 'With our own problems seemingly solved I have been thinking a great deal of Louise. I cannot rest easy knowing she is still in France. There has been no further news from Louise, though Penwithick learned that Etienne is the leader of a group of *sans-culottes* in the Loire valley who are demanding the end of the monarchy. These *sans-culottes* are a dangerous force, especially in Paris. Twenty thousand of them ran riot through the Tuileries last month.'

'Poor Louise.' Amelia looked worried. 'Why is there again so much unrest in France?'

'It is because the Austrians have invaded. They would secure King Louis's throne. It has increased the people's hatred for the Austrian queen even more. They fear the Austrians will march on Paris. All citizens have been issued with arms.'

'Then you must see that Louise is safe,' Elspeth insisted. 'I do not trust Etienne. He is concerned only with his own future. She may have no one but ourselves to protect her.'

'The *Pegasus* is ready to sail at any time,' Adam offered.

'You must not go alone. It is too dangerous.' Edward was adamant. 'Unfortunately I have too much to do at the yard, which makes it impractical for me to travel at this time. St John will accompany you and I saw Japhet last month when he was visiting Cecily. He is willing to accompany you, but you will have to contact him in Truro. I assume he is still at the address I was given. I'll get Fraddon to send word to him to join you here in three days.'

'I can be reprovisioned by then and if the wind and fortune is with us we should be back in England with Aunt Louise within three weeks.'

Edward put his hand on his son's shoulder, his expression drawn. 'I pray so, my son, but France grows steadily more unstable. A ship such as *Pegasus* will draw too much attention in a, strange port. It would be better to get one of the fishermen to sail you over.'

'Japhet thrives on danger, but how will St John accept such a venture?' Adam queried.

'If he can work with the smugglers and sneak off to Guernsey when I am from home, and he thinks I will not know what he is up to, he can face the hazards of bringing his aunt to safety. He owes his mother that much to save her sister.'

The gong was sounded to announce dinner and as the family went ahead to the dining room,

481

Adam called his father to one side.

'Sir, there is a matter I must discuss and I would rather it was before we dine.'

Edward nodded for Adam to continue.

Adam cleared his throat, suddenly nervous, 'Sir, once I return from France I need to consider my future. I would like your blessing to ask Senara Polglase to be my wife.'

Edward pursed his lips and regarded Adam gravely. 'Clearly, you have great affection for this woman, but she is not of our kind. St John married beneath him. I had expected you to be more aware of ancestry, and consider marriage within our own class.'

'I will one day be master of a shipwright's yard and proudly so. St John will inherit Trevowan. It is through his children that our line will continue to be the custodians of this land.'

'St John has yet to produce an heir. Cheg-widden did not think that Meriel would bear another child,' Edward reminded him. 'You, or your sons, will inherit Trevowan. Bluntly, I would not see their blood tainted by that of a gypsy.'

Adam flushed. 'You would deny me the happiness you found with first my mother, and then Amelia?'

'I did not look outside my class for the woman who would carry my heirs. Keep the Polglase woman as your mistress. No one will condemn you.'

'Senara deserves better than to be branded a whore.'

Edward shook his head. 'And what of her? From what I have heard of the woman she is not as Meriel. She knows her place. Do you truly believe that she will fit in amongst our friends and neighbours?'

'She is more suitable than Meriel. I have had great trouble persuading her to accept my proposal.'

'Then she is wiser than you.'

Adam was resolute. 'I came to you out of respect. Your blessing is important to me, but I will marry her without your blessing if I must, sir.'

Edward mastered his emotion. He had expected more from Adam than this. 'Taking aside Senara's lowly birth, have you considered the implications of her gypsy blood?' He put up his hands to stop the interruption that was forming on Adam's lips. 'By that I mean their nomadic way of life. How long has Senara lived in any one place? She has the gypsy way with herbs and their healing, and her life is certainly unconventional. She does not visit a church and is often seen wandering the moor and other heathenish places.'

'That is part of why I love Senara,' Adam replied. 'When have the Lovedays been entirely conventional? I could not be content with a woman like Roslyn Druce, whose only thoughts are of fashion and aggrandisement.'

'Gwendolyn has many qualities and you have appeared to enjoy her company in the past.'

'But I love Senara. If I do not marry her, then I will not marry.'

Edward faced his son and his eyes sparked with anger. 'It is your duty to marry as befits your position.'

Adam's anger matched his father's. 'I am sorry you feel that way, sir. I agreed to wed Lisette out of family duty. I could never have known the happiness with her that I have with Senara.'

'And if I were to disinherit you for this unsuitable match?'

'Would you treat me with less acceptance than you did St John? If so, then I would not be chained to tyranny. I can make a living as a sea captain if I must.'

Edward let out a harsh breath. 'I am bitterly disappointed. You have proved that you are more than worthy to inherit the yard. So I would urge you to wait upon making this decision until after your next voyage to America.'

'That will not be for eighteen months if I do not set sail before the end of August. I would not risk the *Pegasus* through the winter storms. I cannot make that promise.'

Edward nodded sadly. 'Then at least consider what I said. Are you certain that Senara can settle in one place for the rest of her life? One day she may not be able to resist the power of her ancestors' nomadic blood.'

Adam had so accepted Senara that he had given no thought to her gypsy heritage; he did not see it as a barrier. He believed that if she loved him, as he loved her, they could overcome any obstacles.

The night before Adam sailed for France with his brother and cousin, Senara weakened under her lover's persuasion to marry him. She had gone to

Mariner's House at his request to dine that evening. After they had made love, Adam was insistent that she marry him, refusing to drop the matter.

She wavered, but on the very point of agreeing she started to sneeze a dozen times for no reason. It made her hesitate. Gypsy-bred, she was by nature superstitious. It was as though she had been prevented from answering.

'My love, you cannot refuse me.' Adam held her against his naked chest as they lay in his bedchamber. 'My family will accept you in time. Father shall not deny me the happiness only you can give me.'

'Which means they have not yet accepted me. They hope that you will lose interest in an unsuitable woman.' She guessed their reaction and forced a teasing note into her voice to cover her sadness. 'And no doubt you have been asked to wait until after another voyage.'

He gave her a sidelong look. 'Good God, you are uncanny. Perhaps I should have you read my fortune.' He held out his palm. 'It must be written there that I will revere and honour you above all women. And bring you happiness and joy.'

'I have seen your hand many times, Adam. It tells of travel and your strength to overcome any adversity. Fortune will smile on you and you will achieve your goals.'

'Is that an acceptance?' He rolled on his side to study her.

Her heart was bursting with love for him. Yet a shadow remained, a feeling she could not dispel or ignore. For so long she had been strong, and accepted the barriers of birth and station in life. But the betrayal by her army captain had left her too suspicious of all Adam's class. If their love was meant to be, a few more weeks would make no difference. 'Ask me again when you return from France.'

Adam groaned and sank his head into the pillow. 'You are a perverse wench.' He raised himself to regard her and sighed. 'Must I again teach you how much I adore you?'

He began to kiss her and make love to her with such thoroughness she almost fainted from pleasure. In the early hours of the morning, Senara lay for a long time watching Adam as he slept, and knew what her answer would be when he returned from France.

The Loveday men had persuaded Harry Sawle to sail them to Dieppe in his lugger. From the moment they docked they sensed an antagonism about the people. They had thought to slip unobtrusively into the harbour, but it seemed that any strange vessel was being viewed with suspicion.

'Why do I feel that I have leprosy from the way we are being stared at?' St John surveyed the wary glances from the fishermen and people on the quay.

'I can smell where trouble is brewing and we are not welcome here,' Japhet observed.

Harry also looked uncomfortable. 'Aye, I'm not happy about waiting here until you return.'

They all spoke in whispers, aware that an

English voice would increase the fishermen's suspicions. Adam studied the quay and people and knew the others were right. There was an oppressive atmosphere in the town.

'How well do you know this coast, Harry?'

'There be a fishing village some miles to the west. The headland looks like a lobster pot. There be a cove next to it which is fairly desolate. It be a better place to meet.'

'I know the headland,' Adam answered. 'We shall join you there in five nights. That should give us enough time.'

'I'll wait a further night. Then I'll assume something has happened and you are on your own. I will be taking my own risks in these waters.'

'That is fair enough.' Adam shook his hand. 'Thank you, Harry.'

Two days later they reached the convent. They had hired a covered wagon which they loaded with sacks of flour they had brought with them from England. The road was dry and dusty and the heat oppressive as they travelled. Many of the châteaux they passed looked deserted. In those that were not, the peasants worked lethargically in the fields. So many of the fields which should be full of ripening corn lay unploughed; other crops were poorly tended or showed signs of having been plundered or burned. If the peasants were starving, as their ravaged bodies showed them, why was the land neglected? But it was land owned by the aristocracy, who spent all their time at the Tuileries.

The porteress on the door of the convent was

reluctant to allow them to enter. Three men in their twenties obviously filled the elderly woman with distrust. Finally, she agreed that only Adam could visit Louise Riviere.

'We will meet you in the tavern opposite the pond,' Japhet said, looking relieved, and wiped the sweat forming in the July heat from his brow. They had travelled in their work clothes to avoid looking too prosperous and were in shirts and sleeveless leather jerkins. For protection each man had a pistol tucked into his waistband, and a dagger in a sheath at his waist. Two muskets were hidden below the driving board of the wagon.

The high-walled convent was across a narrow river from the village and reached by a stone bridge. St John had been scanning the lane from the village as they waited for entry.

'I don't care for the way we are being watched,' St John announced. 'Perhaps we should wait under the trees by the river bank.'

On the edge of the village a group of a dozen men had gathered, several armed with staves.

'You would be wise to forgo your ale and wait here,' Adam suggested. 'We have drawn attention throughout our journey and already have fought our way out of a similar village. With rumours spreading that the Austrians are advancing through France, it is to be expected that the people are antagonistic towards strangers.'

St John nodded. 'Those men look like they could cause trouble. It may be difficult to get Aunt Louise away without rousing the villagers against us. We are not about to do anything untoward, are we?' St John eyed Japhet meaning-fully.

'I have no wish for a fight,' Japhet returned.

St John turned to Adam, 'Show the nun the money Pa gave you for the convent, and tell her we have sacks of flour in the wagon. That should gain us admittance. I do not like the mood of those men.'

Japhet had been pacing in front of the oak-studded door of the convent, and his usual bluster had abated as a group of men formed a barricade across the lane leading to the village. 'St John is right. They look murderous.'

He rubbed his side where he had been hit by a cudgel yesterday and his ribs were badly bruised.

When the door was opened by the porteress, Adam was insistent. 'Sister, it would be better if you allowed my companions to enter. There are a dozen sacks of flour for the needy in the wagon. It may cause a riot if the villagers see us unloading them.'

For a moment it seemed she would close the door in Adam's face as she glanced nervously at the men on the bridge. Then it widened. 'Be quick.'

'We mean you no harm,' Adam reassured. 'We have brought alms for the sisters to dispense to the poor or use for the benefit of the convent.'

The nun was short and wrinkled, her habit hanging loosely on her where once she had been much stouter. Her face was vaguely familiar to Adam. He held out the pouch of coins and shook it. 'The Mother Superior knows our family. My father, myself and my cousin visited Louise

489

Riviere when she was first brought here. My father left money then.'

The nun nodded. 'I remember you. It is good you have brought flour. We can bake bread for the villagers to be distributed each day. I will enquire if the Prioress will allow you all to see your aunt. We have little food to spare but you may share what we have and drink from the well and tend to your horses.'

'We have some food for ourselves in the wagon.' They had not risked staying at inns on the journey and had slept in the wagon by the roadside.

By the time they had watered the two horses and tethered them to an iron ring set in the wall out of the heat of the sun, the porteress returned. 'You may attend Madame Riviere. She is in the cloisters. First you must leave any weapons on the stone bench there. This is a house of God, a place of peace.'

They reluctantly complied, feeling defenceless without them. Japhet kept rubbing his hand across his empty dagger sheath, clearly more ill at ease than his cousins at being deprived of the means to protect himself.

The nun led them through to the shaded cloisters which were refreshingly cool after the heat of the courtyard. Two women in plain gowns were seated near a statue of the Virgin Mary in the shadows. The tread of the visitors' boots drew the attention of one, who rose unsteadily to her feet and leaned on a crutch for support. The other ignored their approach.

'Adam. St John. Japhet. Can this be true? Or is

it but a dream?' Aunt Louise stared at them with tears running down her cheeks. Her hair was completely white, one side of her face was twisted down, and her speech was slurred. She held one hand close to her chest but the other was extended towards them.

Adam embraced her frail figure and was distressed to see her looking so weak and old. 'It is us, Aunt. We have come to take you to England, if you will permit us. There is a home for you at Trevowan, and you will receive loving care.'

St John held her more stiffly, his expression shocked at the change in her. 'We should have come sooner. It is so long since we heard from you.'

'I have sent letters, but they say there is much unrest. I doubt they got through.' Louise turned to Japhet, who took both her hands and raised them to his lips.

'Dear Aunt, how can you forgive us for abandoning you for so long?'

'My recovery has been slow. I could not have travelled until recently. Nor would have left France without–' She broke off and held out a hand to her companion. 'None of you has greeted Lisette. She has been here two months.'

Lisette made no move. She was staring straight in front of her, her hands locked together in her lap.

'Lisette, my dear,' Louise gently prompted, 'we have visitors. Look, it is St John, Japhet and Adam. Will you not greet them?'

There was no response. The three men stared

at their cousin in alarm. She wore a high-necked, grey linen gown and she was so thin that her tiny form looked like that of a twelve-year-old. A large white linen mobcap covered her head, and the skin stretched over her cheeks was pale and transparent, showing the network of veins.

'Lisette,' Adam was shocked by her appearance. When she did not respond, he spoke her name again, then squatted down beside her and reached out to cover her hand with his.

She started and threw off his hand as though he had thrown boiling water over her. Then, even more alarming, her eyes became round spheres of terror and she began to pant and make a strangled sound in her throat.

'Oh, I should have warned you,' Louise cried, distraught. 'She cannot bear to be touched.'

Adam felt nausea rise to his gullet. St John and Japhet had backed away, but he remained crouched in front of Lisette and spoke to her in a gentle tone: 'Lisette, there is nothing to fear. It is I, Adam. You know I would never harm you.'

He repeated the words and his name several times and slowly her panting subsided and the wildness left her eyes. Throughout Aunt Louise sobbed.

'She has been like this ever since she arrived. The horrors she must have seen no one knows. They even shaved her head to further humiliate her.'

'How did she get here?' St John asked.

'Etienne brought her one night. He said Gramont had been dragged out of his château and murdered before the peasants set fire to it.

Lisette had for some time lived separately from her husband. Etienne did not say where, only that he had managed to get her away.'

Adam shuddered. 'How could she have agreed to wed Gramont? She was terrified of him.'

Louise hung her head. 'It was Etienne who forced her. Adam, it pains me to say this but he was so against your marriage to Lisette. He was ambitious and felt Gramont would give her a better life.'

'You mean have more influence to further Etienne's career,' Adam raged. He saw the pain in his aunt's eyes and knew it would only distress her further for him to rail against her son. 'But why did Lisette agree?'

'She was given no choice.' Aunt Louise dabbed at her eyes with a handkerchief. 'When Claude died Etienne locked Lisette in a room and would give her no food until she agreed to wed the Marquis. But my brave darling would not give in. She, who was always so frail, held out against her brother. When she became feverish, Etienne took her away telling me it was to consult a physician—'

She broke off and the tears streamed from her eyes and she could not look at the Loveday men. 'He had her married to Gramont while the poor girl was virtually unconscious. The Marquis took her to Auvergne and once the marriage was consummated, what could I do? When Etienne told me I fell ill and he brought me here.'

'So Etienne was responsible for your seizure,' Japhet growled. 'Horsewhipping would be too good for him.'

493

Aunt Louise lifted her red-rimmed eyes to Adam. 'I am so sorry. It was my dearest wish that you two would marry.'

'Where is Etienne now?' Adam allowed his anger to surge. He was guilty that they had not done more to search for Lisette when they learned of the marriage, but it had all seemed so pointless and Etienne was then his sister's guardian.

Aunt Louise dabbed her eyes. 'Etienne did not stay more than an hour when he brought Lisette. His wife and her parents fled to England some months ago, but Etienne is now involved with the insurrectionists in some way. I do not understand what is happening in France today.'

'How can you speak so calmly of that monster?' Japhet demanded.

Louise sighed and turned sorrowful eyes upon him. 'He is my son. I love him but for what he did to Lisette I cannot forgive.'

Adam swallowed his anger at Etienne. Louise looked ill after so much emotionally charged talking. There was no point in making matters worse for her. 'Dear Aunt, these are troubled times. You would be safer in England,' Adam reasoned.

'Etienne is saving his own hide by the sounds of it,' Japhet raged.

'You wrong him,' Louise defended. 'He is loyal to France. He risked much to save Lisette and he did not bring her empty-handed. Her jewels are sewn into her petticoats.'

'Why did he not get you both out of France when his wife and family left?' Adam demanded.

She made a dismissive gesture with her hand. 'I would not leave. Not without Lisette.' Aunt Louise wiped her eyes. 'My poor lamb. What have they done to her, to make her this way?'

Adam continued to speak softly to Lisette. If they were to get them out of France, the dangers would be too great if Lisette reacted to every man as she had to him.

'Lisette. Surely you do not fear me?' he continued. 'Look at me. I am Adam. I have come for you.'

'A-d-a-m,' she breathed his name slowly. Her eyes focused upon him. 'Adam. Oh, Adam! You have come to save me.' She flung herself into his arms, her sobs hysterical. 'I knew you would not let them keep me from you. You have come. I knew you still loved me. Would not fail me. All will be well now. Now we can marry.'

Adam stiffened. 'You were married, Lisette. I am no longer your fiancé.'

Her eyes were glazed as she stared at him. 'Yes, we will wed in September as we planned. I knew you would come.'

Adam stared at his aunt. Louise shrugged. 'Her mind has been disturbed. Please humour her, Adam. She has suffered so much.'

'We have come to take you to England,' St John said. 'We have a covered wagon for you to travel in. The situation in France is getting worse by the week. We should leave tonight.'

'It is safe here,' Louise became agitated. 'This is now my home. Etienne said we have lost the warehouse and house in Paris.'

'It is not wise to stay here,' Japhet advised. 'In

495

times of revolution, the people lose their respect for religion and God. The nuns cannot protect you. At Trevowan you can live in comfort. It is a two-day journey to the coast where we have a ship to take us to Cornwall.'

Lisette was clinging to Adam and babbling, 'My love, why do you not kiss me? I have yearned for you. At last I can be your wife.' She stroked his face and ran her hands over his chest. He gently took her hands in his. 'First we must travel to England. We will leave when it is dark.'

St John tapped Adam's arm and gestured for him to step away from the women. Aunt Louise was comforting and calming her daughter.

'This is going to be more difficult than we thought. Aunt Louise is frail and Lisette... Clearly she has lost her wits. She could so easily betray us.'

'We have no choice. You have seen the mood of the people. I do not think they will survive if we leave them here.'

Lisette became more distressed. She held out her arms to Adam. 'My love. Why do you not hold me? I have prayed for you to come. I knew you would not desert me.' She screamed his name.

Adam felt as though his guts had been impaled.

Aunt Louise turned to beg, 'Adam take her. Tell her all is well.'

Two nuns had come running. 'You men must leave. You are upsetting Madame. Go. Go. Go now!'

'We cannot abandon them,' Japhet insisted. 'We have come all this way for Aunt Louise. Thank

God, we have been given the chance to save Lisette as well. Tricky situation, though. Looks like you will have to humour her, Adam, at least until we get her on board ship. She will be docile enough if kept calm. Better play the amorous lover.'

Reluctantly, Adam took Lisette in his arms. Immediately, she sank against him and went quiet. Japhet used his charm to pacify the nuns and St John tried to console Aunt Louise, who had put her hands over her eyes as though it was all too much for her.

The three cousins were white and shaken by the meeting and none of them knew how they would succeed in getting these two women to the coast safely or, for that matter, themselves.

Chapter Twenty-Eight

When Keziah heard the rumours about Senara, she roared with laughter. 'Where do these women get their notions? Senara bain't no more a witch than I be.'

'What about her morals? Adam Loveday, Gideon Meadows, Harry Sawle all be interested in her.' Nell Rundle, the daughter of Ginny, sucked in her lips in a prim manner. She was a thin, melancholic woman with a face which looked as though she had a mouthful of aloes. 'They all be interested in her. A man don't sniff round a woman if she bain't encouraging them.

Reckon she be playing Cap'n Loveday for a fool.'

They were in the cheese room of Keziah's house, where women from the village who had discovered how good her cheese was would come to purchase it. Keziah let the women of Penruan buy it cheaper than they could get it in any shop. The room faced north and was cool even in summer. It was fitted out simply with two scrubbed tables and a sink. Two wooden buckets filled with water drawn from the garden pump stood on the sink draining board. There was also a large vat where Keziah separated the goat's-milk curds from the whey. Leading off from the cheese room was the storeroom lined with wooden shelves on which rounds of cheese the size of a man's fist were laid out to mature.

'From what I've seen of Cap'n Loveday no woman in her right mind would want any but him in her bed,' Keziah chuckled. 'And Senara is a lovely looking woman. 'Tis only natural that men will pursue her.'

Nell gave a condemning snort. 'Senara do be a gypsy. They bain't got no morals. Shiftless lot of thieves and beggars to a man and woman.'

'I've not heard that Senara has ever stole nothing, or begged. She do run a regular business with her pottery. You'll go a long way to find any as fine,' Keziah defended. She hated gossip and the way these rumours were spreading had a nasty turn to them. 'Best remember that Captain Loveday is an important man. He bain't gonna take kindly to gossip about his woman. Especially some of the other things those ignorant women be saying.'

'You mean about her magic.'

Keziah put up her hands. 'I won't listen to no talk of that. 'Tis evil and unfounded. As I see it, she's helped a lot of people. And she lives quietly, never causing no trouble.'

'But don't you find it odd the way she lives with so many animals around her? How do we know they bain't the devil's familiars?'

Keziah flushed with angry colour. 'Then they might as well accuse me of such rites. Baltasar follows me round like a dog. Reared him from a kid, I did. He never got it into his head he's a goat. 'Cepting when it comes to mating, then he takes a shine to the nannies.'

Nell Rundle eyed the large woman sceptically. She had been wet nurse to Rowena Loveday when her own child had died a week before Rowena was born. She now had two boys, and like all the women in Penruan, had speculated on the arrival of Zack Sawle in Keziah and Clem's house. The talk of taking him from an orphanage struck them as strange, but then Keziah did have some funny ways.

As though to prove this, Baltasar began to chew at the laces of Nell's boots. She sprang away. 'That creature bain't safe in the company of decent folk, Keziah.'

'He do a lot less harm than idle gossip,' Keziah retorted. 'And I'd have thought gossip was the first thing the families of Penruan would avoid. They all have their secrets and their stash of goods no excise has been paid on.'

Nell Rundle left Keziah to find more interested ears.

The forthcoming wedding of Thomas and Georganna in September was a favourite topic at Trevowan. The July afternoon was warm and the family were taking Sunday tea on the lawn. The women all wore dresses of pale-coloured muslin and large-brimmed straw hats to shield their faces from the sun.

'Trust Thomas not to choose a conventional heiress.' Elspeth leaned towards Amelia and squinted against the sunlight, her voice accusing. 'How will Margaret take to having the daughter of a playwright in the family? I cannot see that it will help the reputation of Mercer's Bank.'

'Mercer and Lascalles Bank, as it will now be known,' reminded Amelia. 'And you forget that Thomas has his own aspirations to write plays.'

'Then this year should have brought him to his senses,' Elspeth snorted.

'You are hard on the boy,' Edward interceded. 'I am proud of him. This year has not been easy.'

'Do you think this marriage will solve your financial problems, Edward?' Joshua asked as he drew his brother away from the women.

'We seem to be over the worst. But it will take some years to recoup all that was lost.'

The two men looked across the cliff top to the cove where Richard was sailing Adam's dinghy. Joshua's younger son, Peter, was sitting on a rock reading the Bible. Since his return from the seminary school, Peter had been aloof, only speaking to condemn a member of his family for lack of religious principles or failings in the sight of the Lord. Edward tried to be tolerant of

Peter's fervour, but Joshua was often at logger-heads with him.

'I fear Peter is a bigot,' Joshua confided in his brother. 'He sees only sin in people and has no tolerance or compassion. I have forbidden him to preach in my parish, or approach any of my congregation.'

Peter had long been nicknamed Pious Peter by the family, and Edward had always hoped that he would grow out of his obsession with religion. Now, at twenty, he was as tall as his cousins, but thin from an abstemious life. He was more rigid in his beliefs than ever.

Meriel was approaching from the Dower House; with her were Rowena and Gwendolyn Druce.

'Gwendolyn is a remarkable woman,' Joshua observed. 'She comes to the Rectory twice a week to help Cecily with her parish work. Yet she is not particularly devout.'

'Living at Traherne Hall cannot be easy,' Edward commented. 'Her sister can be a shrew.'

'I am not complaining,' Joshua laughed. 'I enjoy her company and once she loses her shyness, she is a witty woman. I cannot understand why she had not been snapped up by some worthy gentleman. They could do a lot worse. Pretty little thing. I had not realised how so until this year. Nicely turned ankles and a trim figure.'

'Shame on you, Josh,' Edward teased. 'A man of God should be above noticing such things.'

'Not until I am in my coffin,' Joshua laughed. 'Peter may regard beauty as a sin but I see it as

501

one of the Lord's blessings and therefore to be appreciated.'

Meriel joined the women and took care to sit on the wooden seat which circled a cedar tree well out of the sun. She was proud of the pale skin which proclaimed her genteel lifestyle. Lady Traherne had told her that only the fishermen's and workers' wives showed their lowly status by allowing their skin to be darkened by the sun. Once seated she interrupted Amelia and Elspeth's conversation on the fruits to be preserved that summer to talk of Thomas's wedding.

'How long will we be staying in London, Amelia? There is so much I want to see. And I shall need several new gowns. We are so behind the fashions here in Cornwall.'

'She talks of gowns as though we had money to spare. If we could afford such extravagances I would have bought back all of my darling mares.' Elspeth regarded Meriel gravely. 'There will be expenses enough if we all go to London, without the purchase of new gowns. Especially this year. Money may be less tight but we have not recovered all that was lost.'

Meriel pouted and Gwendolyn intervened before her friend could offer a tart reply. 'I am sure that Mrs Mercer is delighted at the news. Georganna will be company for her. Will they all be living together in the Strand?'

'Of course, it is a large house,' Amelia said. 'And Margaret's last letter was full of plans for the wedding. She had despaired that Thomas would ever wed.'

'Perhaps now my Japhet will settle down,'

Cecily sighed. 'Except he spends too long in the company of the wrong set of people.'

'Then you must ensure to introduce him to the right woman.' Meriel cast a sly glance at Gwendolyn. Her friend blushed. To cover her discomfort, Gwendolyn knelt on the blanket which had been placed on the grass, on which Rafe was kicking his legs beneath his long skirts.

Meriel was impatient that her matchmaking between Gwendolyn and Japhet had come to nothing. True, Japhet flirted with Gwendolyn whenever he encountered her, but then he flirted with any available woman. But he so rarely came to Trevowan. Still, she had not given up. At least her machinations had worked with Harry and Hester. They were seeing each other whenever Lanyon left Penruan on business. Meriel remained confident that she would achieve the same success with Japhet and Gwendolyn. It was frustrating that Japhet had gone to France, but Meriel had used the time wisely, schooling Gwendolyn in the ways a woman could capture the attention of a man like Japhet. She would have to devise more means to get them together on his return.

It was a new and heady power that she had discovered in her ability to manipulate others to her will. When she had heard the rumours being spread about Senara Polglase, she had been delighted.

A shadow fell across the group.

'So much idleness and gossip, cousins.' Peter Loveday regarded the women with disdain. He wore black to proclaim his lay calling and his dark hair was cropped above his collar. 'The devil rejoices in idle hands.'

'But on the Sabbath are we not meant to rest from our labours?' Meriel retorted.

'On the Lord's Day it is no sin to work and keep the devil from tempting us to sloth.' Peter puffed out his chest in self-importance. He was almost as tall as his brother Japhet, and would be considered equally. handsome were it not for his permanent sneer of disapproval.

'Then why are you not doing something useful, instead of annoying people with your pontificating?' Elspeth accused. 'Pomposity is as much a sin as vanity. If you cannot be civil, go away, Peter.'

With an offended air, for Peter was in awe of Elspeth, he sidled away. He opened his Bible and approached Jenna Biddick, who was bringing out a tray of cakes and a fresh pot of tea.

'And do not lecture the servants, Peter!' Elspeth called after him. 'Your father's sermon was quite adequate to restore our souls on such a hot day.'

'Elspeth, you are too hard on the young man,' Amelia chided. 'He means well. It is unfortunate that he is so enthusiastic in his piety.'

'Piety is for inside a church. How can a still wet-behind-the-ears sobersides like him presume to lecture on sin?' Elspeth returned. 'At least Joshua lived a worldly life before he took to the Church. I will listen to sermons on temptation only from one who has overcome it. There are times when I am ashamed to own Pious Peter as a Loveday.'

While Aunt Louise packed her possessions, the Loveday cousins had to re-evaluate their chances of getting to the coast.

'We cannot risk stopping at any village,' Adam decided. 'The women will have to sleep in the wagon and we will manage as best we can.'

'It is Lisette I am concerned over.' In his agitation St John's fingers drummed on one of the stone pillars which supported the arches around the cloisters. 'What if she starts screaming when we are on the road? She could get us all killed.'

'I shall ask the nuns if they have some opiate to sedate her,' Adam said.

'She is quiet enough when you comfort her, Adam,' Japhet let his humour surface. 'Your pretty cousin is still in love with you.'

'It is no jesting matter,' Adam groaned. 'I find her conduct embarrassing.'

'I would not mind her nestling up to me,' Japhet was undeterred. 'Humour the wench. I see no other way until we reach England. Once she is pampered and rested at Trevowan she will recover her wits.'

Adam remained worried. 'I will speak with the nun in the infirmary for her advice on the matter. It will be dark in an hour. We will leave as soon as we can.'

The infirmary held six beds, two of which were occupied by elderly women. It was a stark room with little light penetrating the high windows, the only relieving feature a painted statue of the Virgin ringed by candles.

Sister Augustine provided Adam with a phial of tincture for Lisette. 'Give her no more than six drops; it is very strong. It will make her sleep.'

'Do you know what is wrong with her?'

'Your cousin has been here two months. When we examined her, it was obvious that she had been brutally raped. That can be enough to derange any woman's mind. There were also old scars around her wrists and ankles as though she had been a prisoner of some kind.'

'She has suffered greatly.' Adam tried to blot out his imaginings of the horrors of Lisette's violation. It was impossible. The Marquis du Gramont was capable of tying up a woman to inflict his perversions upon her. Adam felt sick with disgust, and guilt hammered him that they had not done more to search for Lisette.

Sister Augustine continued, 'Madame Riviere said her daughter's constitution had always been delicate. We have done what we can, but food is scarce and she needs proper nourishment to recover. I think it is good that you have come at this time. She needs to be far away from the horrors she has experienced, and in the protection of a loving family.'

'And you think both my aunt and she are strong enough to travel?'

'It will be hazardous for them; Madame Riviere tires easily and her daughter... I could not say. Lisette seems to believe that you are some kind of saviour. She should be pliable enough on the journey. To be honest, this is not an institution for the insane. And there have been times when Lisette has needed restraining and strong drugs

506

to subdue her. This we have kept from Madame Riviere because of her condition. If you do not take Lisette from here, the Prioress has been considering committing her to an asylum.'

Adam shuddered. He had heard terrible things about such places, where the patients were chained to their beds, given freezing baths, or hot cups placed on their heads or stomachs which blistered the skin to allow the demon which had entered their body to escape. And they were the milder treatments. He could not allow that to happen to Lisette.

'We are leaving as soon as it is dark. Thank you for your advice, sister.'

'May God go with you.' Sister Augustine made the sign of the cross in front of him.

When Adam went to collect Lisette she was in her cell sitting in the same trance-like state as on their arrival. Louise was beseeching her to heed them.

'Why can I not reach her? She can be like this for hours – days sometimes.' Louise was holding a small bundle of clothes for their journey.

'I suppose it is her mind's way of coping with the ordeal she has endured.' Adam carried a cup of water with several drops of the opiate in it. It would be easier if Lisette slept through the journey.

When he held the cup to her lips she did not appear to notice. It took several minutes of his coaxing to get her to swallow some.

'We are going on a journey, Lisette. Shall I carry you or can you walk?'

'Carry her, Adam,' Aunt Louise said. 'That is if

she will permit you to touch her.'

'Lisette, it is Adam. I am going to carry you to the wagon.' She did not resist as he slid his arms around her and lifted her. She was so light that he scarcely noticed her weight as he strode through the convent.

Japhet had climbed the church bell-tower and returned to say that the men were still across the river by the bridge.

'Is there another road out of here?' Adam asked the porteress, who had come to open the gates for them.

The nun shook her head. 'We have been baking bread all afternoon with the flour you brought. Wait another hour and the loaves will be ready. Three of the sisters will leave by the wicket gate at the side of the convent. They will distribute the bread by the market cross which should draw those men away from the bridge. Take the road away from the village and a league further on is a track which will skirt the village. It will be a rough ride for the wagon, but the track is passable.'

'Thank you, sister.'

An hour later the nuns left the convent and there was a shout from the bridge. The nuns had given the travellers six loaves for their journey and a cask of fresh water. The porteress, who had been peering through the spyhole in the door, signalled for them to come forward and hurried to open the gates. They had crossed the bridge when a shout from the village alerted them that they had been spotted. Japhet, who was driving the wagon, brought the whip down on the horses' backs and they broke into a canter. They careered along the road and he was forced to swerve abruptly when they almost missed the track. Fortunately, they had not been pursued and he slowed the horses to a walk.

'How are the women?' he called back to Adam who, to keep Lisette calm, had travelled inside the wagon.

'Lisette has finally fallen asleep. Aunt Louise is eager to reach the coast as soon as possible, and says you are not to slow down on account of her.'

Japhet cracked the whip. St John sat beside him with the flintlock musket close by his feet in case of trouble. The moon was full and they could make good progress by its light. By keeping Lisette drugged, the three men took it in turns to drive the wagon while one of then slept inside on the floor. It was decided that no stops would be made unless they could not be avoided.

Because Joshua Loveday had forbidden Peter to preach in his parish, Peter had taken to visiting the surrounding villages to preach in the open.

It was his first visit to Penruan. The fishing fleet had been in an hour and the women were busy on the quay, gutting and sorting the fish.

He stood in front of the sheds, a yard or so from the edge of the quay. 'Good women of Penruan, the Lord is with you in your work. All things work for good to them that love God. Praise his name and his blessings will be upon you. Sin and you shall be judged.'

For the most part the women ignored him, though one or two of the younger ones giggled as

509

they appraised him. He possessed the Loveday rakish dark looks, despite his thin figure and sober dress. They found it amusing that Japhet, who had such a devilish reputation, should have such a pious brother.

Senara rarely came to Penruan, but Bridie had worn down the heels of her specially built-up boots and they needed repair. With Bridie riding on Wilful, Senara led the donkey down into the village towards Joseph Roche's cottage. Rachel Glasson, who had been sent by Meriel to buy mackerel for supper, saw her. She made the sign of the cross as she passed. As Senara entered the cobbler's cottage, Rachel ran down to the quay, going first into Lanyon's shop and then to the women in the fish sheds.

When Senara emerged from Joseph Roche's cottage with Bridie, there was no sign of Wilful, whom she had tethered outside. Angel had been inside with her and had not barked.

'Did you not hear Wilful wander off, Angel?'

Senara had begun to suspect that the mastiff's old scar tissue from the battered side of his face was causing the dog to lose his hearing. He rarely was far from her side during a walk, and if he did run ahead, he kept looking back as though to check she was still with him. There was a loud braying from the direction of the quay.

'So that is where Wilful has wandered to. It is not like him to go so far. How did he get free?' she said to Bridie. 'I am sure I tied him securely. Do you want to wait here while I fetch him?'

'No, I'll come with you,' her sister replied. She

510

had just been fitted for another pair of boots as Joseph Roche had declared that she had grown out of her old ones. 'Can we afford a pair of my special boots?'

'The money is not important if they help you to walk properly. You get little enough spent on you.' Senara held her sister's hand as they walked, her stride slow to match Bridie's hobbling gait.

Wilful's bridle was being held by one of the fishermen's young sons. Senara went to thank him. He dropped the reins and then spat at her feet. Shocked, Senara stared after the boy as he ran away. She picked up Wilful's reins and was about to help Bridie on to his back when she saw the group of women gathered around a young man who was preaching.

She recognised Peter Loveday who, earlier in the week, had tried to preach at Trevowan Hard. Senara had gone to pick Bridie up from the school and had seen Edward Loveday ordering his nephew from the shipyard, accusing him of disrupting the men at their work. Adam had often mocked his cousin for a zealot.

Peter Loveday was working himself into a frenzy as he preached. He flung his arms wide and looked up to heaven. 'The Bible tells us: "Wide is the gate, and broad is the way, that leadeth to destruction, and many there be that go in thereat."'

One daughter of a fisherman who had lain with Japhet many times, giggled, 'Look to your own family, preacher. Your brother has done his fair share of sinning.'

Peter ignored her. It was a constant trial to him to have to answer to his brother's sins. 'Repent of your sins. Ask the Lord's forgiveness for your evil ways.'

Rachel Glasson stood at the front of the crowd. 'It bain't us who be the sinners. 'Tis her, preacher. Your cousin's whore. And whore to others, if the truth be known.'

Senara felt the first shiver of unease. She pulled on Wilful's reins, but someone had thrown some carrot tops on the ground and he was too interested in eating them to obey her.

'See, she don't deny it, preacher,' Rachel screeched. 'And how does she trap such men as your cousin? Why should a man like him want the likes of a gypsy brat? Unless she has put a spell on him.'

'And what of her potions?' Nell Rundle took up the cry. 'What decent woman roams the moors at daybreak collecting herbs and the like? Unless they want them for some secret purpose.'

Wilful would not budge and fear was now pumping through Senara. She lifted Bridie from the donkey. 'Get away from here quickly. Go to Sal at the Dolphin and wait there for me.' She was frightened for her sister as well as herself. She had no one to help her if the villagers became violent. Angel had begun to growl and stood close to her side.

Hester Lanyon had come out of the shop to stand in the doorway and watch the proceedings. Her eyes narrowed with jealousy as she regarded Senara. This woman had seduced her Harry. Harry, who had vowed to save her from Lanyon,

512

and to be true to her, had regularly visited Senara's cottage. And Harry only visited a woman for one reason. Her jealousy made her remark, 'Seems like more than sin is to be questioned here, preacher.'

'Have we a Jezebel in our midst?' Peter Loveday bore down upon Senara. He stopped short when Angel barked. He took several paces back and clutched his Bible to his chest. He belatedly recognised Senara as Adam's mistress, and although he despised whores, he knew Adam would give him a sound beating if he caused trouble for this woman. There was even talk Adam intended to wed the wench.

The village women began to murmur amongst themselves. Angel planted himself in front of Senara, his growls loud and his fangs barred. Saliva drooled from his mouth.

'If that bain't no hellhound, then what is?' Rachel Glasson shouted. ''Tis the devil's beast. No ordinary dog would survive with such scars. He be her familiar. Look at how he protects his mistress.'

Incensed, Senara rounded on the women. She was frightened, but she would not run away. This is what she had feared could happen. 'As any loyal dog would! I do not deny that I have a lover and each of you know who it is. Are my morals less than most of yours?' She stared pointedly at Hester and Rachel. Whilst out gathering comfrey, she had seen Rachel and Baz Tonkin, who worked on the Trevowan estate and lived there with his brother and family, making love behind a tree in the woods.

'When have I harmed any of you?' she went on, fighting to keep her voice calm. 'I have never asked anything from you. Yet when you are ill and cannot afford a physician's fees, you beseech me for a herbal remedy to cure your families of stomach disorders, or the putrid throat and the like. Have I ever charged you for these remedies? No! You willingly offer me some fish in exchange.'

'And how do we know we bain't selling our soul to the devil with these potions you give us?' Rachel saw that the women were losing interest in baiting Senara. 'Is that why you ask nothing? Strikes me it is the work of the devil's hand-maiden using trickery and sorcery. What are you going to do about it, preacher?'

Senara again saw fear and suspicion in the women's eyes. They pressed closer, circling her, the air now oppressive and menacing. Women who had come to her in tears and begged for her help now stared at her with loathing. It was flung over her like a malignant net, her own inner terror trapping her in its web.

'The preacher bain't gonna do nothing,' Hester Lanyon scoffed. 'The Polglase woman is his cousin's whore.'

Peter was sweating under his stock. He had never been in this situation before. These women were all but accusing Senara of being a witch. 'Thou shalt not suffer a witch to live,' the Bible said. But there had been no witch hunts for over a century. He stared at her lovely figure and suddenly visualised her stripped naked as he searched for the devil's mark on her body.

The vision roused his lust and as his body responded he knew himself damned. If she had been any woman but this one, who had won the respect of his family; if he had been anywhere but Penruan where his father would learn of his involvement, he would have been tempted to put her to the test. But he would have been driven as much by lust as by his piety. He had never desired a woman and now knew he was no better than his rakehell brother.

He was still wrestling with temptation when a deep voice thundered, 'What's this I hear from young Bridie, that you be causing trouble for Miss Polglase?' Clem Sawle strode along the quay.

At the sight of him, Rachel Glasson ran into a narrow alley to avoid detection. The Sawles did not take kindly to gossip against their family and she had linked Harry's name with Senara throughout the last month. Many of the other women went back to their work.

'There is nothing you need concern yourself over, Mr Sawle,' Peter Loveday took several steps backwards. 'There is no trouble. A few of the women got rather overheated. Miss Polglase seems to have made enemies in the village.' He noted that those who had shouted loudest had disappeared.

'Bloody bitches!' Clem yelled so the hiding women could hear. 'Don't think I don't know what they've been saying. They had better watch themselves, that's all I can say.' He glared at Hester and his voice lowered. 'I thought you would know better, madam. Are you so

515

innocent?' He gave a taunting laugh. 'Or any of you? And how much suffering has this woman spared your family with her remedies? Ingrates! You should be honouring her for the help she has selflessly given to you. You sicken me with your petty persecution.'

With a sob Hester fled back into the shop and several other women slunk away shame-faced.

Clem advanced towards Peter Loveday. 'And what of your part, preacher man? I haven't much time for church myself. Yet when I see a so-called man of God allowing a woman to be victimised by others, just because she is different and keeps herself to herself, then I can see no reason to enter one.'

Peter gulped and took another four steps backwards. He was now perilously close to the edge of the quay. 'I was trying to calm the women.'

'Is that true, Senara?' Clem asked.

She wanted no more trouble. 'Things got a bit out of hand. There is no problem now. Thank you, Clem.'

''Tis little enough after you saved Harry's life.' Clem rounded on Peter and jabbed a warning finger at him. 'Don't let me hear of anything like this again.'

Peter wiped his brow with his kerchief, and when Clem jabbed out his finger again he stepped back. He had not realised that he was on the edge of the quay, and with a yell he disappeared over the side. There was a dull thud and Clem peered over the edge and burst into laughter.

The tide was going out, and Peter Loveday was lying on his back in thick squelching mud, which had splashed over his clothing and face.

'That will teach you not to persecute the innocent. Mud sticks, don't it, preacher? The Lord does indeed work in mysterious ways.' He gave another roar of laughter.

Senara stared at the preacher and at seeing him covered in the stinking slime, she hid her own laughter. It would have been touched with near-hysteria.

She was shaking from the encounter, and left Penruan in a troubled state of mind. Since Adam had sailed for France she had missed him so much that she had overcome all her earlier misgivings, and had decided that she would marry him.

After today she knew that if she did not marry Adam she would leave her home, as she had left other places before, to protect her family from prejudice and harm. She would never trust these women again.

Chapter Twenty-Nine

The incident in Penruan had shaken Senara, and Leah was troubled. 'It begins again,' Leah said once Bridie was asleep. 'Must we always be plagued by this prejudice?'

In her agitation Leah was rapidly weaving willow sticks around the support struts to a

517

wicker basket as she sat by the window catching the last of the light.

Senara was pounding dried comfrey leaves with a pestle in a mortar. Her face was flushed. 'At least such prejudice will end when I marry Adam.' Senara was now resolute where she had once been so uncertain. 'I love him. Is it not prejudice of my own which has stopped me in the past? No one will act against you or Bridie if you are connected to the Lovedays.'

Leah's hands paused over her work. Senara looked radiant as she spoke of her lover and Leah did not repeat her reservations. If it were not for the differences of their class, Leah would have said that Senara and Captain Loveday were destined for each other. 'I know it is because you love him that you will accept him, and not to save us.'

Senara kept her head bowed, her frustration showing in the terse movements of her hands with the pestle. 'And you will live in comfort. I will never see you or Bridie go without.'

'As long as you are happy, that is all that matters,' Leah said. 'Will you give up your pottery?'

'I doubt it. I enjoy it. Working with such an essential element of the earth connects me to nature in a way I find right and natural. I was born to be a potter.'

Leah laughed. 'There is much of your father in you. He was at one with his environment. He honoured the seasons in the old way and never passed an ancient place, be it a natural well, strange-looking stone or a certain type of hill, without leaving some tribute to the old ones. Spooked me at times, he did, when he spoke of guardians and spirits to be appeased. And your grandmother would never let me pick a herb or berry without giving thanks to the plant or tree. I didn't mind that; it were sort of like blessing food by saying grace before you eat it.'

'There are times when I know what my father would have meant. I feel it too. So did Caleph, though he would not talk of such things. He had the same way with horses as Father.'

Leah regarded her daughter for a long moment. It was not often they spoke of their old life, or of the half-brother they had left behind. Leah had been thinking of Caleph a lot lately.

'Do you miss the old life, Senara? I know you were unhappy when I left and we moved from town to town.'

'I liked the freedom. I miss Caleph, for we were close, but it was not the same after Father was arrested. Caleph was fifteen; he would have seen himself as responsible for us.'

'I could not stay without Darius. I lived that life because I loved him. But I always wanted to settle and have a place of my own. I have that now. This is where I be happy.'

Senara looked around the room with its drying herbs, her potter's wheel and pots waiting to be fired on a bench in the corner. There were three rag rugs on the floor and her mother's wooden rocking chair was new. There were many comforts they had never known before. Living here had been good for them and their simple needs were met. In the bedroom the bed had a proper horsehair mattress, and a colourful patchwork cover was thrown over it. There was a scuffling from the animals who shared their house and she felt a glow of contentment.

'I have been happy here,' Senara said.

'But you do miss Caleph?'

'Yes. And sometimes I miss the companionship of the campfires of an evening. I loved listening to the stories the elders told about our ancestors, and there was the dancing...' She shrugged. 'It was a different world. A different time.'

Leah grinned. 'Then I have a surprise for you. Caleph is camped nearby. I saw him on the road on the way home after finishing my work at Mariner's House. I did not mention it before as you were so upset from what happened in Penruan. Caleph said he would call on us tomorrow. They be moving on in a few days.'

'That is wonderful. How was he? Is he married?'

'He is a fine man. Handsome like his father. In fact he is the image of Darius. I thought I was seeing his ghost! I nearly fainted. And he is married to Maddy. You remember Maddy?'

'Maddy was my friend. She was a wild little devil. I am so pleased for them. It will be good to see Caleph.'

'Are you sure you do not miss that way of life?'

Senara paused before answering. 'Not compared with what I have here.'

The next day Caleph did not come. Senara was despondent.

Leah shrugged. 'He will come when he can. They do not travel on until next week.'

520

The journey to the coast of France took its toll on Louise and Lisette. The heat of the midday sun pressed down on the wagon and on the baked earth of the road. Dust was kicked up by the horses' hoofs and formed a hazy cloud around the wagon. It settled on their hair, skin and clothing, and irritated their eyes and mouths. The men sat with kerchiefs over their faces to protect them. The trees cast some shadows but to spare the horses they were forced to travel at a walk. There was no wind and the heat was oppressive. Drenched in sweat, their energy sapped, and their tempers became malignant in the heat's intensity. Inside the wagon it was worse, the stifling atmosphere and lack of air making the women light-headed. Several times Aunt Louise had fainted.

At least Lisette was asleep though she would soon need some more medicine. When conscious, the demands she made on Adam stretched his patience past its limit. She would cling to him weeping that he had abandoned her, playing on his guilt one moment, then euphoric the next, convinced that they were soon to wed. Her moods were volatile, and only by humouring her could she be calmed. Adam hated the deceit he must resort to but could see no alternative.

They stopped to rest and water the horses by a stream for an hour.

'We cannot delay much longer,' St John paced the stream bank. 'We must reach the coast tonight or Harry Sawle may not wait for us.'

'Harry will not let us down,' Adam replied. 'We

should reach the coast tonight. There is danger for Harry as well as ourselves. And Aunt Louise is suffering in the wagon.'

'At least Lisette has been quiet the last four hours.' Japhet shook his head. 'If she has another one of her tantrums I do not trust myself not to wring her stupid neck. The wench would try the patience of a saint. I think the nuns were right. She is ripe for Bedlam.'

'It is an ordeal for us all,' Adam groaned. 'But I could not live with my conscience if they had been left behind. There are signs of revolution everywhere. We have passed two burned châteaux. Tonight we should be at sea and all this will be behind us.'

They continued their journey for another two hours. Aunt Louise had lost all the colour from her face. Adam passed her the canteen of water. 'Could I have a few drops of Lisette's physic? I have such a headache. It has been getting worse all day.'

'We should reach the coast in four hours and in an hour it will be cooler.' Adam was concerned for her. She had been so uncomplaining through the journey but she did not look well.

Lisette was beginning to stir. She usually remained in a dazed state for upwards of two hours after her sleep. Adam hoped she was not going to be difficult again as the effects of the opiate wore off.

On the outskirts of a village the Loveday wagon was halted by a barricade across the road with armed men standing behind it.

'Confound them!' Japhet said. 'I thought things

were going too well. Yet in two hours we should be at the coast.'

The track was too narrow to turn the wagon around and escape. A dozen armed villagers swamped over the barricade shouting their demands and questions.

Adam was the most fluent in their language, and with an anxious glance at Lisette, who had opened her eyes and was staring trance-like at the roof of the wagon, he swapped places with St John at the front. 'Do nothing to antagonise them,' he warned his brother and cousin. 'Keep the muskets out of sight but to hand in case we need them.'

'Aristos!' the men chanted. They were ragged, dirty, several constantly scratched at lice, all had hatred burning in their eyes and could overrun the wagon at any moment. 'Down with the Aristos. You bleed your people dry and now you seek to flee the country.'

'We are honest citizens,' Adam declared. 'We are carpenters from Rouen. The town is erupting in violence and unrest. We are taking our mother and sister to our relatives where it is more peaceful.'

A thick-set man, with several warts on his face and a thick beard, brandished a musket at them. 'There will be no peace until the Austrians leave France and the King is no more. Long live the Revolution!'

'The Revolution!' With an ambiguous gesture Adam raised his hat.

'You have papers?' the bearded man challenged. Another man with the build and lumbering gait of a bear joined him. There was brutality and little intelligence in his eyes and his stomach gave a thundering rumble of hunger. He gripped the side of the wagon and shook it. There was a squeal of fear from one of the women inside.

'Of course we have papers.' Adam rummaged in a leather pouch to produce some documents Squire Penwithick had supplied. They would pass a cursory glance. He shoved them at the Man, giving them to him upside down.

Another villager held the head of one of the horses. 'These will make good eating,' he growled.

Another came forward and Adam could smell the rancid stench of their unwashed bodies. His own stomach tightened and he took a deep breath to control his fear. Their own lives were in danger but the threat to the women was even more diabolical.

The man who was the leader stared at the papers and finally nodded. Since he had not turned them over, Adam realised that he could not read. 'My mother is ill,' Adam informed him, using a voice of authority but without any arrogance for that would antagonise them further. 'We wish to reach our destination by nightfall, citizen.'

'Not so fast.' The man pointed his musket at Adam. 'To afford such a wagon you must have valuables. Hand them over and we will let you pass.'

'We have no valuables. Just our tools,' Adam was now glad that he had thought to bring some to aid their disguise. He held up his hands which were calloused from his months of working in the yard. 'Do these look like the hands of an aristo? I am a poor carpenter.'

'Let me see the other men's hands.'

St John held out his which, like Adam's, bore the scars of old blisters from working on the land at Trevowan.

'And you, citizen,' he pointed to Japhet.

Adam put his hand over his dagger. Japhet did not have the hands of a workman. He held his breath as his cousin extended his right hand, the reins clasped in his left. To his surprise they were roughened and almost as calloused as his own. Then he realised that Japhet practised his swordplay most days and the constant use of a sword roughened a man's hand.

The leader scowled. 'Hand over your money and valuables and you may pass.'

'This is highway robbery,' Japhet growled. 'I'll be damned if–'

'We have a few sous, no more,' Adam intervened before Japhet did something reckless. 'And three loaves of bread we brought for our journey. You are welcome to those.' He opened his purse and sprinkled the sous on to the road and St John tossed out the bread. Several of the men pounced on the loaves and began fighting.

Other men behind their leader shouted abuse. Two short men carrying pitchforks ran to the back of the wagon and wrenched back the sailcloth which covered it. Suddenly there was a scream behind Adam, and Lisette stuck her head through the front opening of the wagon. She screamed again and her face screwed up in fury as she let forth a stream of abuse and profanities which would have shamed a dockyard whore. She waved her arms erratically and her eyes were wild. She then began to spit at them.

The leader backed away. In many parts of the country madness was regarded with fear, 'Let them through. The woman is no aristo. If my sister were that foul-mouthed I'd be carting her off to stay with relatives.'

Two of the men sniggered but the barricade was pulled aside. Lisette was now hysterical and yelling profanities. Adam grabbed her arms and pushed her back into the wagon. 'You could have got us all killed,' he shouted at her.

Aunt Louise was huddled in a corner, moaning. 'Where can my baby have learned such filth? What have they done to her? Oh, my baby ... my baby...' Louise put her hands to her head and moaned as though in pain.

Adam had no time for his aunt as he tried to calm Lisette. She was staring through him whilst fighting him like a madwoman. Finally he slapped her face, and she reeled back, the obscenities stopped, and her eyes slowly focused.

'Adam, my love. It is you. The *canaille*. The filth of the streets. They wanted to take me. I will kill them before they will touch me again.' Then her eyes became cunning and she wrenched open the front of her bodice, baring her breasts. 'But not you, Adam. I have waited so long for you. Take me. Take me as your wife now.'

Shocked, Adam sat back on his heels and threw a blanket over her to cover her nakedness. 'You

526

have forgotten how a lady behaves.'

There was a strangled cry from Aunt Louise.

Then Lisette began to twitch and pull at her hair. 'I am yours, Adam. Why do you look at me that way?' With a shriek of anguish she burst into hysterical tears.

'Can't you stop that row, Adam?' St John yelled. 'We are drawing the attention of some men searching for birds' eggs to eat.

Adam battled against his own disgust at the creature this once innocent girl had become. The wagon was moving fast and jolting those inside as he tried to calm her. 'Lisette, you must be quiet. All will be well. You have upset your mama. Take some more of your medicine. It will help you. We should be at the coast soon. Tomorrow we will be in England.'

Her tears stopped abruptly and her eyes gleamed with fervour. 'And then we will marry, Adam. Oh, I am so happy.' Her personality changed to that of a coy young girl. 'You were always so kind. I adore you.'

During her frenzied struggle with him, her mobcap had fallen off. Her hair dark, no longer than a fingernail, stuck up in tufts like a tarnished halo. She sat with her hands demurely in her lap, beautiful and frail, but with such scars to her mind. Adam felt pity for her.

'Why do you not tell me you love me, Adam?' Lisette pleaded. 'I have waited so long to hear those words.'

'I want you to sleep, Lisette. We will talk of the future when we are in England.' He raised the phial of opiate to her lips and waited until her lids began to droop.

It was only then, in the silence of the wagon, that he realised how quiet his aunt had become. She was lying on her side with her eyes wide and staring.

'Dear God, no!' Adam groaned and bent over her. The side of Louise Riviere's face had contorted and her right hand was flapping feebly. He made her as comfortable as he could on the floor. She had suffered another seizure and it looked severe. He could do nothing except loosen the collar of her gown and dab some water to her lips and brow. All the while Lisette was whimpering and demanding his attention.

When both women fell asleep Adam took over driving the wagon. He needed the fresh air and some exercise after being cooped in the back for so long. St John had gone inside the wagon to try to sleep.

'Keep an eye on Aunt Louise. There is little we can do. I worry in case she chokes in some way. I wish we could stop to see a physician.'

'They will just bleed her,' St John observed. 'She seems so frail without suffering further loss of blood. Best wait to see what Chegwidden says.'

'Where the devil did Lisette learn such language?' Japhet said. 'She used to be such an innocent. I was shocked. And what was she trying to do in there? Seduce you?'

Adam stared at the darkening road ahead. Just visible on the distant horizon was the sea. 'No wonder the nuns wanted to commit her to an asylum for the insane.'

Japhet gave a low whistle. 'The quiet life at Trevowan will be disrupted. It does not bear thinking about what must have happened to her. The family will be taking on more than they bargained for with Lisette.'

'At least she is safe,' Adam replied. 'It may only need time and a loving family around her to heal Lisette's mind. I am worried about Aunt Louise. Her breathing does not sound right.'

A half-hour later St John called to Adam, 'Get in here. I think Aunt Louise is dying.'

Adam knelt by his aunt's side and took her hand. Her breathing was laboured and strangely wheezing. His aunt opened her eyes and seemed to be staring into the depths of Adam's soul.

'Take ... c ... care ... of ... my ... b ... aby. Prom ... ise ... me.'

'We shall take good care of you both,' Adam agreed. 'Rest. You must regain your strength.'

'Lisette ... c ... care ... for ... her. You ... Adam.'

Adam feared what she was asking. Surely his aunt did not expect him to honour their past betrothal? He could not answer.

'Please...' The word faded and he felt her hand go limp.

Louise Riviere was dead and had bequeathed him a deathbed wish that he knew he could never honour. Yet a part of his conscience told him that he should.

They stopped at the next church and Japhet, who had hidden several silver coins in his boot, gave them to the priest to bury their aunt and provide a headstone. It had been decided that Louise would have preferred to be buried in

French rather than English soil.

Lisette had been roused, but she did not seem aware of what was happening as they left the church. Later, on board Harry Sawle's lugger when the drug wore off, she screamed and ranted and refused to believe her mother was dead.

She sobbed throughout the voyage, refusing any more of her medicine and becoming hysterical if Adam left her side. She was only calm when he held her in his arms.

Chapter Thirty

Senara was on the headland at dawn. Adam had been expected three days ago and she had spent the last two days watching for his arrival. She would do the same today. She sat on the cliff top weaving wicker baskets to pass the time.

Three hours later she sighted Harry Sawle's lugger. It was heading towards Trevowan Hard and not Penruan. She would reach there by the time they docked.

Senara stopped at the cottage long enough to change into her lilac gown and coil her hair high on her head in a more sedate manner than the plait she usually favoured. She fixed a new wide-brimmed straw bonnet over her hair, her hands shaking so much she could hardly tie its green ribbons.

Leah smiled at her daughter. 'You look lovely. Now no more shillyshallying. You accept the captain's proposal. And allow both of you the happiness you deserve.'

'I still wonder sometimes, Ma.'

"'Tis too much wondering that has kept you two apart.' Leah was stern. 'You love him and he loves you. And he loves you enough to cast aside your lowly birth and marry you.'

Senara trembled with excitement. 'If it is meant to be, now is the time.'

'I'll not be expecting you back this evening,' Leah chuckled.

Senara kissed her mother's leathery cheek. Her decision made, she was glowing with happiness and her step was light as she hurried to Trevowan Hard. She was singing to herself as she approached the entrance of the yard. The lugger was drifting towards the dock and she saw Harry Sawle leap ashore to secure it. Edward Loveday was on the dock. The lugger must have been sighted earlier and word sent to Trevowan, for the Loveday carriage was in the yard and Amelia, Meriel and Elspeth were also waiting to greet their French relatives.

It made Senara halt. She had not expected this. She hung back and would wait for the chance to talk to Adam alone. She saw him on deck and her heart swelled with love. Japhet and St John stepped on to the dock and for the first time Senara noticed the petite woman clinging to Adam's arm. She was too young to be Adam's aunt. With a jolt Senara recognised her as his French cousin – the woman he had once been betrothed to.

Queasiness churned through her, together with

531

a feeling of unease. There was a possessiveness to the woman's hold on Adam's arm.

'That be the Cap'ns betrothed! I thought she had jilted him,' one of the shipwrights' wives exclaimed.

'Looks like she got her hooks in him good and proper now,' another laughed.

She turned round and saw Senara and her stare was scathing as she jeered, 'Looks like your man be about to wed his own kind.'

Senara stood rigid, fighting against her fear and nausea. There could be any number of reasons why Lisette was here. She watched as Adam helped Lisette on to the dock and the young woman broke away to run to Edward Loveday and throw her arms around her uncle's neck. Her voice was shrill, carrying clearly. 'Adam came for me! I knew he would. We are to be married! Is it not wonderful? It is as Papa planned.'

Adam stepped forward and spoke to his father but their words were inaudible. Lisette was taken away by the excited, chattering women.

Senara backed off. The men were talking animatedly. Edward put his hand on Adam's shoulder and looked to be congratulating him.

Senara could not bear to witness more. She fled back to the cottage, her heart aching that she had again allowed a man above her in class to take her love and cast it aside when it suited him.

Edward was upset and shocked to hear of Louise's death and continued to look appalled when Adam explained about Lisette.

'But the girl is convinced she is to wed you.'

Edward glanced towards the women who were laughing and embracing Lisette and were clearly delighted at her news. 'It would be like jilting her. Perhaps it would be for the best. It was always what Claude Riviere wanted. The girl has at least some money and what better way to give her our protection?'

'I cannot believe I am hearing this.' Adam grew heated. 'There will be no wedding to Lisette. She got the notion in her head in the convent. I humoured her as it was the only way to calm her. I fear her wits are deranged. She has been acting very strangely on the journey.'

'Then if you had no intention of wedding her, you should not have duped the girl,' Edward returned.

'Adam had no choice, Uncle,' Japhet defended him. 'But Lisette has it fixed in her head they are to marry. At least at Trevowan she can be cared for.'

Edward frowned, his expression troubled. 'I suppose you did what had to be done. But I do not like the girl to have been so misguided. She has babbled the news to all in the yard.'

'And I shall make it known that she was mistaken,' Adam declared. 'I intend to marry Senara within the month.'

Edward rounded on him. 'In the circumstances is that not insensitive towards Lisette? At least give her more time.'

'I have waited long enough. Lisette must accept the truth. It will be easier for her to come to terms with once I am married. She will have to discard the foolish notion.'

He turned to walk away.

'Where are you going?' his father demanded.

'To Senara. I have had my fill of hysterical women for one lifetime.'

'You cannot desert Lisette,' Edward raged. 'If she is as bad as you say, at least wait until Chegwidden has seen her.'

'I have done my duty.' Adam was firm.

'Adam. Adam. Adam! Where are you?' Lisette's voice began to rise with the familiar hysteria. She broke away from the women and ran back to fling her arms around his neck. 'Adam. I was frightened. You were not there.'

Adam disengaged her arms, his face frozen with anger.

She stared at him with horror. 'Why do you look at me like that? Adam, I do not want to go to Trevowan without you. We must tell your family our plans.' Her voice rose and her eyes became wild.

'You cannot abandon her like this.' Edward spoke softly against Adam's ear. 'We should avoid a scene if she is as deranged as you say. Get her back to the house. Is there more of the opiate the nuns gave you? Amelia will get her to rest. Then you can leave to go to your woman, if you must.'

Adam reluctantly agreed. He was embarrassed by the scene. He scanned the curious faces of the people in the yard. The one he sought was not amongst them. At first he was disappointed that Senara had not somehow learned of his return and come today, then he was glad. Lisette had caused a stir; her shrill voice would have carried with the lie that they were to wed.

'I will join you in the coach, Lisette,' he said. When she pouted and would have lingered, he said sharply, 'I will not be disobeyed. I will be with you directly.'

Tears sprang to her eyes at his harshness and he ignored them. His patience with her had long expired.

'I do not want news of these lies spreading to Senara before I can speak with her,' he said to his father. He called to Timmy Wakeley and gave him a coin. 'Go to the Polglase cottage. Tell Miss Polglase that I have returned and request the pleasure of her company at Mariner's House this evening.'

'Aye, aye, Cap'n Loveday.' Timmy ran off.

Adam felt easier as he approached the coach. Lisette was sobbing and Amelia had her arm round her.

'Will you not sit next to Lisette? What have you said to her?' Amelia looked puzzled.

'I shall collect Solomon from the stable here and ride. I need the exercise.'

'But, Adam, I want you beside me,' Lisette wailed.

'I will be with you at Trevowan. I shall ride beside the coach.' He ironed the impatience out of his voice. He should not let his exasperation make him forget his manners. Lisette had suffered a great deal. She must feel more vulnerable than ever now that her mother was dead. But he could not bring himself to suffer even the short journey to Trevowan so close to her.

As he rode he began to feel his frustration

535

dissolve. Tonight all this would be behind him and Senara would be the haven to restore his own sanity.

Timmy Wakeley, in his eagerness to please Adam, took a short cut along the cliff path to the narrow cleft in the rocks where the stream would lead back to the Polglase cottage. He had gone less than a quarter of the distance to the cottage when a buzzard dived out of the sky ahead of him to swoop on a vole. In wonder Timmy watched it soar skywards without breaking his pace. He did not see the rabbit hole, his foot went in it and he fell, severely spraining his ankle. He sat for a long time rubbing it and crying, and then bravely hobbled back to Trevowan Hard to find someone else to deliver Captain Loveday's message.

It was two hours later when Jacob Mumford, the yard overseer's youngest son, arrived at the Polglase cottage. He was greeted by a stony-faced Leah. Bridie was sobbing uncontrollably in the background.

'You can tell Cap'n Loveday that Senara is not available for his beck and call. She has left. Gone for good, she says.'

Jacob returned to Trevowan Hard. Captain Loveday had not returned for Jacob to give him Leah's reply, so Jacob went home.

It was late when Adam arrived back at the yard. It had been dark for two hours, and he was anxious to have kept Senara waiting. He was surprised to see Mariner's House in darkness, and disappointed that Senara was not there. He flopped into a chair and considered riding to the cottage. But his body was heavy and he began to yawn. The week in France had been mentally and physically exhausting. At Trevowan Lisette had been difficult and demanding, until Adam could bear no more and had walked out.

He needed Senara more than ever, but even as he tried to rouse himself to go to her, his eyelids drooped and he fell asleep in the chair. He awoke at dawn and dragged himself up to his bed, too tired to undress, where he slept until midday.

Eventually the hammering in the yard woke him. It was a bright sunny day. He shaved and changed his clothes and only then realised that there was no sign of Leah in the house. She always came on his return to prepare his meals. Was she ill? Is that why Senara had not come to him last night?

There was no food in the house so he walked to the Ship kiddleywink and bought one of Prudence Jansen's large pasties, freshly baked each day for the unmarried shipwrights who lived on their own.

'Don't often have you in here for your food, Cap'n. Leah not learned you be back?'

'I sent word. I hope she is not ill.'

'Strong as a horse is Leah.' Prudence grinned at him. 'I hear we are to congratulate you on your forthcoming wedding, Cap'n. Could be that Leah is not too pleased if she's heard you're to wed your cousin.'

'Your information is wrong. I have no intention of marrying Lisette de Gramont.'

Lucy Mumford entered the kiddleywink and gasped at seeing Adam. 'Oh, Cap'n, I didn't realise you be back from Trevowan. Young Jacob delivered your message yesterday after Timmy hurt his leg.' She looked ill at ease. 'Could I have a word with you outside, Cap'n?'

Puzzled. Adam followed her and she shifted uncomfortably before speaking. 'I didn't like to say anything in front of Pru. But when Jacob gave Leah your message she were real sharp with him. She said Senara had left. Gone for good. I reckon Jacob got it wrong. I saw Senara at the yard yesterday but she looked upset when your cousin declared you were to wed.'

'Senara was here and heard that?' Adam was horrified.

'Aye. Must have been a shock for her, Cap'n.'

'Thank you for telling me Lucy.'

He ran to the stables and mounted Solomon. The gelding was lathered when he drew to a halt by the Polglase cottage.

Leah and Bridie were taking some fired pots from the kiln. Adam sighed with relief as he leapt to the ground.

'Then Lucy Mumford was wrong; Senara was not left.'

Leah regarded him frostily. 'Senara has gone. What else did you expect? Though I never thought you would play her so false.'

'I would never do that to her. Where is she? I must speak with her.'

Bridie limped forward. 'I hate you! I hate you! I thought you were our friend. Now because of you Senara has gone away.' She began to sob and hobbled away to the wood.

Adam was too anxious about Senara to go after

Bridie and he ran into the house. It was empty. Senara's cloak was not hanging on the peg by the door. In the bedroom the only sign of her clothes were the two dresses he had brought her flung on the floor.

Leah was continuing her work when he returned to the kiln. 'Where is she, Leah?'

'A long ways from here by now. You broke that girl's heart. I hope you can live with that.'

'She told you about Lisette?'

'I suppose it's to be expected. It were a cruel way for Senara to find out you are to wed another.'

'Senara is the only woman I will *ever* marry. Lisette lives in the distant past for she cannot face her more recent memories. She has forgotten she was married. The peasants murdered her husband and, I confide this in you, they raped her. When we found her the nuns who were caring for her were about to commit her to an asylum. My family knows that Senara is my chosen bride. There will be no other. Tell me where she is, Leah.'

Leah looked distraught. 'She be gone. There were no stopping her. She went with Caleph. She said she were better off with the gypsies who accepted her for what she is.'

'Had I not accepted her?' Adam ground out, his mind and heart in turmoil.

'This last week has not been easy for her. You'll find out soon enough. The women of Penruan turned on her. Reviled her. Condemned her as a witch. She were not hurt. Clem Sawle saw to that. Though if he had not been there—'

Leah broke off and her condemnation mellowed as she saw the pain and torment in his eyes. 'Perhaps this be for the best. It was what she always feared.'

'Where did they go, Leah? I will find her. I will not rest until she is mine.'

'Caleph did not say whether they were going north for the harvest fairs or east, which be warmer come winter.'

'Then I shall search until I find her, Leah. They cannot be that far away.'

He returned to Trevowan to tell his family his plans. 'I must go after her,' he concluded.

'She is with her own kind, Adam,' Edward counselled. 'Perhaps this is for the best.'

'No. She left because she believed I betrayed her. I have done my duty by my family. I shall return when I find her.'

Edward looked set to argue, then seeing his son's unhappy expression he put up his hands in a gesture of surrender. 'You must do what you feel is right. But I beseech you to remember your duties here. Squire Penwithick was impressed at St John's account of how you rescued Lisette. I got the impression he wanted to use you and the *Pegasus* to help more *émigrés* leave France. It is dangerous work but perhaps it is what you need to take your mind from all this.'

'Nothing can make me forget Senara.' Adam was stiff with affront.

Edward studied Adam. The stubborn tilt of his son's chin warned him he would not be deterred. Edward changed tactics, his voice now neutral. 'By coincidence Thomas has written. There are

540

many French *émigrés* using Mercer's Bank and they talk often of their fears of friends and families left behind. They would pay handsomely to help their countrymen escape. Thomas wanted to know if you would consider the venture. The money would help pay off the loans on the yard.'

Normally such an adventure would have fired Adam's blood. 'I am aware of my duty, but I cannot risk losing Senara.'

Senara's people were adept at avoiding pursuit. Senara suspected that Adam would try to seek her out. She had no intention of allowing him to find her.

As she trudged besides her grandmother's wagon as they travelled through the south of England, her pain intensified. Adam had broken his promise to her and destroyed her trust. It had been heart-rending to acknowledge that he was no different from the rest of his kind. She had been a fool to believe that he had actually intended to go against his family and wed her. That he had finally broken down her resistance and she had been ready to marry him, had made his betrayal harder to bear.

The ache swelled in her breast. Last night she had run from the camp as she saw him ride into the clearing to speak to the elders. From behind a hawthorn bush she had watched him arguing, his stance showing that he believed she was with the troop. Caleph had threatened Adam with a knife to get him to leave. The sight of her lover's shoulders hunched in dejection had almost made her call out. Pride made her resist.

Her tears blurred at the sight of him riding away. She loved him too much to be thrown the scraps of his affection, seeing him only when he stole away from his wife. As the only woman in his life, she had been content as his mistress, but then they had met as equals in love. She would not share him with another woman.

Adam was equally determined that he would be reunited with Senara. He would search if it took him until he must set sail next spring.

Fate had been cruel to them. But fate could be overcome. He was determined to conquer fate as he had triumphed over so many adversities in the last year. He had won Senara's love and he would not lose it. Fate had mocked him, but it would not triumph. He would not abandon her. What they had was too precious.

During the next weeks, her lovely face would dance before him on the road, beckoning but always elusive. One moment her image was twirling with arms outstretched in welcome; the next it was veiled, indistinct beside an ancient oak or Celtic monolith.

He would stop to drink at a stream and see her face reflected in the water. When he turned in expectation he was distraught to find himself alone. Solomon's hoofs pounded the byways and sometimes Adam swore Senara's voice called on the breath of the wind. Yet his answering call was met by silence.

It was not possible for a band of gypsies to disappear without trace. Yet it seemed that they had. Any group he encountered viewed his questions about Caleph and Senara with suspicion. They were a too-close community to disclose the whereabouts of another of their kind. Some even threatened him with violence. He could only use stealth to watch their campsite for some sign of his love. None was revealed.

The trees turned golden and their fallen leaves were a recrimination of his failure. It hardened his resolve. Senara was out there – often he sensed close by. Always she eluded him, yet he remained confident throughout his despair. He would move heaven and earth if that is what it took to find her and make her his bride.

Chapter Thirty-One

The weeks dragged into months. Winter frost whitened the landscape and nipped the air. Adam had not given up his quest but out of duty towards his father and the yard he could not stay away from Trevowan for ever. And there was *Pegasus*. He had ignored his ship and neglected his duty. The family could not afford to have an asset such as his merchant ship lying idle. Christmas was but a fortnight away and his family would be disappointed if he did not spend it with them. Was it time to accept that Senara was lost to him?

He would never be able to forget her but to overcome his aching loss he needed to be at sea. Adam remembered Squire Penwithick and Thomas's suggestions that he work with the *émigrés* needing to escape the new regime in France. The situation had greatly worsened in that country in recent months with the new terror of the guillotine used to murder hundreds of aristocrats.

The idea of helping the *émigrés* appealed to him; the danger and adventure would be a potent balm to his pain. The need to settle his future had taken Adam to Bristol. There he had sold the cargo he had invested in at the beginning of the year which he had intended to sell in America. That money would pay off the interest which was again due on the loan for the yard. It would also relieve Adam of the guilt he felt that he had abandoned his family when they still needed him.

While in Bristol he sent the bank draft to pay off the interest to the lenders by mail coach, and another letter to his father stating what he had done and that he would be home before the end of the Christmas festivities.

The continuing heavy frost made it possible to travel the potholed roads. He wanted one more chance to try to find Senara before he returned to his home. In his months of searching he had relived every conversation with Senara. He had never condemned her for her beliefs in the old ways and her veneration of nature. She had spoken much of the ancient stone temple known as Stonehenge on Salisbury Plain and of a vast complex of stones set in a circle not far from there at a place called Avebury.

As he rode out of Bristol, he had the strangest feeling that Senara was calling to him. He had dreamed of her last night lying by the Druid stone on the moor where they had first made love. The stone took on a new significance. If the weather held, a day and half hard ride would take him to those other ancient stones – places which held an important part in Senara's heart. There he would feel closer to her and, if need be, in such a place he would find the strength to say his goodbye to her, and accept that, at least for now, he had lost her and he must return to take up his life without her.

With each mile it felt right to be making such a detour, a pilgrimage to their love. He arrived at Stonehenge at noon the following day. Salisbury Plain was shrouded in mist and three times he had to ask farm workers the direction of the stones. Finally they rose before him in sombre majesty, grey sarsen towers flecked with golden splashes of lichen, their purpose forgotten and blighted by time. Many of the great monoliths lay on their sides, having long ago fallen. On the isolation of the plain, it was a place of ghosts and spectres and, with the grey misty shroud as a backdrop, a place which echoed to the silenced heartbeats of the dead and not the living.

Adam did not know what he had expected to feel or find, but he dismounted and walked around the circle. The shipbuilding part of his mind marvelled at how such ancient people had managed to bring the stones to this place, let alone had the knowledge to raise their weight and place the transom stones on their top. Senara had told him something of its history which she had gleaned from Gideon Meadows when he had been teaching her. Geoffrey of Monmouth, writing in 1136, had believed they were erected by Merlin. That had appealed to Adam's Cornish pride for as a boy he loved the tales of King Arthur, the Druid wizard Merlin, and the knights of Camelot which had supposedly existed in Cornwall. Gazing at the stones, Adam secretly doubted that anything the great Merlin had erected by magic would have fallen down. The henge was most commonly held to be a Druid temple. It certainly was as impressive as any more modern Gothic-style cathedral.

Yet the place left his heart hollow as a void. He did not feel the unity with Senara he had sought. With a sigh Adam leaned back against one of the great bluestones and closed his eyes.

A heartfelt plea escaped him, 'Whatever gods or goddesses Senara believed were worshipped here, have mercy on us.'

He pushed away from the stone and, in the eerie silence of the mist-veiled moor, threw up his arms and shouted. 'Where is she?'

The release of emotion left him bereft. He returned to Solomon and for a moment rested his head against the warmth of the gelding's neck. A thin cry of a heron made him raise his eyes. It flew low over the stones towards the north in the direction he had been told was Avebury. As Adam swung in to the saddle his heart began to beat faster. Senara had once described a heron as a messenger of the gods. It was a sign she would have heeded. He would not give up until he had visited Avebury.

Light flurries of snow accompanied his ride. Adam hunched his shoulders beneath the triple cape of his greatcoat and bound a muffler over his nose and mouth. The rest of his face was reddened by the cold. The snow stopped after an hour, having transformed the landscape with a dusting of pristine whiteness. The bleat of sheep grazing the open land carried to him. There were more trees dotted in copses over land which dipped and rose like a stormy sea.

The village of Avebury was encircled by the stones but instinct made Adam skirt its boundary He was stunned by the sight before him. It was not just one stone circle; it had smaller ones inside. The number of stones were too vast to estimate as the outer ones remained stretched into the concealing mist. There were also lines of double stones leading away from its centre. The stones were surrounded by ditches and earthworks from a prehistoric time.

He halted on the edge of a copse overlooking the site. Solomon blew a harsh breath through his nostrils, which steamed in the cold air. The sun was low on the horizon, tinting the sky and lingering mist with an ethereal pink light. He surveyed his surroundings, half expecting to see a gypsy camp, but was disappointed. The warmth of the village inn beckoned. The stones maintained their stalwart vigil and he appeared to be the only human outside the village.

Half frozen and with his stomach growling with hunger, Adam admitted that he had been mad to follow such a romantic whim. It had been born of desperation and his quest had

547

again ended in failure.

His body slumped with dejection. By the heat of the inn fire he would get drunk and curse himself for a romantic fool. He touched his feet to Solomon's sides but the horse did not respond. Then Adam saw two cloaked figures and a small child gliding across the whitened grass towards the centre of the ring. The sun was low, almost setting. It was a fiery orange sphere disappearing between two stones towards the west.

The three figures were followed at a distance by a dozen others and they began a low chanting. The cloaked figures raised their hands to the heavens and the rest were silent. It was only then that Adam realised that it was the winter solstice.

The younger of the women tilted back her head towards the setting sun and her hood fell back, revealing unbound hair falling to her hips. Around her head was a garland of woven mistletoe. Someone within the gathering was softly playing a flute, its melodious, haunting sound bringing a beauty to the simple ritual.

The woman turned slowly and her cloak fell back, showing the profile of her body heavily swollen with child. Then she began to sing in praise of ancient spirits, the bounty of mother earth, and of her lover and provider of life the father sun. Heavy with her fertility, the priestess was the manifestation of the goddess on earth. But that voice, low, throaty and earthy, set his body trembling. It was Senara's voice.

The ceremony was short and for Senara immeasurably moving. For the tribe the ritual was part of their heritage, symbolic of life and death as the sun was swallowed by the earth, and the longest night of the year stretched before them. With the dawn of the next day there would be celebrations, for the year would be reborn, the cycle turned once again towards the longer lighter days, heralding rebirth and the continuance of life.

For Senara, who had been asked to officiate at the ceremony with her grandmother, and Caleph's eldest daughter Maura who was seven, it was a special time: a time of transition.

She had felt it when she woke that morning. The day had an air of expectancy about it. For the last week she had thought constantly of Adam, unable to shake his image from her mind. Several times in recent days when she had been walking alone she had called out his name, letting it carry on the wind. Her hand would rest on her stomach and feel the kick of his child in her belly, impatient to be born. She had been hugging the secret of a suspected pregnancy when she had fled Trevowan Hard. In the following months, so deep had been her misery, she had not heeded the changes to her body until the child had quickened, and she had felt the first flutter of movement as it demanded acknowledgement to its life.

There had followed soul-searching months where she was pulled to return to her lover, his memory branded deep within her, yet she had held out against her need. It was better this way. What good to bring a bastard child into the world, forced to share Adam's love with his legitimate children? What child could be happy living on the outskirts of a family of wealth and importance, and knowing they were of the same blood. The taunts of bastardy would follow it through life. Would it not come to resent the lowliness of its own birth? Better to allow it to follow its gypsy heritage, be accepted and loved and to live among equals. It was that thought which had stopped her returning. For had she not tried to break away to her own cost?

For the first time in her life Senara had known jealousy. Not for Lisette, whom she believed would share so much of Adam's life, but for Lisette's children, who would take by right so much from her own child.

Yet that morning as Senara had stepped out of the travelling wagon with its horseshoe-shaped roof, the first sight which had greeted her was two feeding magpies. For her, magpies had always been birds of good fortune and her heart had lightened. She had slept badly and woken with backache. She lifted her face to the watery sun and in that moment sensed that Adam was close. Could it be that he was still searching for her? That was foolish for by now he would have been long wed to his French cousin. With the time of the child's birth so close, she was growing fanciful. Yet the sensation persisted and had stayed with her all day.

To be camped close to the circles of stones had charged her with a restless energy she had not felt in months. If the snow held off there would be singing and dancing around the campfire this night, until they greeted the sun's rebirth at dawn. The camp was hidden from the village by the far earthworks and a copse of hawthorn. When the celebrations were completed with the rising sun, the gypsies would disappear before the villagers started their work for the day.

Senara was thinking of the night ahead and of the new life within which would soon be born, when her grandmother touched her shoulder and nodded towards a rider.

The dark figure was silhouetted against the fading light yet her senses were alerted. A cry of recognition was torn from her, and the rider leapt to the ground, holding the reins of his horse as he advanced towards her. The men of the tribe closed in with menacing intent. Caleph drew a dagger as he took his place as their leader.

'He is a friend, brother,' Senara cried out.

Caleph remained braced and on guard; the raised dagger caught the last red rays of the sunset.

Adam did not even glance at the men, he could only stare at Senara, humbled that finally he had found her. He had to swallow hard against a rock of emotion blocking his throat.

'Senara.' Her name was a caress. She did not run towards him but wrapped her thick cloak more protectively around her.

'This is a strange place to find a sea captain who has but recently wed.' The words were crisper than the frost-sharpened air.

'You were the woman I vowed to wed. There is no other.' He found himself accusing, 'How could you doubt me?'

Still she did not move. Adam's legs felt wooden

551

as he closed the gap between them. It was almost dark now and, though the snow clouds had gone and a full moon turned the landscape silver, he could not see her face shadowed by the crown of mistletoe. 'I have been searching for you since the day you ran off. Sometimes I even thought I was close, but always you eluded me.'

'Have you truly been searching for so many months?'

Adam hid his impatience that she still seemed to doubt him. 'Why else would I be here? You know the situation within my family. I should be at sea or helping in the yard.'

The moonlight showed the sparkle of tears on her cheeks. His restraint broke and he gathered her in his arms.

'Get back from her,' the gypsy leader challenged.

'It is all right, Caleph,' Senara said with a muffled sob. 'Adam and I need to talk.' With that a pain cut through her so sharply that she gasped, and she would have stumbled had not Adam held her tight.

The old woman cackled, 'Looks like your talking will have to wait, there's birthing to be done first.'

Adam lifted Senara on to Solomon's saddle and turned to find the gypsy men pressed close around him. 'I mean her no harm. I came here to take her home as my bride. Now I find I shall be made a father this night. Have I not the right to be with her?'

'If she wants you to stay,' Caleph challenged. The gypsy was some four inches shorter than

Adam, with wild curling black hair, olive skin and obsidian-black eyes. He looked more than ready to give Adam a beating for all the wrongs he believed Adam had done his half-sister.

'I would have Adam here,' Senara answered as another pain ripped through her.

'Will you men stand back so we can get Senara to her wagon?' her grandmother shouted. 'She has been in labour all day but would not miss the ritual.'

The stoop-shouldered crone peered up at Adam. Her face was crisscrossed with wrinkles but there was a serenity and glow of wisdom about the woman. Adam was subjected to a long assessing stare, then she nodded as though in approval. 'You'll do. You've an honest face. It's time that headstrong granddaughter of mine were taken in hand.' She hobbled away and the others followed.

The night hours dragged slowly for Adam. He spent most of them pacing the outer rim of the campfire. The gypsies were ringed about the fire, the orange light flickering over their faces showing them watchful as wolves assessing their prey. One of the rabbits which had been cooking over the fire on spits was snapped in half and a portion handed to Adam, together with a cup of strong cider. He ate and drank without tasting, his stare constantly returning to the wagon with the light in the window, and he was racked by the thought of the pain Senara was enduring. Yet there were no screams, just a toing and froing from the woman carrying hot water from a smaller fire outside.

All night a fiddler had played, accompanied by a man on the flute. By the early hours the men had seemed to accept Adam's company and began to dance. One or two of the younger women clicked their fingers and banged on tambourines with long flowing ribbons attached, then they leapt to their feet and began to twirl and dance around the fire. Others clapped and sang in a language which Adam could not understand.

Inside the wagon Senara heard the music and bit her lips against the pain. She refused to cry out, wanting her child to come into the world to the sound of rejoicing and celebration, not her agonised screams. The herbs her grandmother had brewed had eased the worst of her pain and at the first tinge of lightening sky, her child was born.

Maddie, Caleph's wife and Senara's childhood friend, came to touch Adam's arm as he absently watched the dancers. 'Your child is born. Senara wishes to see you.'

Adam ran to the wagon as the last of the women tending Senara left.

A lantern hanging from the roof beam illuminated Senara propped up on a narrow cot bed, the child nestled against her breast. They were bathed in a golden glow and when her gaze lifted to him, it was filled with such radiance he was transfixed.

'Behold your son, Adam. Is he not perfect?' She held the baby, wrapped in a green shawl edged with a cream border, towards him. Absently he noted it was the shawl he had bought Senara in

Bristol, but his full attention was on the child. He had a cap of dark hair and his eyes were open, staring up at him. Adam felt humbled by the marvel of life and, when his gaze lifted to meet Senara's, there were tears in his eyes and he found his voice was a hoarse croak.

'He is indeed perfect, like his mother.' He knelt at the bedside. 'You can no longer deny your right to be my wife. I love you, Senara. There never was any question of me marrying Lisette,' he began to gabble in his urgency to reassure her. 'What you heard from Lisette on the quay was talk from her deluded mind. She has been unstable in her wits since her chateau was attacked. She could not remember the horrors she was subjected to in France and had forgotten that she had been married to another. It is you I love. Even my father has accepted that you are the only woman I would marry. I have missed you so much.'

Senara reached up and touched the side of Adam's face where he bore the pale crescent-shaped scar he had acquired in saving Bridie's life. The birth of their child as the solstice dawn was heralding the birth of a new year – a time of new beginnings – had been a powerful omen for their future. She had put civilisation before her faith for so many years, but the two were intricate parts of herself – she understood that now. And Adam had seen her performing the secret ritual without condemning her. That acceptance meant a great deal. Also she knew that life without Adam would be to live with her heart torn asunder.

'Yes, I will marry you, my love, but since for your world to accept me as your wife I must enter your church, would you take your vows with me within the great circle at the moment that the new sun is fully reborn? It would be a sign of the rebirth of our love and a blessing on our future. There is time, for the sun has not yet risen above the horizon.'

'But surely you are too weak?'

She shook her head. 'Take me there on Solomon.'

'And we will then have a wedding performed by Uncle Joshua for I will have no one doubt that our marriage is legal. Do you agree?'

She kissed him. 'Joshua Loveday is a priest of great understanding and little hypocrisy. If he will agree to marry us, I shall be happy for him to perform the ceremony.'

They reached the circle as the lightening blue sky shimmered with a growing gold. Then the sun was on the horizon, its rays gilding the snow which covered the grass and trees. Senara had refused to be parted from the baby. Adam lifted her, still holding the child, from Solomon and held her in the protection of his arms.

They stood before the tallest of the central stones and in a clear voice Adam proudly proclaimed, 'Here before you all, I, Adam Loveday take this woman Senara to be my wife. I will love and revere her above all women, and protect her to the end of my days.'

Senara stared at him with adoration, her own voice firm: 'I, Senara, take this most honourable of men Adam Loveday to be my husband. I will love and cherish him, and serve him faithfully and with joyful heart until the end of my days. Blessed be our union and love.'

Their vows were sealed with a kiss. Caleph stepped forward and clasped Adam's hand. 'You have done right by Senara. Long may you both be happy. But if you fail her...' The unspoken threat hung between them.

Adam took no offence. 'I would give my life for Senara.'

He lifted his wife and child on to Solomon's back. 'Have you thought of a name for our son?'

'Would you not like to choose?'

Adam laughed. 'I am sure that you have given it a great deal of consideration, whereas I have rather been taken by surprise by his arrival. Tell me your choice.'

'I had thought of Nathan.'

'Nathan Loveday has the ring of a fine shipbuilder of the future about it.'

'And what if my blood is the stronger and he becomes a rover by nature?'

Adam grinned. 'There's many a Loveday roved the seas to make his fortune. Nathan Loveday he shall be. You have chosen well.'

Adam took Solomon's bridle. 'We will rest for a few days at an inn before journeying to Cornwall.' As he led the horse his heart was too full of joy to worry about any recriminations from his family over his marriage. He had his father's blessing and that was enough. Fortune had blessed them, and he and Senara would live at Mariner's House. Together they would overcome any conflicts or dissent which lay ahead.

The publishers hope that this book has given you enjoyable reading. Large Print Books are especially designed to be as easy to see and hold as possible. If you wish a complete list of our books please ask at your local library or write directly to:

Magna Large Print Books
Magna House, Long Preston,
Skipton, North Yorkshire.
BD23 4ND

This Large Print Book for the partially sighted, who cannot read normal print, is published under the auspices of

THE ULVERSCROFT FOUNDATION